ict

BOOK ONE IN THE ĐESCENDANTS SERIES

WITHDRAWN

The Isle of the Lost

The
Graphic Novel

#1 *New York Times* best-selling author
Melissa đe la Cruz
Based on *Descendants* written by
Josann McGibbon & Sara Parriott

Adapted by
ROBERT VENDITTI

Art by
KAT FAJARDO

Letter
LEIGH

Adapted from the novel *The Isle of the Lost*
Copyright © 2018 by Disney Enterprises, Inc.

First Edition, September 2018
10 9 8 7 6 5 4 3 2 1
FAC-038091-18201
Printed in the United States of America

A special thank-you to Krzysztof Chalik for all his help with this book

ISBN (hardcover) 978-1-368-03981-9
ISBN (paperback) 978-1-368-04051-8
Reinforced binding
Visit DisneyBooks.com
and DisneyDescendants.com

SUSTAINABLE FORESTRY INITIATIVE

Certified Sourcing
www.sfiprogram.org
SFI-00993

Logo Applies to Text Stock Only

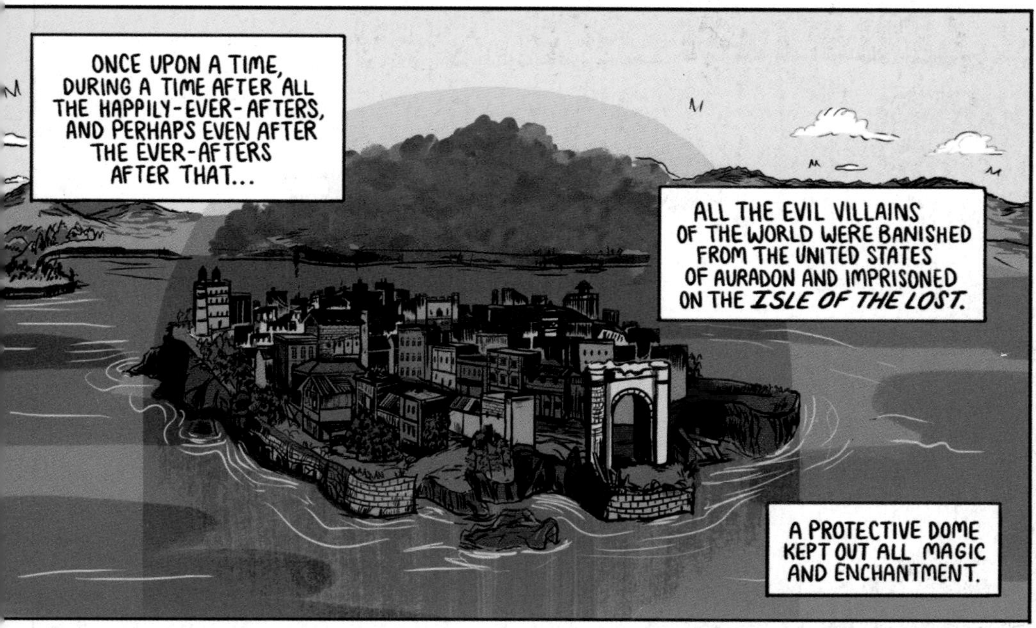
ONCE UPON A TIME, DURING A TIME AFTER ALL THE HAPPILY-EVER-AFTERS, AND PERHAPS EVEN AFTER THE EVER-AFTERS AFTER THAT...
ALL THE EVIL VILLAINS OF THE WORLD WERE BANISHED FROM THE UNITED STATES OF AURADON AND IMPRISONED ON THE *ISLE OF THE LOST*.
A PROTECTIVE DOME KEPT OUT ALL MAGIC AND ENCHANTMENT.

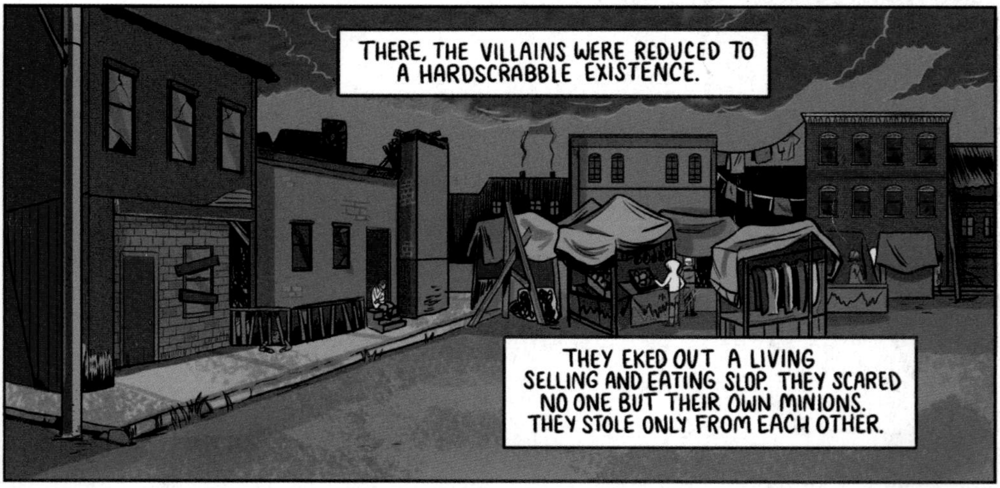
THERE, THE VILLAINS WERE REDUCED TO A HARDSCRABBLE EXISTENCE.
THEY EKED OUT A LIVING SELLING AND EATING SLOP. THEY SCARED NO ONE BUT THEIR OWN MINIONS. THEY STOLE ONLY FROM EACH OTHER.

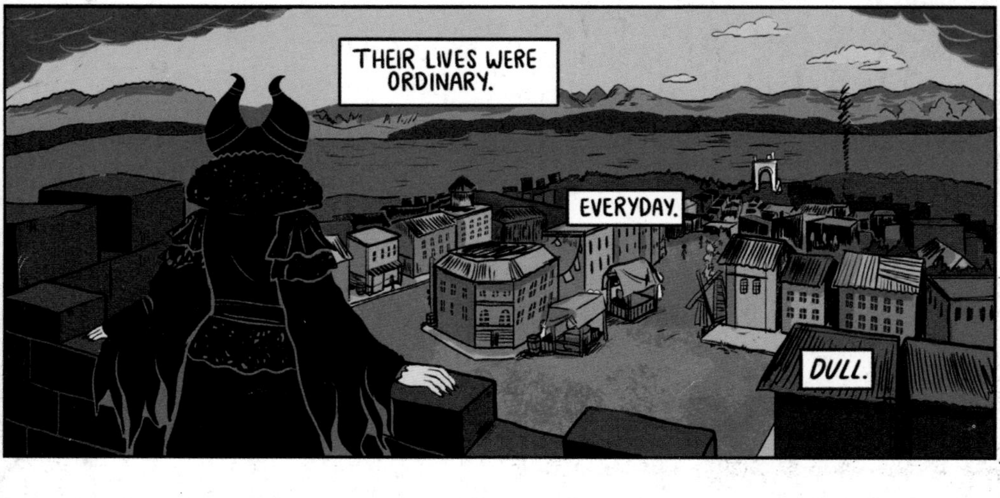
THEIR LIVES WERE ORDINARY.
EVERYDAY.
DULL.

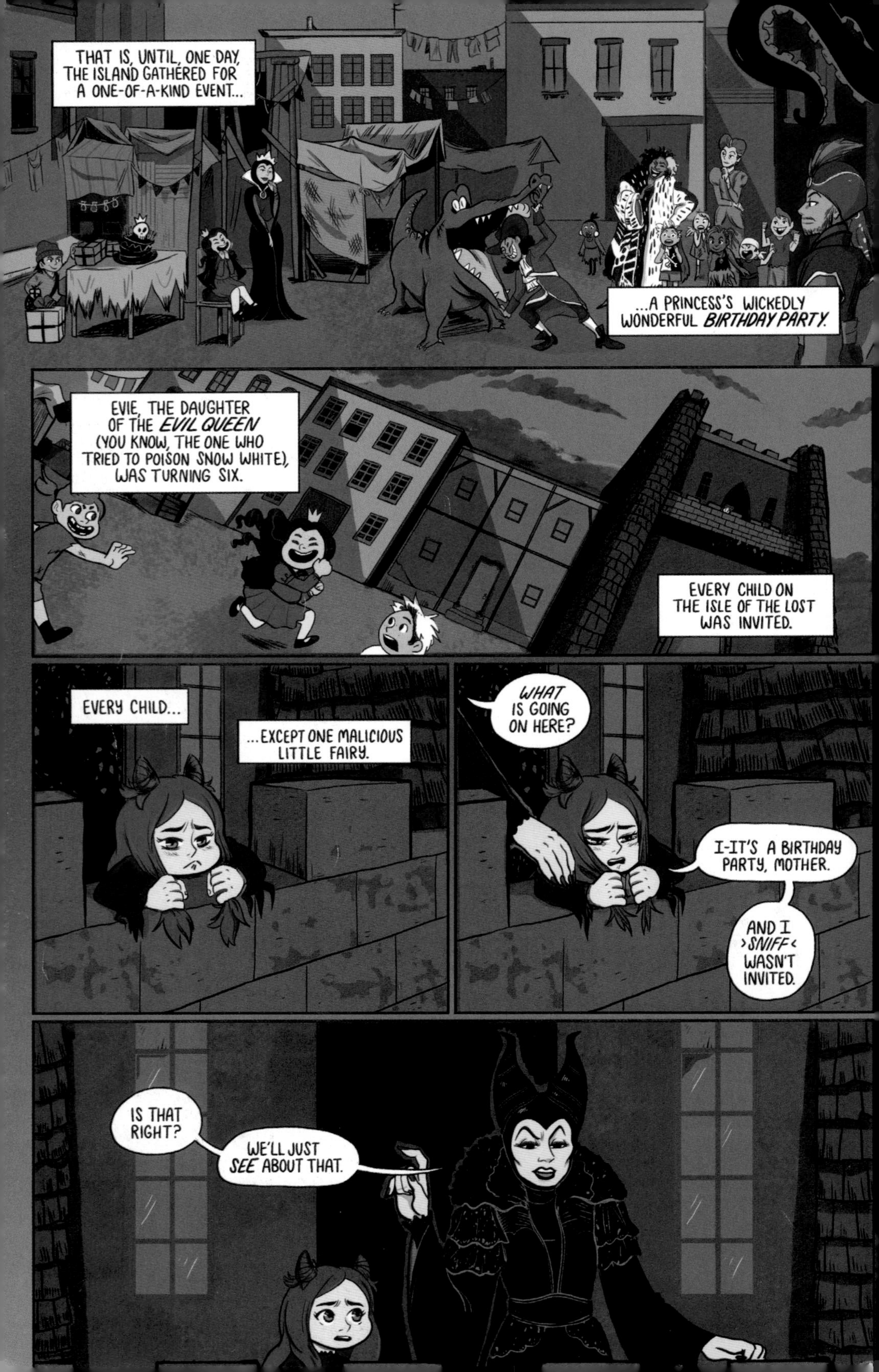
THAT IS, UNTIL, ONE DAY, THE ISLAND GATHERED FOR A ONE-OF-A-KIND EVENT...
...A PRINCESS'S WICKEDLY WONDERFUL *BIRTHDAY PARTY*.
EVIE, THE DAUGHTER OF THE *EVIL QUEEN* (YOU KNOW, THE ONE WHO TRIED TO POISON SNOW WHITE), WAS TURNING SIX.
EVERY CHILD ON THE ISLE OF THE LOST WAS INVITED.
EVERY CHILD...
...EXCEPT ONE MALICIOUS LITTLE FAIRY.
WHAT IS GOING ON HERE?
I-IT'S A BIRTHDAY PARTY, MOTHER.
AND I >*SNIFF*< WASN'T INVITED.
IS THAT RIGHT?
WE'LL JUST *SEE* ABOUT THAT.

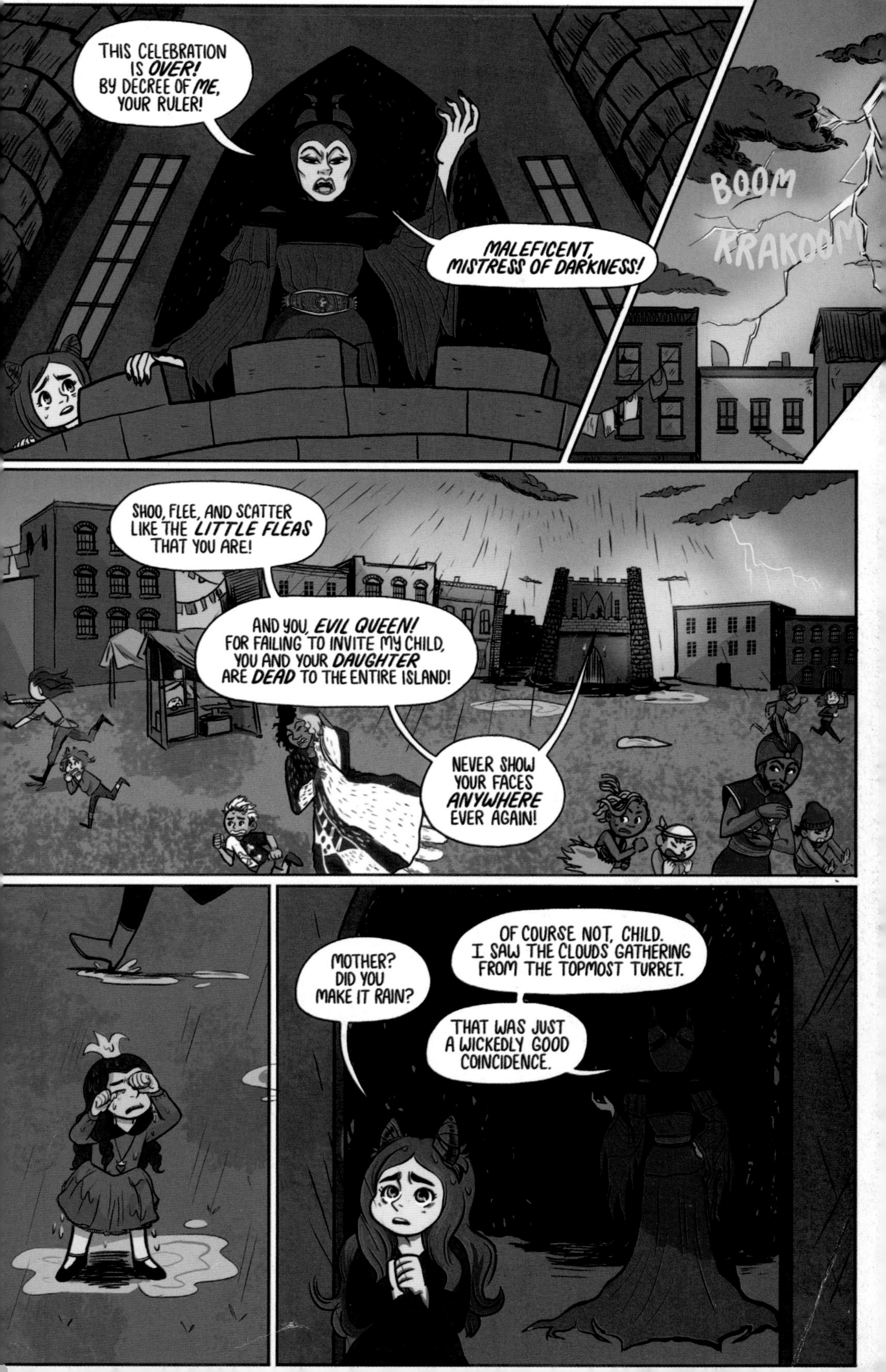
THIS CELEBRATION IS OVER! BY DECREE OF ME, YOUR RULER!
MALEFICENT, MISTRESS OF DARKNESS!
BOOM
KRAKOOM
SHOO, FLEE, AND SCATTER LIKE THE LITTLE FLEAS THAT YOU ARE!
AND YOU, EVIL QUEEN! FOR FAILING TO INVITE MY CHILD, YOU AND YOUR DAUGHTER ARE DEAD TO THE ENTIRE ISLAND!
NEVER SHOW YOUR FACES ANYWHERE EVER AGAIN!
MOTHER? DID YOU MAKE IT RAIN?
OF COURSE NOT, CHILD. I SAW THE CLOUDS GATHERING FROM THE TOPMOST TURRET.
THAT WAS JUST A WICKEDLY GOOD COINCIDENCE.

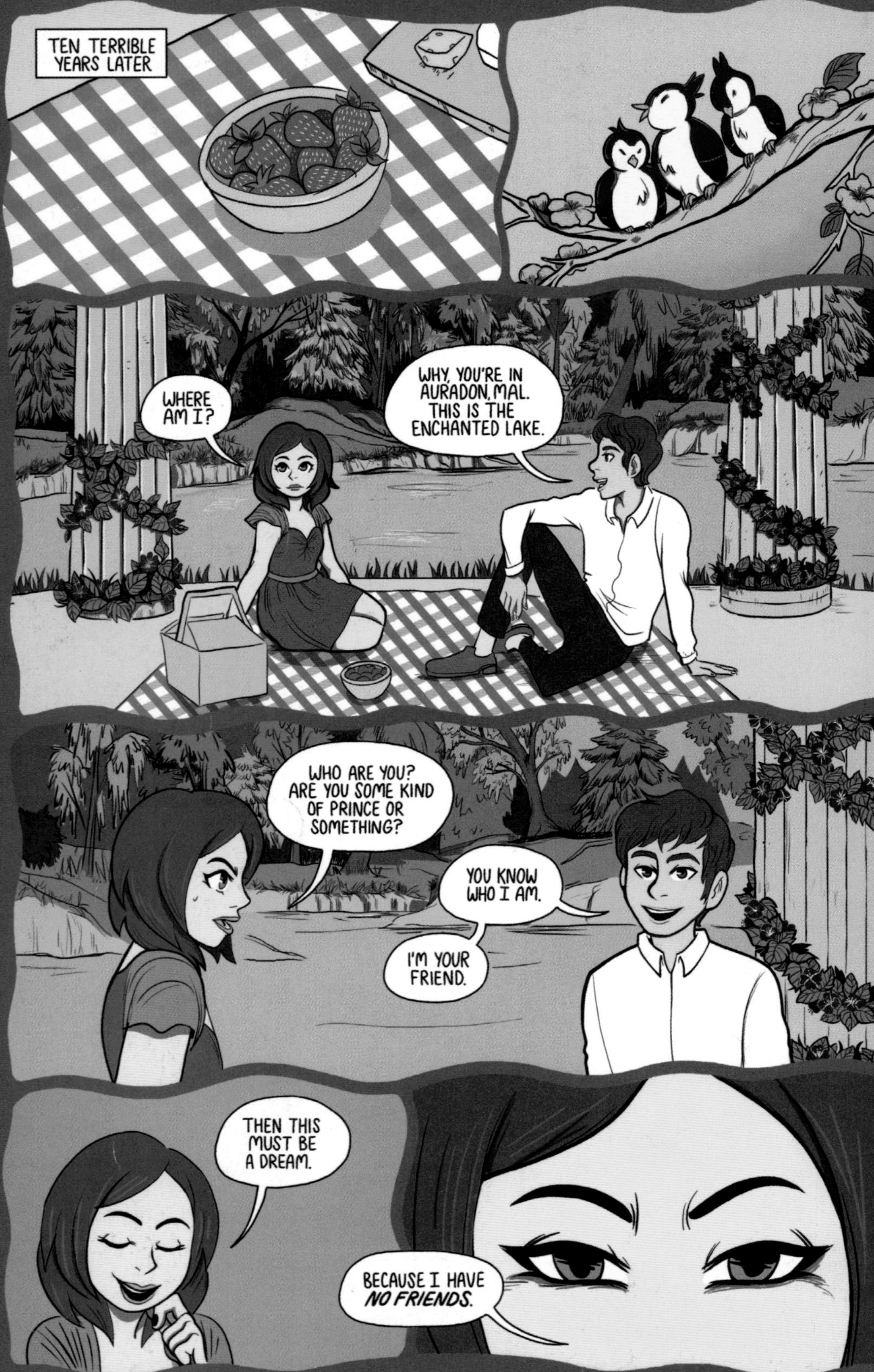
TEN TERRIBLE YEARS LATER
WHERE AM I?
WHY, YOU'RE IN AURADON, MAL. THIS IS THE ENCHANTED LAKE.
WHO ARE YOU? ARE YOU SOME KIND OF PRINCE OR SOMETHING?
YOU KNOW WHO I AM.
I'M YOUR FRIEND.
THEN THIS MUST BE A DREAM.
BECAUSE I HAVE *NO FRIENDS.*

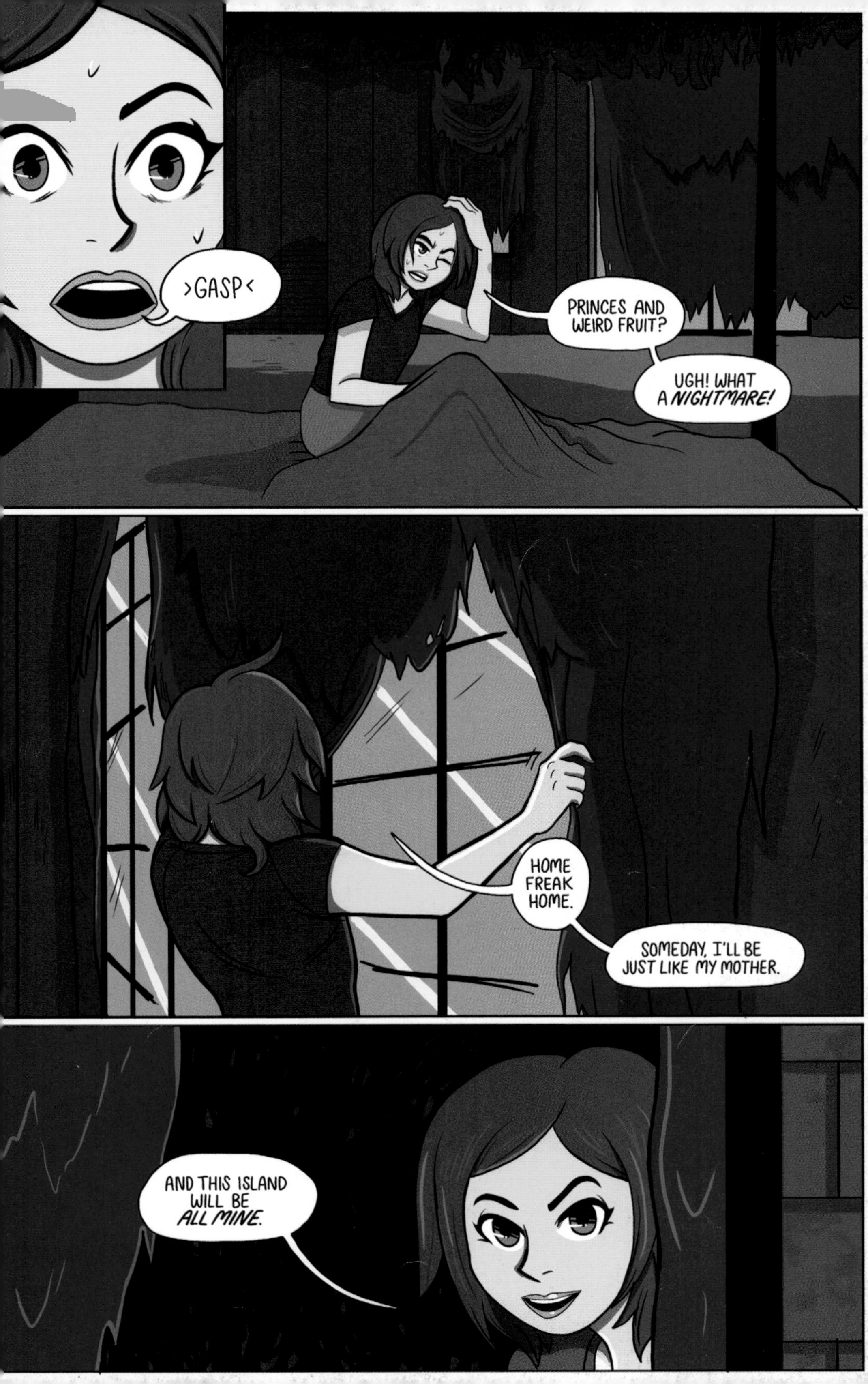
>GASP<
PRINCES AND WEIRD FRUIT?
UGH! WHAT A NIGHTMARE!
HOME FREAK HOME.
SOMEDAY, I'LL BE JUST LIKE MY MOTHER.
AND THIS ISLAND WILL BE ALL MINE.

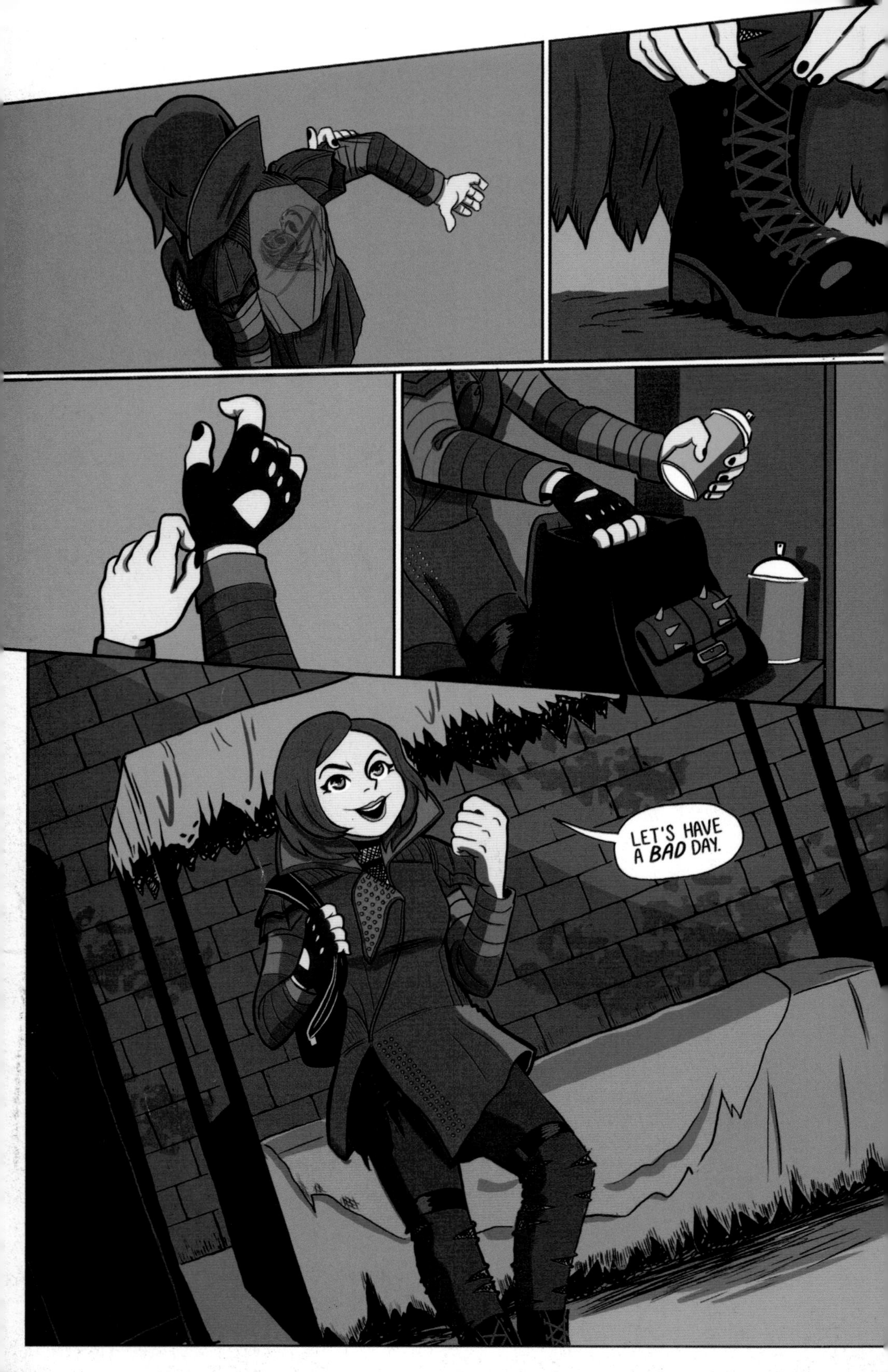
LET'S HAVE A *BAD* DAY.

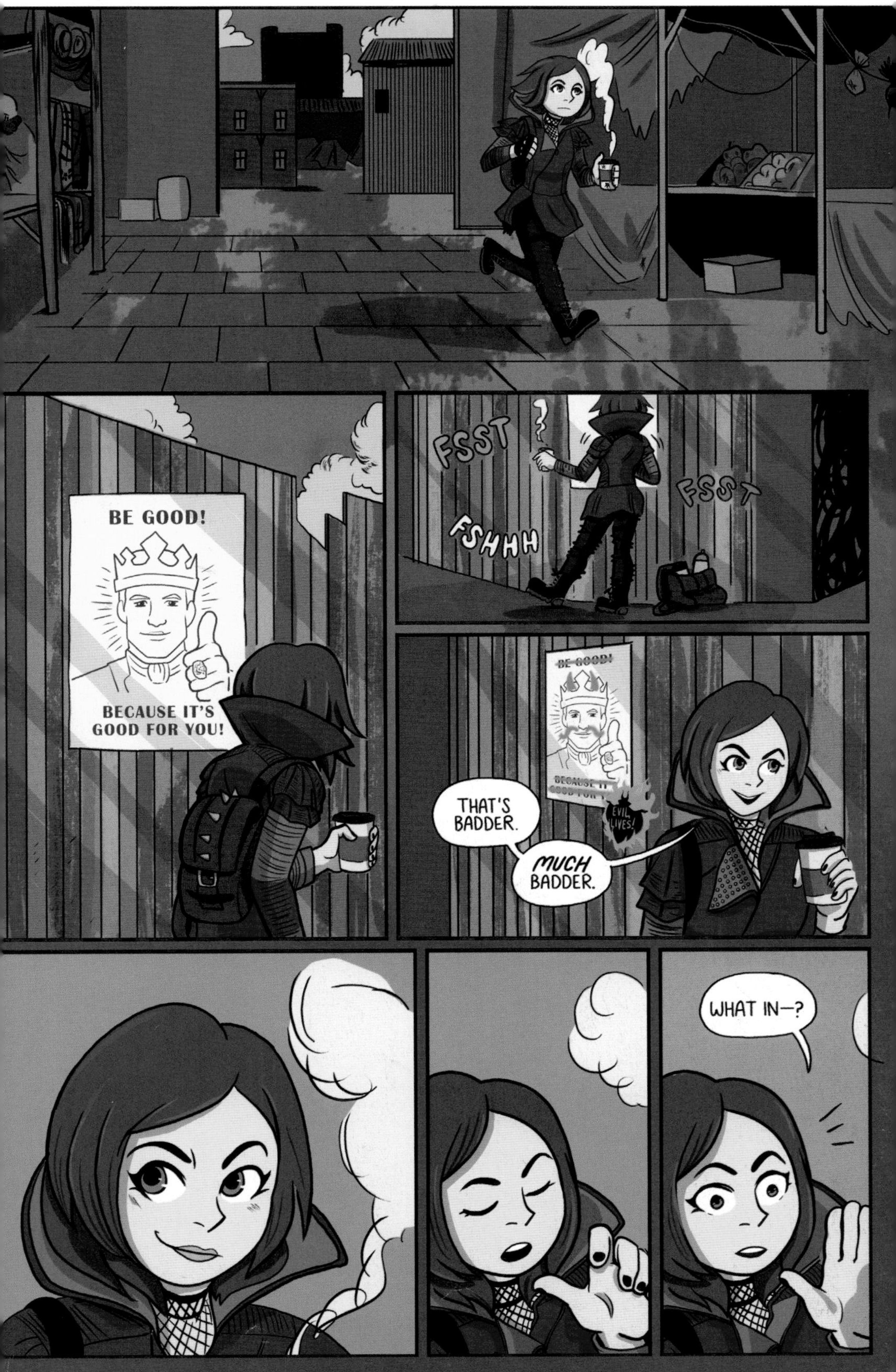

BE GOOD!
BECAUSE IT'S GOOD FOR YOU!
FSST
FSHHH
FSST
THAT'S BADDER.
MUCH BADDER.
EVIL LIVES!
WHAT IN—?

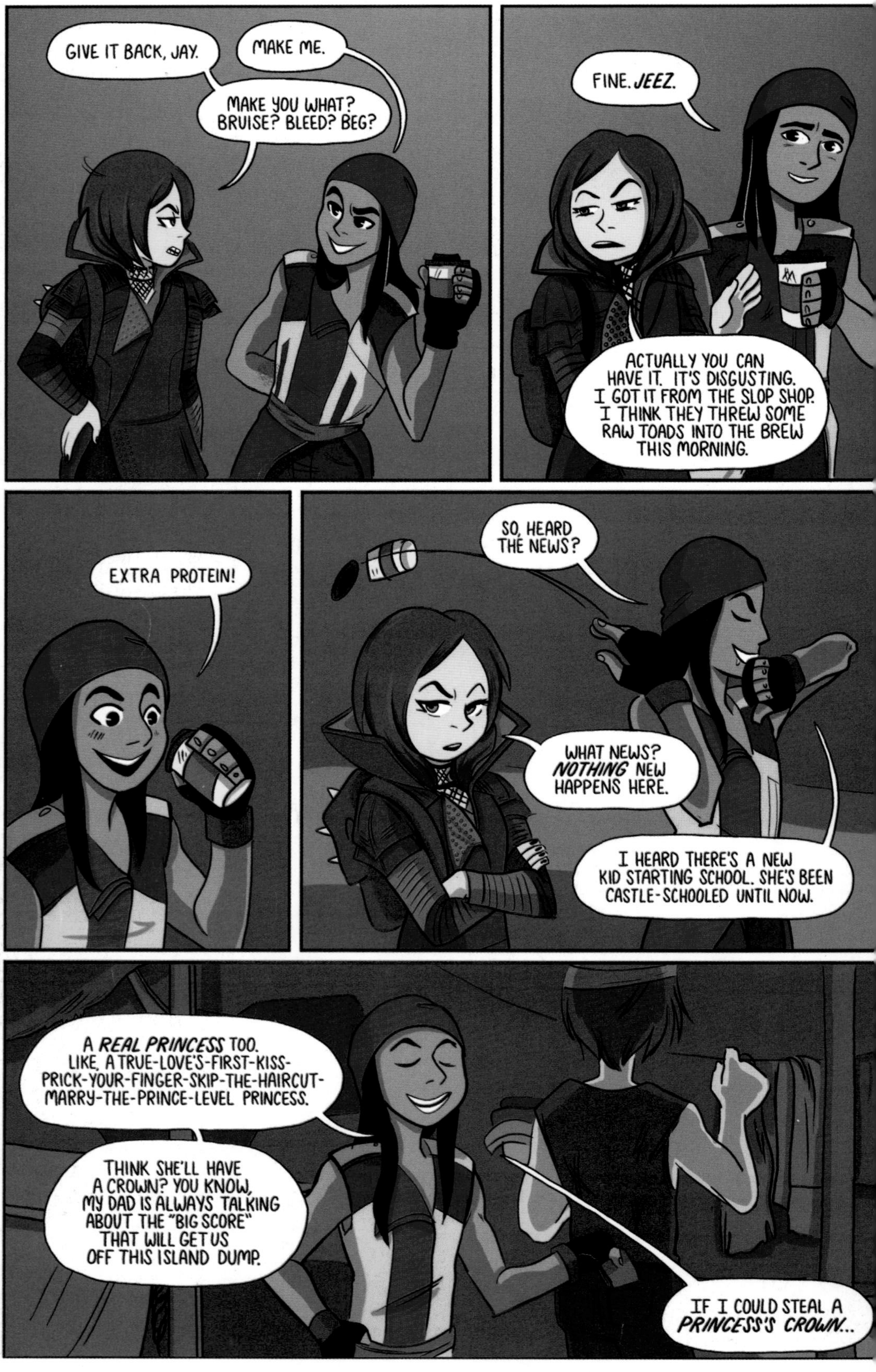
GIVE IT BACK, JAY.
MAKE ME.
MAKE YOU WHAT? BRUISE? BLEED? BEG?
FINE. *JEEZ.*
ACTUALLY YOU CAN HAVE IT. IT'S DISGUSTING. I GOT IT FROM THE SLOP SHOP. I THINK THEY THREW SOME RAW TOADS INTO THE BREW THIS MORNING.
EXTRA PROTEIN!
SO, HEARD THE NEWS?
WHAT NEWS? *NOTHING* NEW HAPPENS HERE.
I HEARD THERE'S A NEW KID STARTING SCHOOL. SHE'S BEEN CASTLE-SCHOOLED UNTIL NOW.
A *REAL PRINCESS* TOO. LIKE, A TRUE-LOVE'S-FIRST-KISS-PRICK-YOUR-FINGER-SKIP-THE-HAIRCUT-MARRY-THE-PRINCE-LEVEL PRINCESS.
THINK SHE'LL HAVE A CROWN? YOU KNOW, MY DAD IS ALWAYS TALKING ABOUT THE "BIG SCORE" THAT WILL GET US OFF THIS ISLAND DUMP.
IF I COULD STEAL A *PRINCESS'S CROWN...*

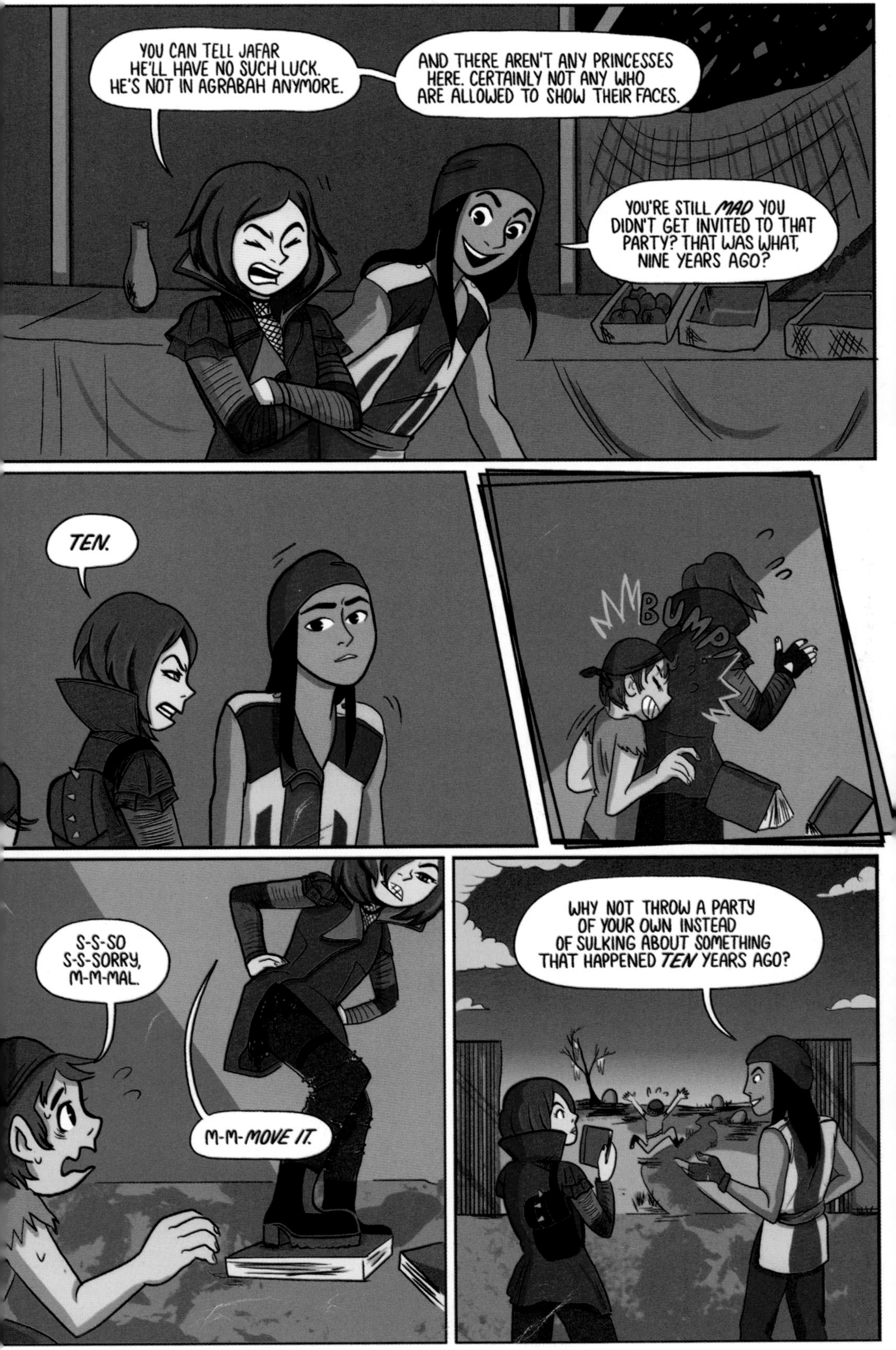
YOU CAN TELL JAFAR HE'LL HAVE NO SUCH LUCK. HE'S NOT IN AGRABAH ANYMORE.
AND THERE AREN'T ANY PRINCESSES HERE. CERTAINLY NOT ANY WHO ARE ALLOWED TO SHOW THEIR FACES.
YOU'RE STILL *MAD* YOU DIDN'T GET INVITED TO THAT PARTY? THAT WAS WHAT, NINE YEARS AGO?
TEN.
BUMP!
S-S-SO S-S-SORRY, M-M-MAL.
M-M-*MOVE IT.*
WHY NOT THROW A PARTY OF YOUR OWN INSTEAD OF SULKING ABOUT SOMETHING THAT HAPPENED *TEN* YEARS AGO?

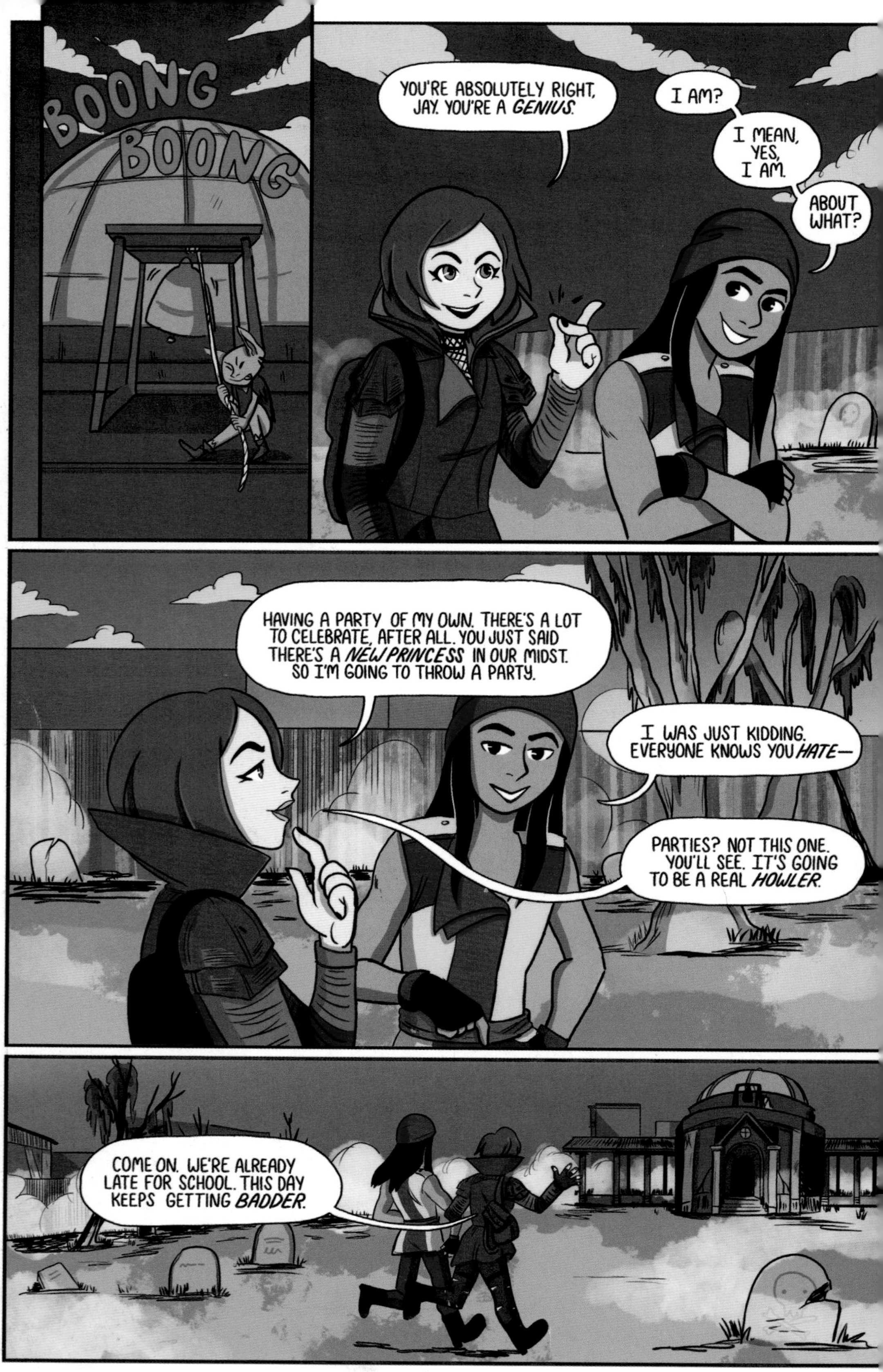
BOONG
BOONG
YOU'RE ABSOLUTELY RIGHT, JAY. YOU'RE A GENIUS.
I AM?
I MEAN, YES, I AM.
ABOUT WHAT?
HAVING A PARTY OF MY OWN. THERE'S A LOT TO CELEBRATE, AFTER ALL. YOU JUST SAID THERE'S A NEW PRINCESS IN OUR MIDST. SO I'M GOING TO THROW A PARTY.
I WAS JUST KIDDING. EVERYONE KNOWS YOU HATE—
PARTIES? NOT THIS ONE. YOU'LL SEE. IT'S GOING TO BE A REAL HOWLER.
COME ON. WE'RE ALREADY LATE FOR SCHOOL. THIS DAY KEEPS GETTING BADDER.

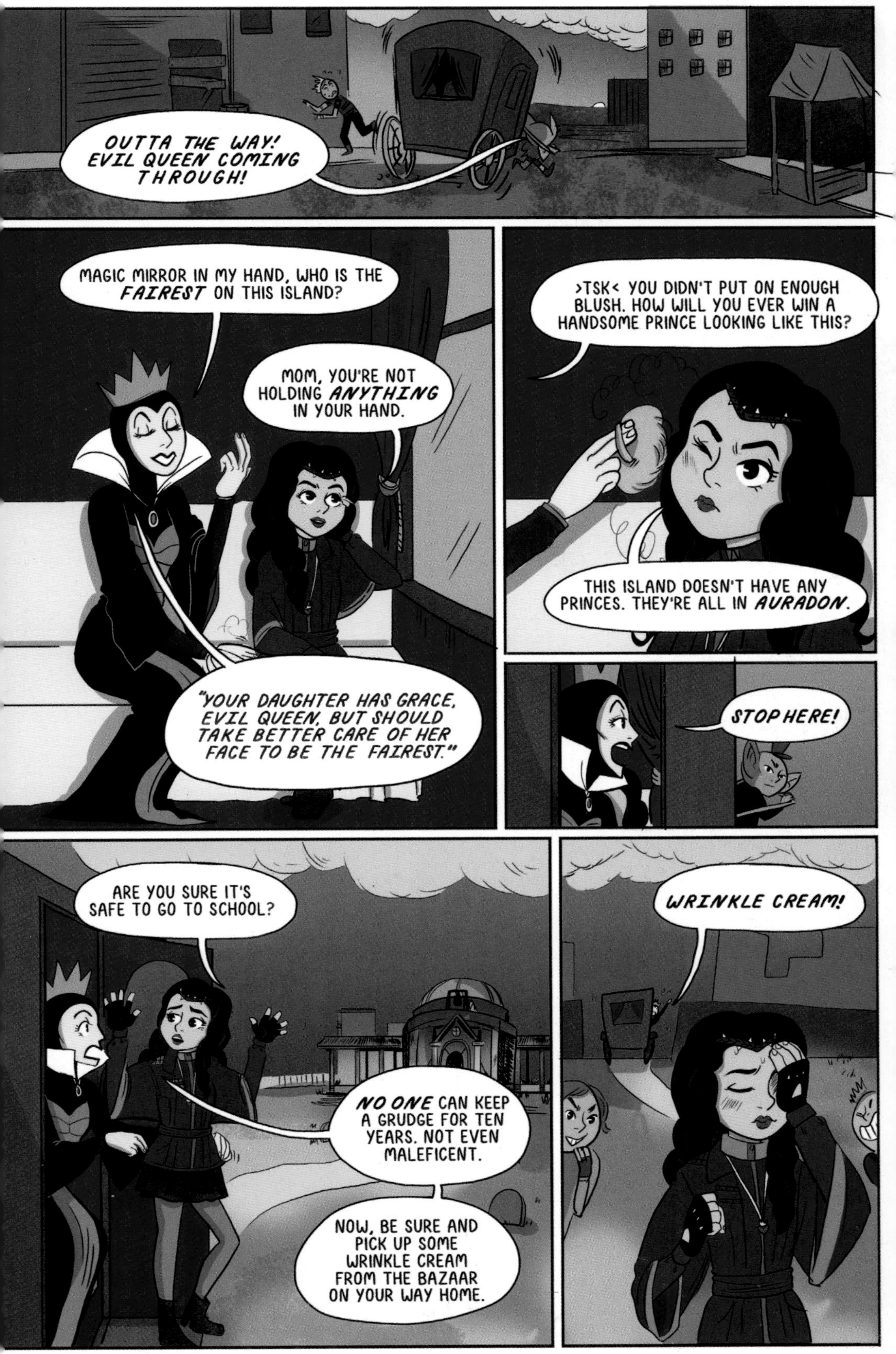
OUTTA THE WAY! EVIL QUEEN COMING THROUGH!
MAGIC MIRROR IN MY HAND, WHO IS THE *FAIREST* ON THIS ISLAND?
MOM, YOU'RE NOT HOLDING *ANYTHING* IN YOUR HAND.
"YOUR DAUGHTER HAS GRACE, EVIL QUEEN, BUT SHOULD TAKE BETTER CARE OF HER FACE TO BE THE FAIREST."
>TSK< YOU DIDN'T PUT ON ENOUGH BLUSH. HOW WILL YOU EVER WIN A HANDSOME PRINCE LOOKING LIKE THIS?
THIS ISLAND DOESN'T HAVE ANY PRINCES. THEY'RE ALL IN *AURADON*.
STOP HERE!
ARE YOU SURE IT'S SAFE TO GO TO SCHOOL?
NO ONE CAN KEEP A GRUDGE FOR TEN YEARS. NOT EVEN MALEFICENT.
NOW, BE SURE AND PICK UP SOME WRINKLE CREAM FROM THE BAZAAR ON YOUR WAY HOME.
WRINKLE CREAM!

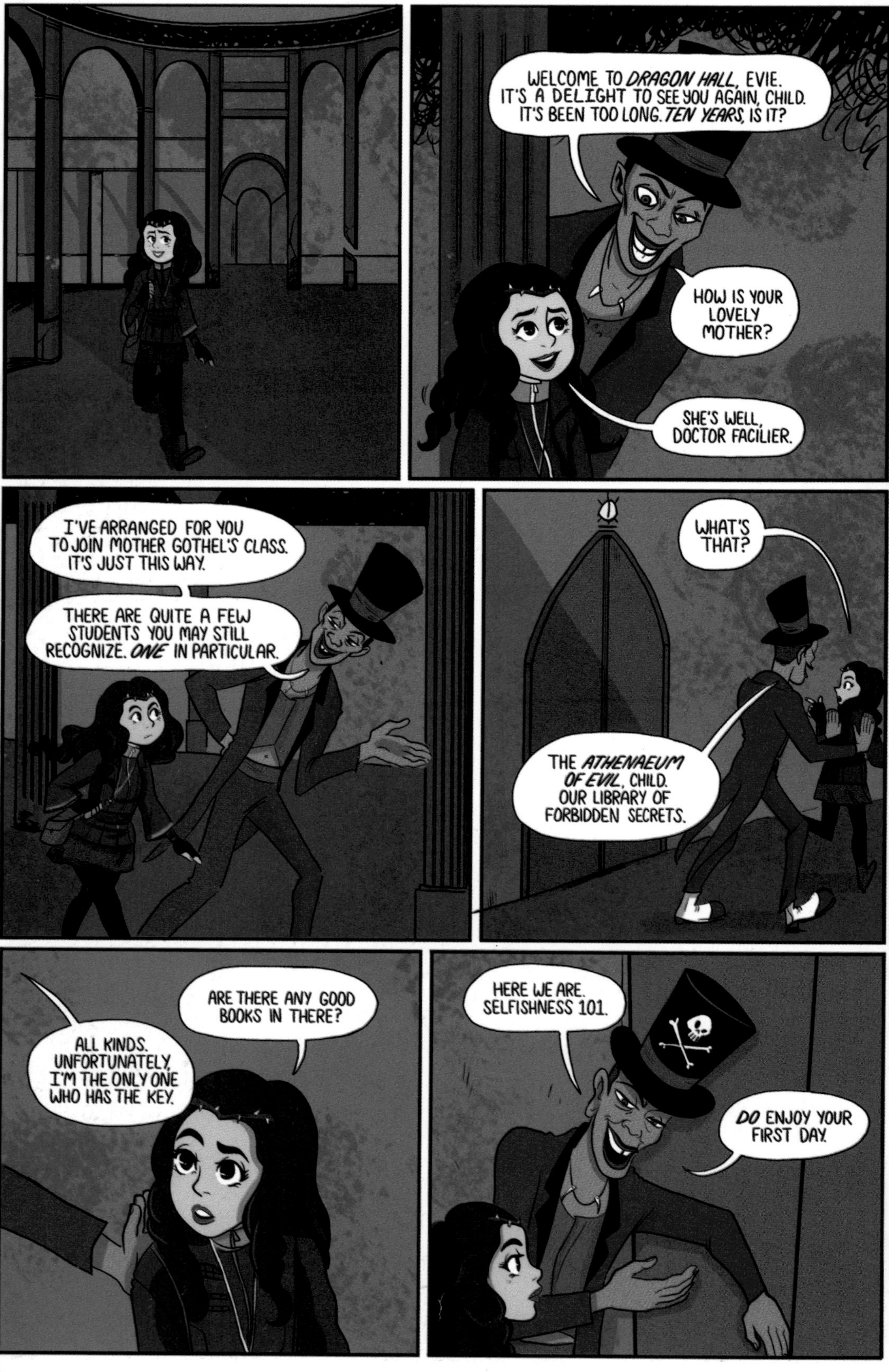
WELCOME TO DRAGON HALL, EVIE. IT'S A DELIGHT TO SEE YOU AGAIN, CHILD. IT'S BEEN TOO LONG. TEN YEARS, IS IT?
HOW IS YOUR LOVELY MOTHER?
SHE'S WELL, DOCTOR FACILIER.
I'VE ARRANGED FOR YOU TO JOIN MOTHER GOTHEL'S CLASS. IT'S JUST THIS WAY.
THERE ARE QUITE A FEW STUDENTS YOU MAY STILL RECOGNIZE. ONE IN PARTICULAR.
WHAT'S THAT?
THE ATHENAEUM OF EVIL, CHILD. OUR LIBRARY OF FORBIDDEN SECRETS.
ARE THERE ANY GOOD BOOKS IN THERE?
ALL KINDS. UNFORTUNATELY, I'M THE ONLY ONE WHO HAS THE KEY.
HERE WE ARE. SELFISHNESS 101.
DO ENJOY YOUR FIRST DAY.

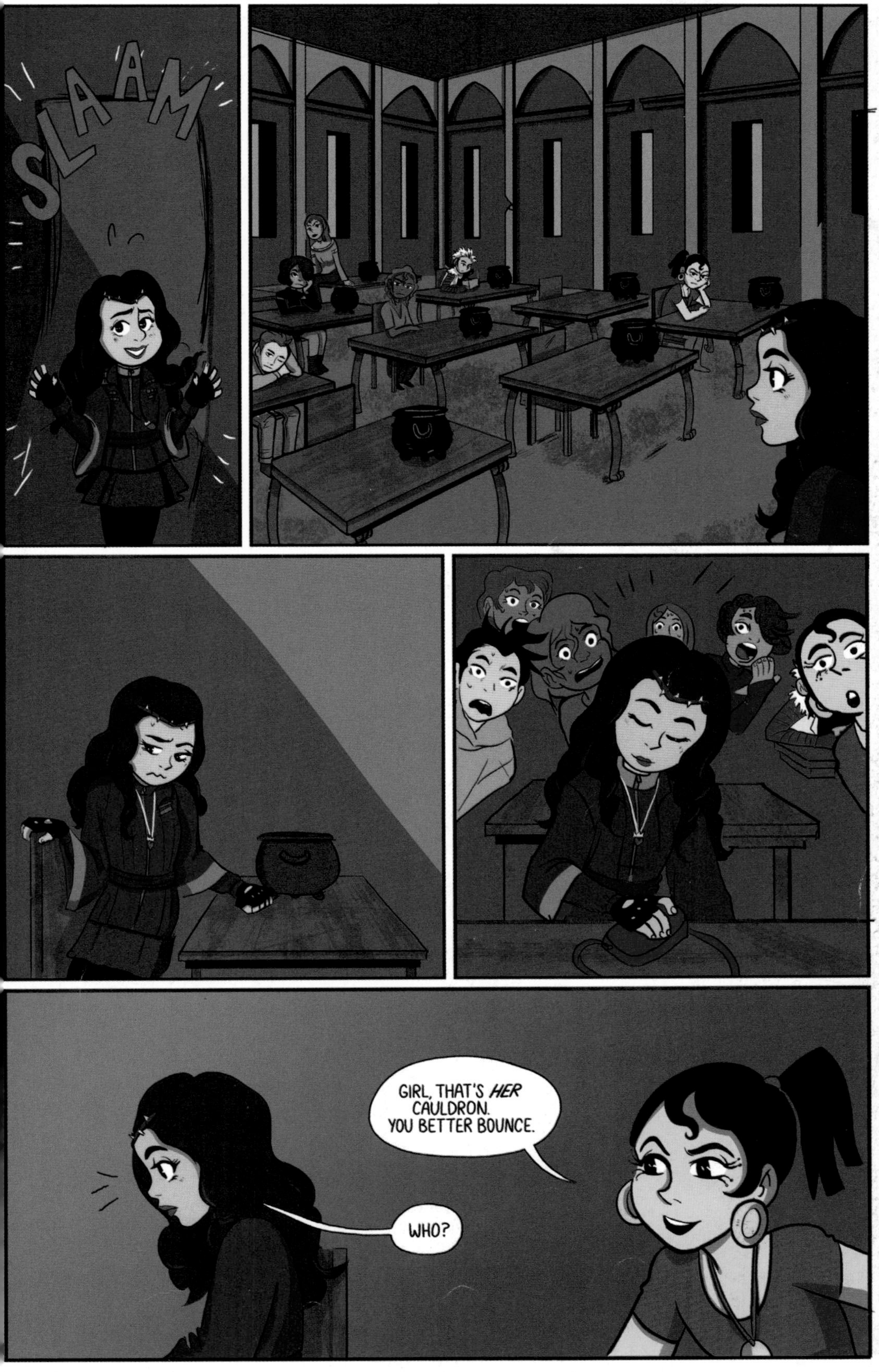
SLAAM
GIRL, THAT'S *HER* CAULDRON. YOU BETTER BOUNCE.
WHO?

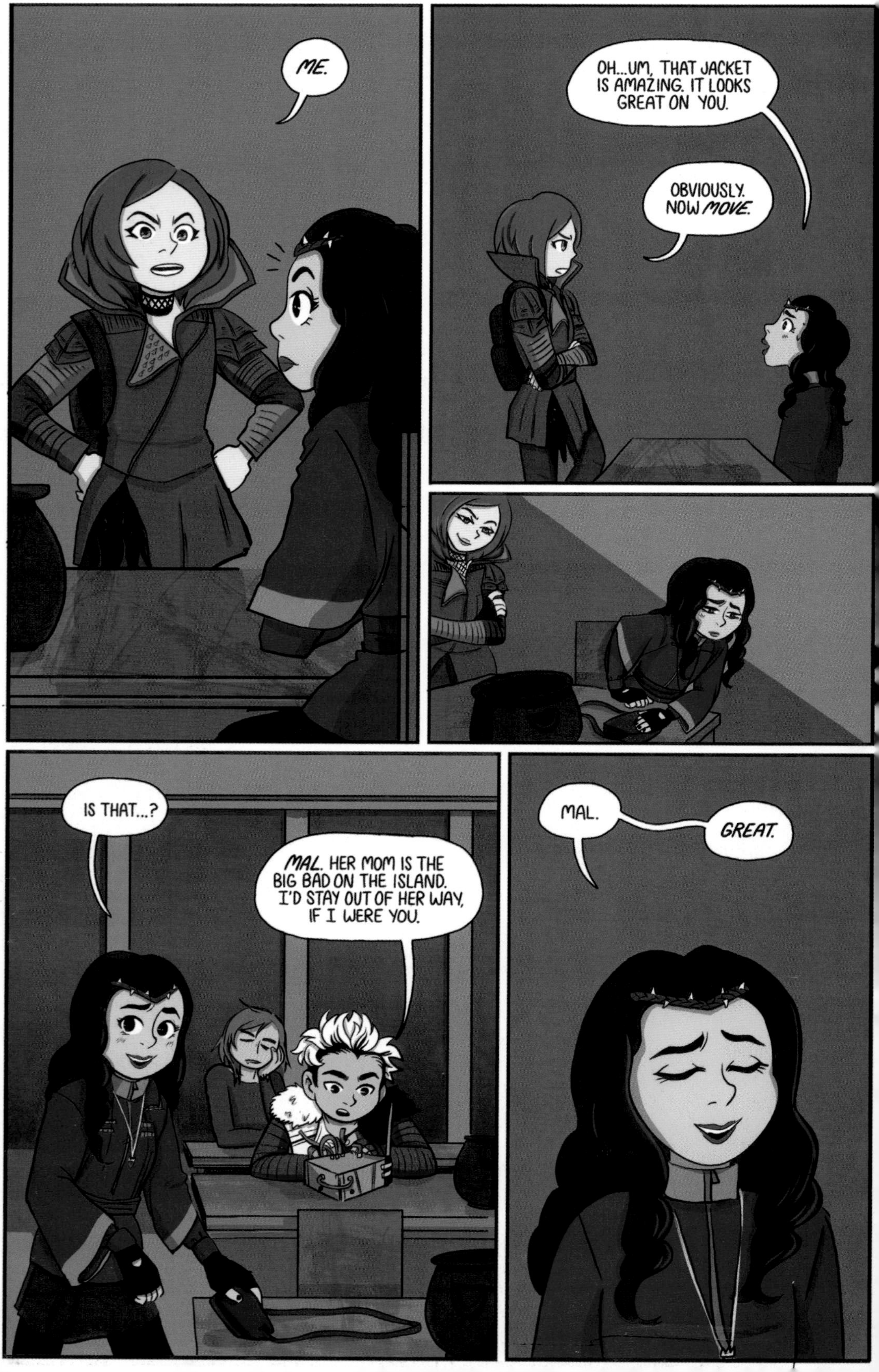
ME.
OH...UM, THAT JACKET IS AMAZING. IT LOOKS GREAT ON YOU.
OBVIOUSLY. NOW MOVE.
IS THAT...?
MAL. HER MOM IS THE BIG BAD ON THE ISLAND. I'D STAY OUT OF HER WAY, IF I WERE YOU.
MAL.
GREAT.

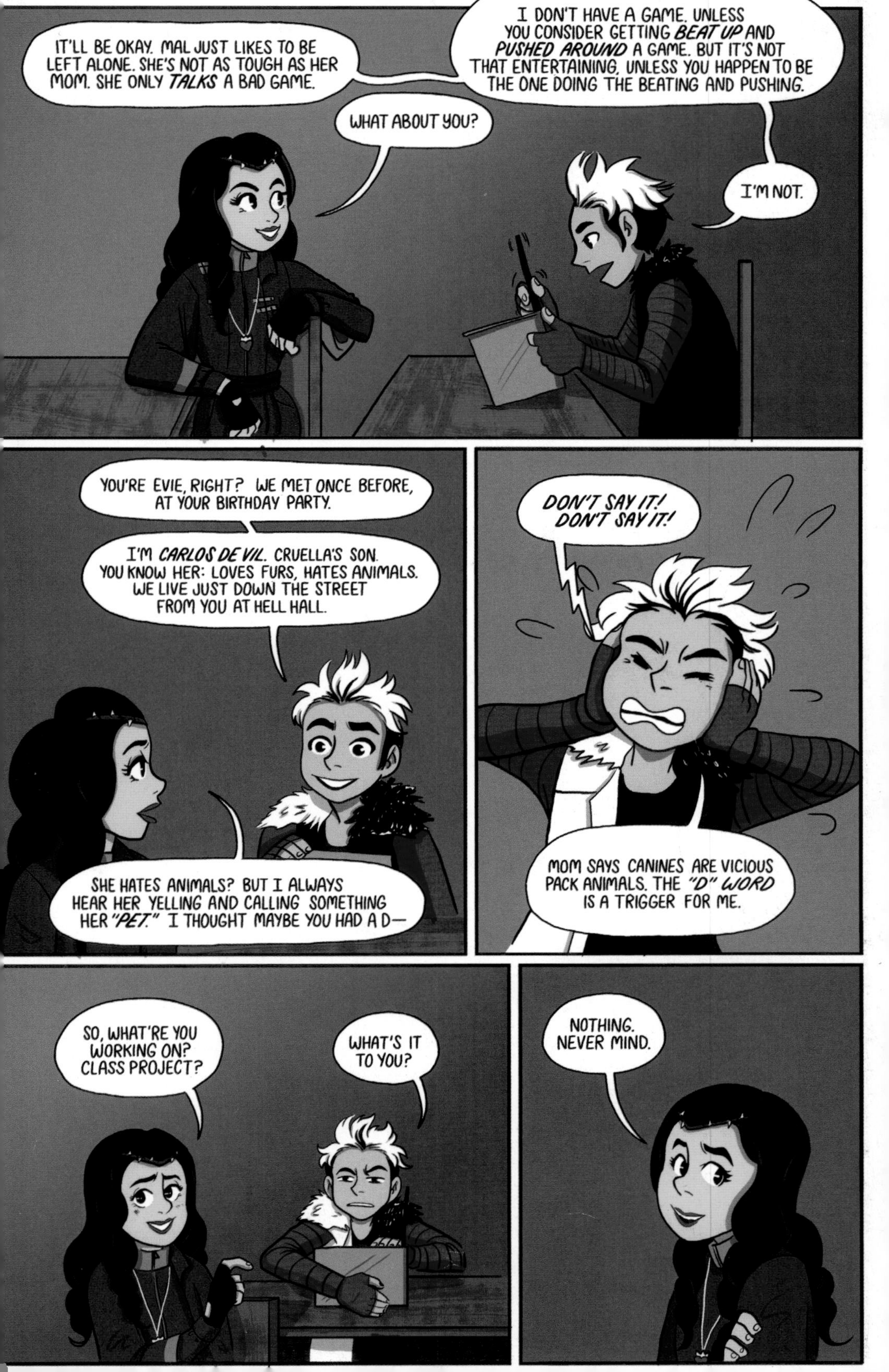
IT'LL BE OKAY. MAL JUST LIKES TO BE LEFT ALONE. SHE'S NOT AS TOUGH AS HER MOM. SHE ONLY *TALKS* A BAD GAME.
WHAT ABOUT YOU?
I DON'T HAVE A GAME. UNLESS YOU CONSIDER GETTING *BEAT UP* AND *PUSHED AROUND* A GAME. BUT IT'S NOT THAT ENTERTAINING, UNLESS YOU HAPPEN TO BE THE ONE DOING THE BEATING AND PUSHING.
I'M NOT.
YOU'RE EVIE, RIGHT? WE MET ONCE BEFORE, AT YOUR BIRTHDAY PARTY.
I'M *CARLOS DE VIL*. CRUELLA'S SON. YOU KNOW HER: LOVES FURS, HATES ANIMALS. WE LIVE JUST DOWN THE STREET FROM YOU AT HELL HALL.
SHE HATES ANIMALS? BUT I ALWAYS HEAR HER YELLING AND CALLING SOMETHING HER *"PET."* I THOUGHT MAYBE YOU HAD A D—
DON'T SAY IT! DON'T SAY IT!
MOM SAYS CANINES ARE VICIOUS PACK ANIMALS. THE *"D" WORD* IS A TRIGGER FOR ME.
SO, WHAT'RE YOU WORKING ON? CLASS PROJECT?
WHAT'S IT TO YOU?
NOTHING. NEVER MIND.

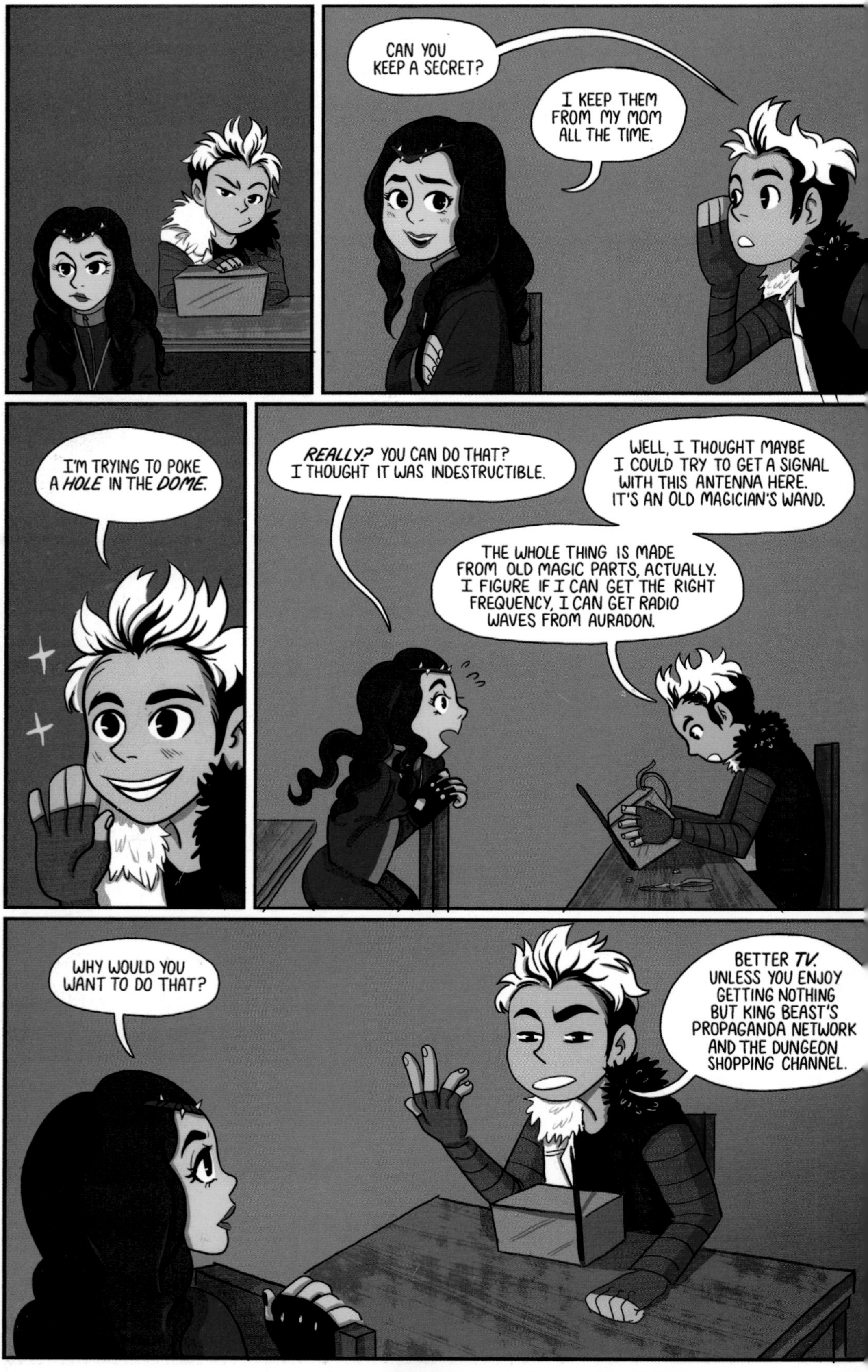
CAN YOU KEEP A SECRET?
I KEEP THEM FROM MY MOM ALL THE TIME.
I'M TRYING TO POKE A *HOLE* IN THE *DOME*.
REALLY? YOU CAN DO THAT? I THOUGHT IT WAS INDESTRUCTIBLE.
WELL, I THOUGHT MAYBE I COULD TRY TO GET A SIGNAL WITH THIS ANTENNA HERE. IT'S AN OLD MAGICIAN'S WAND.
THE WHOLE THING IS MADE FROM OLD MAGIC PARTS, ACTUALLY. I FIGURE IF I CAN GET THE RIGHT FREQUENCY, I CAN GET RADIO WAVES FROM AURADON.
WHY WOULD YOU WANT TO DO THAT?
BETTER *TV.* UNLESS YOU ENJOY GETTING NOTHING BUT KING BEAST'S PROPAGANDA NETWORK AND THE DUNGEON SHOPPING CHANNEL.

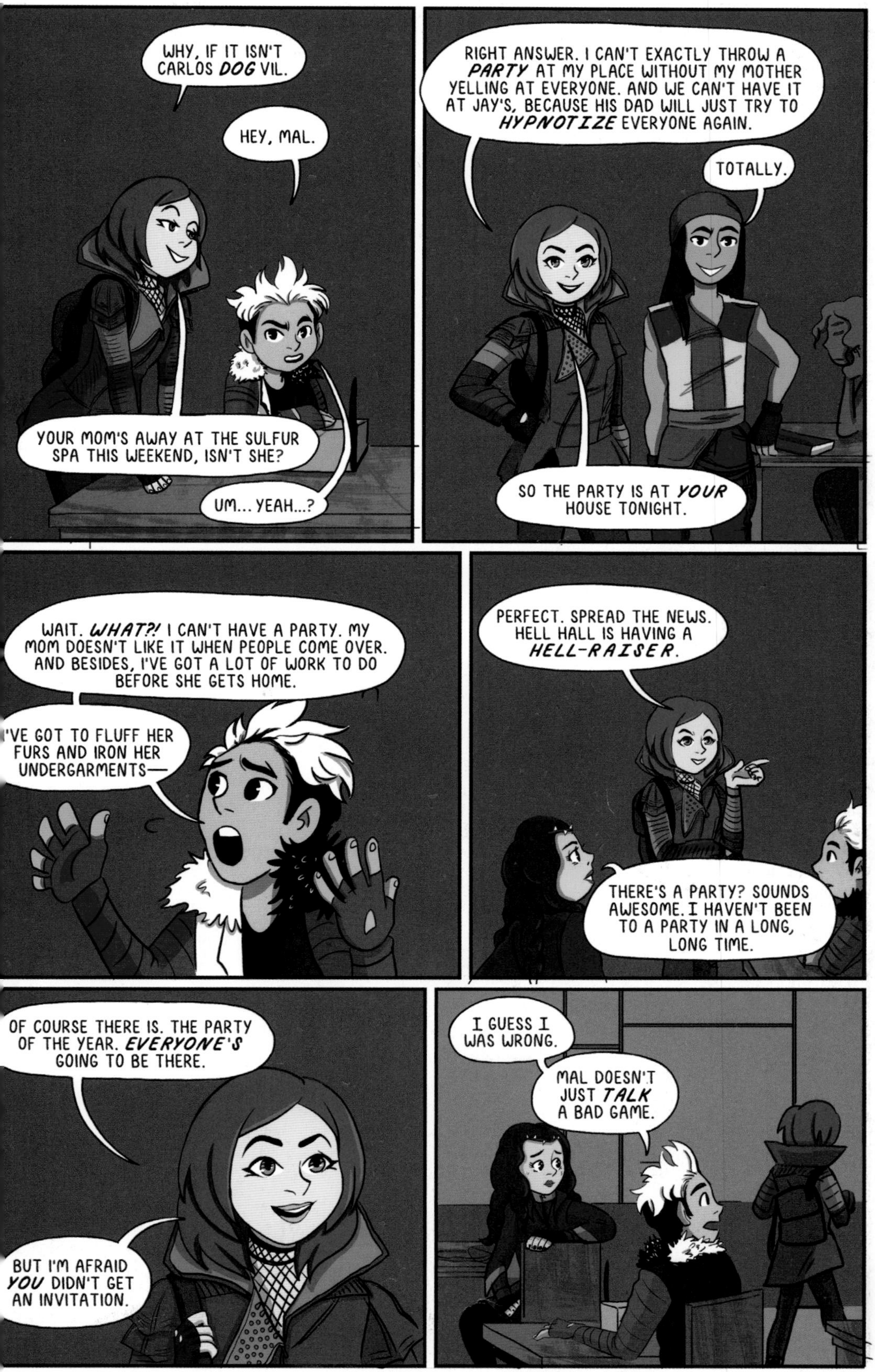

WHY, IF IT ISN'T CARLOS *DOG* VIL.
HEY, MAL.
YOUR MOM'S AWAY AT THE SULFUR SPA THIS WEEKEND, ISN'T SHE?
UM... YEAH...?
RIGHT ANSWER. I CAN'T EXACTLY THROW A *PARTY* AT MY PLACE WITHOUT MY MOTHER YELLING AT EVERYONE. AND WE CAN'T HAVE IT AT JAY'S, BECAUSE HIS DAD WILL JUST TRY TO *HYPNOTIZE* EVERYONE AGAIN.
TOTALLY.
SO THE PARTY IS AT *YOUR* HOUSE TONIGHT.
WAIT. *WHAT?!* I CAN'T HAVE A PARTY. MY MOM DOESN'T LIKE IT WHEN PEOPLE COME OVER. AND BESIDES, I'VE GOT A LOT OF WORK TO DO BEFORE SHE GETS HOME.
I'VE GOT TO FLUFF HER FURS AND IRON HER UNDERGARMENTS—
PERFECT. SPREAD THE NEWS. HELL HALL IS HAVING A *HELL-RAISER*.
THERE'S A PARTY? SOUNDS AWESOME. I HAVEN'T BEEN TO A PARTY IN A LONG, LONG TIME.
OF COURSE THERE IS. THE PARTY OF THE YEAR. *EVERYONE'S* GOING TO BE THERE.
BUT I'M AFRAID *YOU* DIDN'T GET AN INVITATION.
I GUESS I WAS WRONG.
MAL DOESN'T JUST *TALK* A BAD GAME.

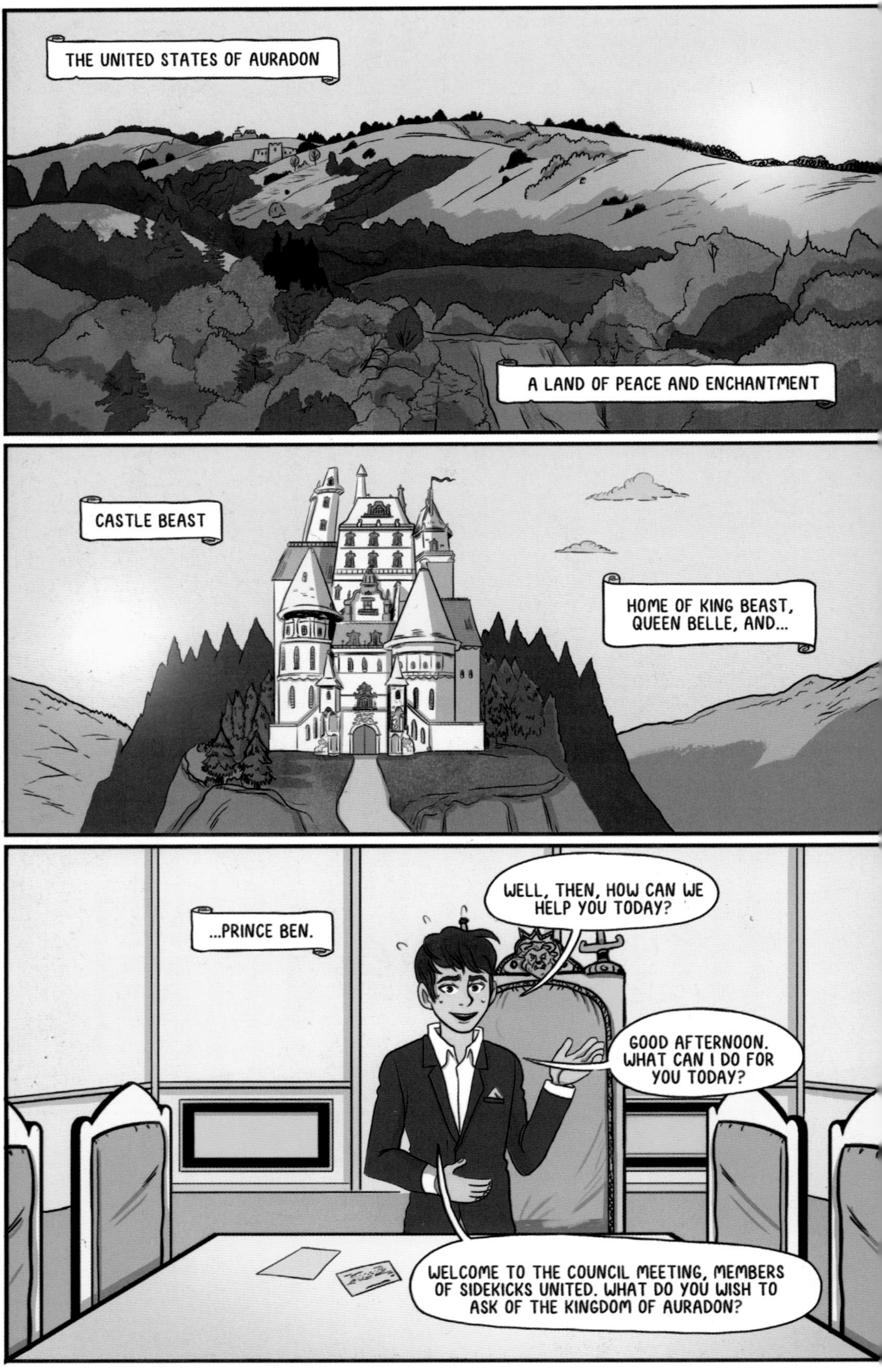
THE UNITED STATES OF AURADON
A LAND OF PEACE AND ENCHANTMENT
CASTLE BEAST
HOME OF KING BEAST, QUEEN BELLE, AND...
...PRINCE BEN.
WELCOME TO THE COUNCIL MEETING, MEMBERS OF SIDEKICKS UNITED. WHAT DO YOU WISH TO ASK OF THE KINGDOM OF AURADON?
GOOD AFTERNOON. WHAT CAN I DO FOR YOU TODAY?
WELL, THEN, HOW CAN WE HELP YOU TODAY?

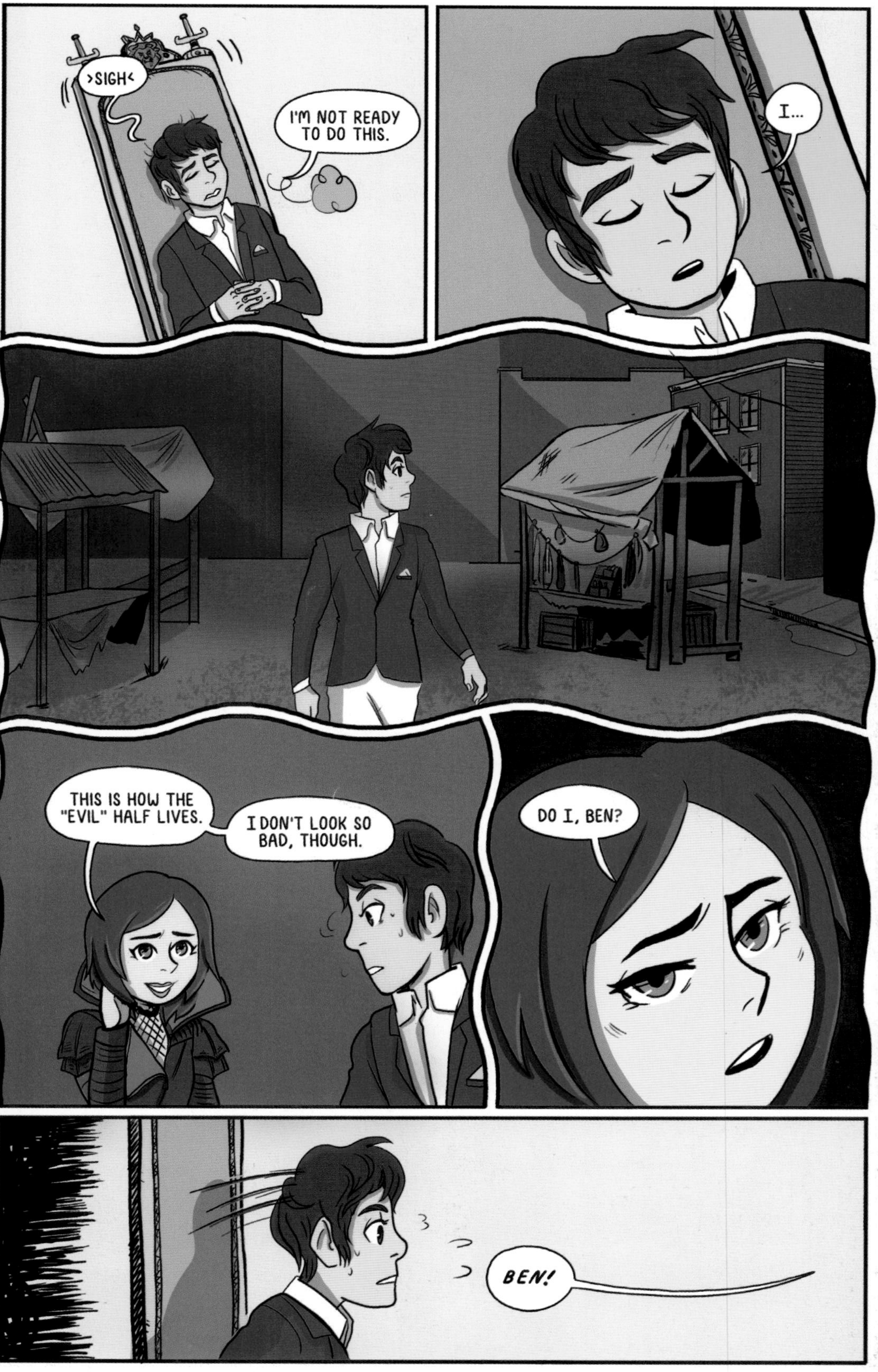
>SIGH<
I'M NOT READY TO DO THIS.
I...
THIS IS HOW THE "EVIL" HALF LIVES.
I DON'T LOOK SO BAD, THOUGH.
DO I, BEN?
BEN!

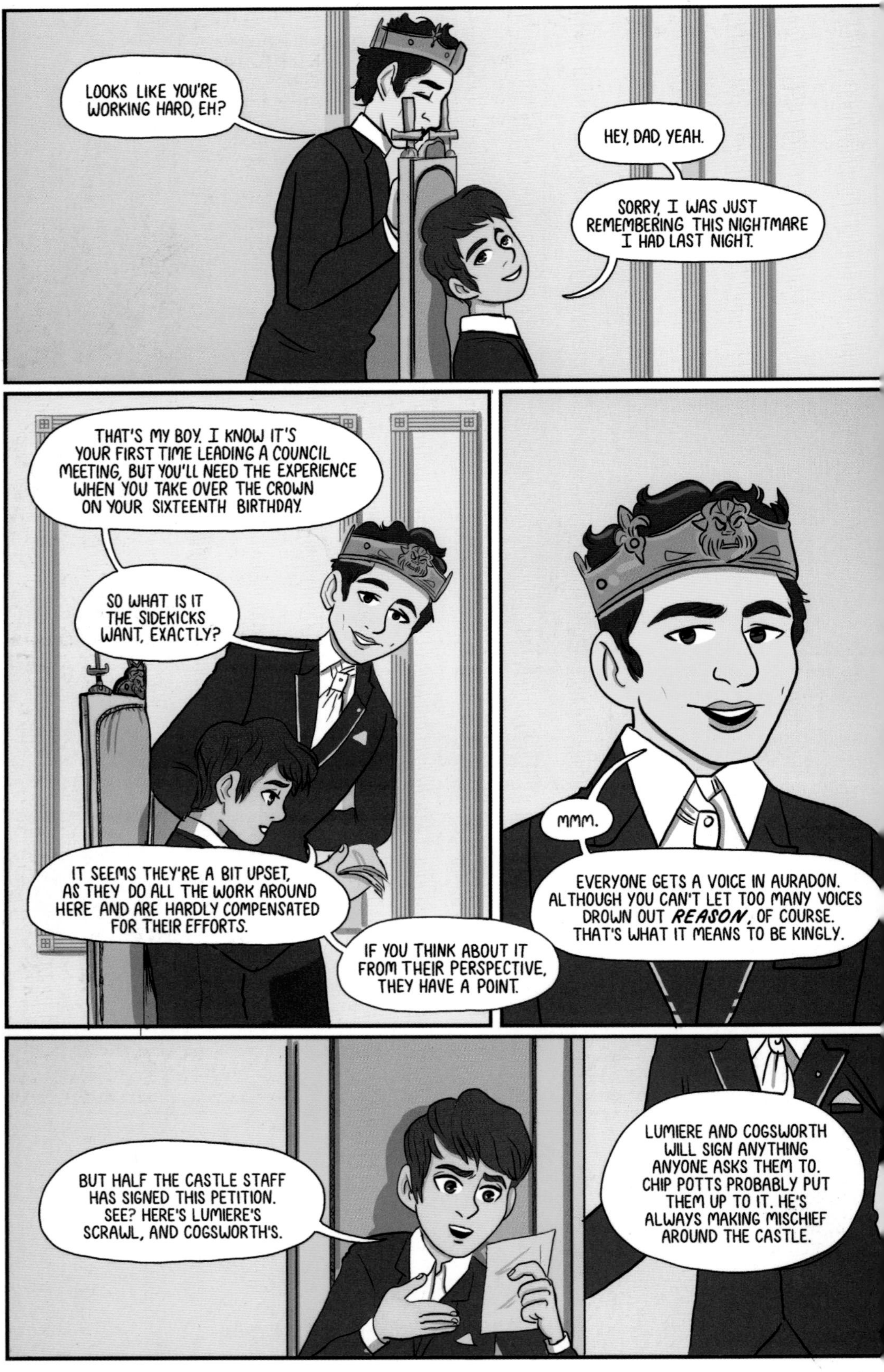
LOOKS LIKE YOU'RE WORKING HARD, EH?
HEY, DAD, YEAH.
SORRY, I WAS JUST REMEMBERING THIS NIGHTMARE I HAD LAST NIGHT.
THAT'S MY BOY. I KNOW IT'S YOUR FIRST TIME LEADING A COUNCIL MEETING, BUT YOU'LL NEED THE EXPERIENCE WHEN YOU TAKE OVER THE CROWN ON YOUR SIXTEENTH BIRTHDAY.
SO WHAT IS IT THE SIDEKICKS WANT, EXACTLY?
IT SEEMS THEY'RE A BIT UPSET, AS THEY DO ALL THE WORK AROUND HERE AND ARE HARDLY COMPENSATED FOR THEIR EFFORTS.
IF YOU THINK ABOUT IT FROM THEIR PERSPECTIVE, THEY HAVE A POINT.
MMM.
EVERYONE GETS A VOICE IN AURADON. ALTHOUGH YOU CAN'T LET TOO MANY VOICES DROWN OUT *REASON*, OF COURSE. THAT'S WHAT IT MEANS TO BE KINGLY.
BUT HALF THE CASTLE STAFF HAS SIGNED THIS PETITION. SEE? HERE'S LUMIERE'S SCRAWL, AND COGSWORTH'S.
LUMIERE AND COGSWORTH WILL SIGN ANYTHING ANYONE ASKS THEM TO. CHIP POTTS PROBABLY PUT THEM UP TO IT. HE'S ALWAYS MAKING MISCHIEF AROUND THE CASTLE.

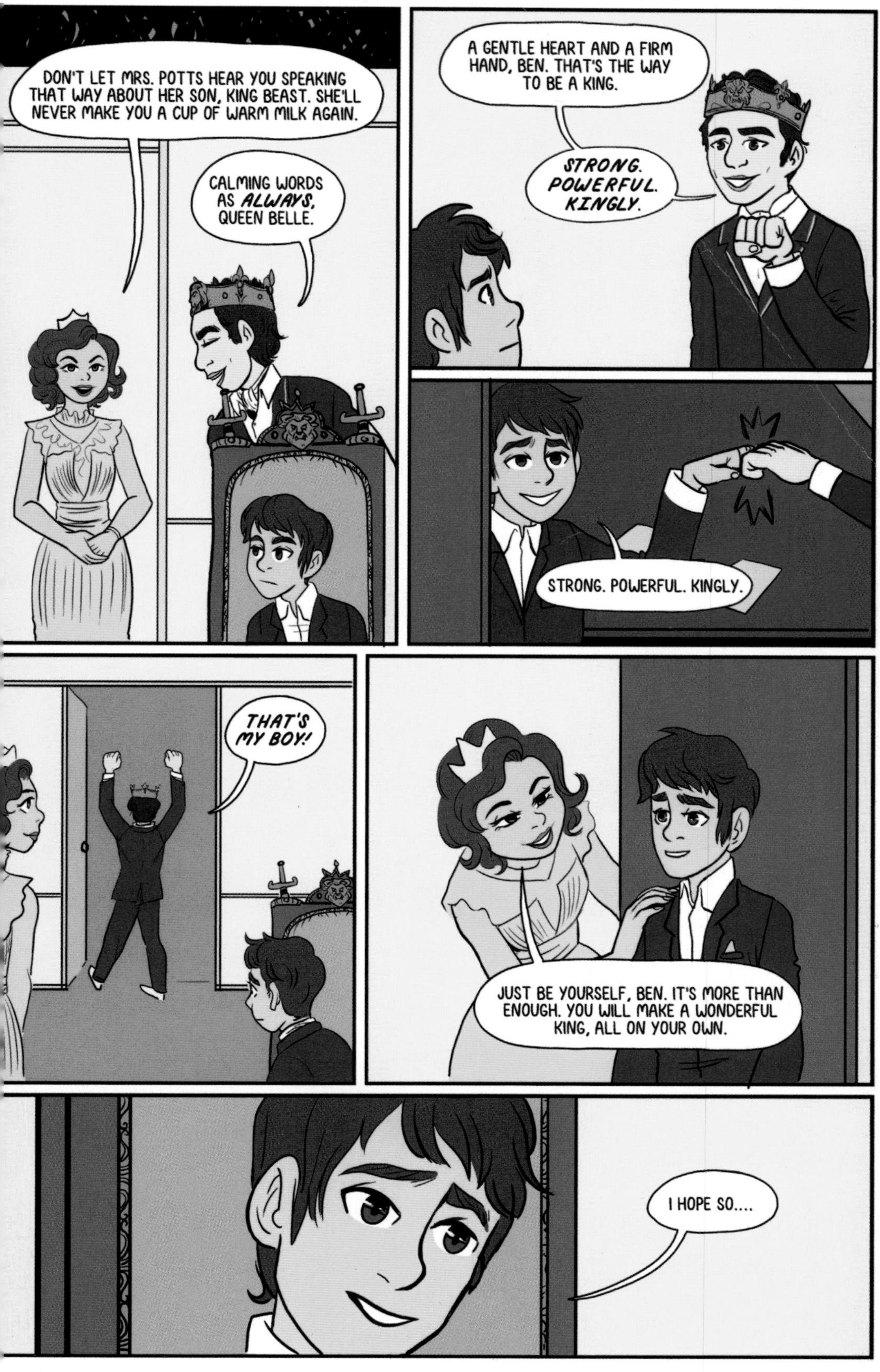
DON'T LET MRS. POTTS HEAR YOU SPEAKING THAT WAY ABOUT HER SON, KING BEAST. SHE'LL NEVER MAKE YOU A CUP OF WARM MILK AGAIN.
CALMING WORDS AS ALWAYS, QUEEN BELLE.
A GENTLE HEART AND A FIRM HAND, BEN. THAT'S THE WAY TO BE A KING.
STRONG. POWERFUL. KINGLY.
STRONG. POWERFUL. KINGLY.
THAT'S MY BOY!
JUST BE YOURSELF, BEN. IT'S MORE THAN ENOUGH. YOU WILL MAKE A WONDERFUL KING, ALL ON YOUR OWN.
I HOPE SO....

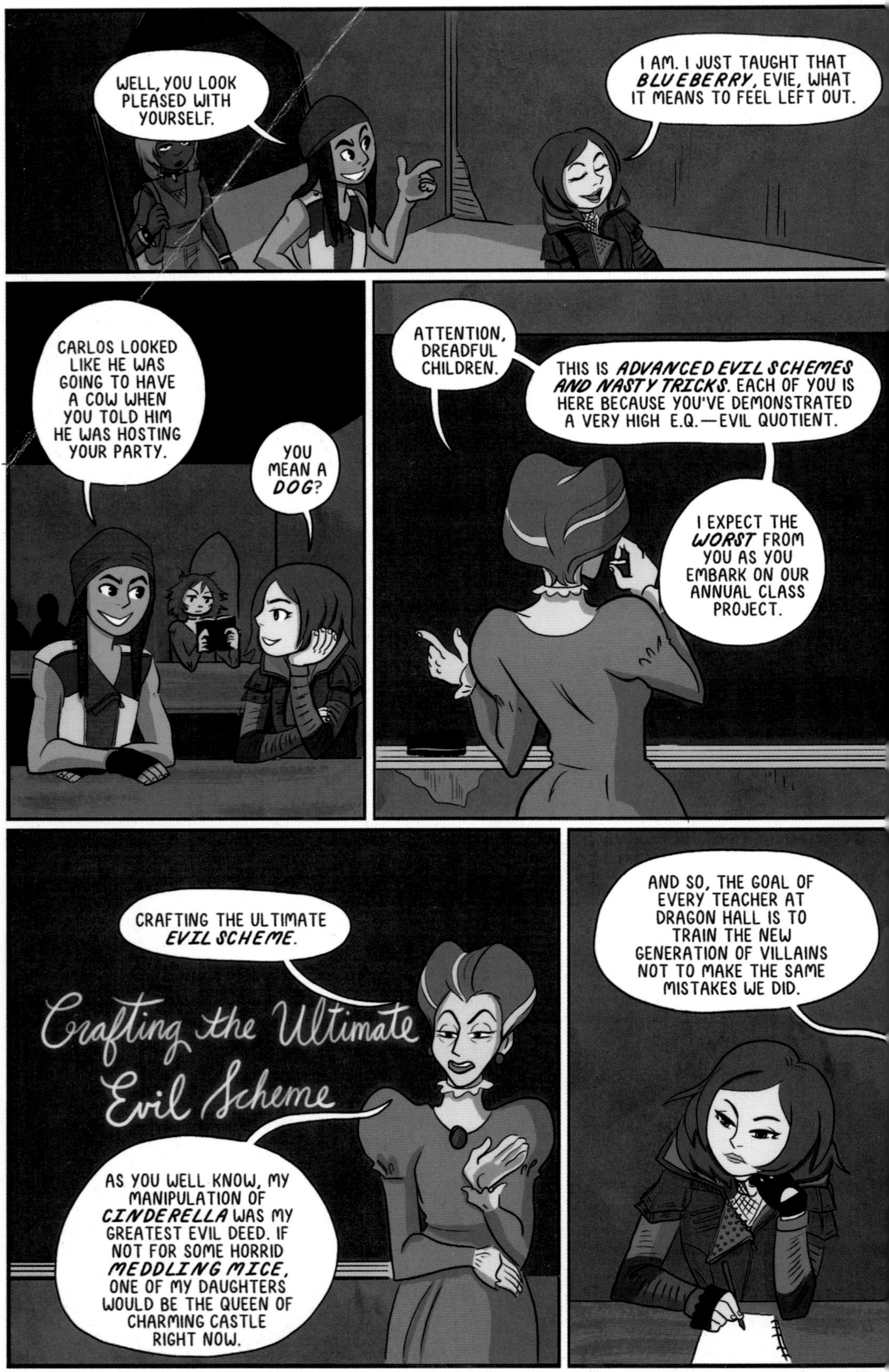
WELL, YOU LOOK PLEASED WITH YOURSELF.
I AM. I JUST TAUGHT THAT BLUEBERRY, EVIE, WHAT IT MEANS TO FEEL LEFT OUT.
CARLOS LOOKED LIKE HE WAS GOING TO HAVE A COW WHEN YOU TOLD HIM HE WAS HOSTING YOUR PARTY.
YOU MEAN A DOG?
ATTENTION, DREADFUL CHILDREN.
THIS IS ADVANCED EVIL SCHEMES AND NASTY TRICKS. EACH OF YOU IS HERE BECAUSE YOU'VE DEMONSTRATED A VERY HIGH E.Q.—EVIL QUOTIENT.
I EXPECT THE WORST FROM YOU AS YOU EMBARK ON OUR ANNUAL CLASS PROJECT.
CRAFTING THE ULTIMATE EVIL SCHEME.
Crafting the Ultimate Evil Scheme
AS YOU WELL KNOW, MY MANIPULATION OF CINDERELLA WAS MY GREATEST EVIL DEED. IF NOT FOR SOME HORRID MEDDLING MICE, ONE OF MY DAUGHTERS WOULD BE THE QUEEN OF CHARMING CASTLE RIGHT NOW.
AND SO, THE GOAL OF EVERY TEACHER AT DRAGON HALL IS TO TRAIN THE NEW GENERATION OF VILLAINS NOT TO MAKE THE SAME MISTAKES WE DID.

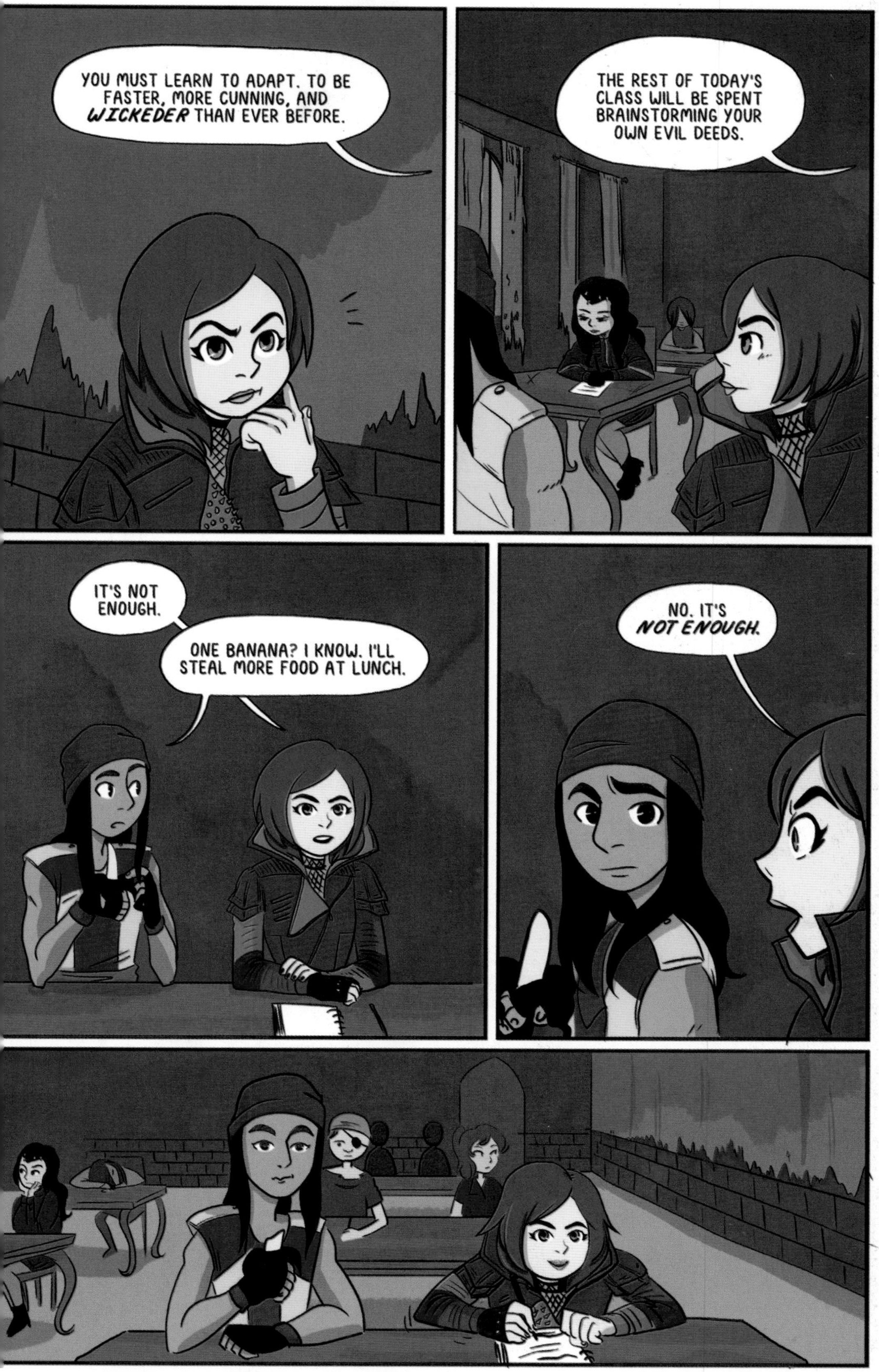
YOU MUST LEARN TO ADAPT. TO BE FASTER, MORE CUNNING, AND *WICKEDER* THAN EVER BEFORE.
THE REST OF TODAY'S CLASS WILL BE SPENT BRAINSTORMING YOUR OWN EVIL DEEDS.
IT'S NOT ENOUGH.
ONE BANANA? I KNOW. I'LL STEAL MORE FOOD AT LUNCH.
NO. IT'S *NOT ENOUGH.*

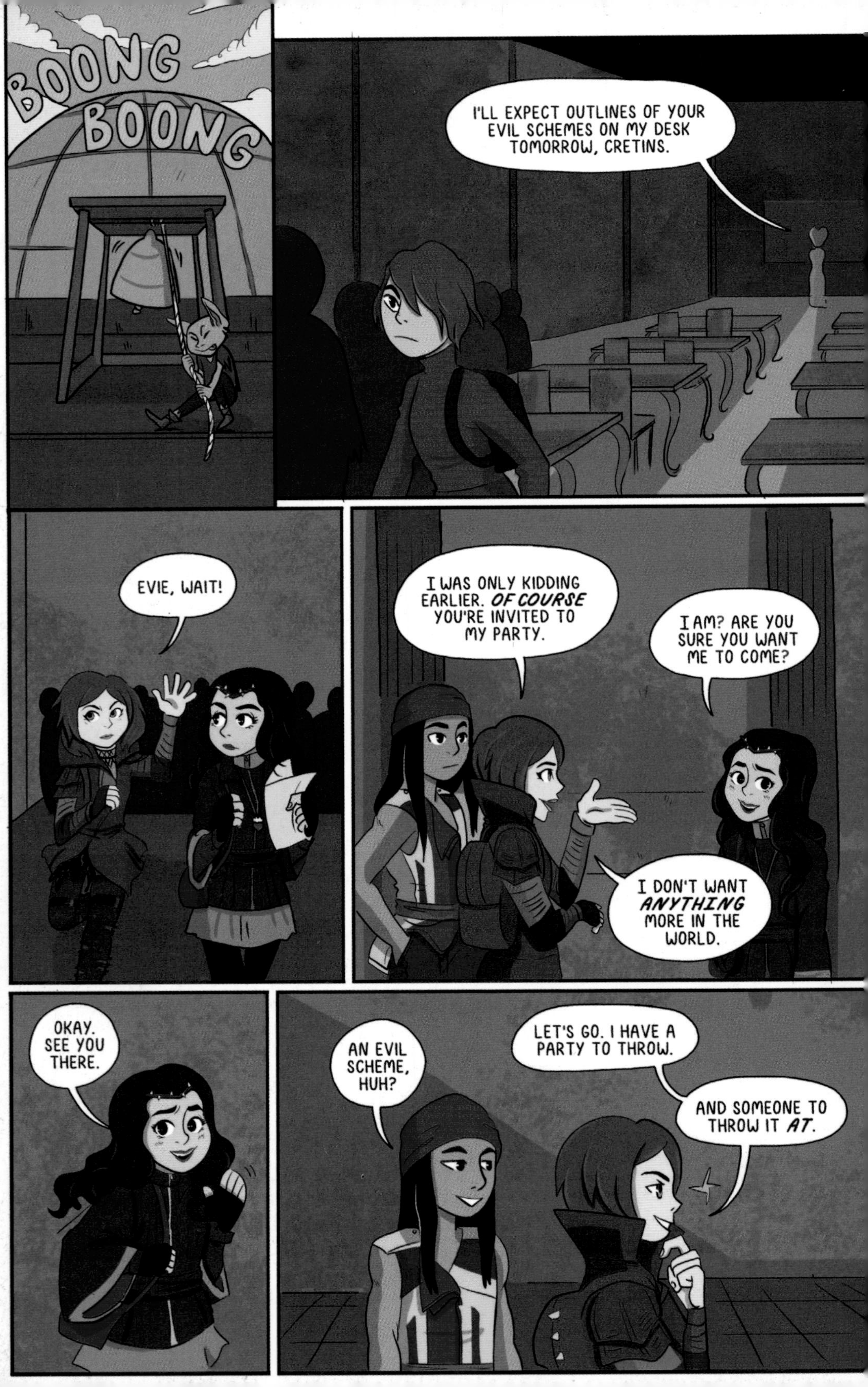
BOONG
BOONG
I'LL EXPECT OUTLINES OF YOUR EVIL SCHEMES ON MY DESK TOMORROW, CRETINS.
EVIE, WAIT!
I WAS ONLY KIDDING EARLIER. *OF COURSE* YOU'RE INVITED TO MY PARTY.
I AM? ARE YOU SURE YOU WANT ME TO COME?
I DON'T WANT *ANYTHING* MORE IN THE WORLD.
OKAY. SEE YOU THERE.
AN EVIL SCHEME, HUH?
LET'S GO. I HAVE A PARTY TO THROW.
AND SOMEONE TO THROW IT *AT*.

LUNCH

DID YOU HEAR *MAL* IS THROWING A PARTY AT HELL HALL? I HEARD IF YOU DON'T GO, SHE'LL COME *FIND YOU.*

FINAL PERIOD

BE THERE, OR MAL WILL *FIND YOU* AND *BAN YOU* FROM THE CITY STREETS.

AFTER SCHOOL

BE THERE, OR MAL WILL *FIND YOU* AND *BAN YOU* AND MAKE EVERYONE FORGET YOU *EVER EXISTED,* AND FROM THIS DAY FORWARD YOU WILL BE KNOWN ONLY BY THE NAME OF *SLOP!*

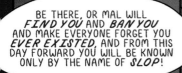

PARTY TIME

I DON'T WANT TO BE HERE....

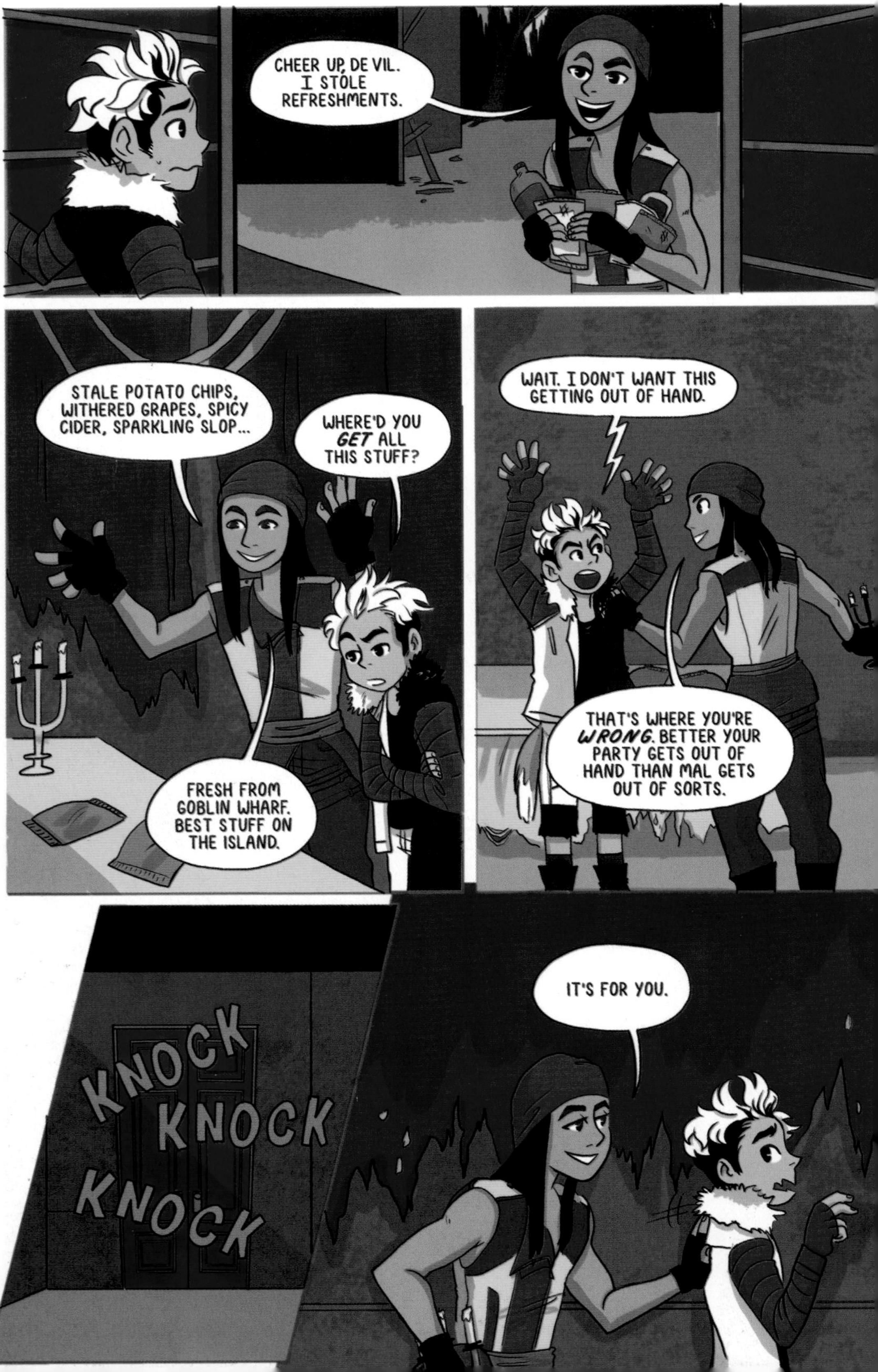
CHEER UP, DE VIL. I STOLE REFRESHMENTS.
STALE POTATO CHIPS, WITHERED GRAPES, SPICY CIDER, SPARKLING SLOP...
WHERE'D YOU GET ALL THIS STUFF?
FRESH FROM GOBLIN WHARF. BEST STUFF ON THE ISLAND.
WAIT. I DON'T WANT THIS GETTING OUT OF HAND.
THAT'S WHERE YOU'RE WRONG. BETTER YOUR PARTY GETS OUT OF HAND THAN MAL GETS OUT OF SORTS.
KNOCK
KNOCK
KNOCK
IT'S FOR YOU.

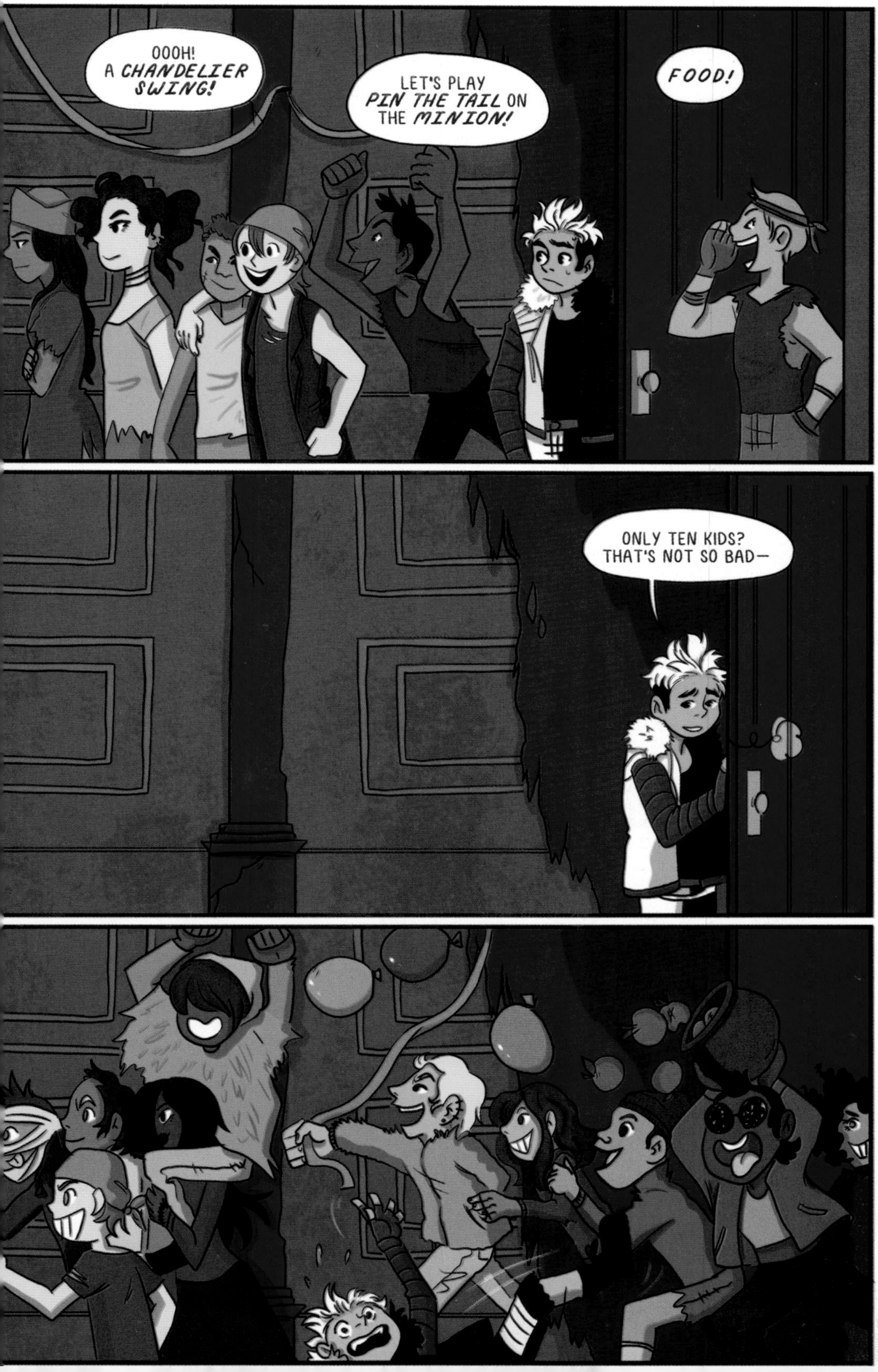
OOOH! A CHANDELIER SWING!
LET'S PLAY PIN THE TAIL ON THE MINION!
FOOD!
ONLY TEN KIDS? THAT'S NOT SO BAD—

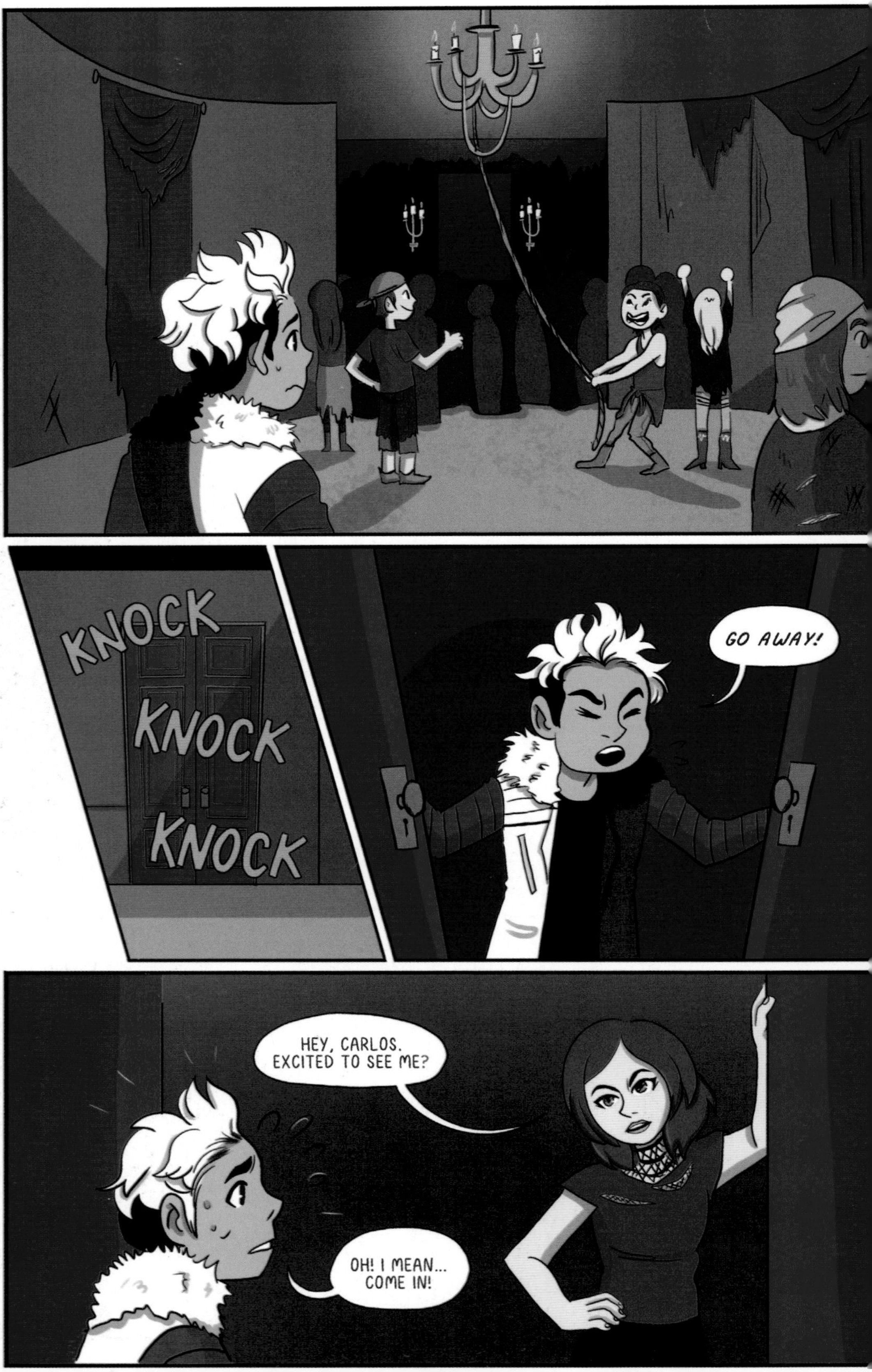
KNOCK
KNOCK
KNOCK
GO AWAY!
HEY, CARLOS.
EXCITED TO SEE ME?
OH! I MEAN...
COME IN!

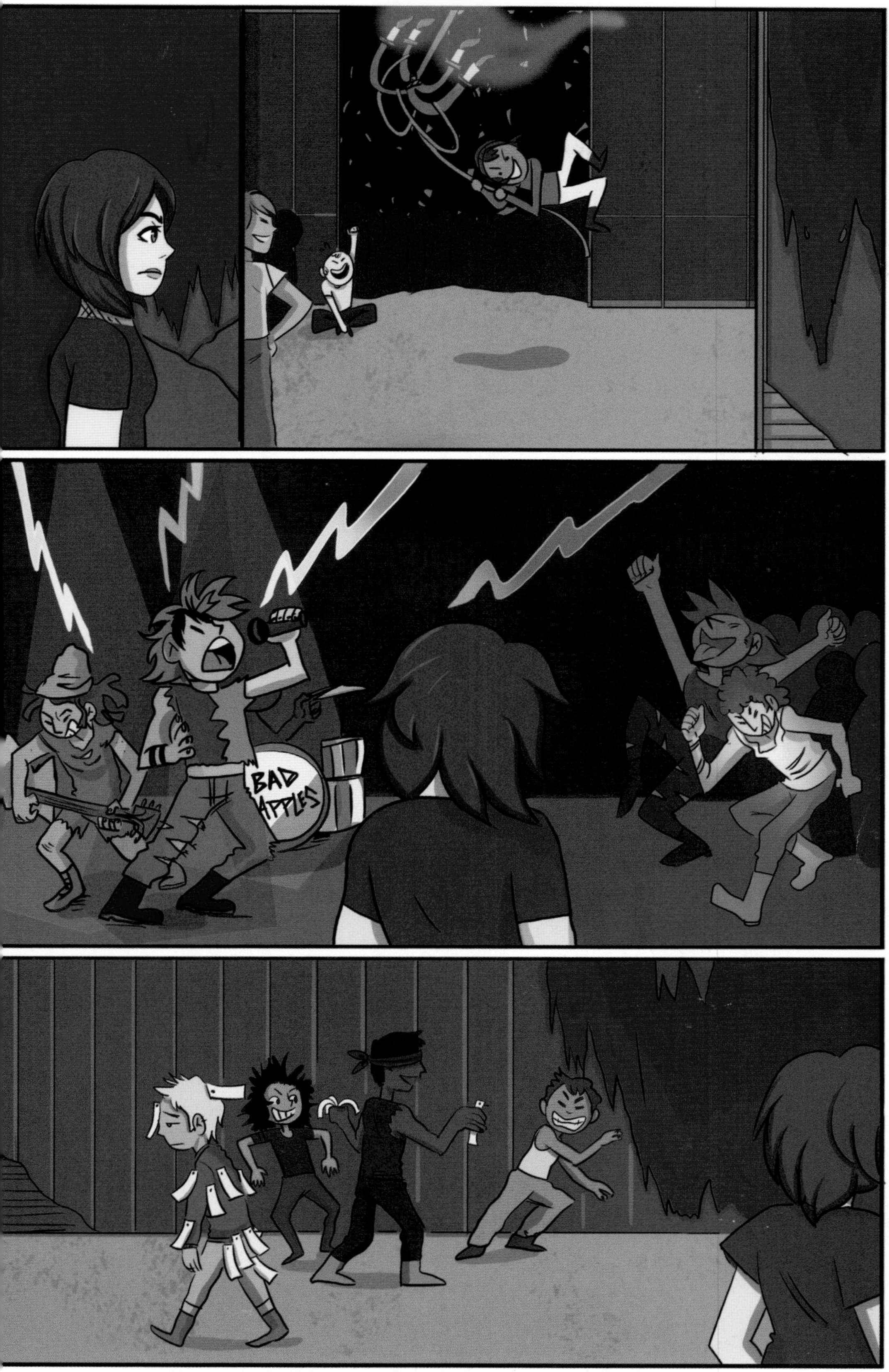
BAD
APPLES

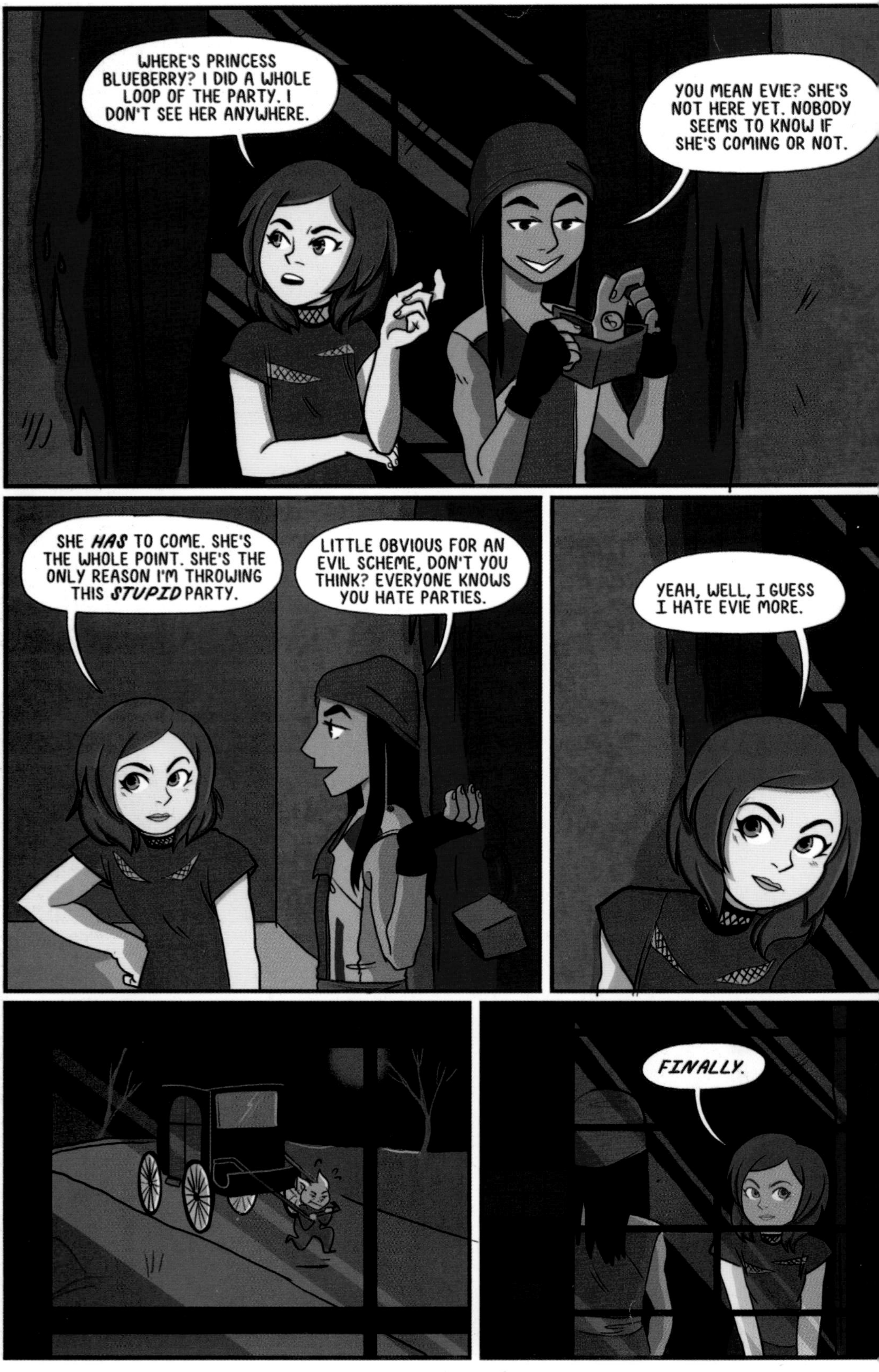
WHERE'S PRINCESS BLUEBERRY? I DID A WHOLE LOOP OF THE PARTY. I DON'T SEE HER ANYWHERE.
YOU MEAN EVIE? SHE'S NOT HERE YET. NOBODY SEEMS TO KNOW IF SHE'S COMING OR NOT.
SHE *HAS* TO COME. SHE'S THE WHOLE POINT. SHE'S THE ONLY REASON I'M THROWING THIS *STUPID* PARTY.
LITTLE OBVIOUS FOR AN EVIL SCHEME, DON'T YOU THINK? EVERYONE KNOWS YOU HATE PARTIES.
YEAH, WELL, I GUESS I HATE EVIE MORE.
FINALLY.

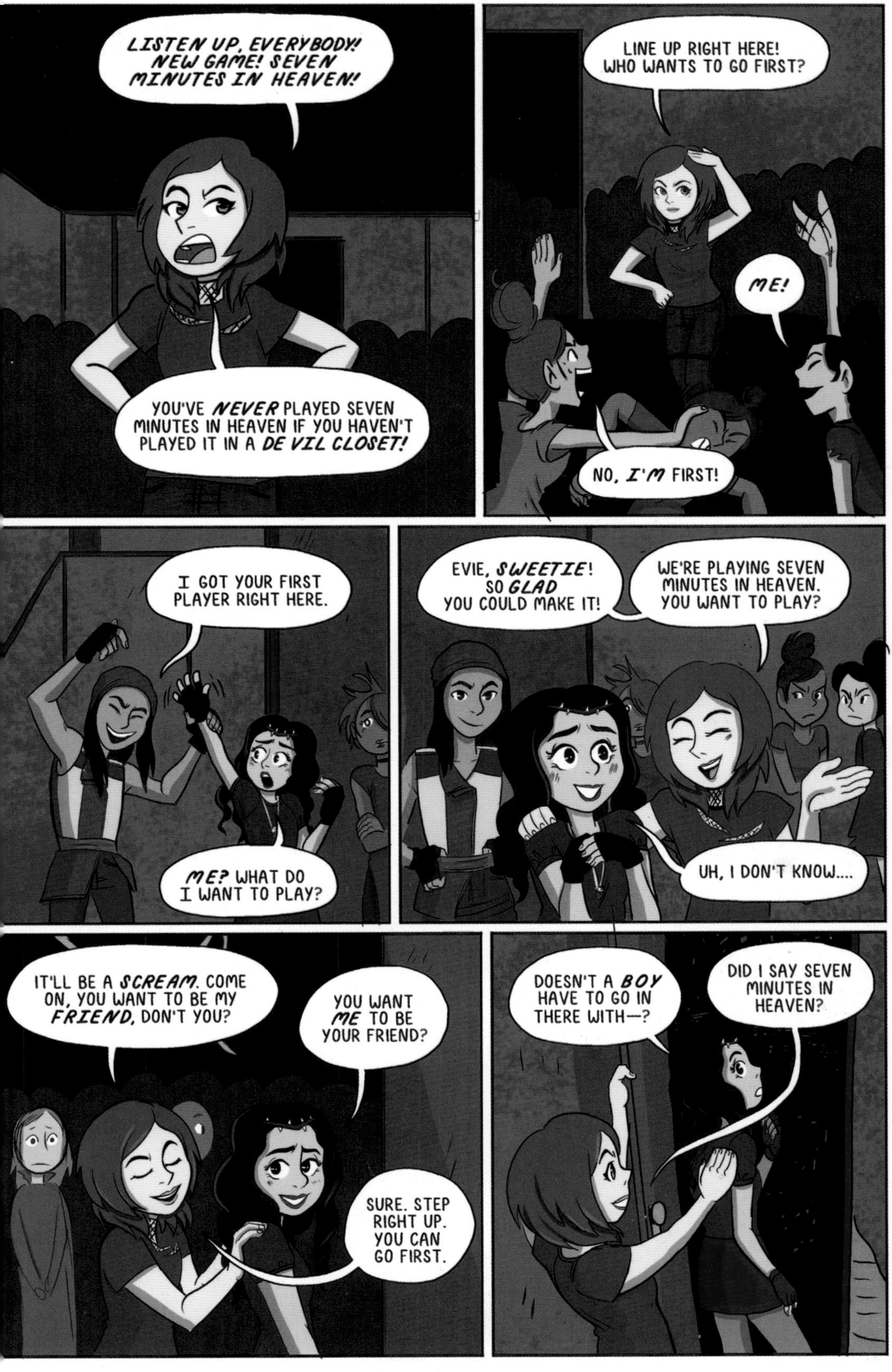
LISTEN UP, EVERYBODY! NEW GAME! SEVEN MINUTES IN HEAVEN!
YOU'VE *NEVER* PLAYED SEVEN MINUTES IN HEAVEN IF YOU HAVEN'T PLAYED IT IN A *DE VIL CLOSET!*
LINE UP RIGHT HERE! WHO WANTS TO GO FIRST?
ME!
NO, *I'M* FIRST!
I GOT YOUR FIRST PLAYER RIGHT HERE.
ME? WHAT DO I WANT TO PLAY?
EVIE, *SWEETIE*! SO *GLAD* YOU COULD MAKE IT!
WE'RE PLAYING SEVEN MINUTES IN HEAVEN. YOU WANT TO PLAY?
UH, I DON'T KNOW....
IT'LL BE A *SCREAM*. COME ON, YOU WANT TO BE MY *FRIEND*, DON'T YOU?
YOU WANT *ME* TO BE YOUR FRIEND?
SURE. STEP RIGHT UP. YOU CAN GO FIRST.
DOESN'T A *BOY* HAVE TO GO IN THERE WITH—?
DID I SAY SEVEN MINUTES IN HEAVEN?

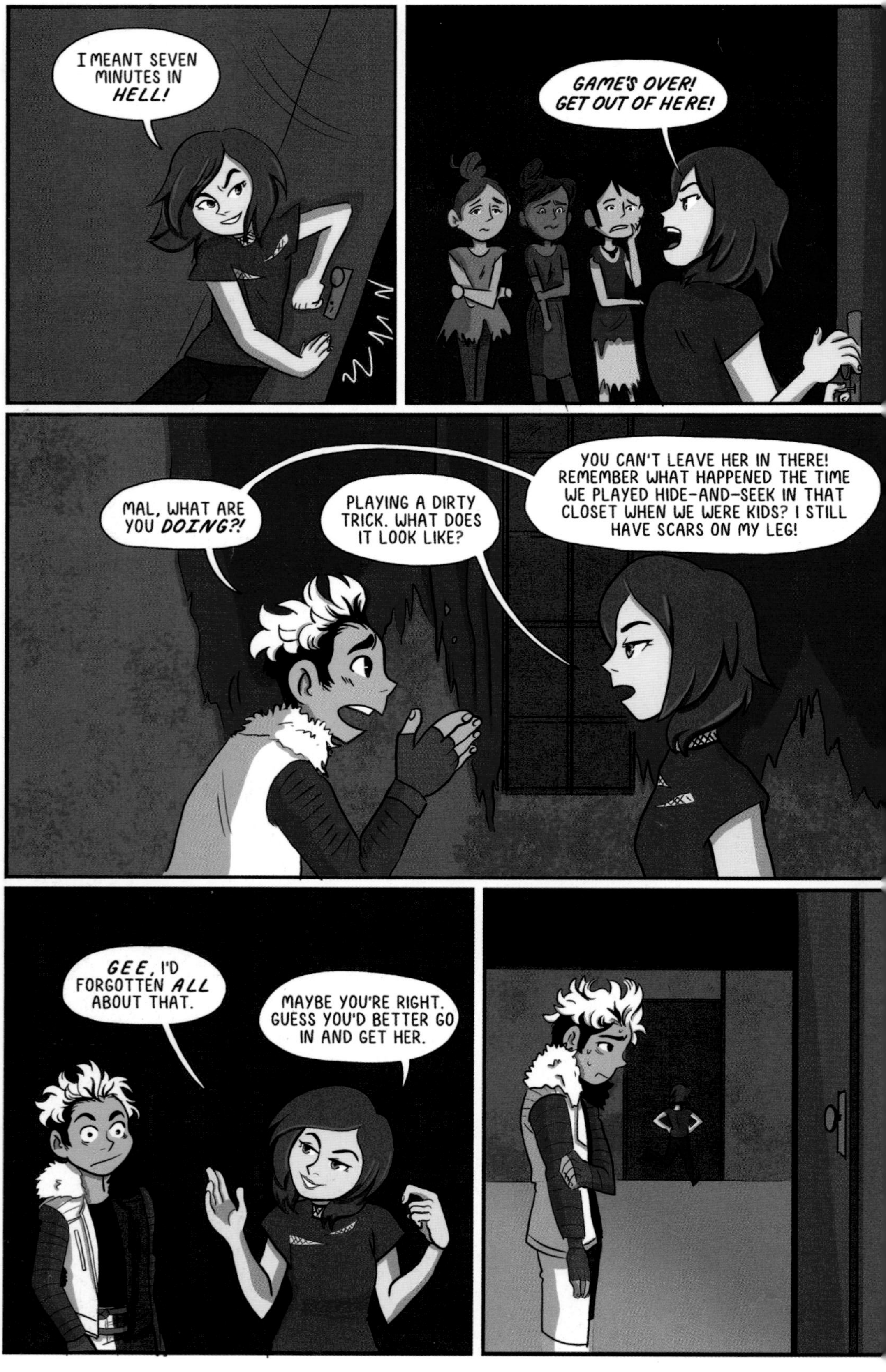
I MEANT SEVEN MINUTES IN *HELL!*
GAME'S OVER! GET OUT OF HERE!
MAL, WHAT ARE YOU *DOING?!*
PLAYING A DIRTY TRICK. WHAT DOES IT LOOK LIKE?
YOU CAN'T LEAVE HER IN THERE! REMEMBER WHAT HAPPENED THE TIME WE PLAYED HIDE-AND-SEEK IN THAT CLOSET WHEN WE WERE KIDS? I STILL HAVE SCARS ON MY LEG!
GEE, I'D FORGOTTEN *ALL* ABOUT THAT.
MAYBE YOU'RE RIGHT. GUESS YOU'D BETTER GO IN AND GET HER.

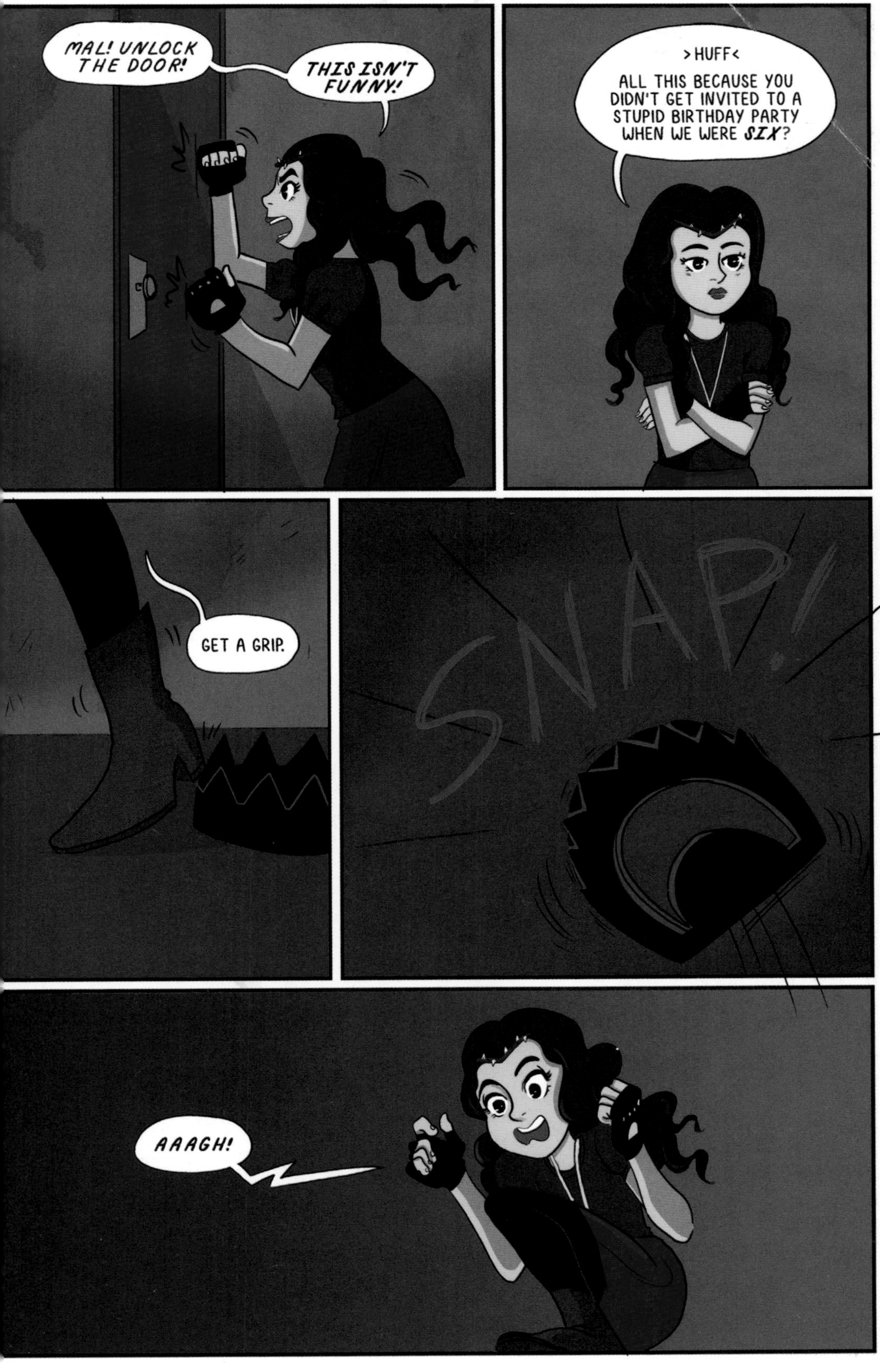
MAL! UNLOCK THE DOOR!
THIS ISN'T FUNNY!
>HUFF<
ALL THIS BECAUSE YOU DIDN'T GET INVITED TO A STUPID BIRTHDAY PARTY WHEN WE WERE SIX?
GET A GRIP.
SNAP!
AAAGH!

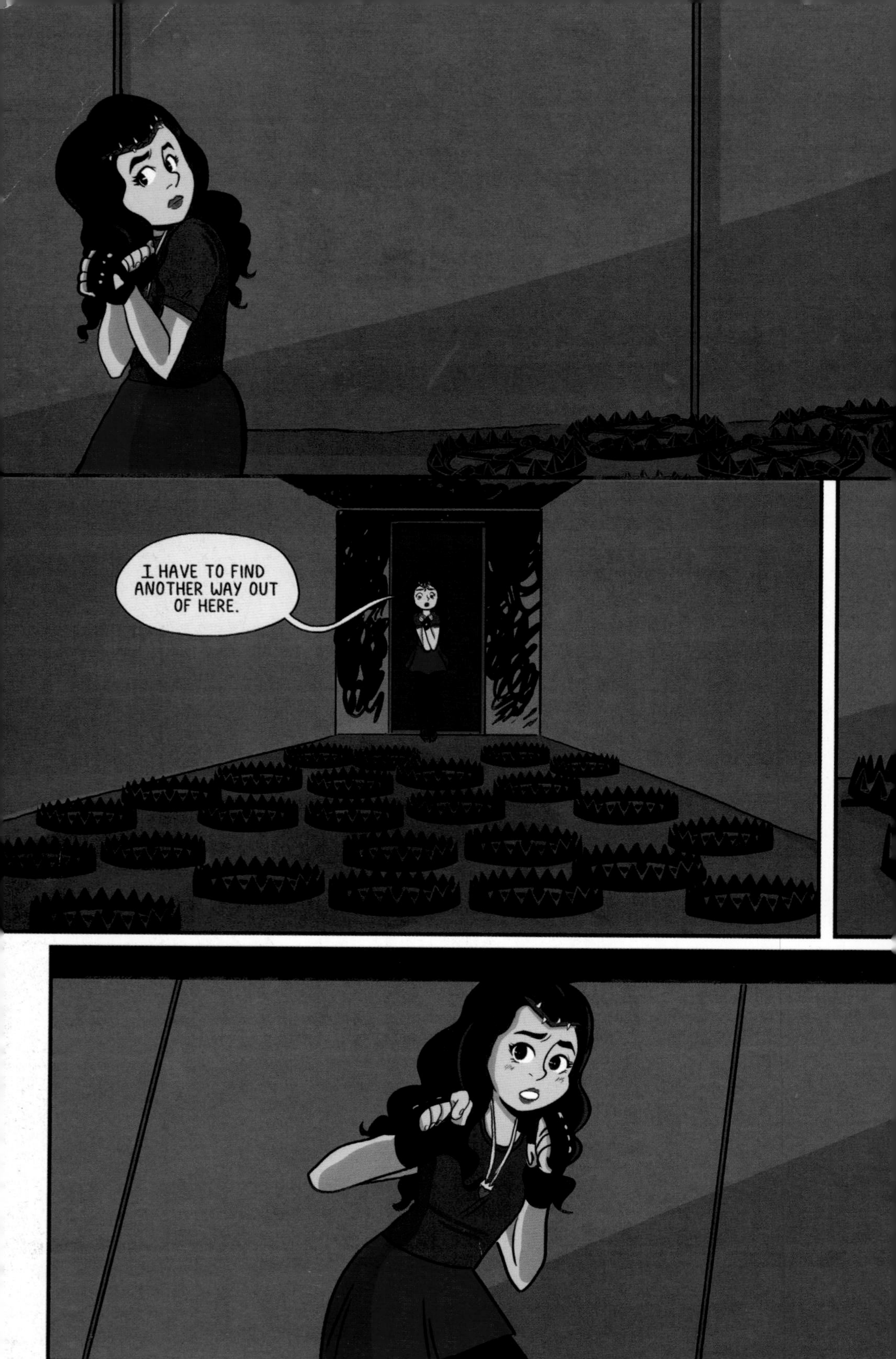
I HAVE TO FIND ANOTHER WAY OUT OF HERE.

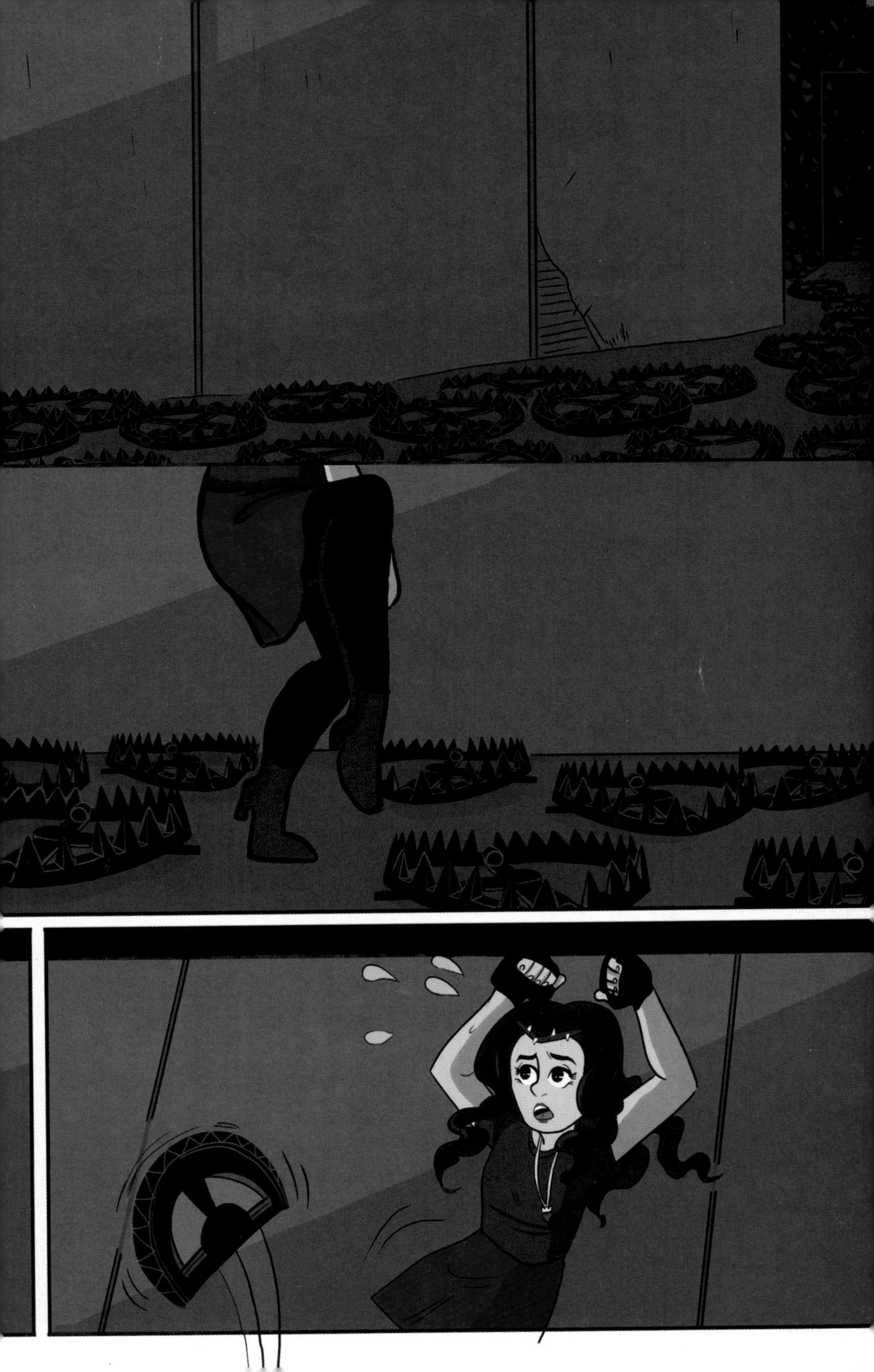

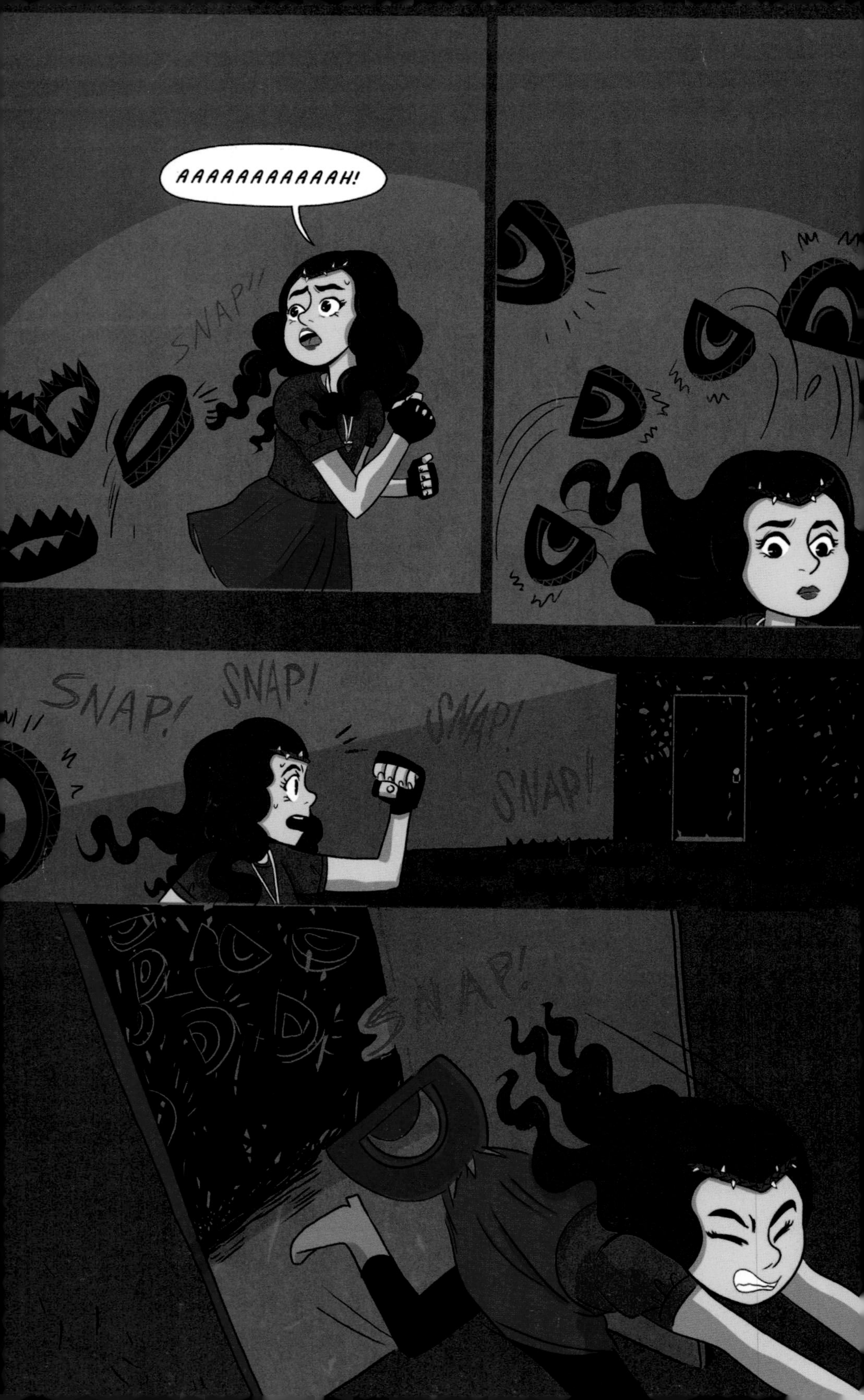
AAAAAAAAAAAH!
SNAP!!
SNAP!
SNAP!
SNAP!
SNAP!
SNAP!

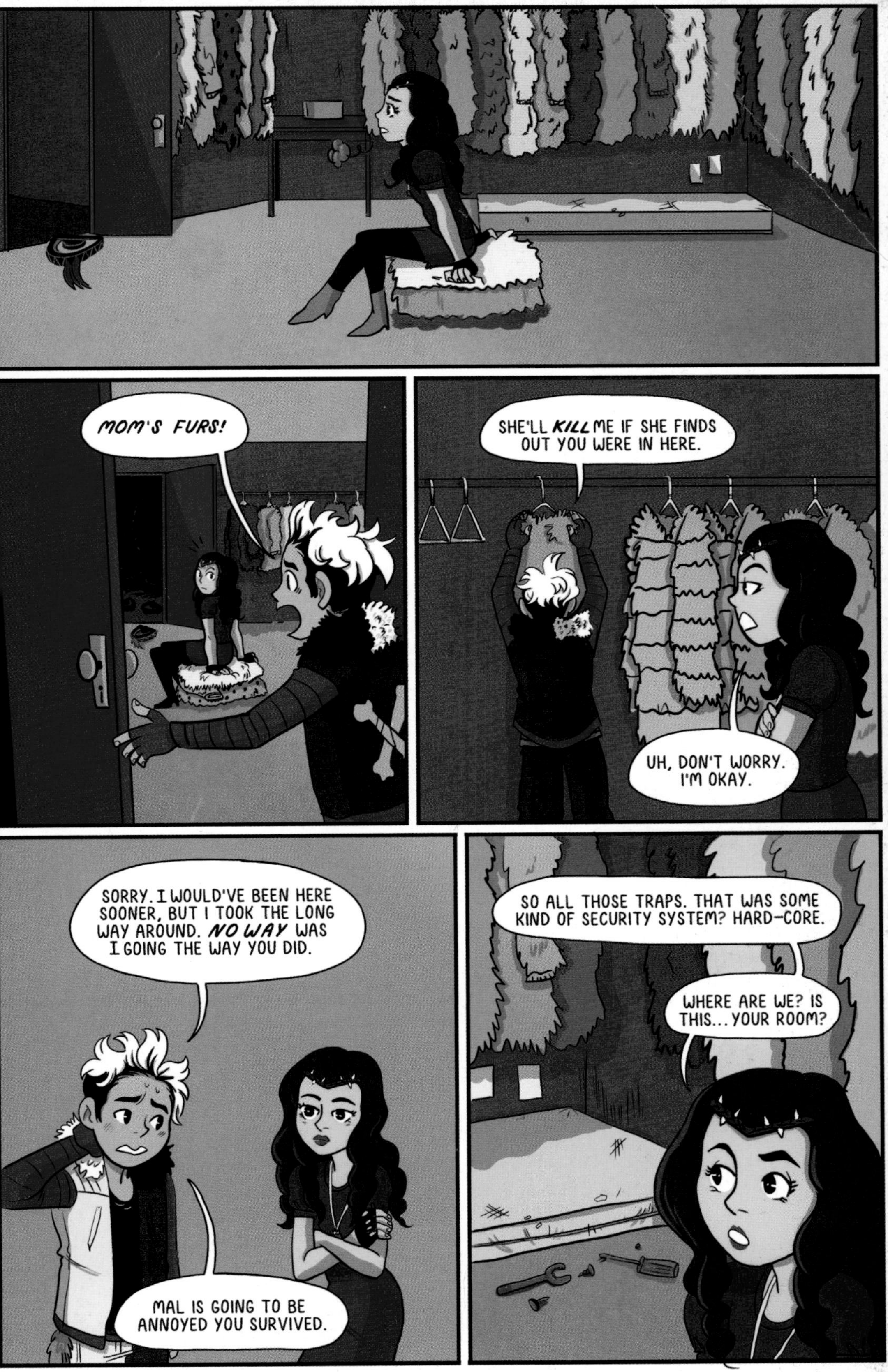
MOM'S FURS!
SHE'LL KILL ME IF SHE FINDS OUT YOU WERE IN HERE.
UH, DON'T WORRY. I'M OKAY.
SORRY. I WOULD'VE BEEN HERE SOONER, BUT I TOOK THE LONG WAY AROUND. NO WAY WAS I GOING THE WAY YOU DID.
MAL IS GOING TO BE ANNOYED YOU SURVIVED.
SO ALL THOSE TRAPS. THAT WAS SOME KIND OF SECURITY SYSTEM? HARD-CORE.
WHERE ARE WE? IS THIS... YOUR ROOM?

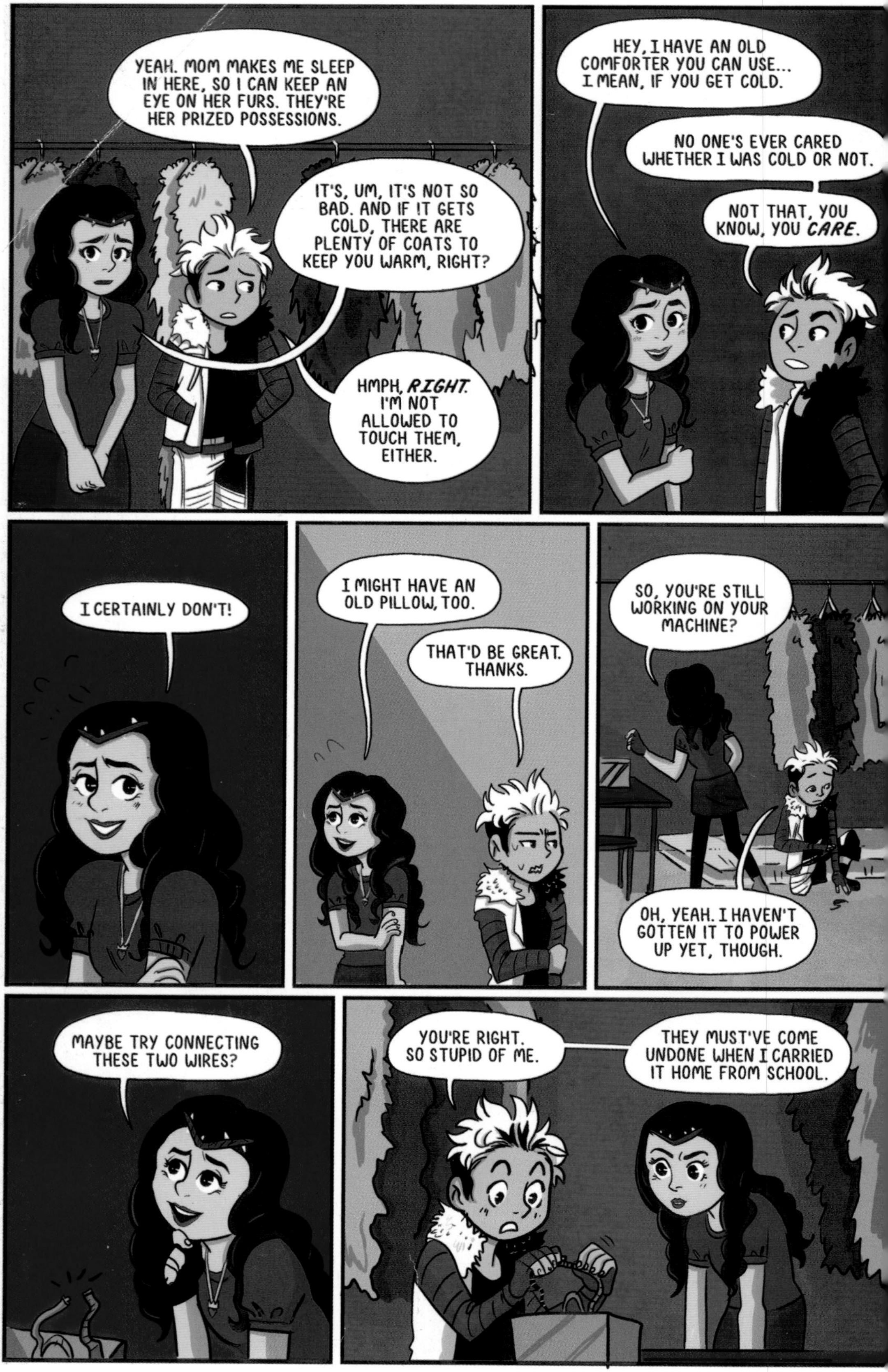
YEAH. MOM MAKES ME SLEEP IN HERE, SO I CAN KEEP AN EYE ON HER FURS. THEY'RE HER PRIZED POSSESSIONS.
IT'S, UM, IT'S NOT SO BAD. AND IF IT GETS COLD, THERE ARE PLENTY OF COATS TO KEEP YOU WARM, RIGHT?
HMPH, *RIGHT.* I'M NOT ALLOWED TO TOUCH THEM, EITHER.
HEY, I HAVE AN OLD COMFORTER YOU CAN USE... I MEAN, IF YOU GET COLD.
NO ONE'S EVER CARED WHETHER I WAS COLD OR NOT.
NOT THAT, YOU KNOW, YOU *CARE*.
I CERTAINLY DON'T!
I MIGHT HAVE AN OLD PILLOW, TOO.
THAT'D BE GREAT. THANKS.
SO, YOU'RE STILL WORKING ON YOUR MACHINE?
OH, YEAH. I HAVEN'T GOTTEN IT TO POWER UP YET, THOUGH.
MAYBE TRY CONNECTING THESE TWO WIRES?
YOU'RE RIGHT. SO STUPID OF ME.
THEY MUST'VE COME UNDONE WHEN I CARRIED IT HOME FROM SCHOOL.

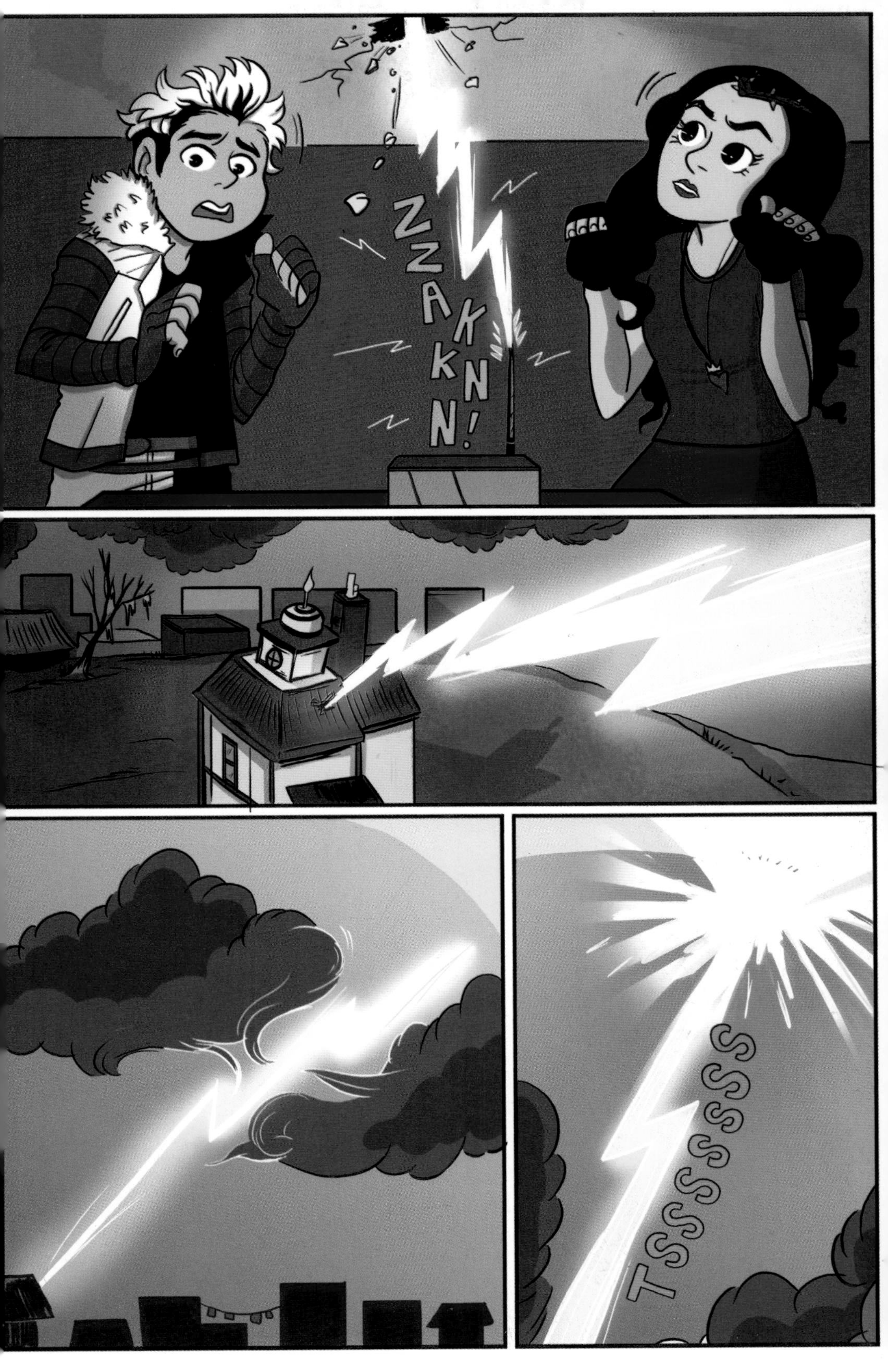
ZZAKKNN!
TSSSSSSS

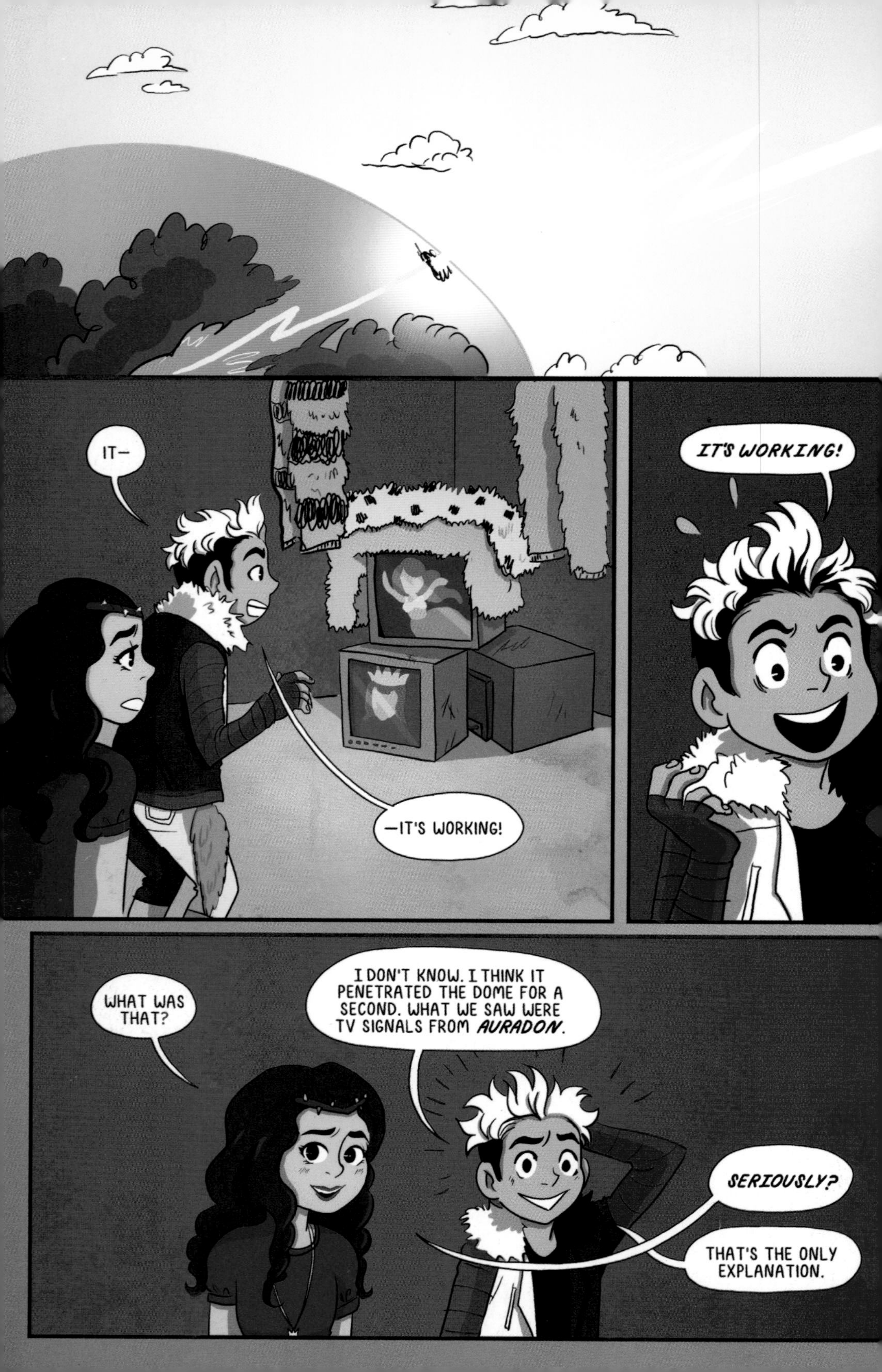

IT—
—IT'S WORKING!
IT'S WORKING!
WHAT WAS THAT?
I DON'T KNOW. I THINK IT PENETRATED THE DOME FOR A SECOND. WHAT WE SAW WERE TV SIGNALS FROM AURADON.
SERIOUSLY?
THAT'S THE ONLY EXPLANATION.

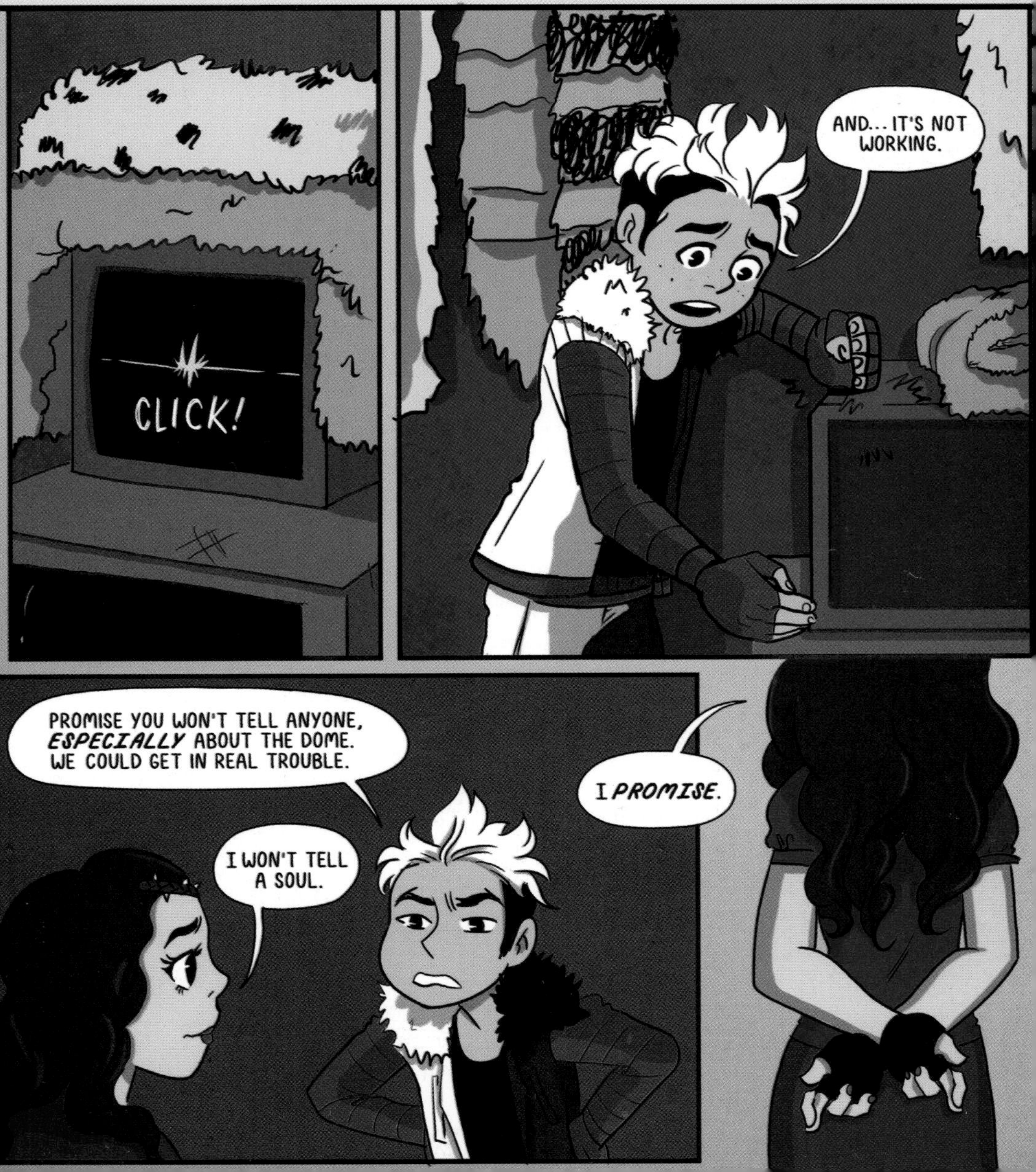
CLICK!
AND... IT'S NOT WORKING.
PROMISE YOU WON'T TELL ANYONE, *ESPECIALLY* ABOUT THE DOME. WE COULD GET IN REAL TROUBLE.
I WON'T TELL A SOUL.
I *PROMISE*.

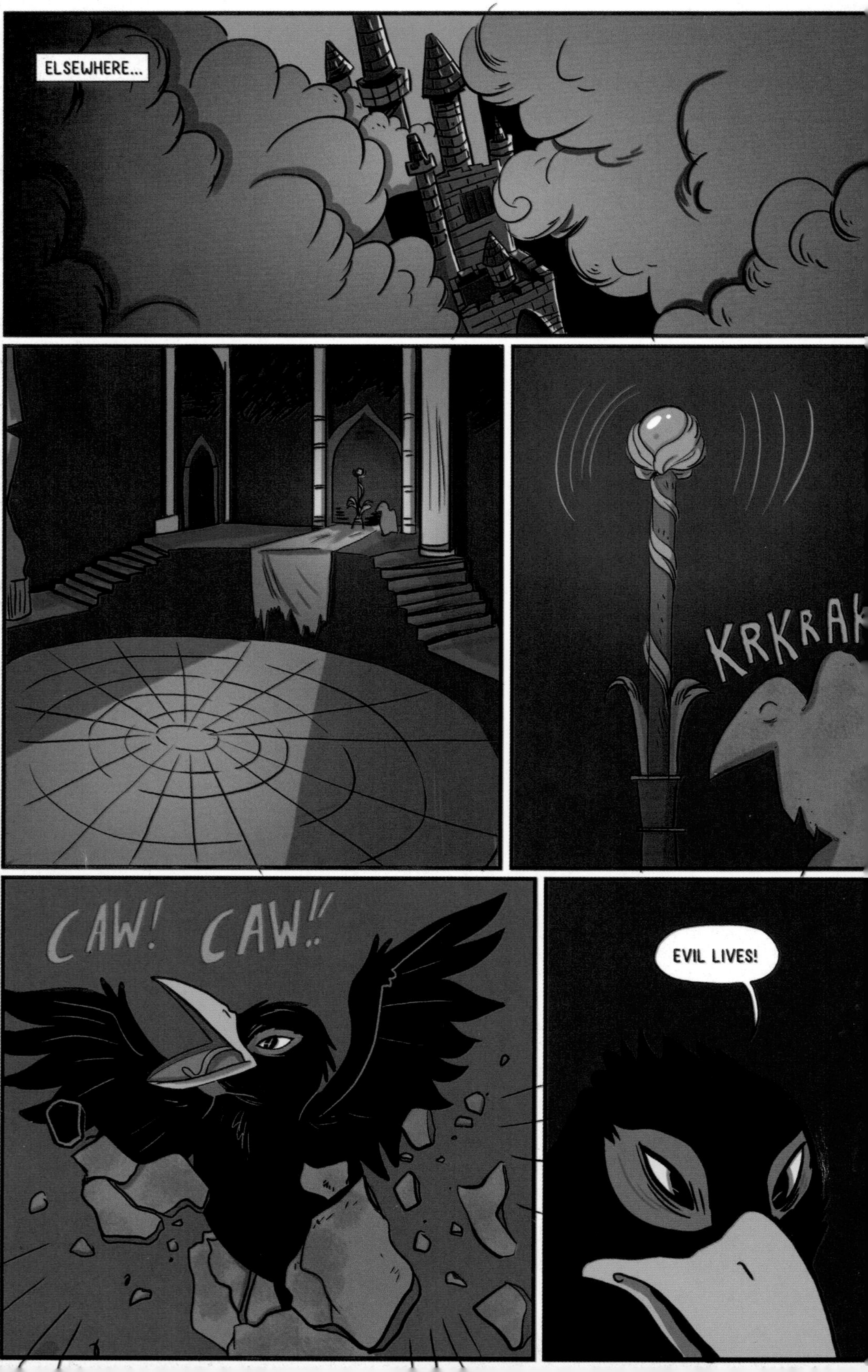
ELSEWHERE...
KRKRAK
CAW! CAW!!
EVIL LIVES!

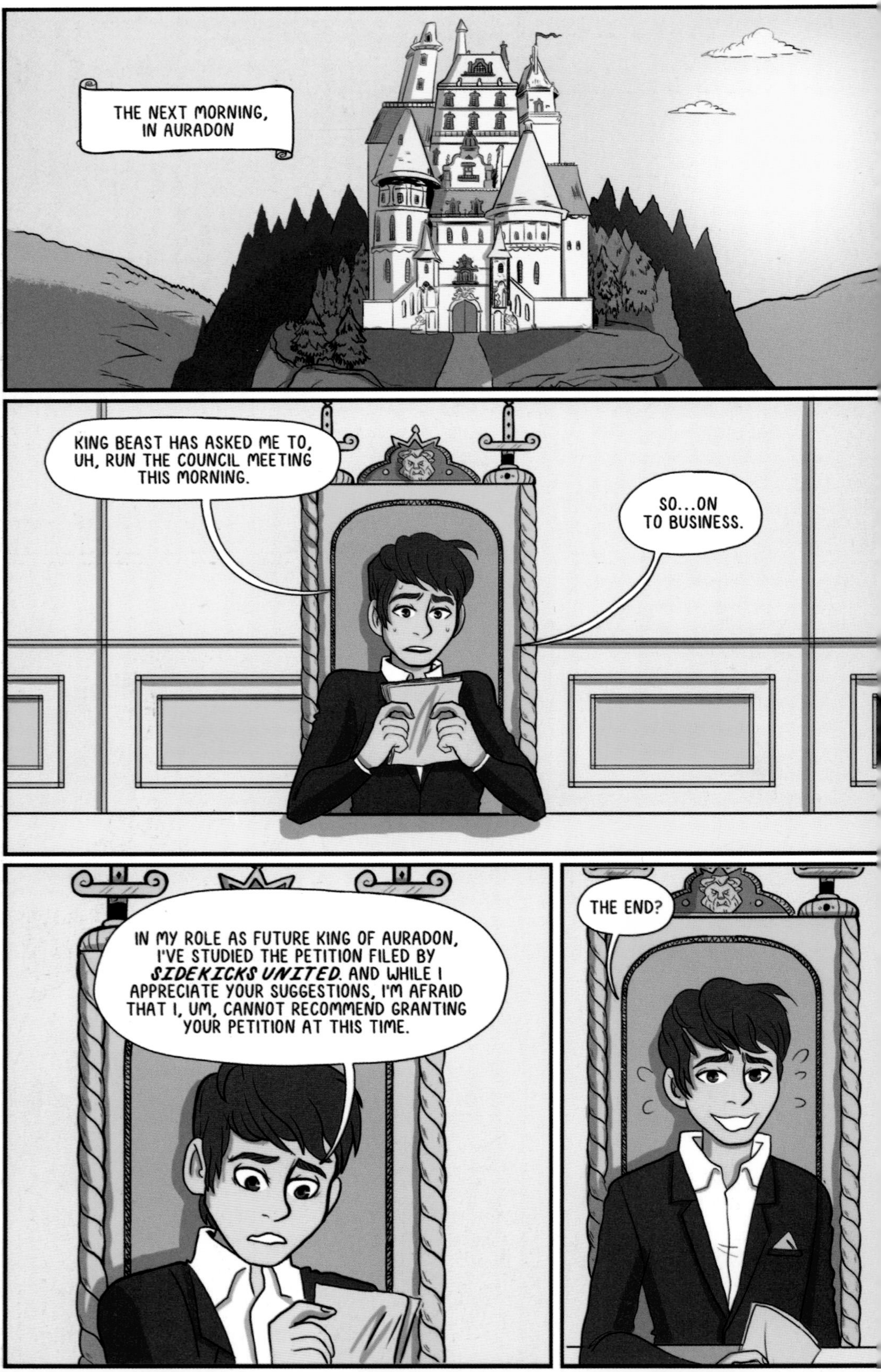
THE NEXT MORNING, IN AURADON
KING BEAST HAS ASKED ME TO, UH, RUN THE COUNCIL MEETING THIS MORNING.
SO...ON TO BUSINESS.
IN MY ROLE AS FUTURE KING OF AURADON, I'VE STUDIED THE PETITION FILED BY SIDEKICKS UNITED. AND WHILE I APPRECIATE YOUR SUGGESTIONS, I'M AFRAID THAT I, UM, CANNOT RECOMMEND GRANTING YOUR PETITION AT THIS TIME.
THE END?

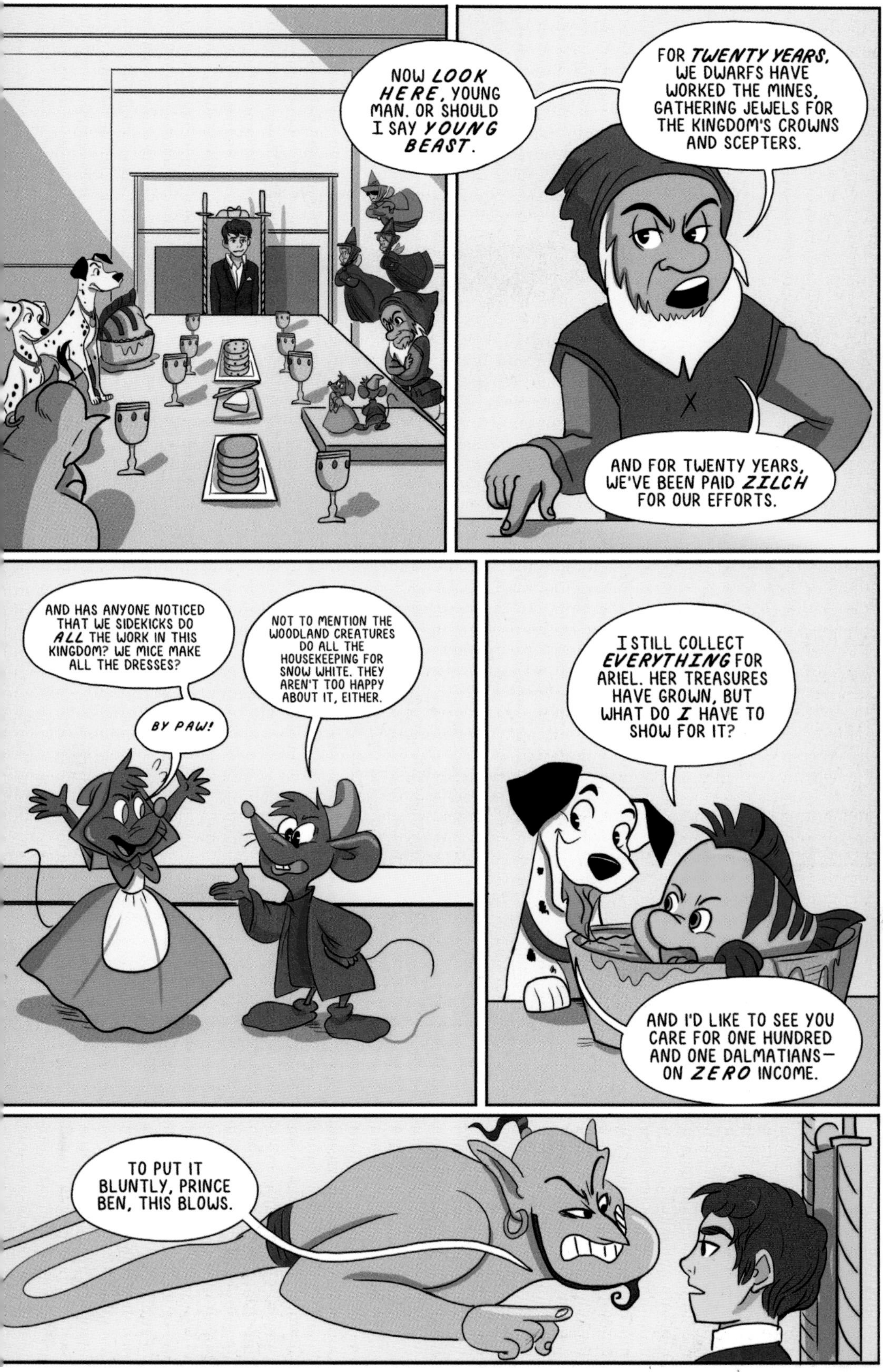
NOW LOOK HERE, YOUNG MAN. OR SHOULD I SAY YOUNG BEAST.
FOR TWENTY YEARS, WE DWARFS HAVE WORKED THE MINES, GATHERING JEWELS FOR THE KINGDOM'S CROWNS AND SCEPTERS.
AND FOR TWENTY YEARS, WE'VE BEEN PAID ZILCH FOR OUR EFFORTS.
AND HAS ANYONE NOTICED THAT WE SIDEKICKS DO ALL THE WORK IN THIS KINGDOM? WE MICE MAKE ALL THE DRESSES?
BY PAW!
NOT TO MENTION THE WOODLAND CREATURES DO ALL THE HOUSEKEEPING FOR SNOW WHITE. THEY AREN'T TOO HAPPY ABOUT IT, EITHER.
I STILL COLLECT EVERYTHING FOR ARIEL. HER TREASURES HAVE GROWN, BUT WHAT DO I HAVE TO SHOW FOR IT?
AND I'D LIKE TO SEE YOU CARE FOR ONE HUNDRED AND ONE DALMATIANS— ON ZERO INCOME.
TO PUT IT BLUNTLY, PRINCE BEN, THIS BLOWS.

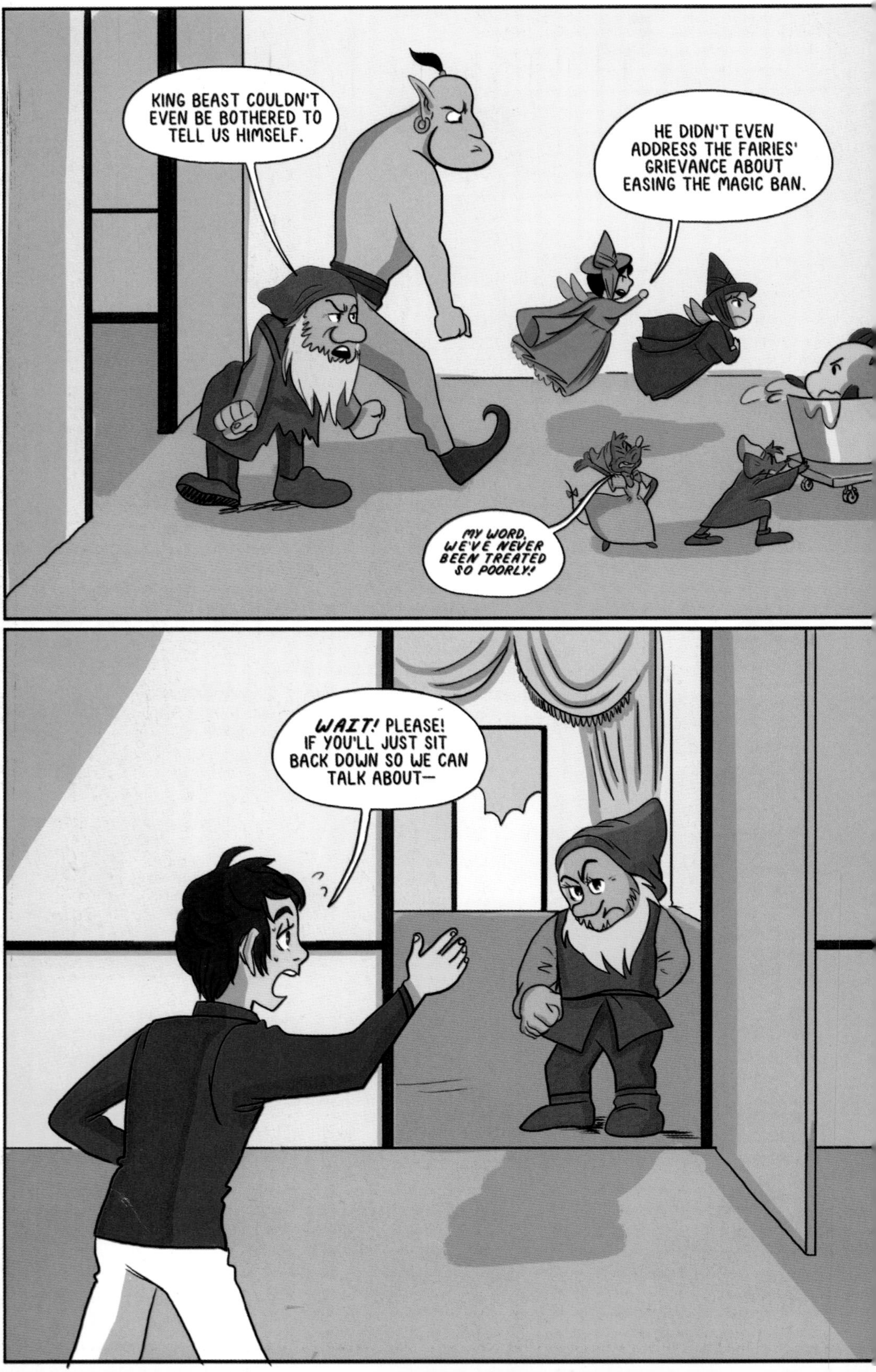
KING BEAST COULDN'T EVEN BE BOTHERED TO TELL US HIMSELF.
HE DIDN'T EVEN ADDRESS THE FAIRIES' GRIEVANCE ABOUT EASING THE MAGIC BAN.
MY WORD, WE'VE NEVER BEEN TREATED SO POORLY!
WAIT! PLEASE! IF YOU'LL JUST SIT BACK DOWN SO WE CAN TALK ABOUT—

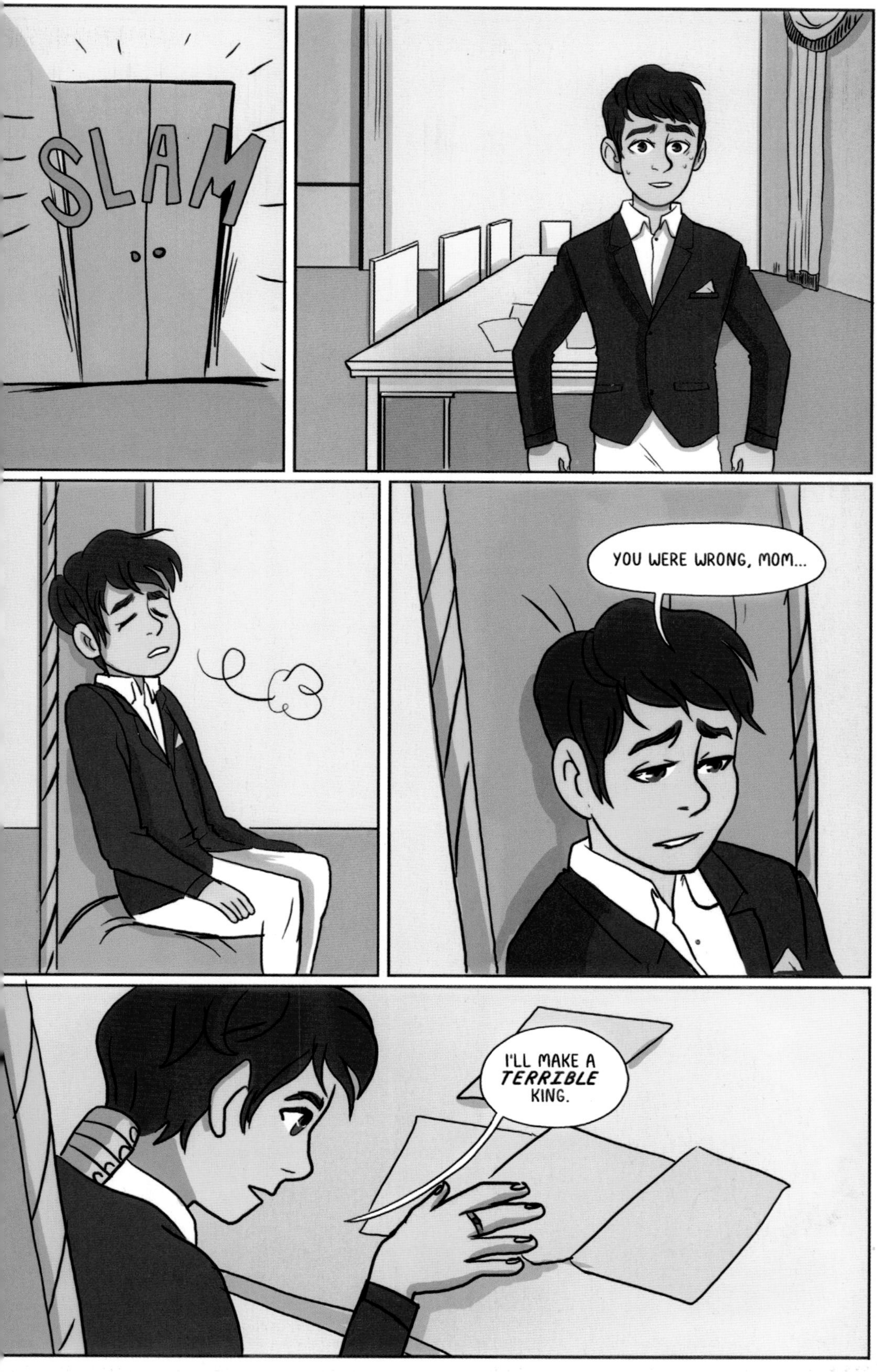
SLAM
YOU WERE WRONG, MOM...
I'LL MAKE A *TERRIBLE* KING.

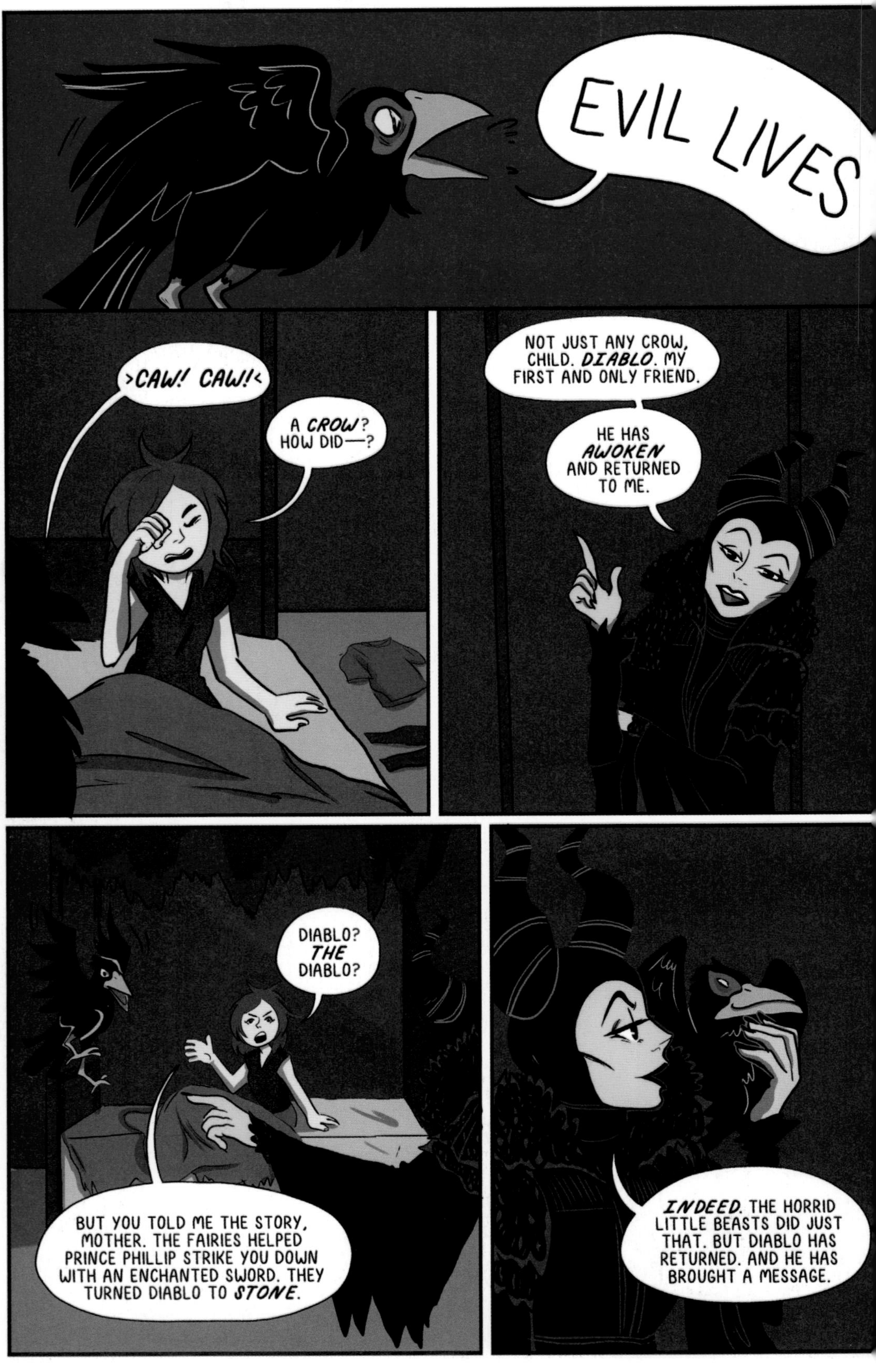
EVIL LIVES
>CAW! CAW!<
A CROW? HOW DID—?
NOT JUST ANY CROW, CHILD. DIABLO. MY FIRST AND ONLY FRIEND.
HE HAS AWOKEN AND RETURNED TO ME.
DIABLO? THE DIABLO?
BUT YOU TOLD ME THE STORY, MOTHER. THE FAIRIES HELPED PRINCE PHILLIP STRIKE YOU DOWN WITH AN ENCHANTED SWORD. THEY TURNED DIABLO TO STONE.
INDEED. THE HORRID LITTLE BEASTS DID JUST THAT. BUT DIABLO HAS RETURNED. AND HE HAS BROUGHT A MESSAGE.

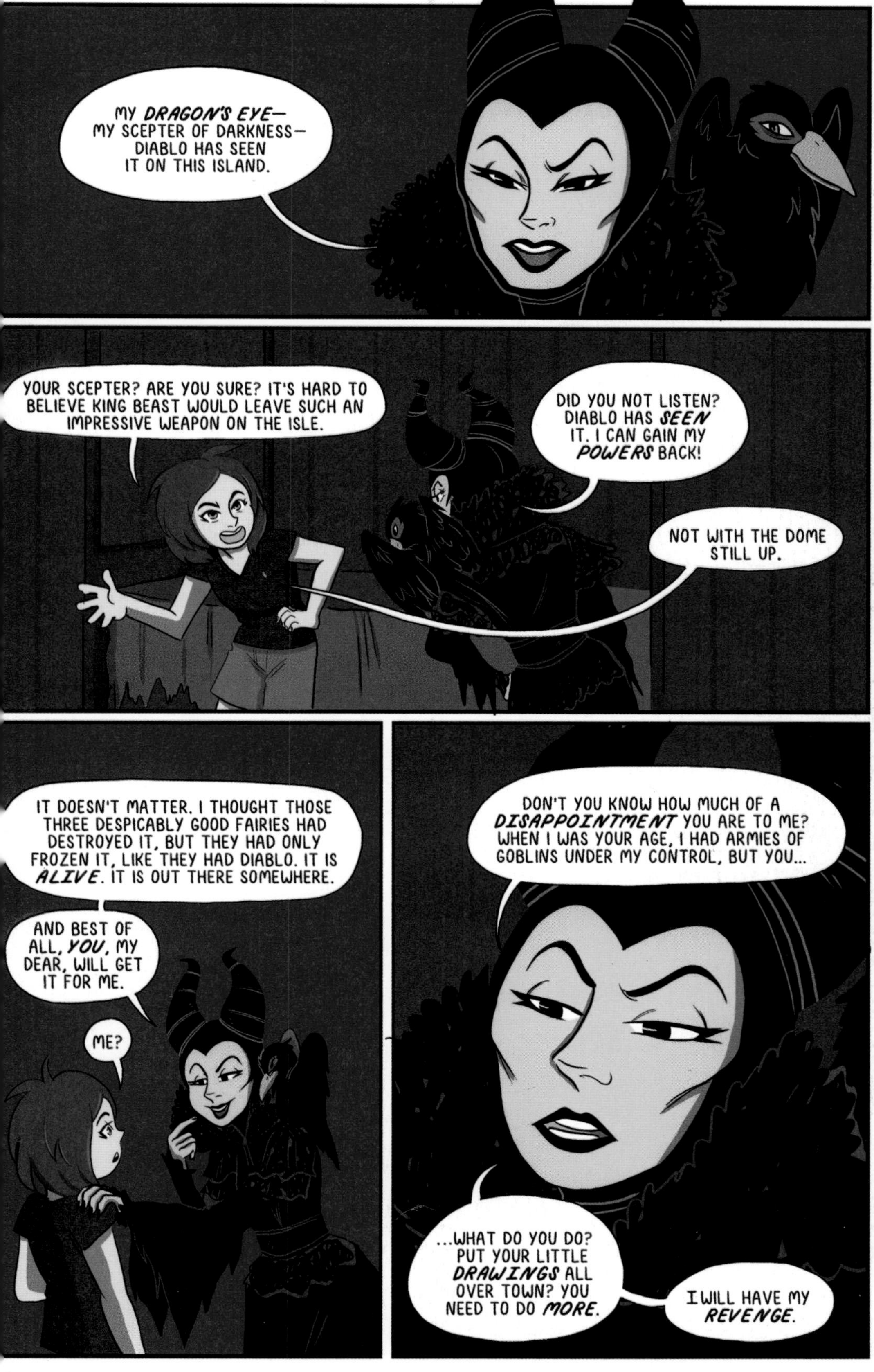
MY DRAGON'S EYE— MY SCEPTER OF DARKNESS— DIABLO HAS SEEN IT ON THIS ISLAND.
YOUR SCEPTER? ARE YOU SURE? IT'S HARD TO BELIEVE KING BEAST WOULD LEAVE SUCH AN IMPRESSIVE WEAPON ON THE ISLE.
DID YOU NOT LISTEN? DIABLO HAS SEEN IT. I CAN GAIN MY POWERS BACK!
NOT WITH THE DOME STILL UP.
IT DOESN'T MATTER. I THOUGHT THOSE THREE DESPICABLY GOOD FAIRIES HAD DESTROYED IT, BUT THEY HAD ONLY FROZEN IT, LIKE THEY HAD DIABLO. IT IS ALIVE. IT IS OUT THERE SOMEWHERE.
AND BEST OF ALL, YOU, MY DEAR, WILL GET IT FOR ME.
ME?
DON'T YOU KNOW HOW MUCH OF A DISAPPOINTMENT YOU ARE TO ME? WHEN I WAS YOUR AGE, I HAD ARMIES OF GOBLINS UNDER MY CONTROL, BUT YOU...
...WHAT DO YOU DO? PUT YOUR LITTLE DRAWINGS ALL OVER TOWN? YOU NEED TO DO MORE.
I WILL HAVE MY REVENGE.

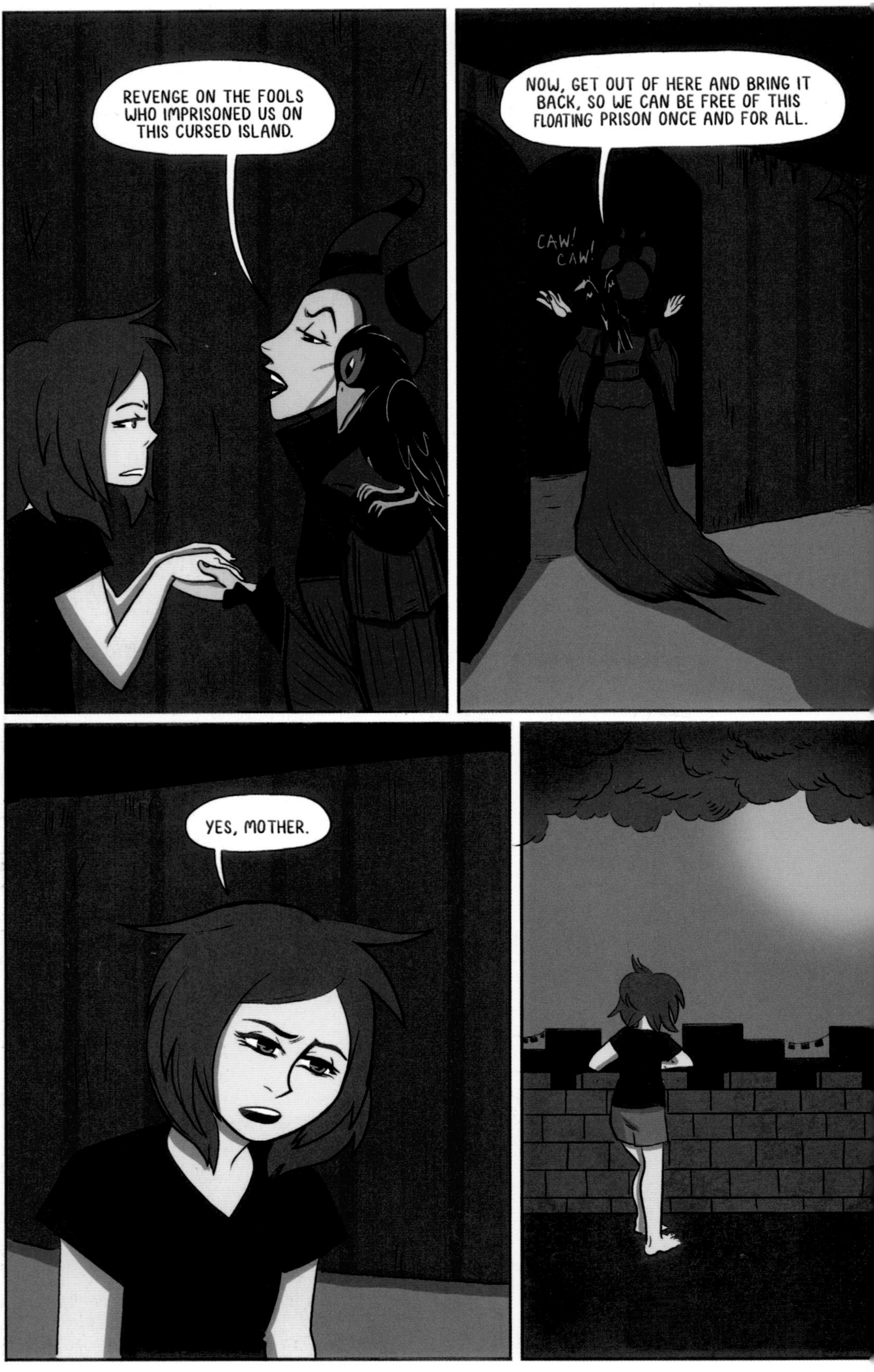
REVENGE ON THE FOOLS WHO IMPRISONED US ON THIS CURSED ISLAND.
NOW, GET OUT OF HERE AND BRING IT BACK, SO WE CAN BE FREE OF THIS FLOATING PRISON ONCE AND FOR ALL.
CAW! CAW!
YES, MOTHER.

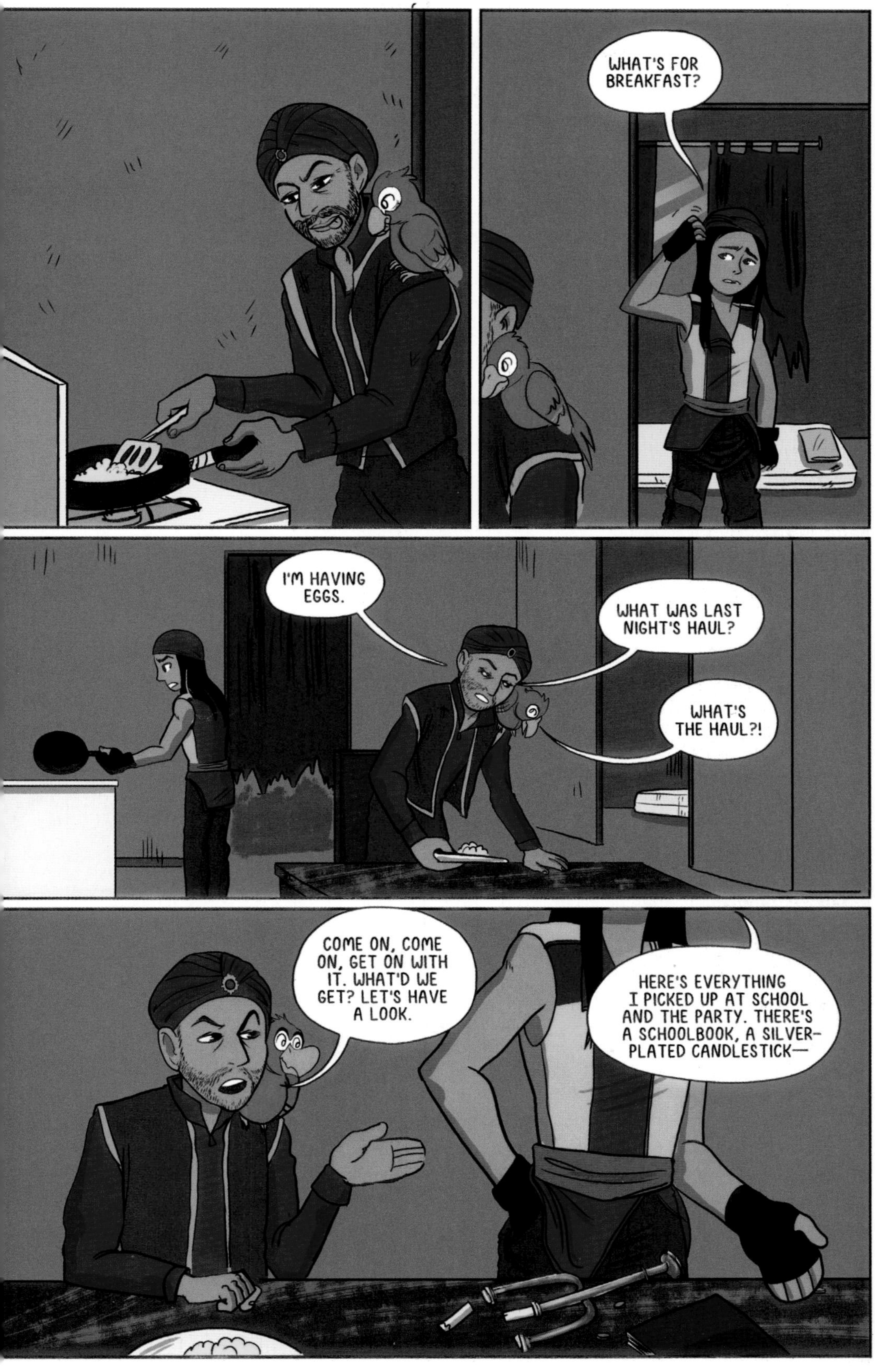
WHAT'S FOR BREAKFAST?
I'M HAVING EGGS.
WHAT WAS LAST NIGHT'S HAUL?
WHAT'S THE HAUL?!
COME ON, COME ON, GET ON WITH IT. WHAT'D WE GET? LET'S HAVE A LOOK.
HERE'S EVERYTHING I PICKED UP AT SCHOOL AND THE PARTY. THERE'S A SCHOOLBOOK, A SILVER-PLATED CANDLESTICK—

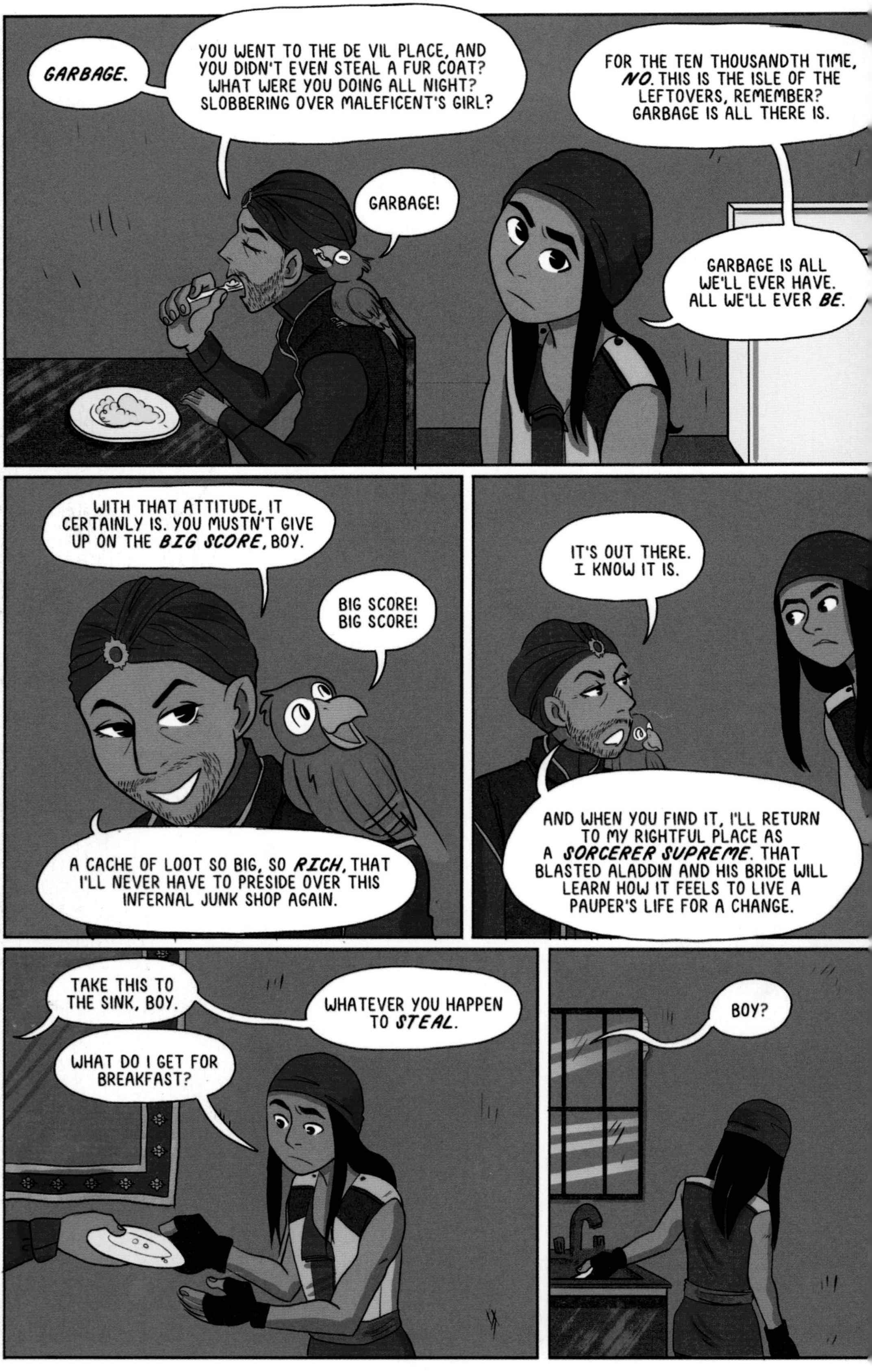
GARBAGE.
YOU WENT TO THE DE VIL PLACE, AND YOU DIDN'T EVEN STEAL A FUR COAT? WHAT WERE YOU DOING ALL NIGHT? SLOBBERING OVER MALEFICENT'S GIRL?
GARBAGE!
FOR THE TEN THOUSANDTH TIME, *NO*. THIS IS THE ISLE OF THE LEFTOVERS, REMEMBER? GARBAGE IS ALL THERE IS.
GARBAGE IS ALL WE'LL EVER HAVE. ALL WE'LL EVER *BE*.
WITH THAT ATTITUDE, IT CERTAINLY IS. YOU MUSTN'T GIVE UP ON THE *BIG SCORE*, BOY.
BIG SCORE! BIG SCORE!
A CACHE OF LOOT SO BIG, SO *RICH*, THAT I'LL NEVER HAVE TO PRESIDE OVER THIS INFERNAL JUNK SHOP AGAIN.
IT'S OUT THERE. I KNOW IT IS.
AND WHEN YOU FIND IT, I'LL RETURN TO MY RIGHTFUL PLACE AS A *SORCERER SUPREME*. THAT BLASTED ALADDIN AND HIS BRIDE WILL LEARN HOW IT FEELS TO LIVE A PAUPER'S LIFE FOR A CHANGE.
TAKE THIS TO THE SINK, BOY.
WHAT DO I GET FOR BREAKFAST?
WHATEVER YOU HAPPEN TO *STEAL*.
BOY?

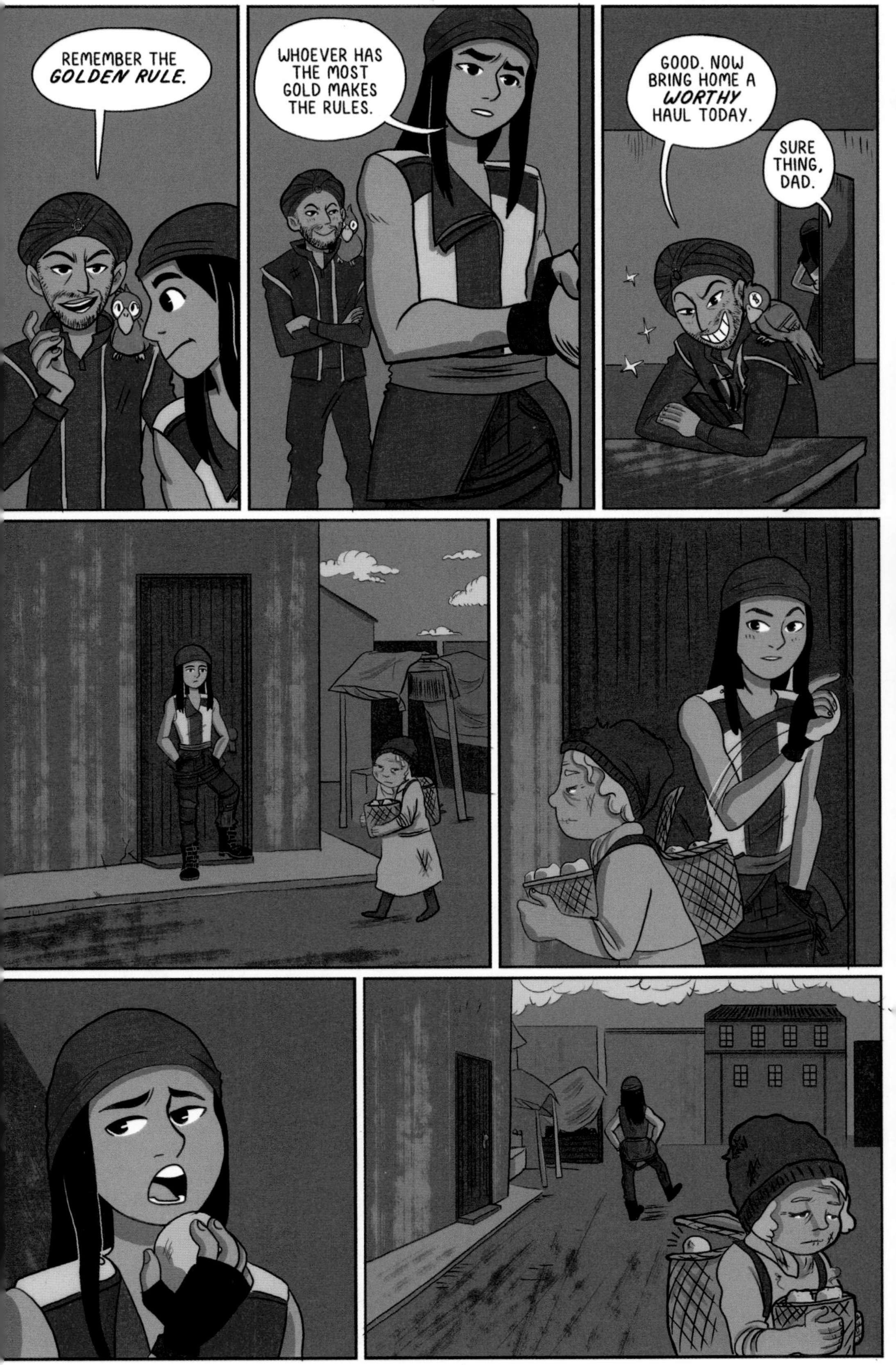
REMEMBER THE GOLDEN RULE.
WHOEVER HAS THE MOST GOLD MAKES THE RULES.
GOOD. NOW BRING HOME A WORTHY HAUL TODAY.
SURE THING, DAD.

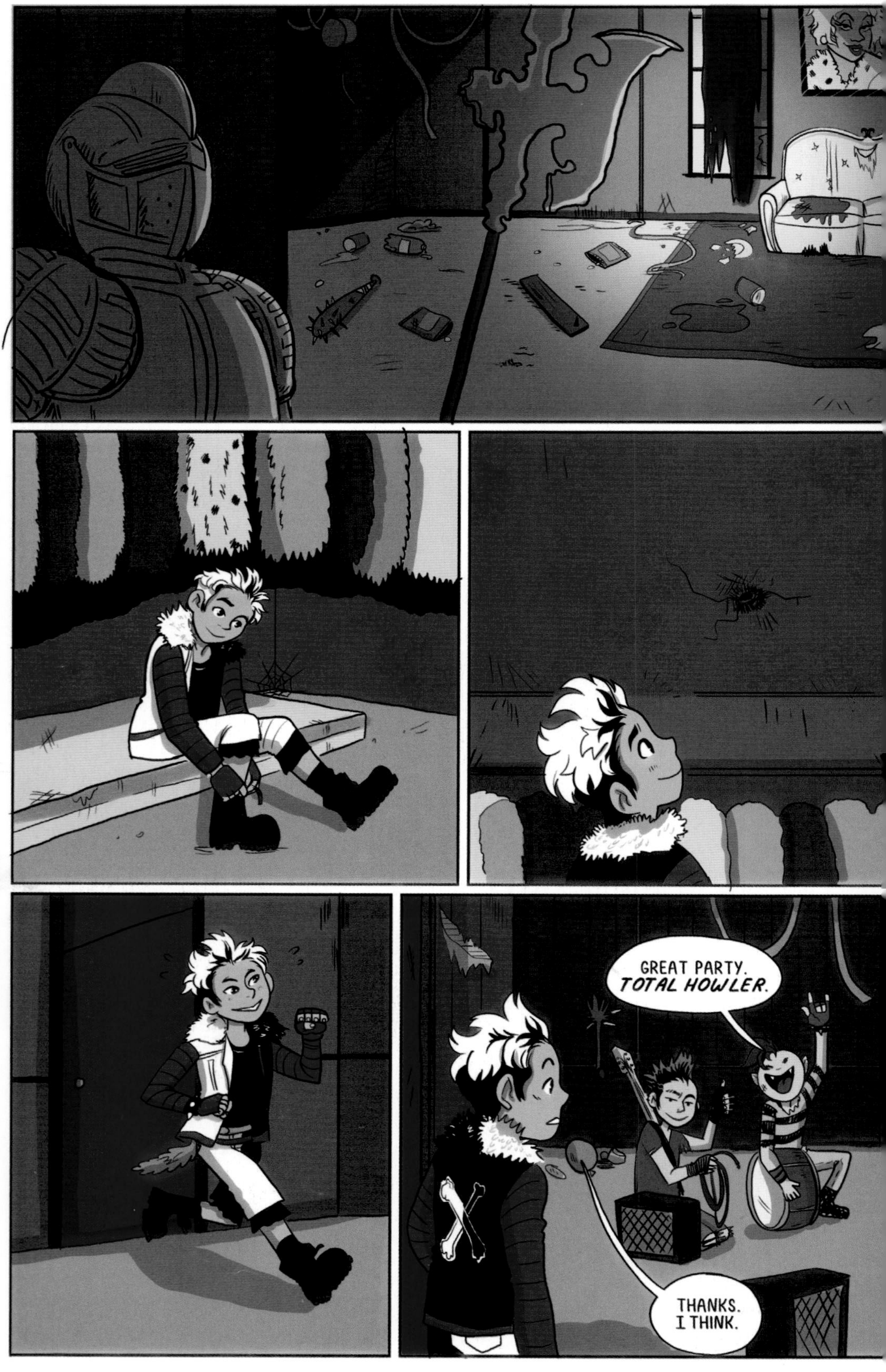
GREAT PARTY.
TOTAL HOWLER.
THANKS.
I THINK.

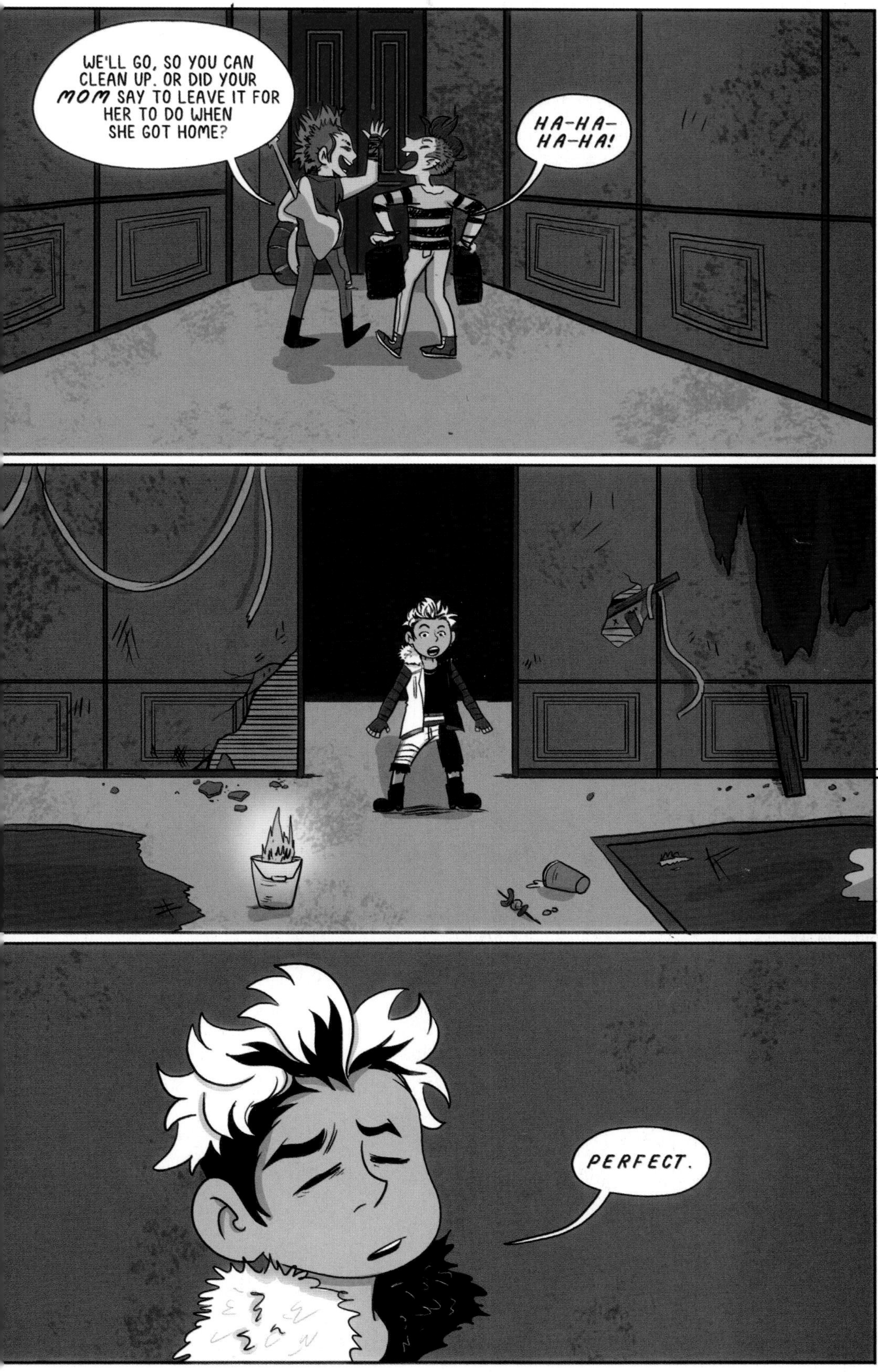
WE'LL GO, SO YOU CAN CLEAN UP. OR DID YOUR MOM SAY TO LEAVE IT FOR HER TO DO WHEN SHE GOT HOME?
HA-HA-HA-HA!
PERFECT.

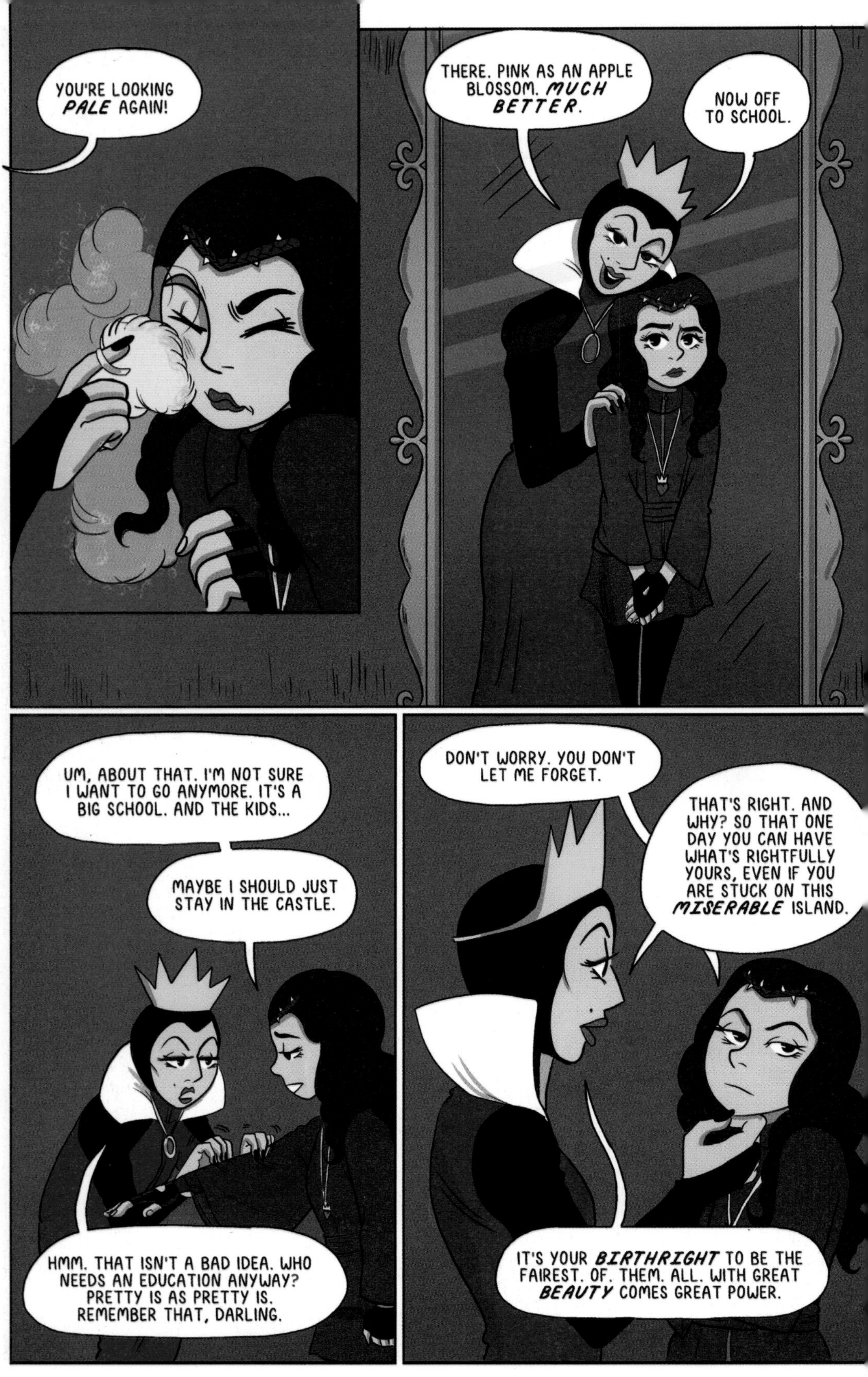
YOU'RE LOOKING PALE AGAIN!
THERE. PINK AS AN APPLE BLOSSOM. MUCH BETTER.
NOW OFF TO SCHOOL.
UM, ABOUT THAT. I'M NOT SURE I WANT TO GO ANYMORE. IT'S A BIG SCHOOL. AND THE KIDS...
MAYBE I SHOULD JUST STAY IN THE CASTLE.
HMM. THAT ISN'T A BAD IDEA. WHO NEEDS AN EDUCATION ANYWAY? PRETTY IS AS PRETTY IS. REMEMBER THAT, DARLING.
DON'T WORRY. YOU DON'T LET ME FORGET.
THAT'S RIGHT. AND WHY? SO THAT ONE DAY YOU CAN HAVE WHAT'S RIGHTFULLY YOURS, EVEN IF YOU ARE STUCK ON THIS MISERABLE ISLAND.
IT'S YOUR BIRTHRIGHT TO BE THE FAIREST. OF. THEM. ALL. WITH GREAT BEAUTY COMES GREAT POWER.

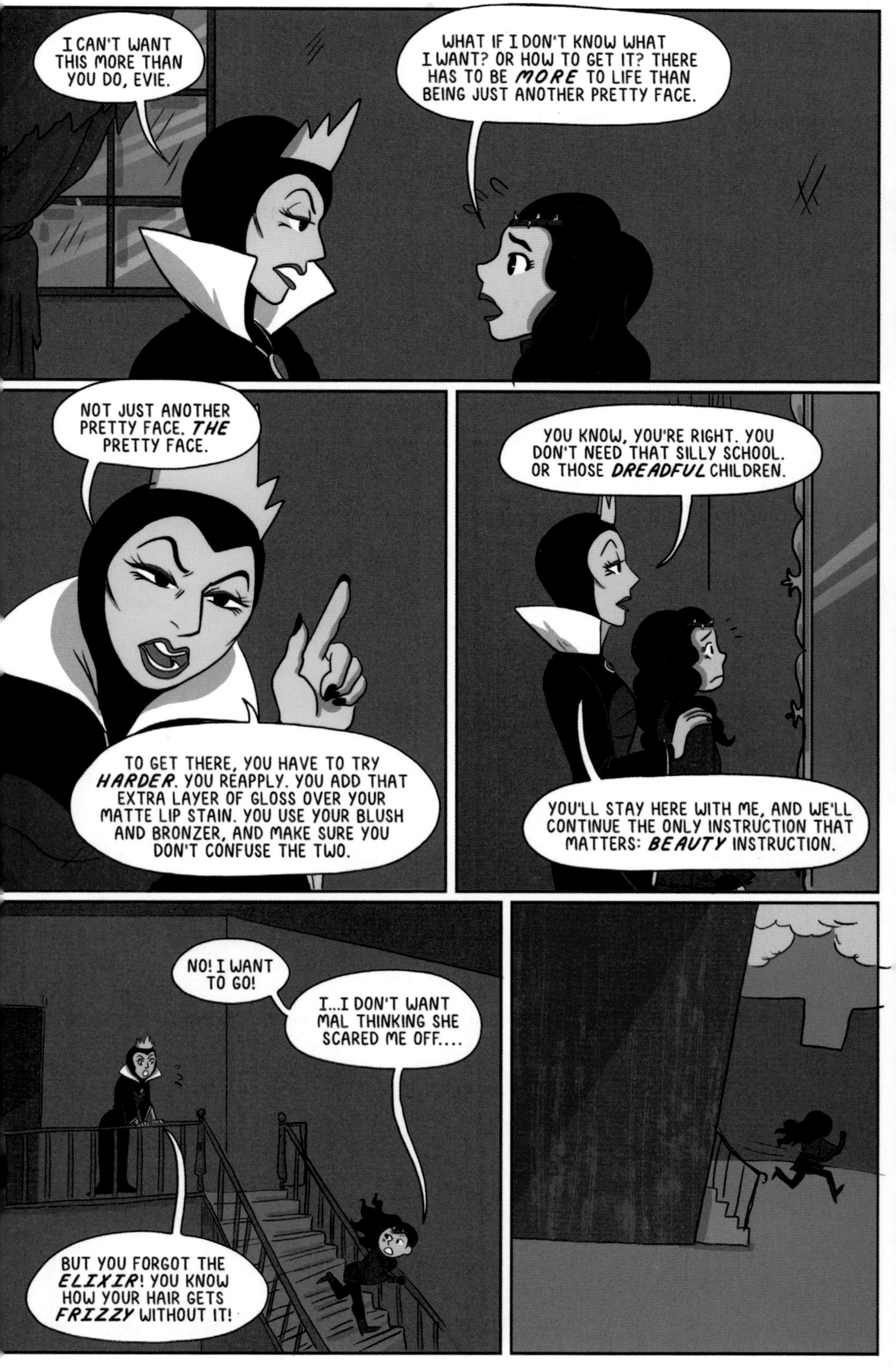
I CAN'T WANT THIS MORE THAN YOU DO, EVIE.
WHAT IF I DON'T KNOW WHAT I WANT? OR HOW TO GET IT? THERE HAS TO BE *MORE* TO LIFE THAN BEING JUST ANOTHER PRETTY FACE.
NOT JUST ANOTHER PRETTY FACE. *THE* PRETTY FACE.
TO GET THERE, YOU HAVE TO TRY *HARDER*. YOU REAPPLY. YOU ADD THAT EXTRA LAYER OF GLOSS OVER YOUR MATTE LIP STAIN. YOU USE YOUR BLUSH AND BRONZER, AND MAKE SURE YOU DON'T CONFUSE THE TWO.
YOU KNOW, YOU'RE RIGHT. YOU DON'T NEED THAT SILLY SCHOOL. OR THOSE *DREADFUL* CHILDREN.
YOU'LL STAY HERE WITH ME, AND WE'LL CONTINUE THE ONLY INSTRUCTION THAT MATTERS: *BEAUTY* INSTRUCTION.
NO! I WANT TO GO!
I...I DON'T WANT MAL THINKING SHE SCARED ME OFF....
BUT YOU FORGOT THE *ELIXIR*! YOU KNOW HOW YOUR HAIR GETS *FRIZZY* WITHOUT IT!

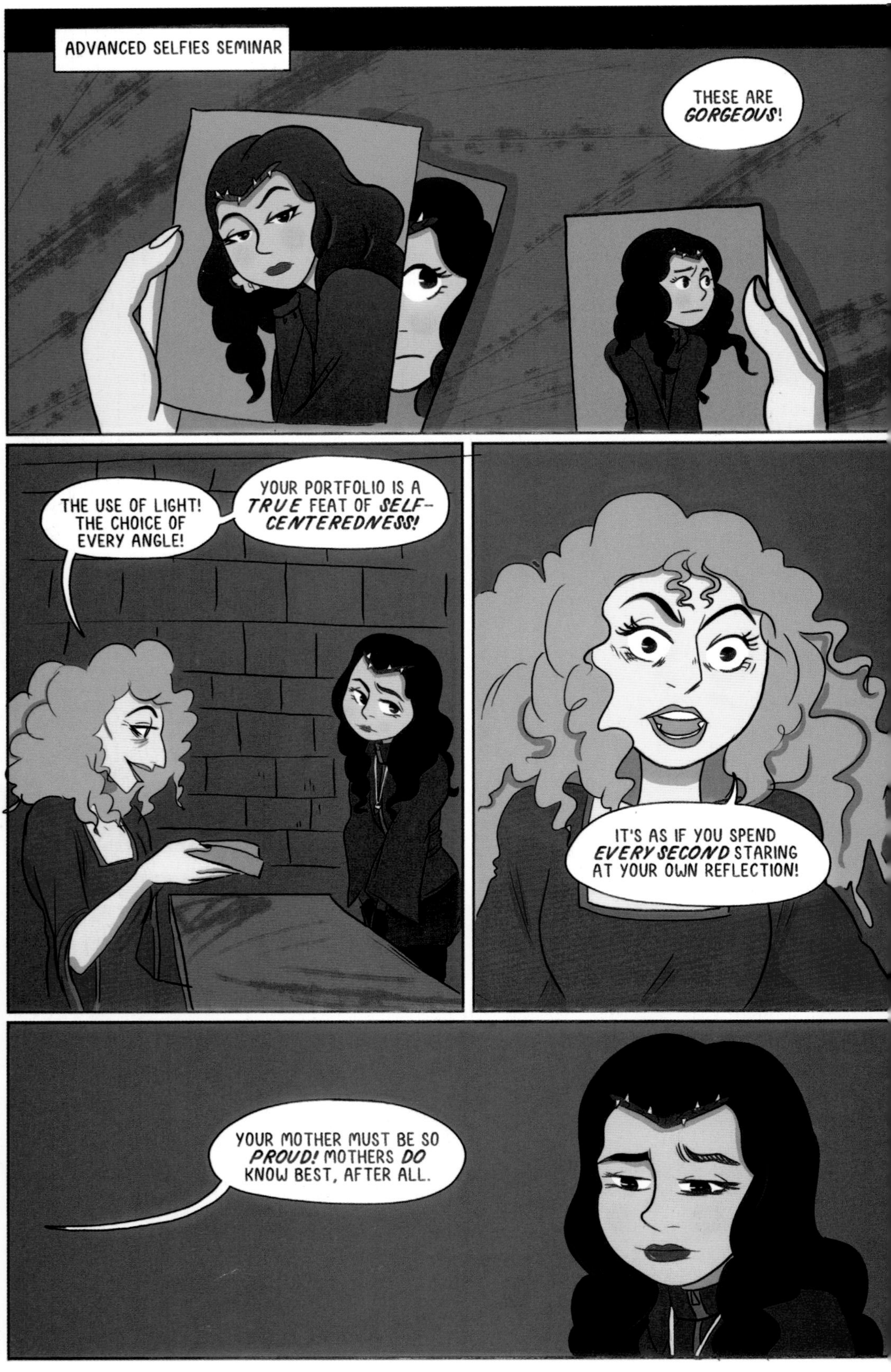
ADVANCED SELFIES SEMINAR
THESE ARE *GORGEOUS*!
THE USE OF LIGHT! THE CHOICE OF EVERY ANGLE!
YOUR PORTFOLIO IS A *TRUE* FEAT OF *SELF-CENTEREDNESS!*
IT'S AS IF YOU SPEND *EVERY SECOND* STARING AT YOUR OWN REFLECTION!
YOUR MOTHER MUST BE SO *PROUD!* MOTHERS *DO* KNOW BEST, AFTER ALL.

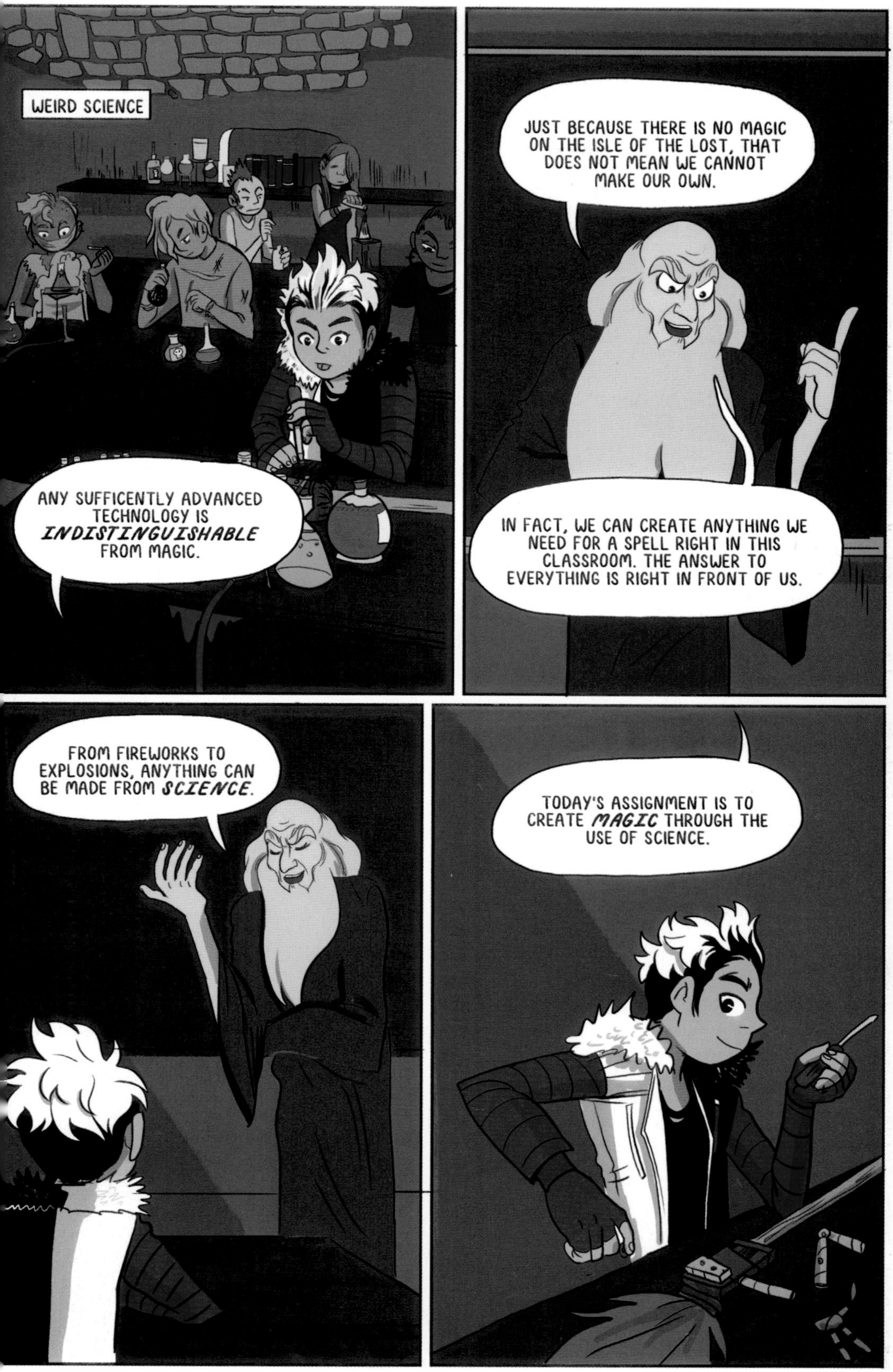
WEIRD SCIENCE
ANY SUFFICENTLY ADVANCED TECHNOLOGY IS *INDISTINGUISHABLE* FROM MAGIC.
JUST BECAUSE THERE IS NO MAGIC ON THE ISLE OF THE LOST, THAT DOES NOT MEAN WE CANNOT MAKE OUR OWN.
IN FACT, WE CAN CREATE ANYTHING WE NEED FOR A SPELL RIGHT IN THIS CLASSROOM. THE ANSWER TO EVERYTHING IS RIGHT IN FRONT OF US.
FROM FIREWORKS TO EXPLOSIONS, ANYTHING CAN BE MADE FROM *SCIENCE*.
TODAY'S ASSIGNMENT IS TO CREATE *MAGIC* THROUGH THE USE OF SCIENCE.

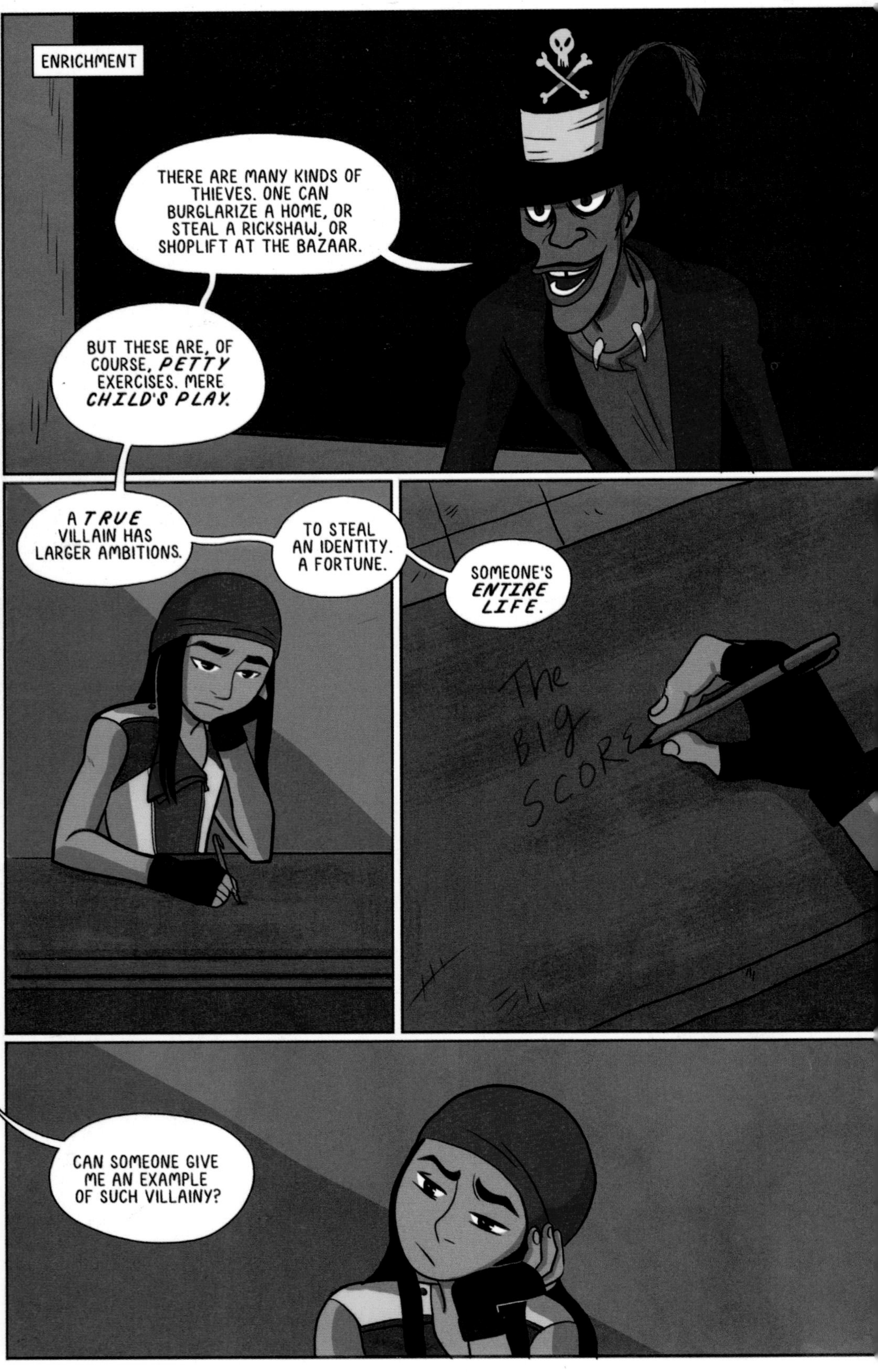
ENRICHMENT
THERE ARE MANY KINDS OF THIEVES. ONE CAN BURGLARIZE A HOME, OR STEAL A RICKSHAW, OR SHOPLIFT AT THE BAZAAR.
BUT THESE ARE, OF COURSE, PETTY EXERCISES. MERE CHILD'S PLAY.
A TRUE VILLAIN HAS LARGER AMBITIONS.
TO STEAL AN IDENTITY. A FORTUNE.
SOMEONE'S ENTIRE LIFE.
The BIG SCORE
CAN SOMEONE GIVE ME AN EXAMPLE OF SUCH VILLAINY?

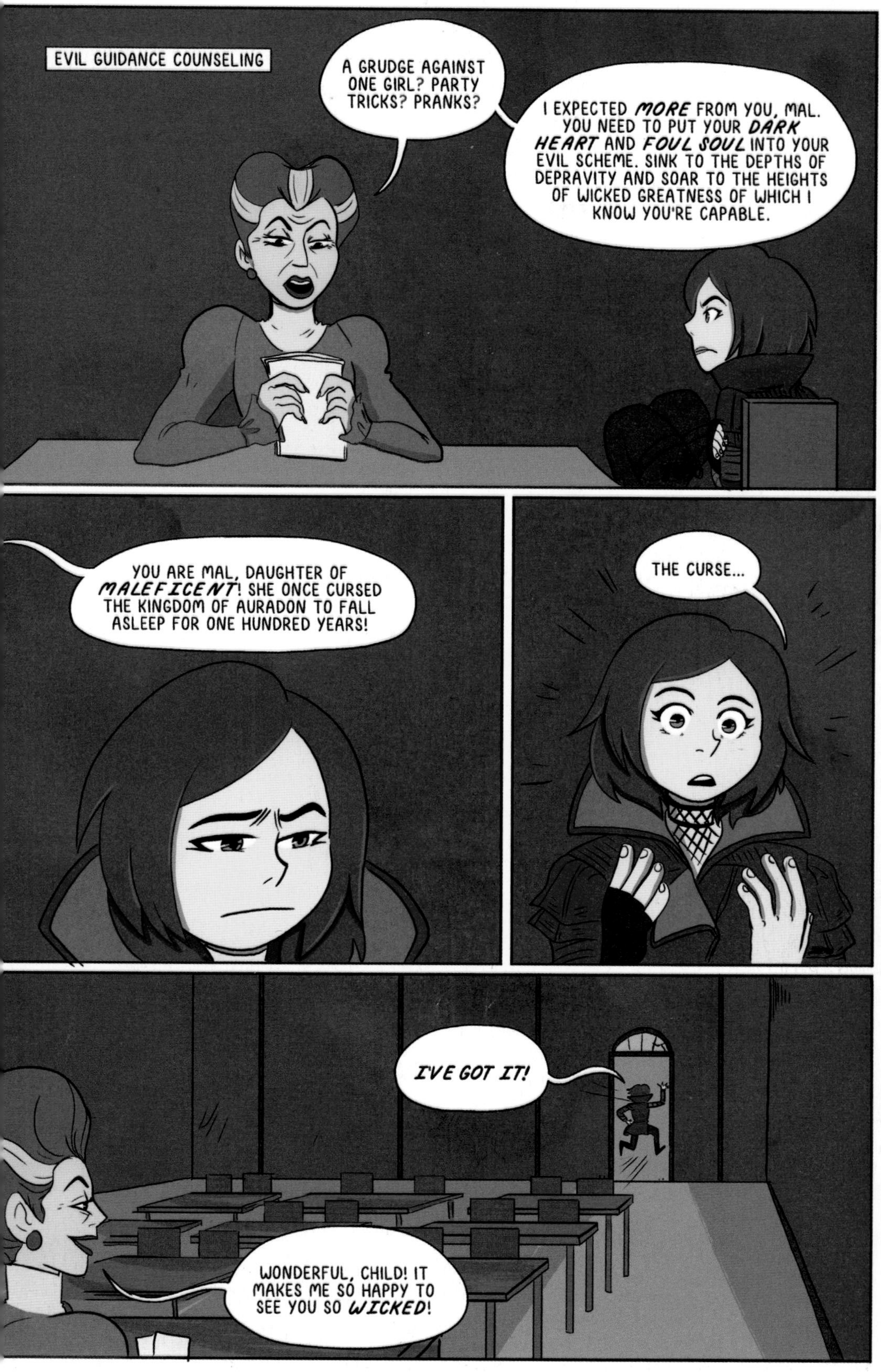
EVIL GUIDANCE COUNSELING
A GRUDGE AGAINST ONE GIRL? PARTY TRICKS? PRANKS?
I EXPECTED MORE FROM YOU, MAL. YOU NEED TO PUT YOUR DARK HEART AND FOUL SOUL INTO YOUR EVIL SCHEME. SINK TO THE DEPTHS OF DEPRAVITY AND SOAR TO THE HEIGHTS OF WICKED GREATNESS OF WHICH I KNOW YOU'RE CAPABLE.
YOU ARE MAL, DAUGHTER OF MALEFICENT! SHE ONCE CURSED THE KINGDOM OF AURADON TO FALL ASLEEP FOR ONE HUNDRED YEARS!
THE CURSE...
I'VE GOT IT!
WONDERFUL, CHILD! IT MAKES ME SO HAPPY TO SEE YOU SO WICKED!

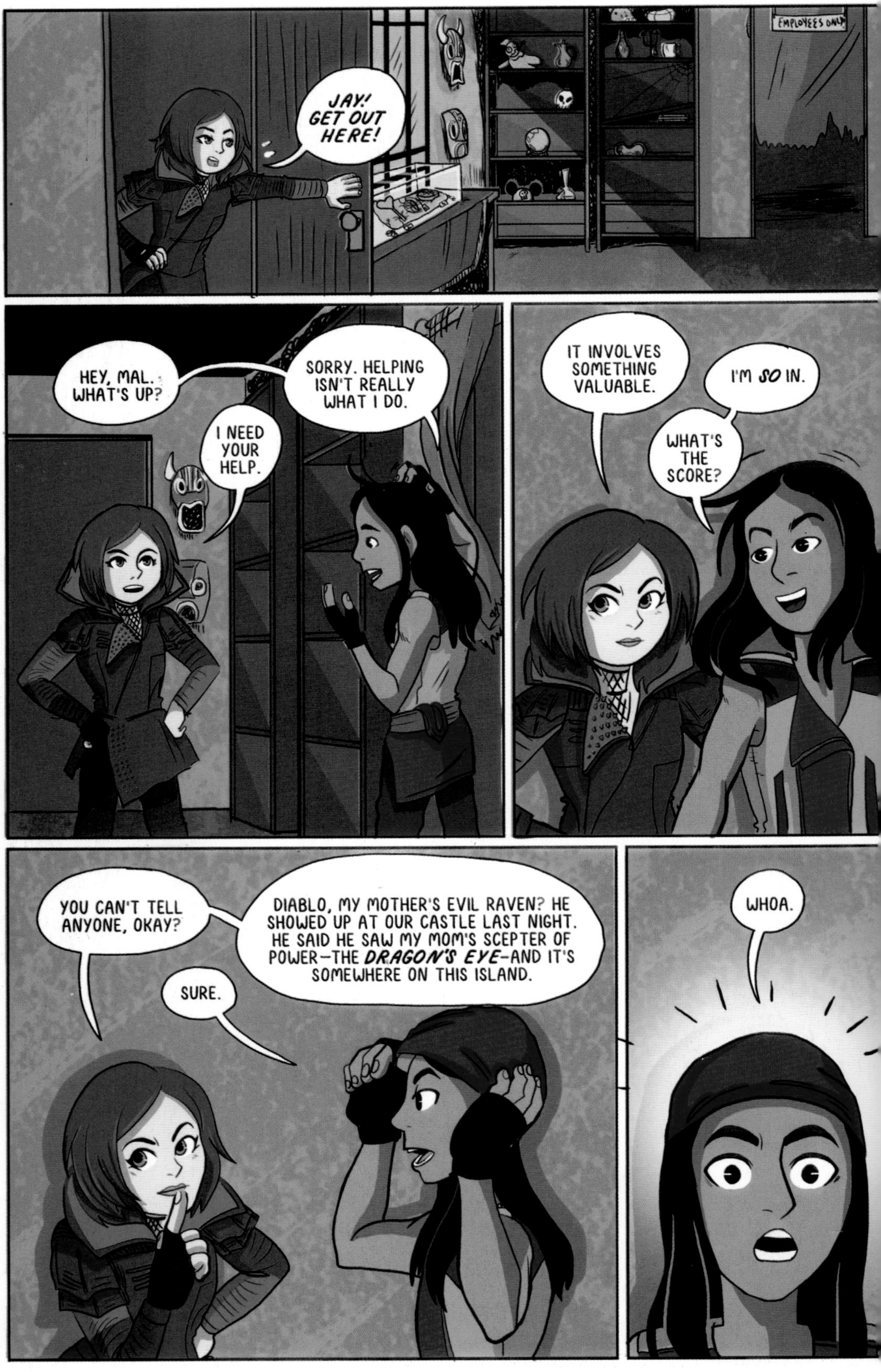
EMPLOYEES ONLY
JAY! GET OUT HERE!
HEY, MAL. WHAT'S UP?
I NEED YOUR HELP.
SORRY. HELPING ISN'T REALLY WHAT I DO.
IT INVOLVES SOMETHING VALUABLE.
I'M *SO* IN.
WHAT'S THE SCORE?
YOU CAN'T TELL ANYONE, OKAY?
SURE.
DIABLO, MY MOTHER'S EVIL RAVEN? HE SHOWED UP AT OUR CASTLE LAST NIGHT. HE SAID HE SAW MY MOM'S SCEPTER OF POWER—THE ***DRAGON'S EYE***—AND IT'S SOMEWHERE ON THIS ISLAND.
WHOA.

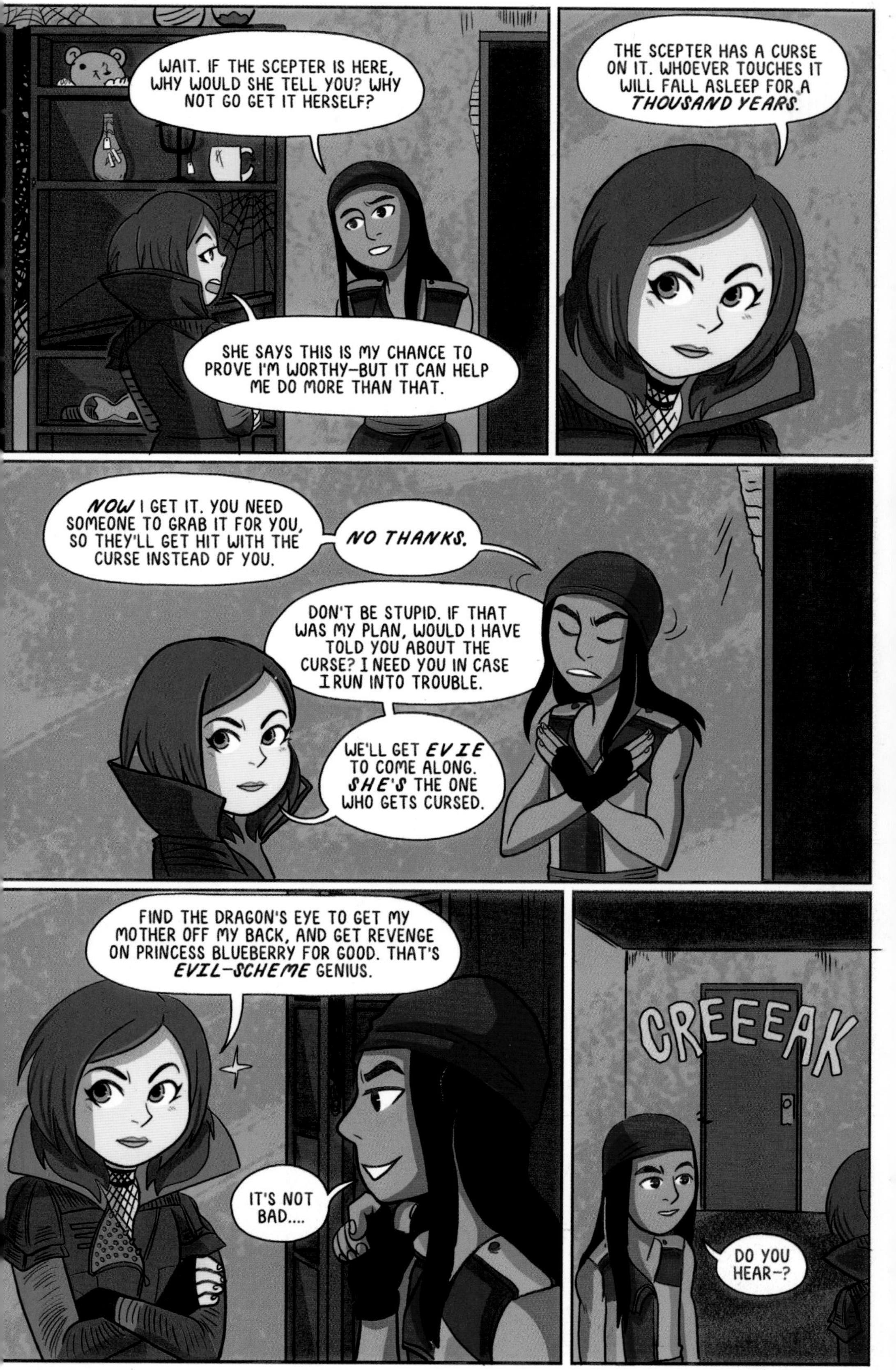
WAIT. IF THE SCEPTER IS HERE, WHY WOULD SHE TELL YOU? WHY NOT GO GET IT HERSELF?
SHE SAYS THIS IS MY CHANCE TO PROVE I'M WORTHY—BUT IT CAN HELP ME DO MORE THAN THAT.
THE SCEPTER HAS A CURSE ON IT. WHOEVER TOUCHES IT WILL FALL ASLEEP FOR A THOUSAND YEARS.
NOW I GET IT. YOU NEED SOMEONE TO GRAB IT FOR YOU, SO THEY'LL GET HIT WITH THE CURSE INSTEAD OF YOU.
NO THANKS.
DON'T BE STUPID. IF THAT WAS MY PLAN, WOULD I HAVE TOLD YOU ABOUT THE CURSE? I NEED YOU IN CASE I RUN INTO TROUBLE.
WE'LL GET EVIE TO COME ALONG. SHE'S THE ONE WHO GETS CURSED.
FIND THE DRAGON'S EYE TO GET MY MOTHER OFF MY BACK, AND GET REVENGE ON PRINCESS BLUEBERRY FOR GOOD. THAT'S EVIL-SCHEME GENIUS.
IT'S NOT BAD....
CREEEAK
DO YOU HEAR—?

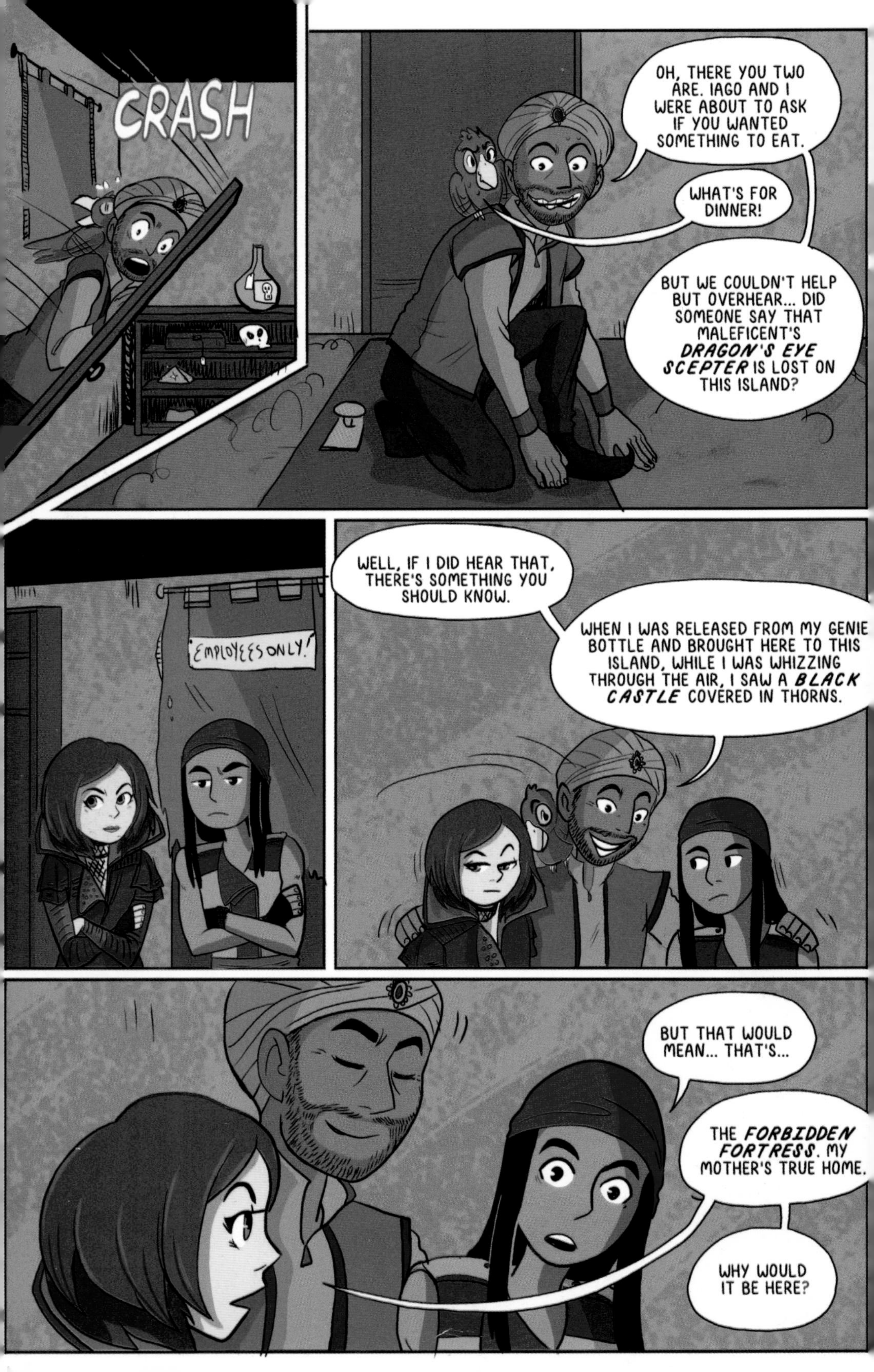
CRASH
OH, THERE YOU TWO ARE. IAGO AND I WERE ABOUT TO ASK IF YOU WANTED SOMETHING TO EAT.
WHAT'S FOR DINNER!
BUT WE COULDN'T HELP BUT OVERHEAR... DID SOMEONE SAY THAT MALEFICENT'S *DRAGON'S EYE SCEPTER* IS LOST ON THIS ISLAND?
EMPLOYEES ONLY!
WELL, IF I DID HEAR THAT, THERE'S SOMETHING YOU SHOULD KNOW.
WHEN I WAS RELEASED FROM MY GENIE BOTTLE AND BROUGHT HERE TO THIS ISLAND, WHILE I WAS WHIZZING THROUGH THE AIR, I SAW A *BLACK CASTLE* COVERED IN THORNS.
BUT THAT WOULD MEAN... THAT'S...
THE *FORBIDDEN FORTRESS*. MY MOTHER'S TRUE HOME.
WHY WOULD IT BE HERE?

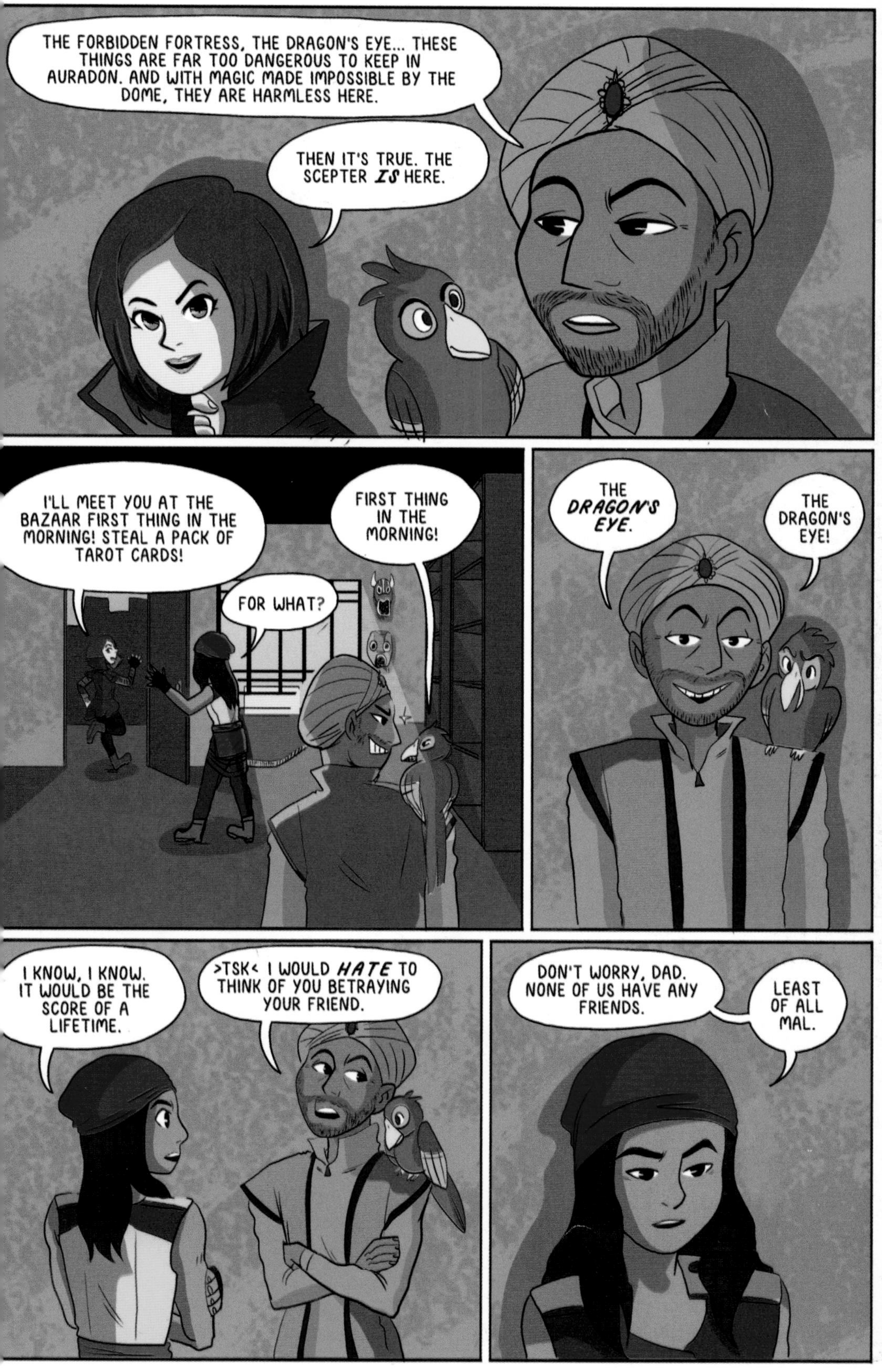
THE FORBIDDEN FORTRESS, THE DRAGON'S EYE... THESE THINGS ARE FAR TOO DANGEROUS TO KEEP IN AURADON. AND WITH MAGIC MADE IMPOSSIBLE BY THE DOME, THEY ARE HARMLESS HERE.
THEN IT'S TRUE. THE SCEPTER *IS* HERE.
I'LL MEET YOU AT THE BAZAAR FIRST THING IN THE MORNING! STEAL A PACK OF TAROT CARDS!
FOR WHAT?
FIRST THING IN THE MORNING!
THE *DRAGON'S EYE*.
THE DRAGON'S EYE!
I KNOW, I KNOW. IT WOULD BE THE SCORE OF A LIFETIME.
>TSK< I WOULD *HATE* TO THINK OF YOU BETRAYING YOUR FRIEND.
DON'T WORRY, DAD. NONE OF US HAVE ANY FRIENDS.
LEAST OF ALL MAL.

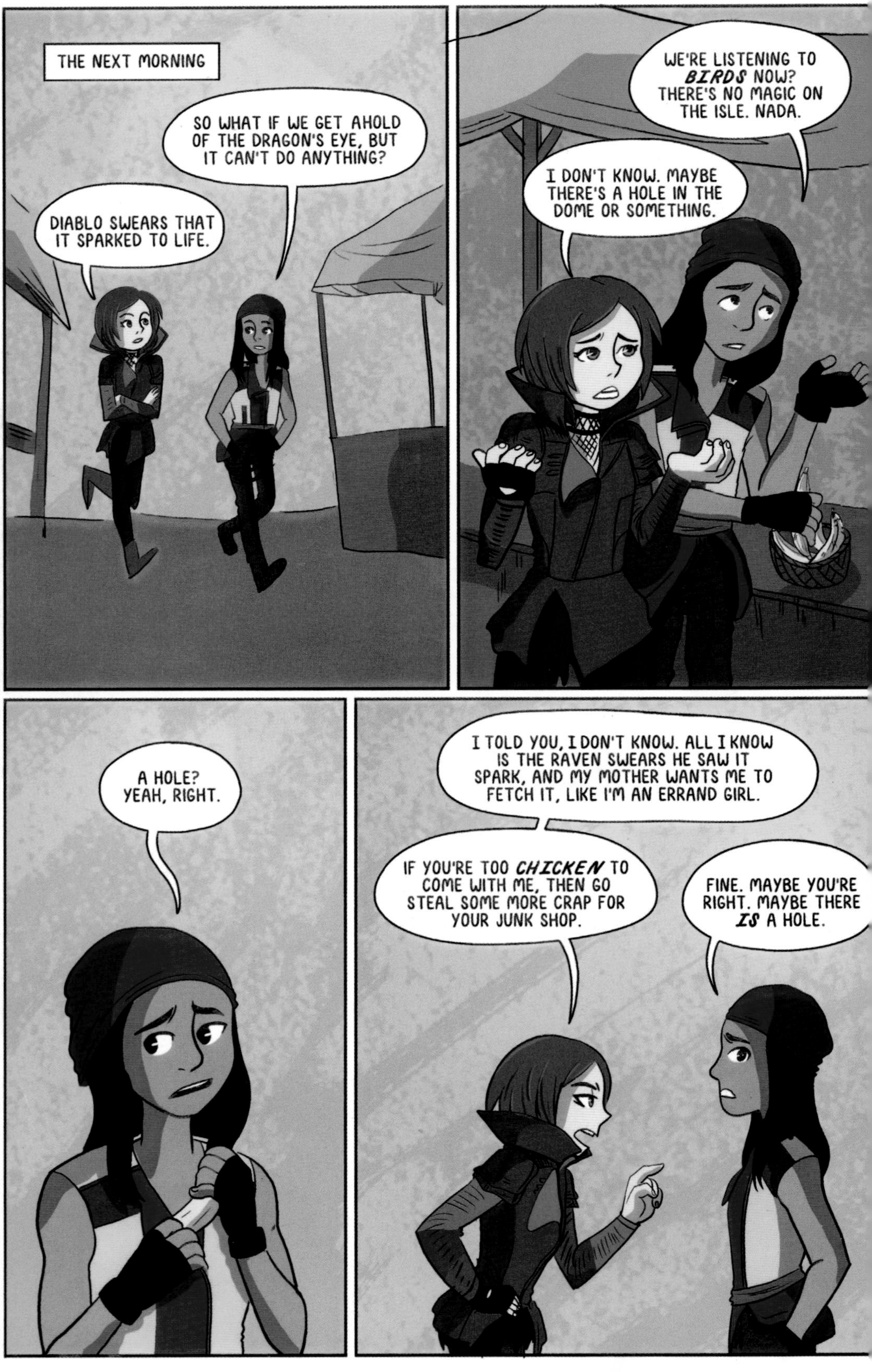
THE NEXT MORNING
SO WHAT IF WE GET AHOLD OF THE DRAGON'S EYE, BUT IT CAN'T DO ANYTHING?
DIABLO SWEARS THAT IT SPARKED TO LIFE.
WE'RE LISTENING TO BIRDS NOW? THERE'S NO MAGIC ON THE ISLE. NADA.
I DON'T KNOW. MAYBE THERE'S A HOLE IN THE DOME OR SOMETHING.
A HOLE? YEAH, RIGHT.
I TOLD YOU, I DON'T KNOW. ALL I KNOW IS THE RAVEN SWEARS HE SAW IT SPARK, AND MY MOTHER WANTS ME TO FETCH IT, LIKE I'M AN ERRAND GIRL.
IF YOU'RE TOO CHICKEN TO COME WITH ME, THEN GO STEAL SOME MORE CRAP FOR YOUR JUNK SHOP.
FINE. MAYBE YOU'RE RIGHT. MAYBE THERE IS A HOLE.

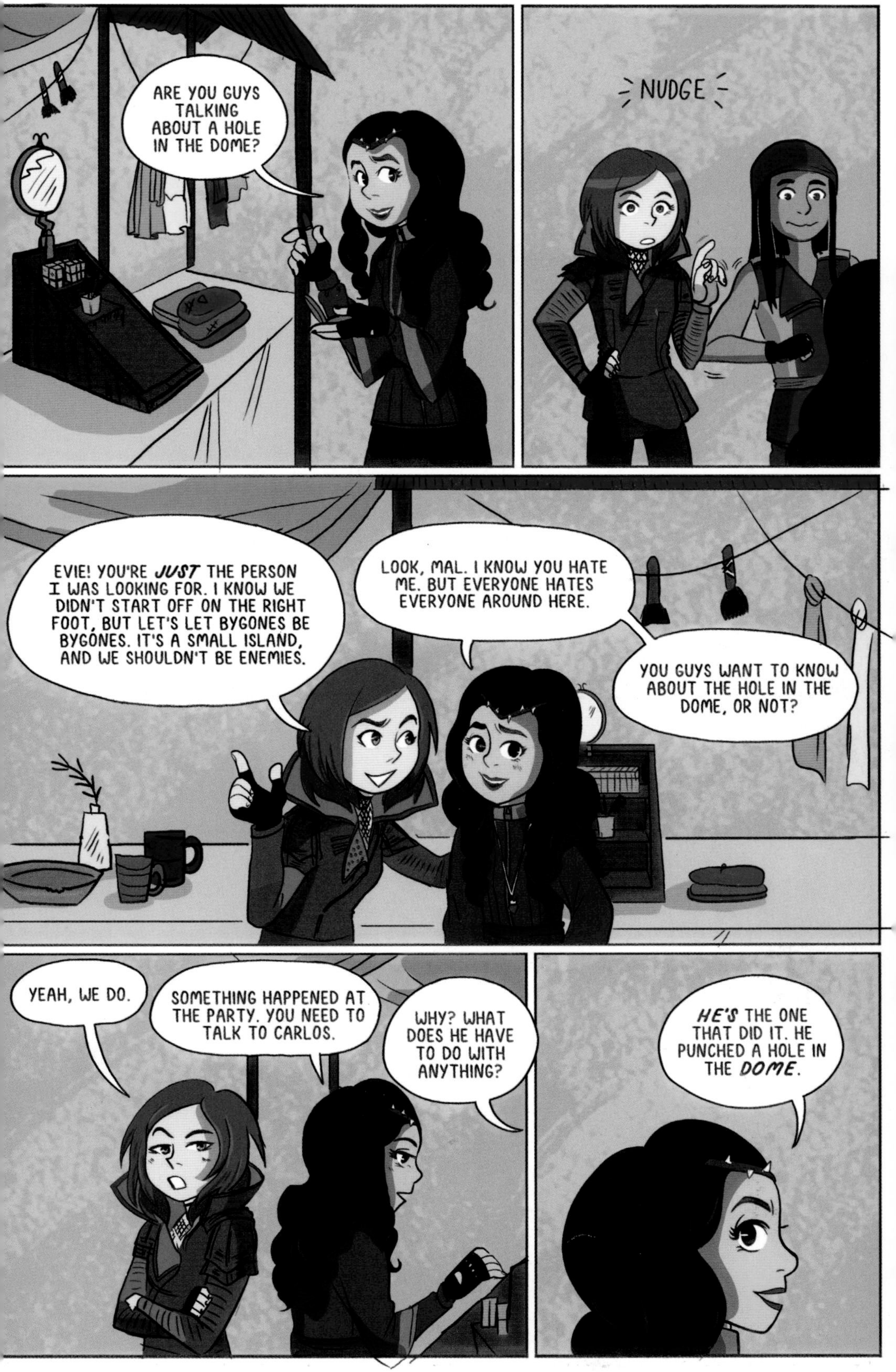
ARE YOU GUYS TALKING ABOUT A HOLE IN THE DOME?
NUDGE
EVIE! YOU'RE *JUST* THE PERSON I WAS LOOKING FOR. I KNOW WE DIDN'T START OFF ON THE RIGHT FOOT, BUT LET'S LET BYGONES BE BYGONES. IT'S A SMALL ISLAND, AND WE SHOULDN'T BE ENEMIES.
LOOK, MAL. I KNOW YOU HATE ME. BUT EVERYONE HATES EVERYONE AROUND HERE.
YOU GUYS WANT TO KNOW ABOUT THE HOLE IN THE DOME, OR NOT?
YEAH, WE DO.
SOMETHING HAPPENED AT THE PARTY. YOU NEED TO TALK TO CARLOS.
WHY? WHAT DOES HE HAVE TO DO WITH ANYTHING?
HE'S THE ONE THAT DID IT. HE PUNCHED A HOLE IN THE *DOME*.

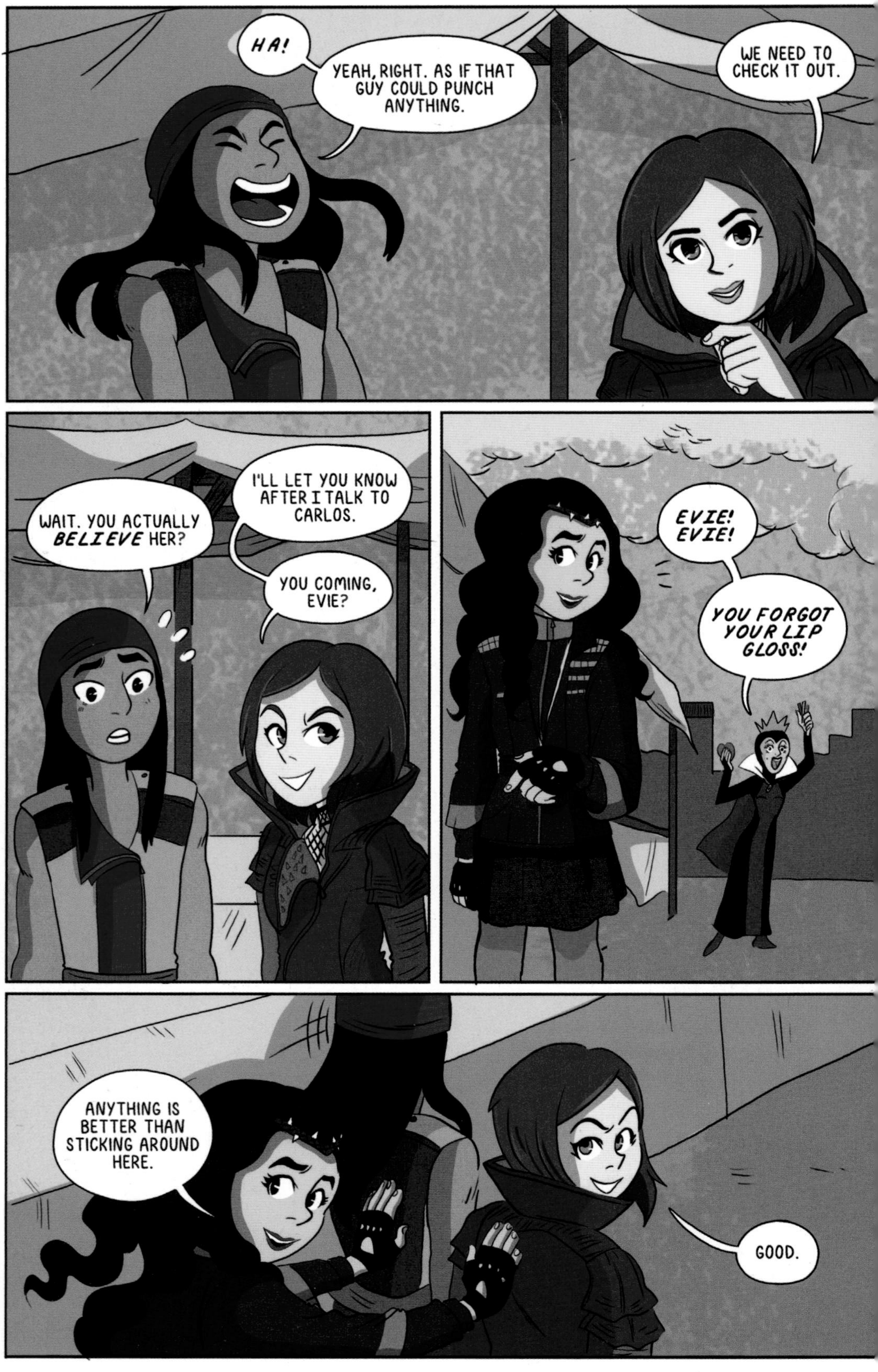
HA!
YEAH, RIGHT. AS IF THAT GUY COULD PUNCH ANYTHING.
WE NEED TO CHECK IT OUT.
WAIT. YOU ACTUALLY BELIEVE HER?
I'LL LET YOU KNOW AFTER I TALK TO CARLOS.
YOU COMING, EVIE?
EVIE! EVIE!
YOU FORGOT YOUR LIP GLOSS!
ANYTHING IS BETTER THAN STICKING AROUND HERE.
GOOD.

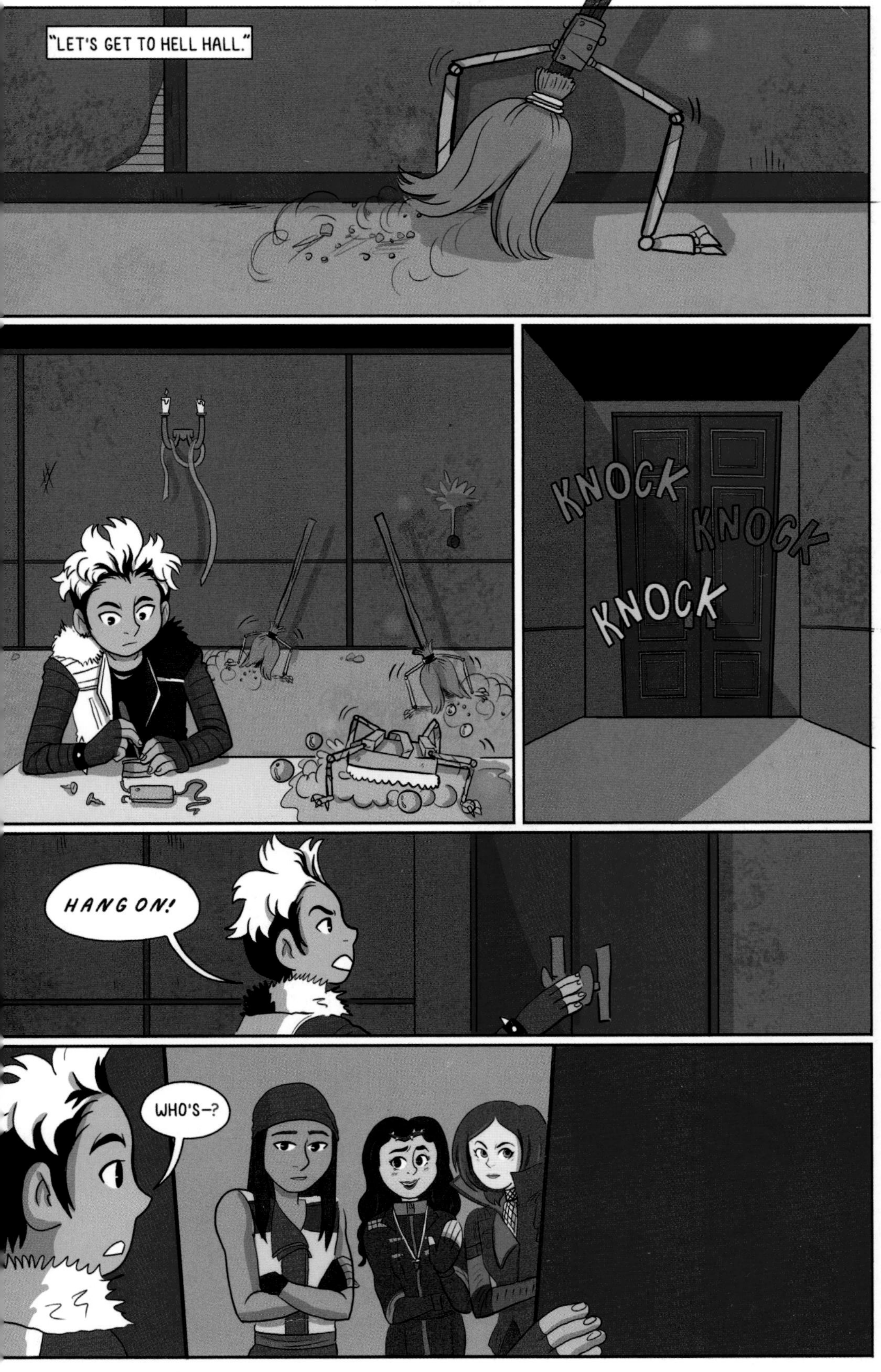
"LET'S GET TO HELL HALL."
KNOCK
KNOCK
KNOCK
HANG ON!
WHO'S—?

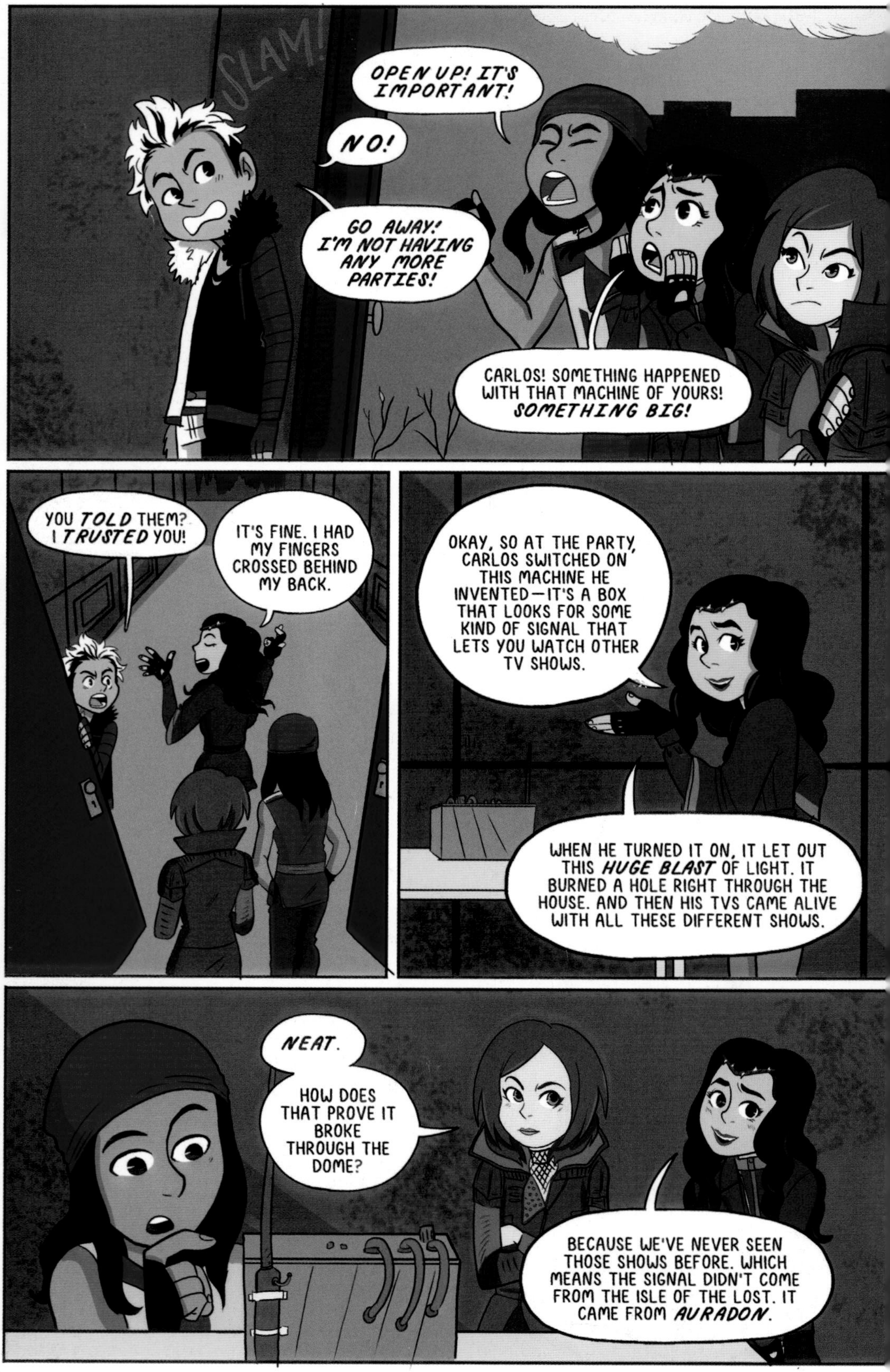
SLAM!
OPEN UP! IT'S IMPORTANT!
NO!
GO AWAY! I'M NOT HAVING ANY MORE PARTIES!
CARLOS! SOMETHING HAPPENED WITH THAT MACHINE OF YOURS! SOMETHING BIG!
YOU TOLD THEM? I TRUSTED YOU!
IT'S FINE. I HAD MY FINGERS CROSSED BEHIND MY BACK.
OKAY, SO AT THE PARTY, CARLOS SWITCHED ON THIS MACHINE HE INVENTED—IT'S A BOX THAT LOOKS FOR SOME KIND OF SIGNAL THAT LETS YOU WATCH OTHER TV SHOWS.
WHEN HE TURNED IT ON, IT LET OUT THIS HUGE BLAST OF LIGHT. IT BURNED A HOLE RIGHT THROUGH THE HOUSE. AND THEN HIS TVS CAME ALIVE WITH ALL THESE DIFFERENT SHOWS.
NEAT.
HOW DOES THAT PROVE IT BROKE THROUGH THE DOME?
BECAUSE WE'VE NEVER SEEN THOSE SHOWS BEFORE. WHICH MEANS THE SIGNAL DIDN'T COME FROM THE ISLE OF THE LOST. IT CAME FROM AURADON.

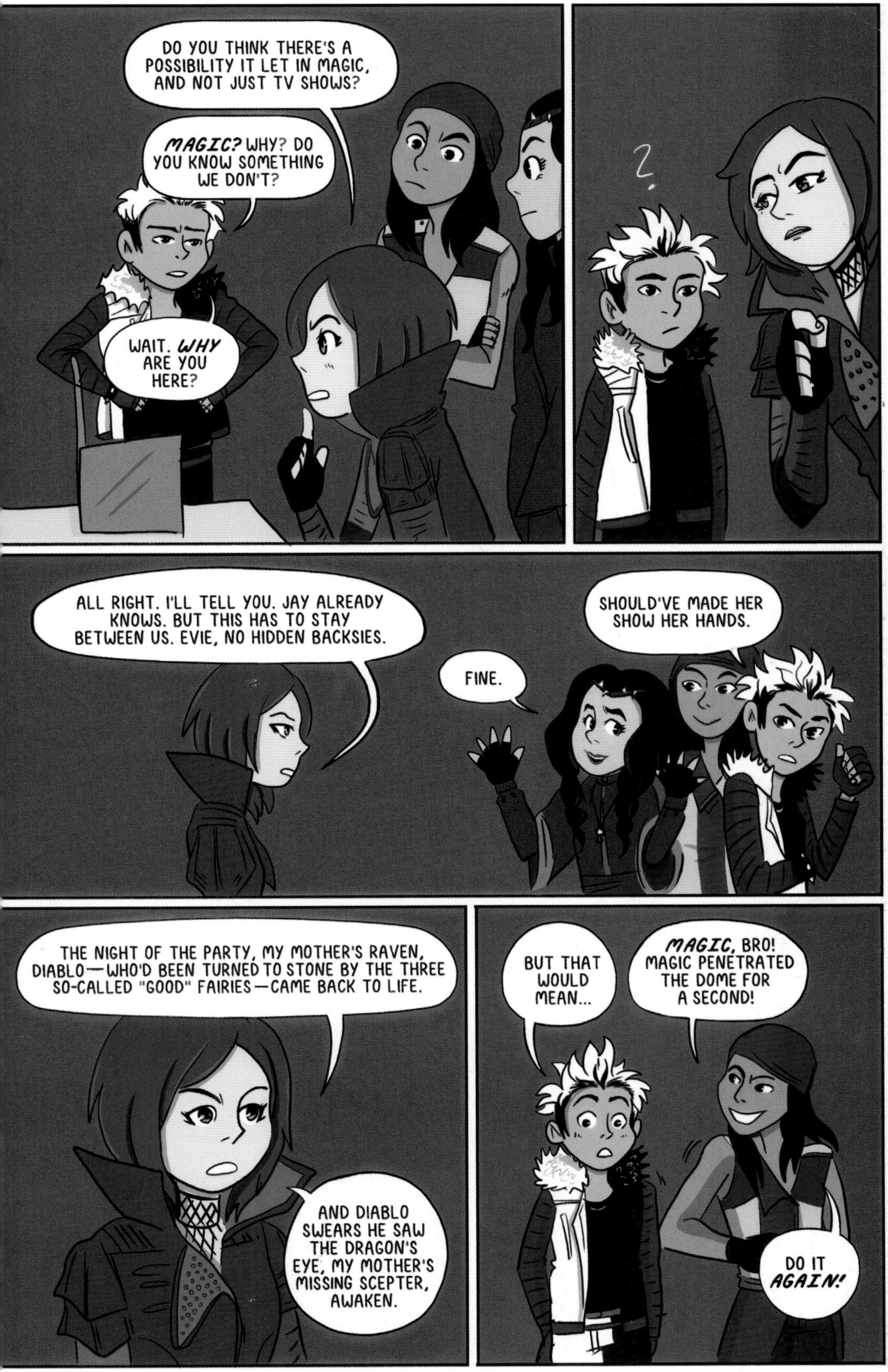
DO YOU THINK THERE'S A POSSIBILITY IT LET IN MAGIC, AND NOT JUST TV SHOWS?
MAGIC? WHY? DO YOU KNOW SOMETHING WE DON'T?
WAIT. WHY ARE YOU HERE?
?
ALL RIGHT. I'LL TELL YOU. JAY ALREADY KNOWS. BUT THIS HAS TO STAY BETWEEN US. EVIE, NO HIDDEN BACKSIES.
FINE.
SHOULD'VE MADE HER SHOW HER HANDS.
THE NIGHT OF THE PARTY, MY MOTHER'S RAVEN, DIABLO—WHO'D BEEN TURNED TO STONE BY THE THREE SO-CALLED "GOOD" FAIRIES—CAME BACK TO LIFE.
AND DIABLO SWEARS HE SAW THE DRAGON'S EYE, MY MOTHER'S MISSING SCEPTER, AWAKEN.
BUT THAT WOULD MEAN...
MAGIC, BRO! MAGIC PENETRATED THE DOME FOR A SECOND!
DO IT AGAIN!

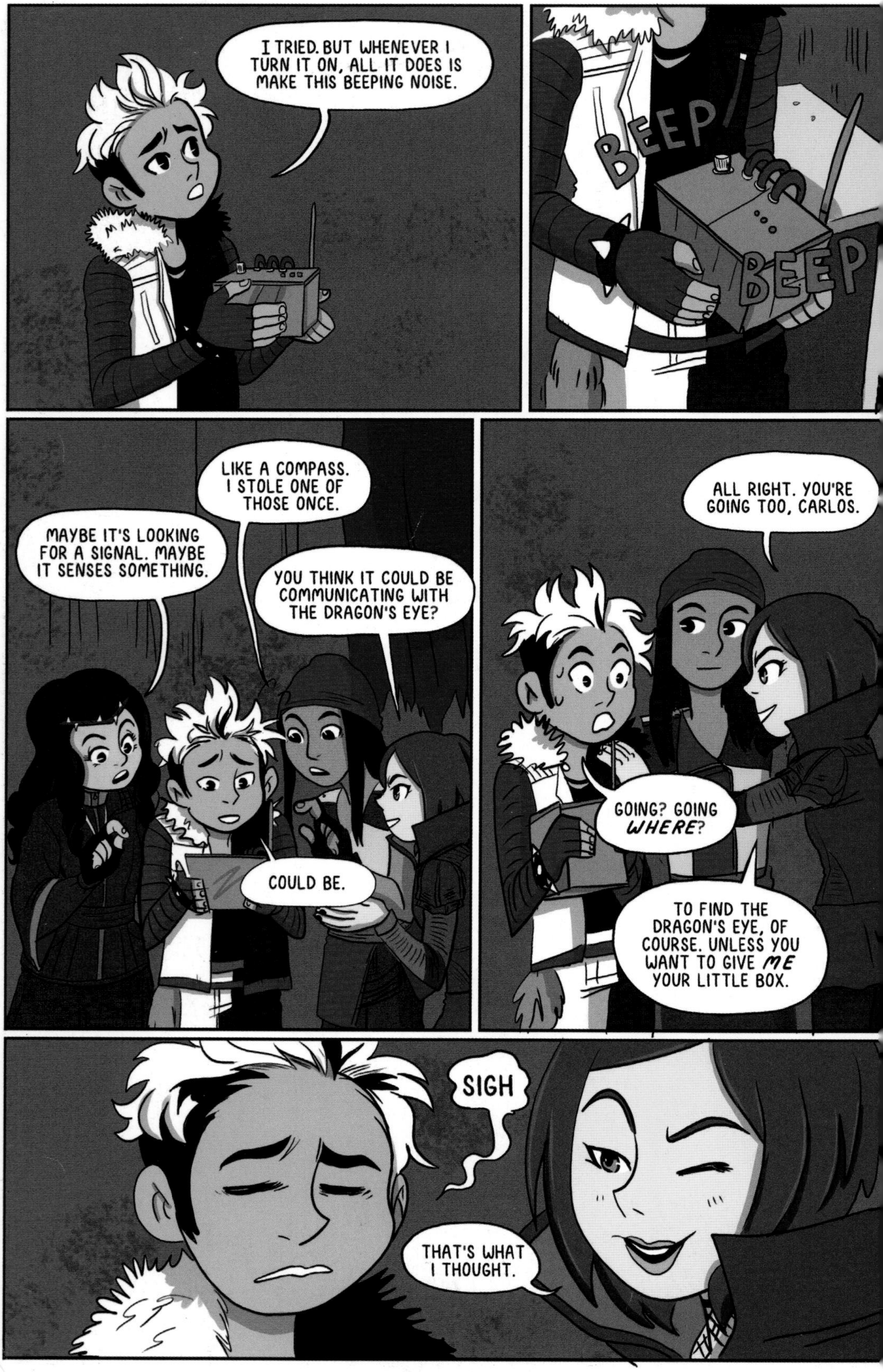
I TRIED. BUT WHENEVER I TURN IT ON, ALL IT DOES IS MAKE THIS BEEPING NOISE.
BEEP
BEEP
MAYBE IT'S LOOKING FOR A SIGNAL. MAYBE IT SENSES SOMETHING.
LIKE A COMPASS. I STOLE ONE OF THOSE ONCE.
YOU THINK IT COULD BE COMMUNICATING WITH THE DRAGON'S EYE?
COULD BE.
ALL RIGHT. YOU'RE GOING TOO, CARLOS.
GOING? GOING *WHERE*?
TO FIND THE DRAGON'S EYE, OF COURSE. UNLESS YOU WANT TO GIVE *ME* YOUR LITTLE BOX.
SIGH
THAT'S WHAT I THOUGHT.

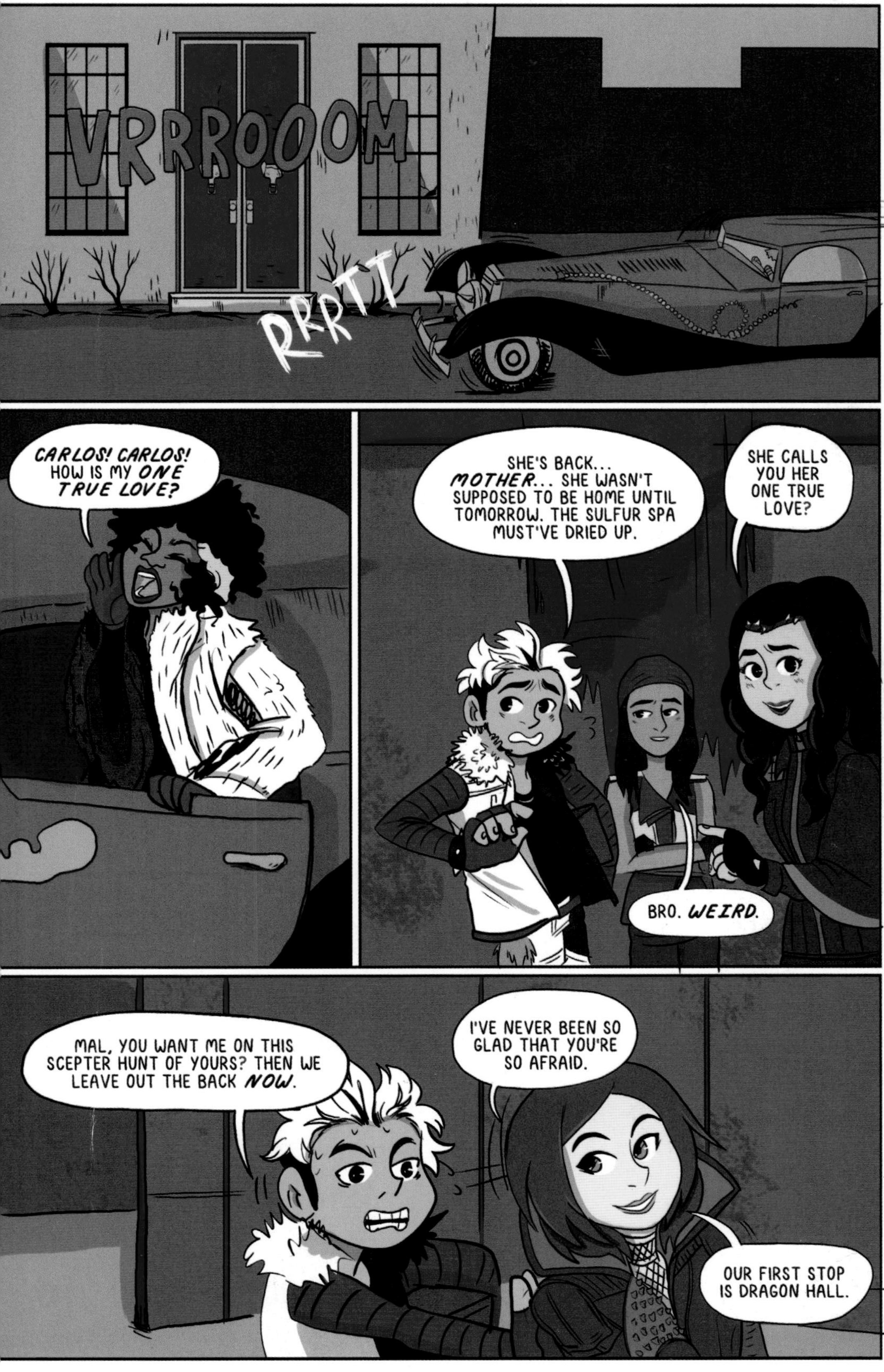
VRRROOOM
RRRTT
CARLOS! CARLOS! HOW IS MY ONE TRUE LOVE?
SHE'S BACK... MOTHER... SHE WASN'T SUPPOSED TO BE HOME UNTIL TOMORROW. THE SULFUR SPA MUST'VE DRIED UP.
SHE CALLS YOU HER ONE TRUE LOVE?
BRO. WEIRD.
MAL, YOU WANT ME ON THIS SCEPTER HUNT OF YOURS? THEN WE LEAVE OUT THE BACK NOW.
I'VE NEVER BEEN SO GLAD THAT YOU'RE SO AFRAID.
OUR FIRST STOP IS DRAGON HALL.

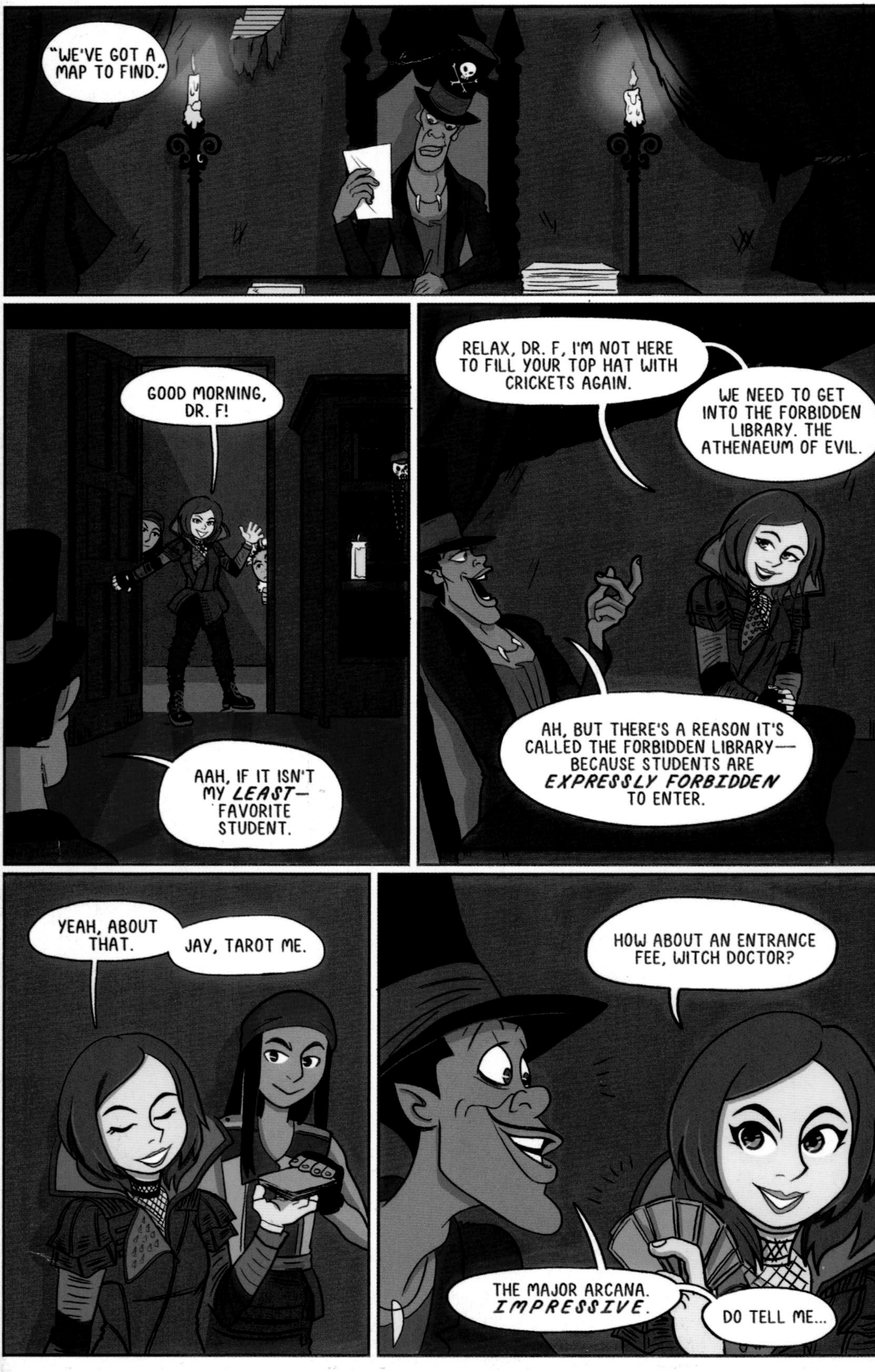
"WE'VE GOT A MAP TO FIND."
GOOD MORNING, DR. F!
AAH, IF IT ISN'T MY *LEAST*— FAVORITE STUDENT.
RELAX, DR. F, I'M NOT HERE TO FILL YOUR TOP HAT WITH CRICKETS AGAIN.
WE NEED TO GET INTO THE FORBIDDEN LIBRARY. THE ATHENAEUM OF EVIL.
AH, BUT THERE'S A REASON IT'S CALLED THE FORBIDDEN LIBRARY— BECAUSE STUDENTS ARE *EXPRESSLY FORBIDDEN* TO ENTER.
YEAH, ABOUT THAT.
JAY, TAROT ME.
HOW ABOUT AN ENTRANCE FEE, WITCH DOCTOR?
THE MAJOR ARCANA. *IMPRESSIVE*.
DO TELL ME...

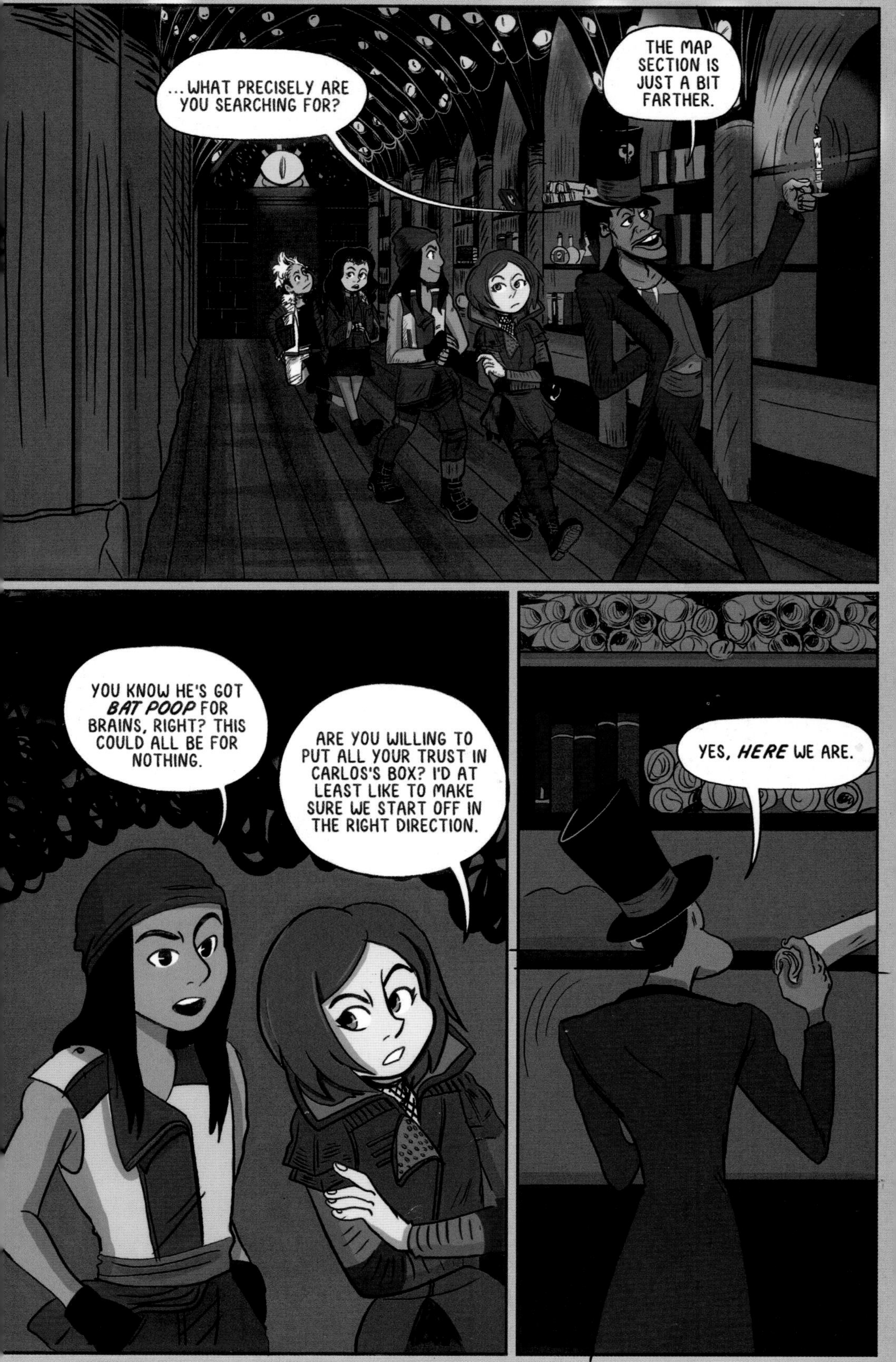
...WHAT PRECISELY ARE YOU SEARCHING FOR?
THE MAP SECTION IS JUST A BIT FARTHER.
YOU KNOW HE'S GOT *BAT POOP* FOR BRAINS, RIGHT? THIS COULD ALL BE FOR NOTHING.
ARE YOU WILLING TO PUT ALL YOUR TRUST IN CARLOS'S BOX? I'D AT LEAST LIKE TO MAKE SURE WE START OFF IN THE RIGHT DIRECTION.
YES, *HERE* WE ARE.

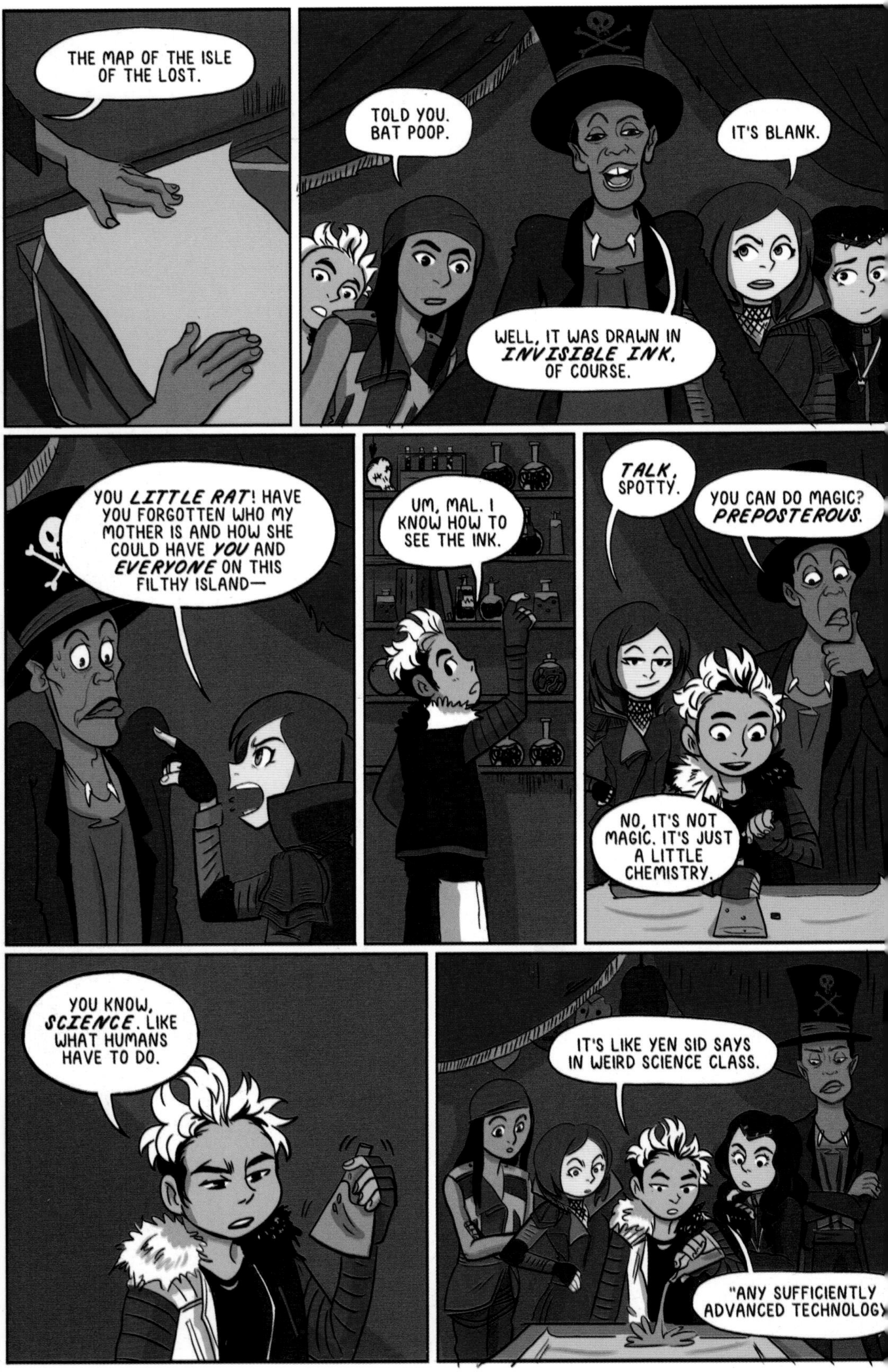
THE MAP OF THE ISLE OF THE LOST.
TOLD YOU. BAT POOP.
IT'S BLANK.
WELL, IT WAS DRAWN IN *INVISIBLE INK*, OF COURSE.
YOU *LITTLE RAT*! HAVE YOU FORGOTTEN WHO MY MOTHER IS AND HOW SHE COULD HAVE *YOU* AND *EVERYONE* ON THIS FILTHY ISLAND—
UM, MAL. I KNOW HOW TO SEE THE INK.
TALK, SPOTTY.
YOU CAN DO MAGIC? *PREPOSTEROUS*.
NO, IT'S NOT MAGIC. IT'S JUST A LITTLE CHEMISTRY.
YOU KNOW, *SCIENCE*. LIKE WHAT HUMANS HAVE TO DO.
IT'S LIKE YEN SID SAYS IN WEIRD SCIENCE CLASS.
"ANY SUFFICIENTLY ADVANCED TECHNOLOGY

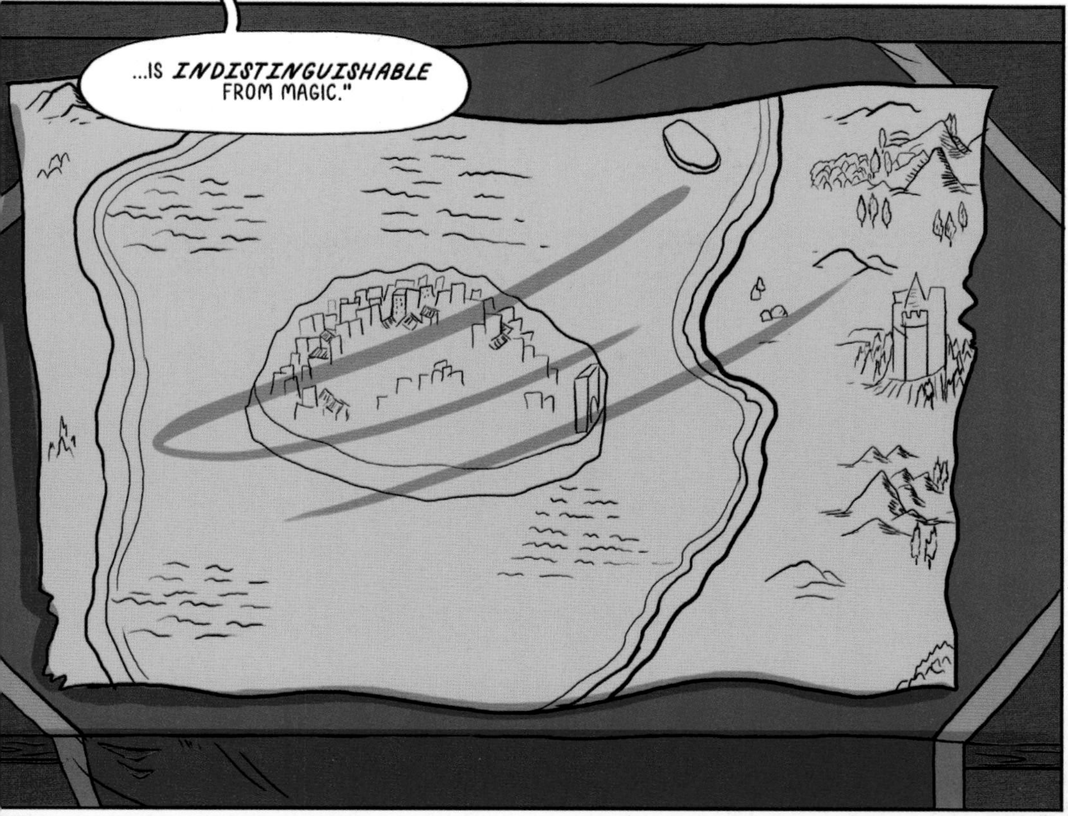
...IS INDISTINGUISHABLE FROM MAGIC."

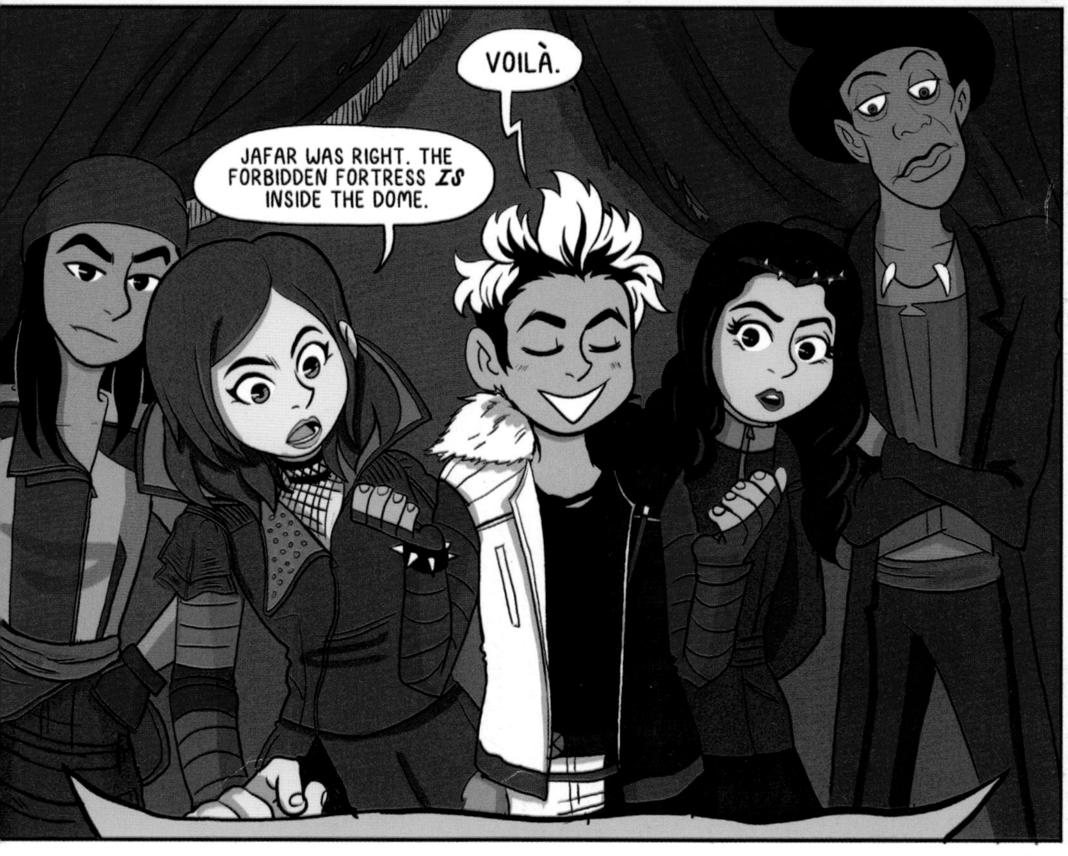
JAFAR WAS RIGHT. THE FORBIDDEN FORTRESS IS INSIDE THE DOME.
VOILÀ.

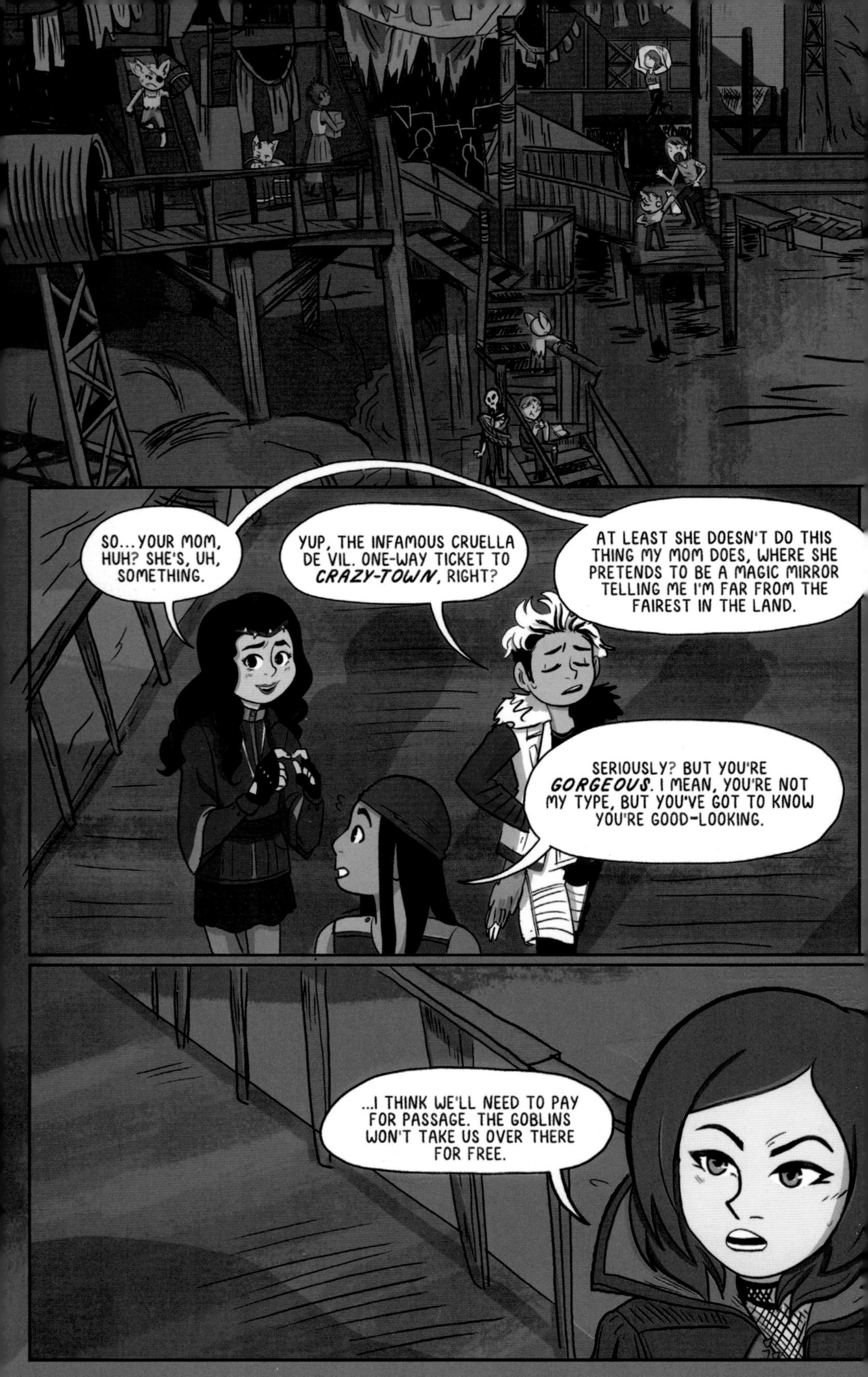

SO...YOUR MOM, HUH? SHE'S, UH, SOMETHING.
YUP, THE INFAMOUS CRUELLA DE VIL. ONE-WAY TICKET TO *CRAZY-TOWN*, RIGHT?
AT LEAST SHE DOESN'T DO THIS THING MY MOM DOES, WHERE SHE PRETENDS TO BE A MAGIC MIRROR TELLING ME I'M FAR FROM THE FAIREST IN THE LAND.
SERIOUSLY? BUT YOU'RE ***GORGEOUS***. I MEAN, YOU'RE NOT MY TYPE, BUT YOU'VE GOT TO KNOW YOU'RE GOOD-LOOKING.
...I THINK WE'LL NEED TO PAY FOR PASSAGE. THE GOBLINS WON'T TAKE US OVER THERE FOR FREE.

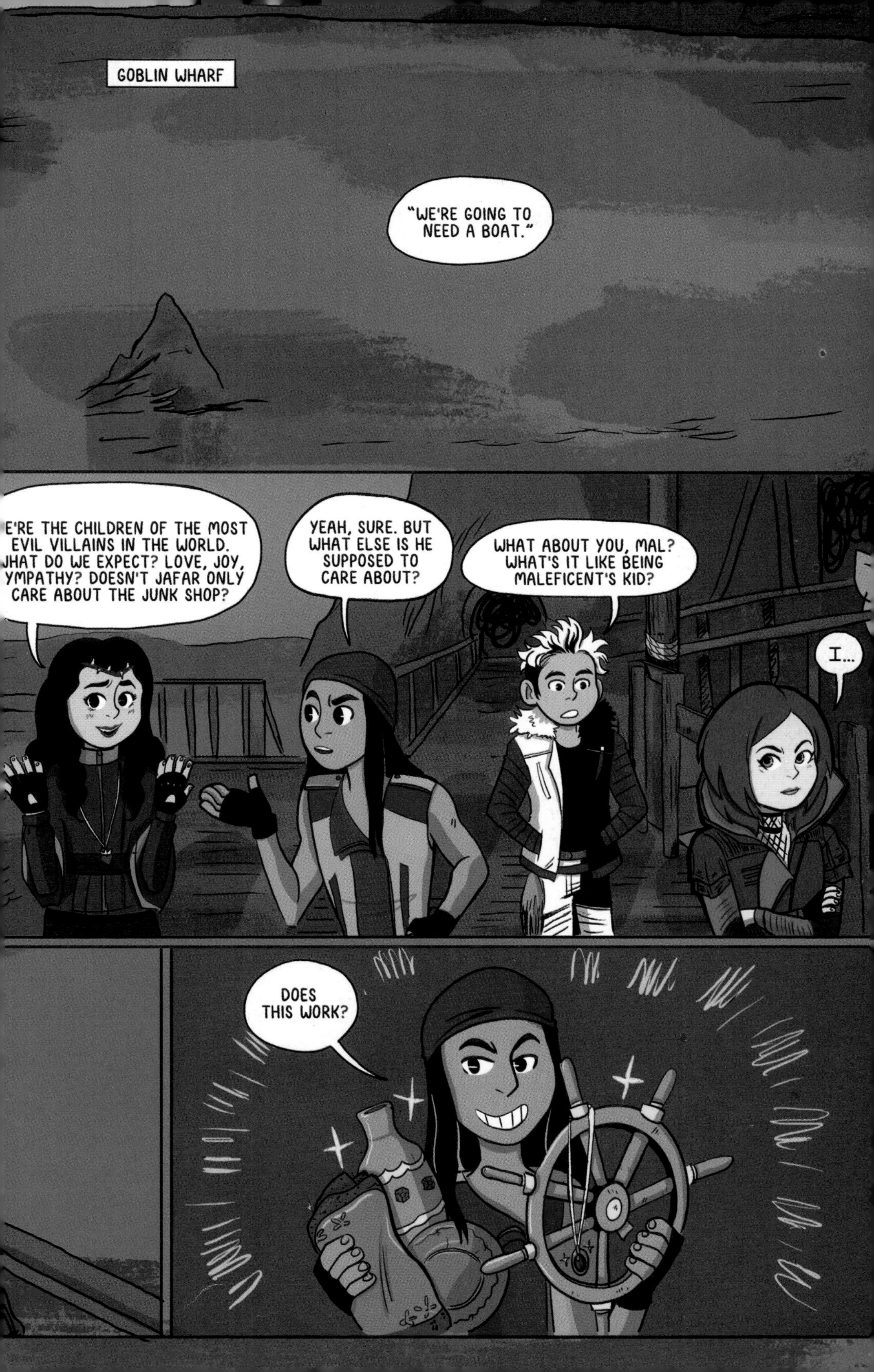
GOBLIN WHARF
"WE'RE GOING TO NEED A BOAT."
E'RE THE CHILDREN OF THE MOST EVIL VILLAINS IN THE WORLD. HAT DO WE EXPECT? LOVE, JOY, YMPATHY? DOESN'T JAFAR ONLY CARE ABOUT THE JUNK SHOP?
YEAH, SURE. BUT WHAT ELSE IS HE SUPPOSED TO CARE ABOUT?
WHAT ABOUT YOU, MAL? WHAT'S IT LIKE BEING MALEFICENT'S KID?
I...
DOES THIS WORK?

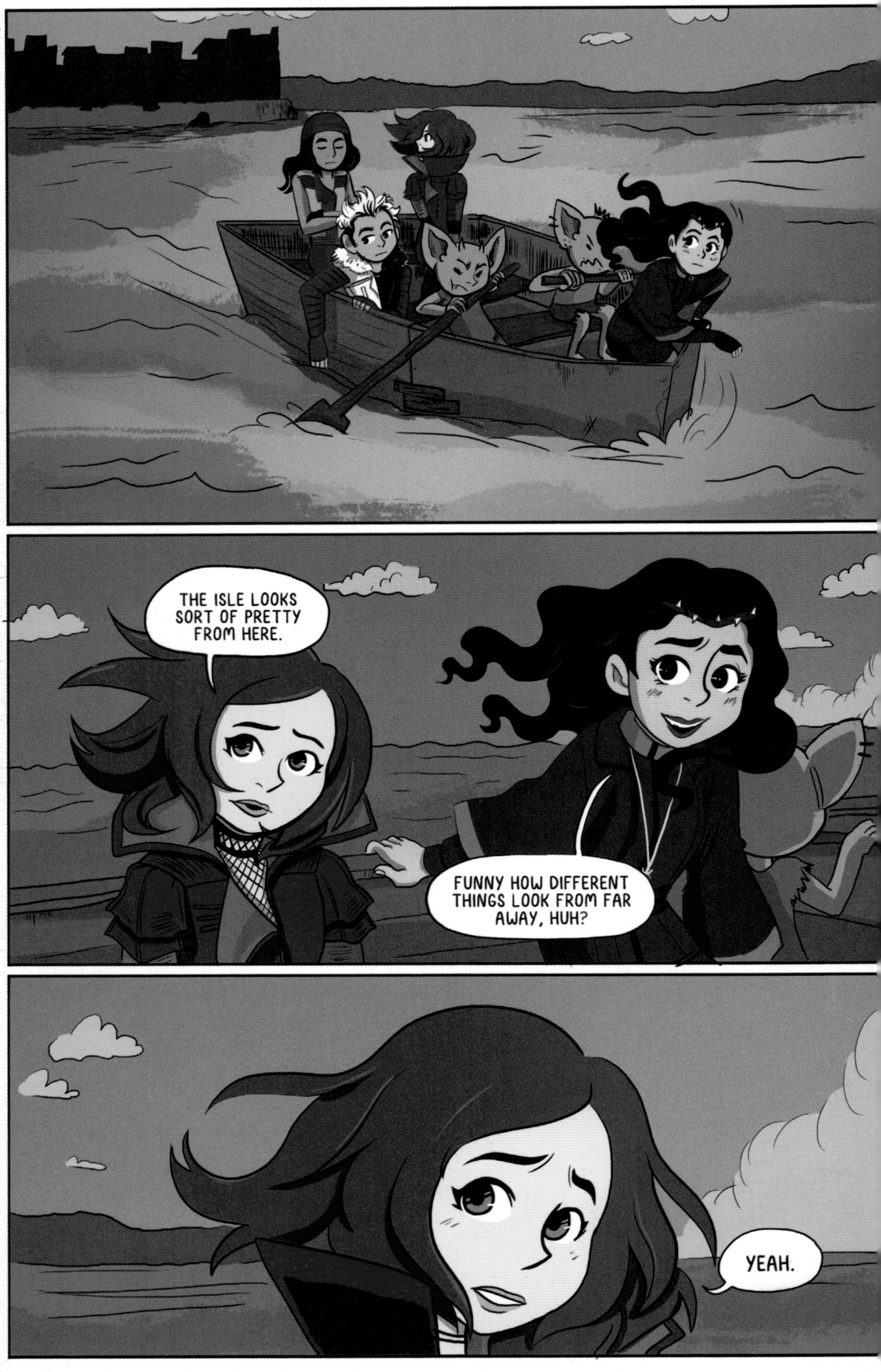
THE ISLE LOOKS SORT OF PRETTY FROM HERE.
FUNNY HOW DIFFERENT THINGS LOOK FROM FAR AWAY, HUH?
YEAH.

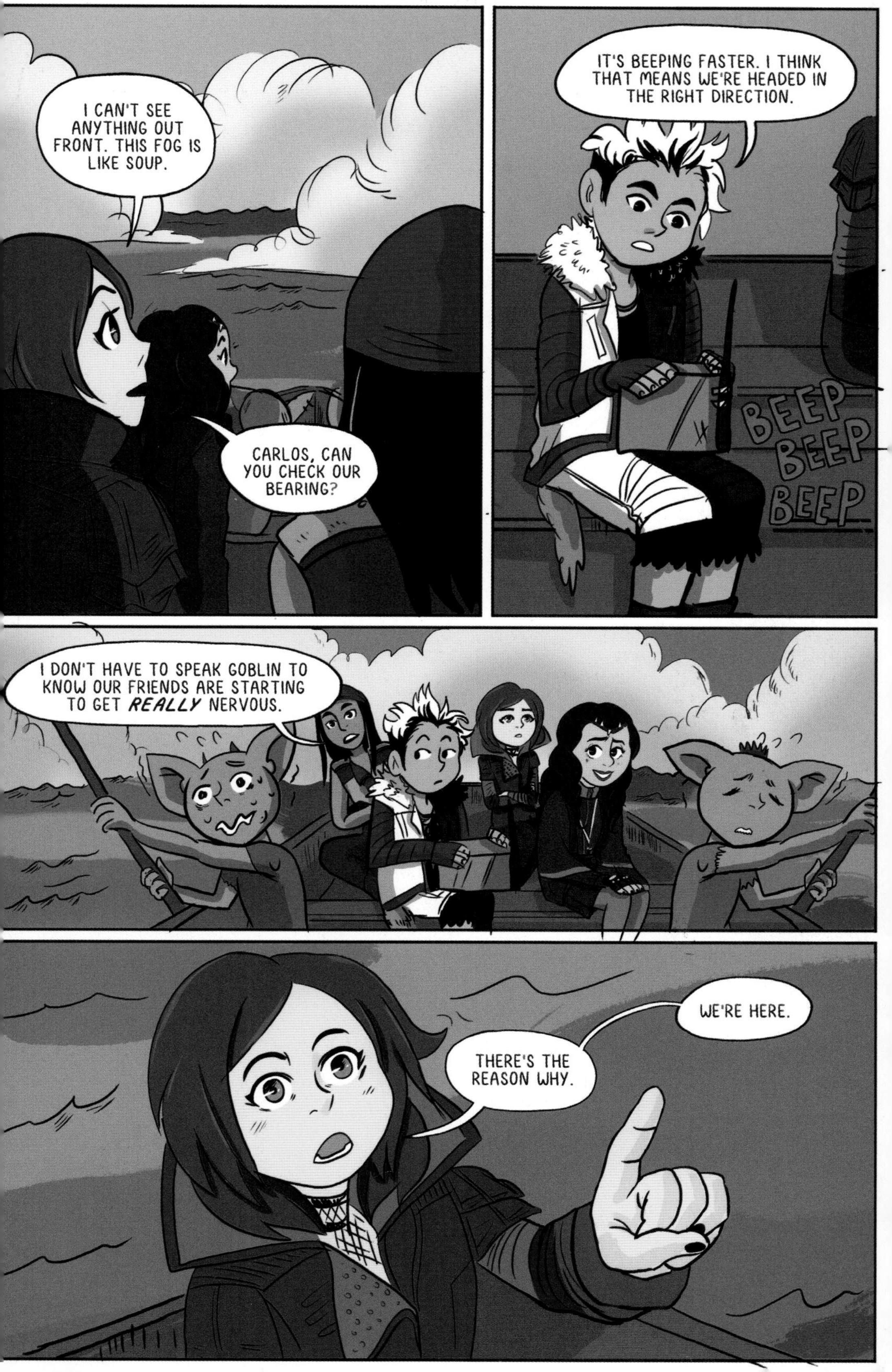
I CAN'T SEE ANYTHING OUT FRONT. THIS FOG IS LIKE SOUP.
CARLOS, CAN YOU CHECK OUR BEARING?
IT'S BEEPING FASTER. I THINK THAT MEANS WE'RE HEADED IN THE RIGHT DIRECTION.
BEEP BEEP BEEP
I DON'T HAVE TO SPEAK GOBLIN TO KNOW OUR FRIENDS ARE STARTING TO GET *REALLY* NERVOUS.
WE'RE HERE.
THERE'S THE REASON WHY.

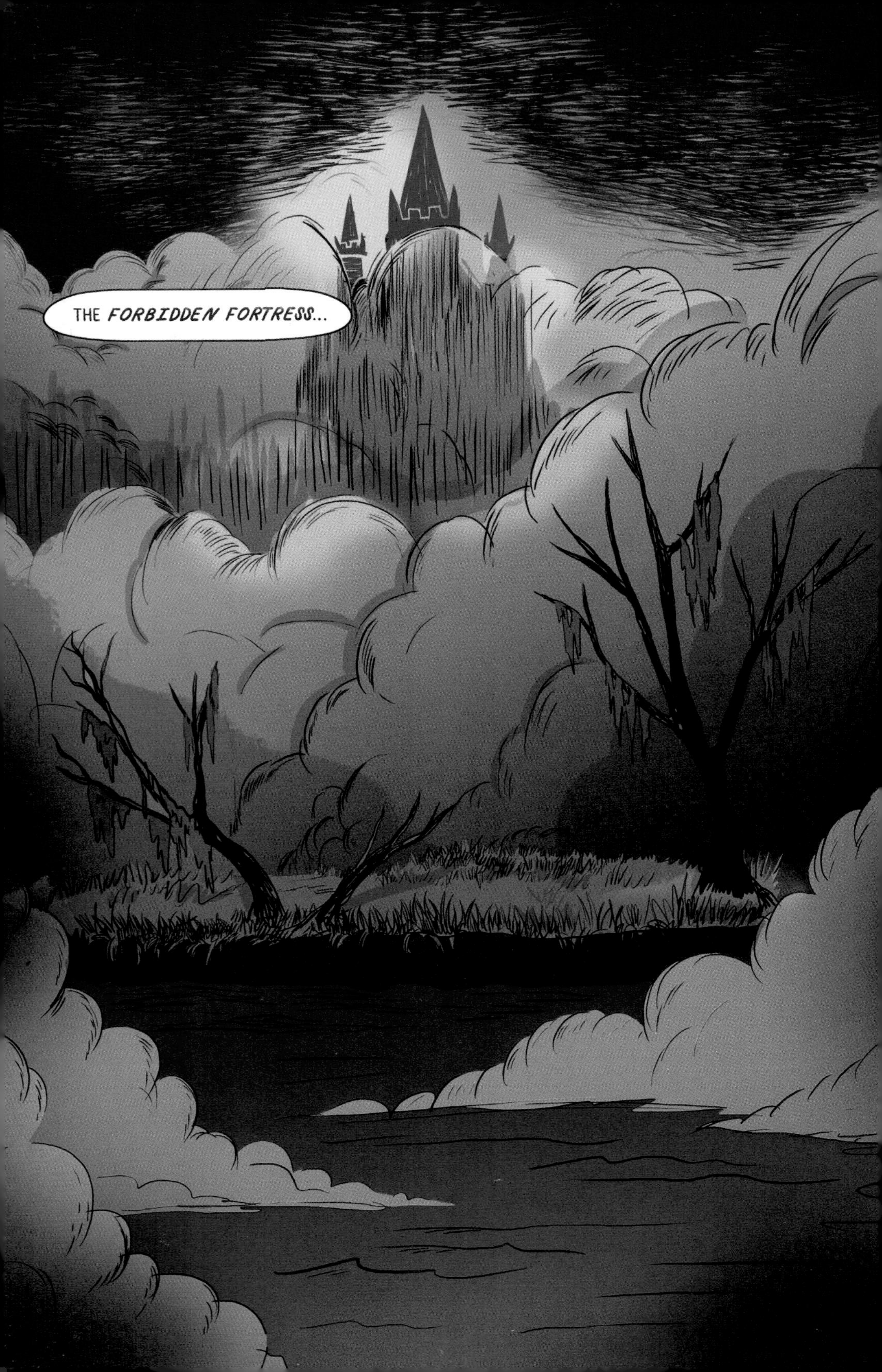
THE FORBIDDEN FORTRESS...

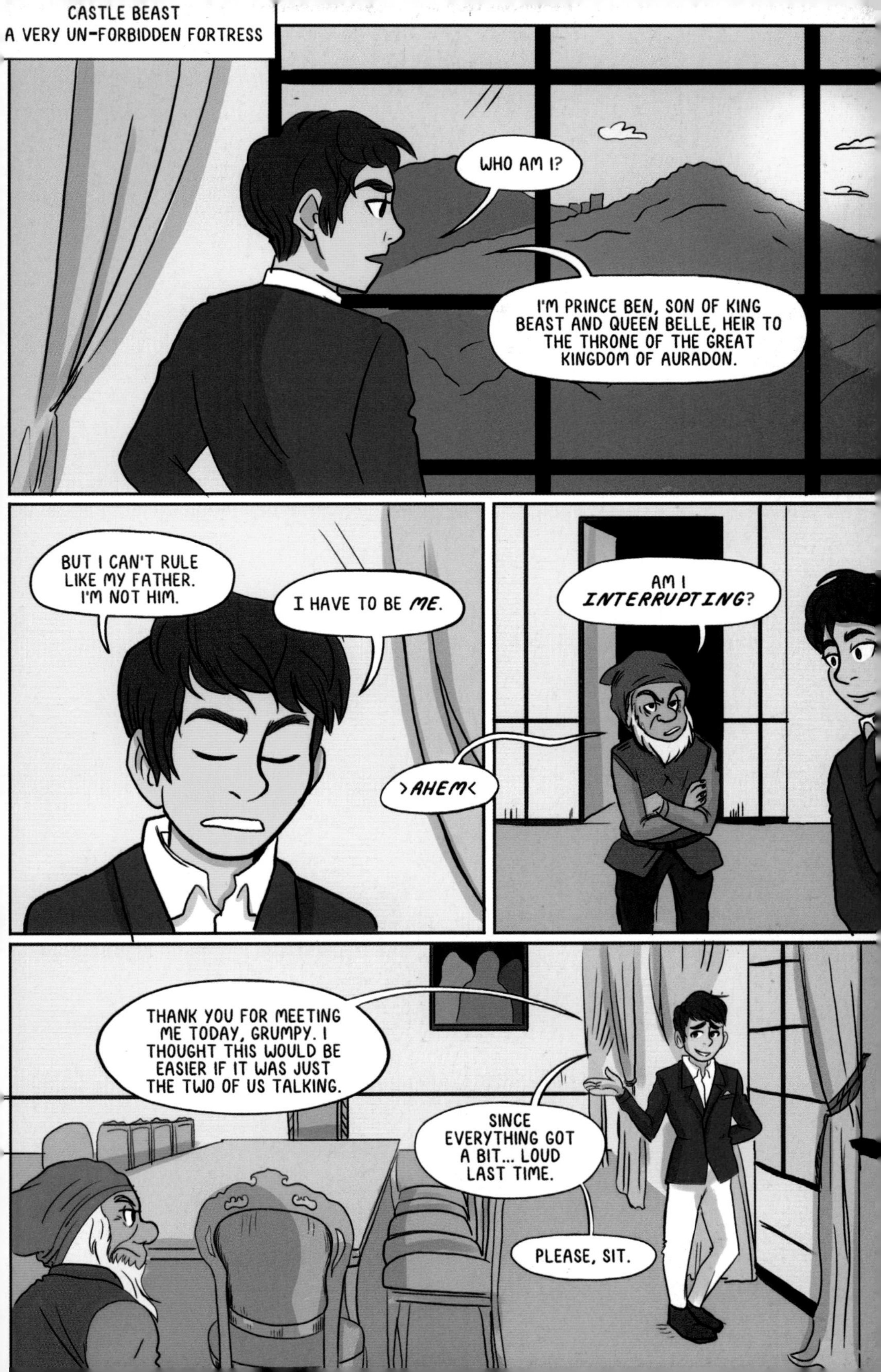
CASTLE BEAST
A VERY UN-FORBIDDEN FORTRESS
WHO AM I?
I'M PRINCE BEN, SON OF KING BEAST AND QUEEN BELLE, HEIR TO THE THRONE OF THE GREAT KINGDOM OF AURADON.
BUT I CAN'T RULE LIKE MY FATHER. I'M NOT HIM.
I HAVE TO BE *ME*.
>AHEM<
AM I *INTERRUPTING*?
THANK YOU FOR MEETING ME TODAY, GRUMPY. I THOUGHT THIS WOULD BE EASIER IF IT WAS JUST THE TWO OF US TALKING.
SINCE EVERYTHING GOT A BIT... LOUD LAST TIME.
PLEASE, SIT.

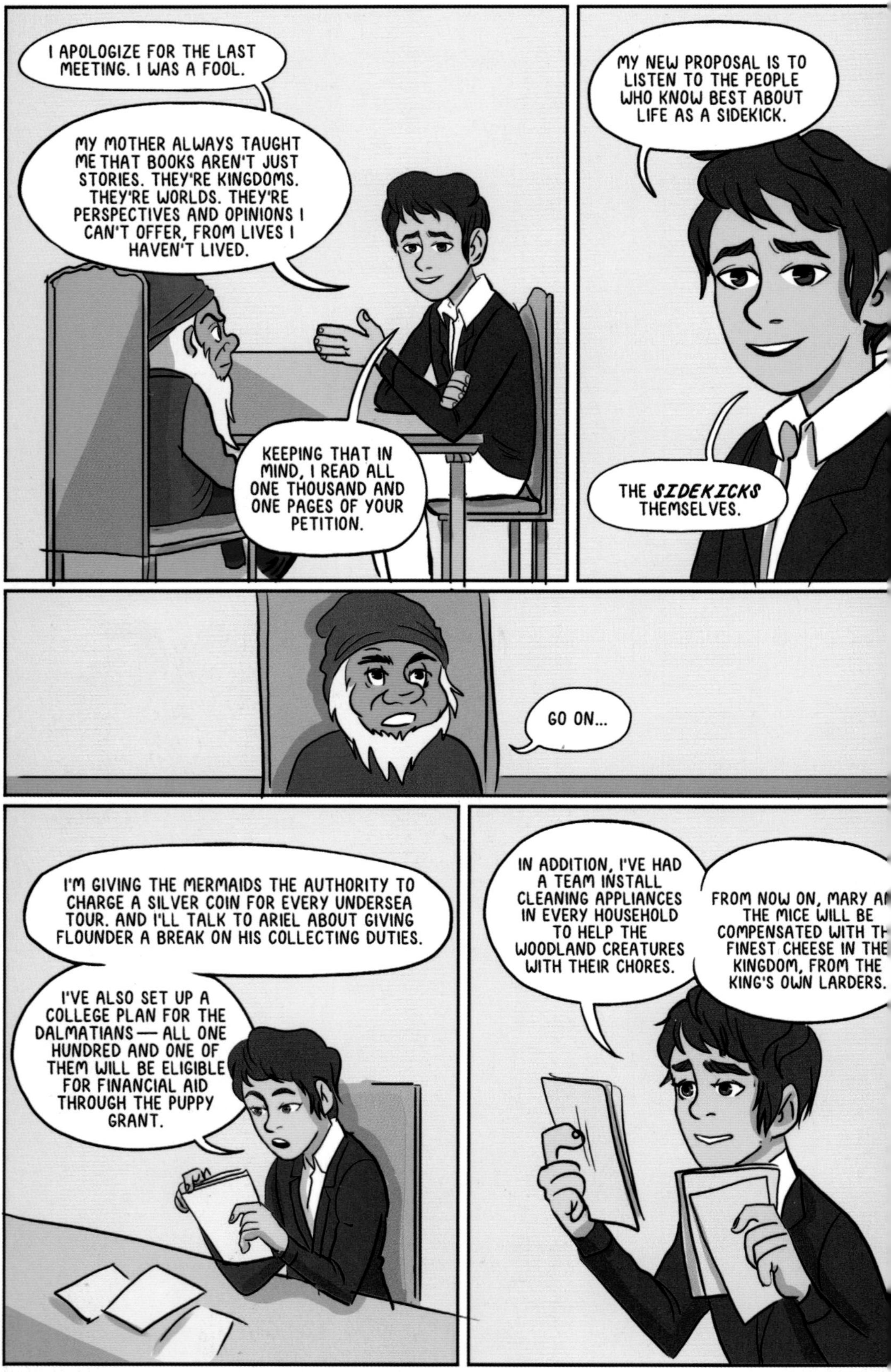
I APOLOGIZE FOR THE LAST MEETING. I WAS A FOOL.
MY MOTHER ALWAYS TAUGHT ME THAT BOOKS AREN'T JUST STORIES. THEY'RE KINGDOMS. THEY'RE WORLDS. THEY'RE PERSPECTIVES AND OPINIONS I CAN'T OFFER, FROM LIVES I HAVEN'T LIVED.
KEEPING THAT IN MIND, I READ ALL ONE THOUSAND AND ONE PAGES OF YOUR PETITION.
MY NEW PROPOSAL IS TO LISTEN TO THE PEOPLE WHO KNOW BEST ABOUT LIFE AS A SIDEKICK.
THE *SIDEKICKS* THEMSELVES.
GO ON...
I'M GIVING THE MERMAIDS THE AUTHORITY TO CHARGE A SILVER COIN FOR EVERY UNDERSEA TOUR. AND I'LL TALK TO ARIEL ABOUT GIVING FLOUNDER A BREAK ON HIS COLLECTING DUTIES.
I'VE ALSO SET UP A COLLEGE PLAN FOR THE DALMATIANS— ALL ONE HUNDRED AND ONE OF THEM WILL BE ELIGIBLE FOR FINANCIAL AID THROUGH THE PUPPY GRANT.
IN ADDITION, I'VE HAD A TEAM INSTALL CLEANING APPLIANCES IN EVERY HOUSEHOLD TO HELP THE WOODLAND CREATURES WITH THEIR CHORES.
FROM NOW ON, MARY A THE MICE WILL BE COMPENSATED WITH TH FINEST CHEESE IN THE KINGDOM, FROM THE KING'S OWN LARDERS.

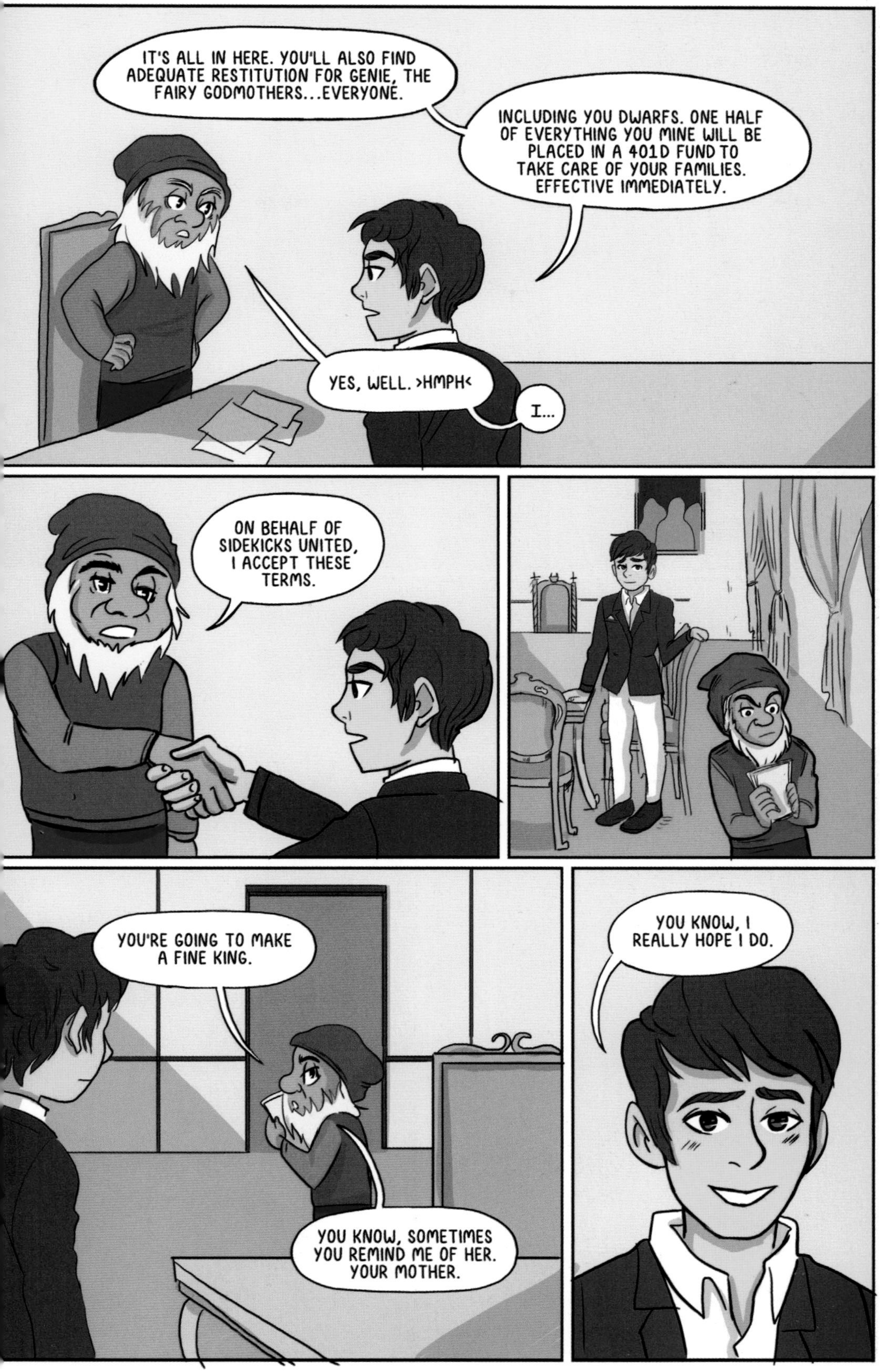
IT'S ALL IN HERE. YOU'LL ALSO FIND ADEQUATE RESTITUTION FOR GENIE, THE FAIRY GODMOTHERS...EVERYONE.
INCLUDING YOU DWARFS. ONE HALF OF EVERYTHING YOU MINE WILL BE PLACED IN A 401D FUND TO TAKE CARE OF YOUR FAMILIES. EFFECTIVE IMMEDIATELY.
YES, WELL. >HMPH<
I...
ON BEHALF OF SIDEKICKS UNITED, I ACCEPT THESE TERMS.
YOU'RE GOING TO MAKE A FINE KING.
YOU KNOW, SOMETIMES YOU REMIND ME OF HER. YOUR MOTHER.
YOU KNOW, I REALLY HOPE I DO.

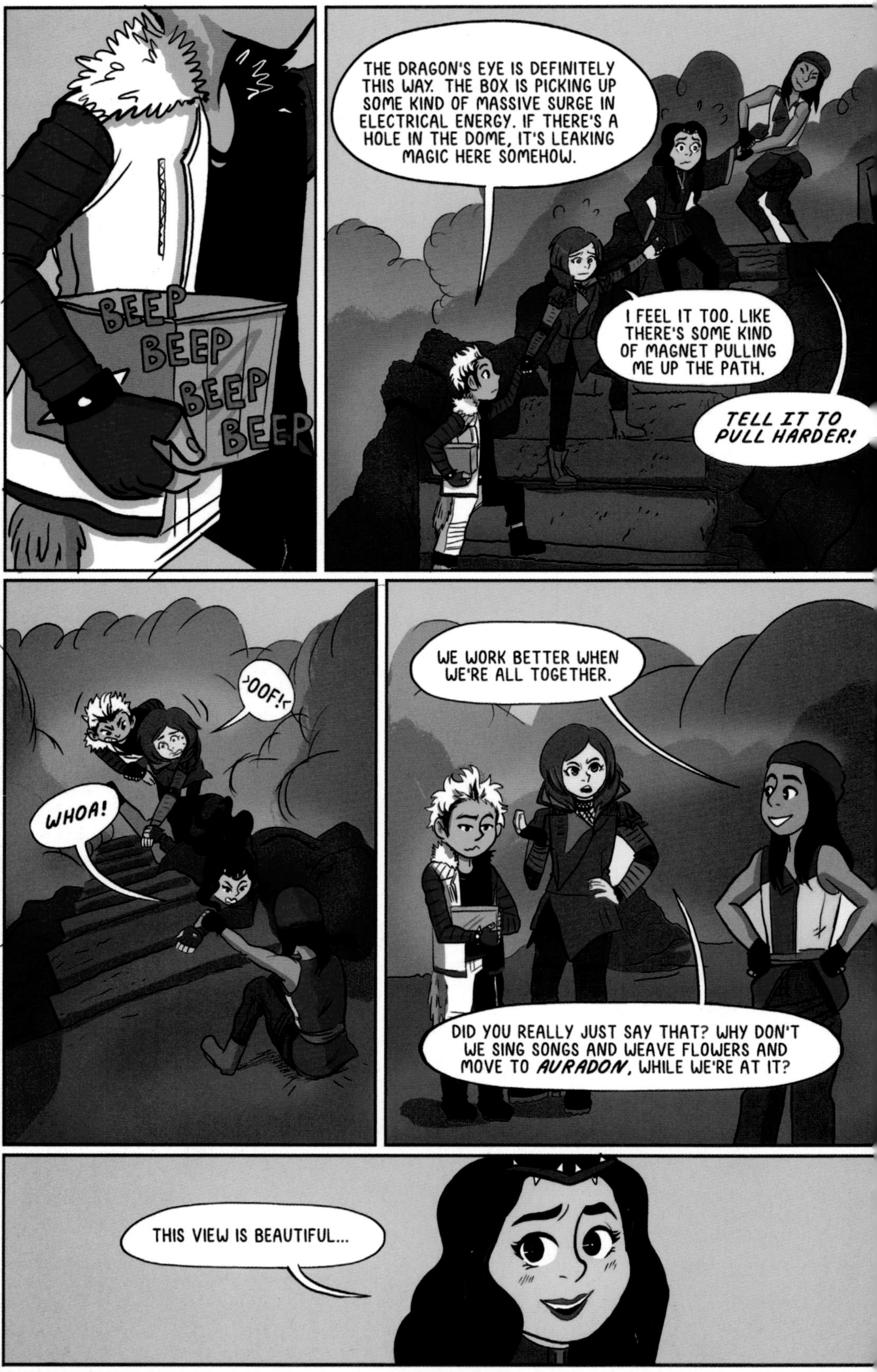
BEEP
BEEP
BEEP
BEEP
THE DRAGON'S EYE IS DEFINITELY THIS WAY. THE BOX IS PICKING UP SOME KIND OF MASSIVE SURGE IN ELECTRICAL ENERGY. IF THERE'S A HOLE IN THE DOME, IT'S LEAKING MAGIC HERE SOMEHOW.
I FEEL IT TOO. LIKE THERE'S SOME KIND OF MAGNET PULLING ME UP THE PATH.
TELL IT TO PULL HARDER!
OOF!
WHOA!
WE WORK BETTER WHEN WE'RE ALL TOGETHER.
DID YOU REALLY JUST SAY THAT? WHY DON'T WE SING SONGS AND WEAVE FLOWERS AND MOVE TO AURADON, WHILE WE'RE AT IT?
THIS VIEW IS BEAUTIFUL...

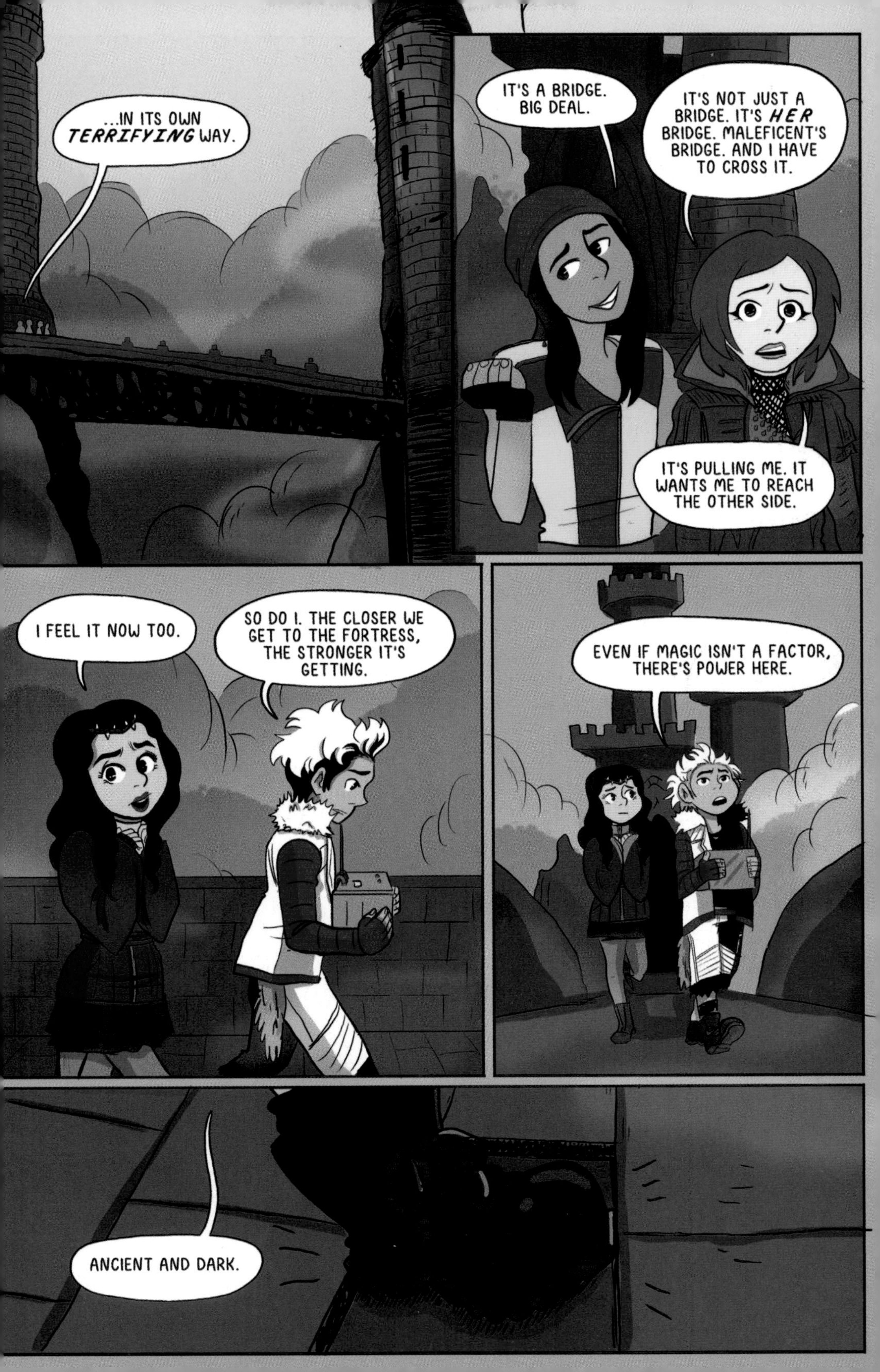
...IN ITS OWN TERRIFYING WAY.
IT'S A BRIDGE. BIG DEAL.
IT'S NOT JUST A BRIDGE. IT'S HER BRIDGE. MALEFICENT'S BRIDGE. AND I HAVE TO CROSS IT.
IT'S PULLING ME. IT WANTS ME TO REACH THE OTHER SIDE.
I FEEL IT NOW TOO.
SO DO I. THE CLOSER WE GET TO THE FORTRESS, THE STRONGER IT'S GETTING.
EVEN IF MAGIC ISN'T A FACTOR, THERE'S POWER HERE.
ANCIENT AND DARK.

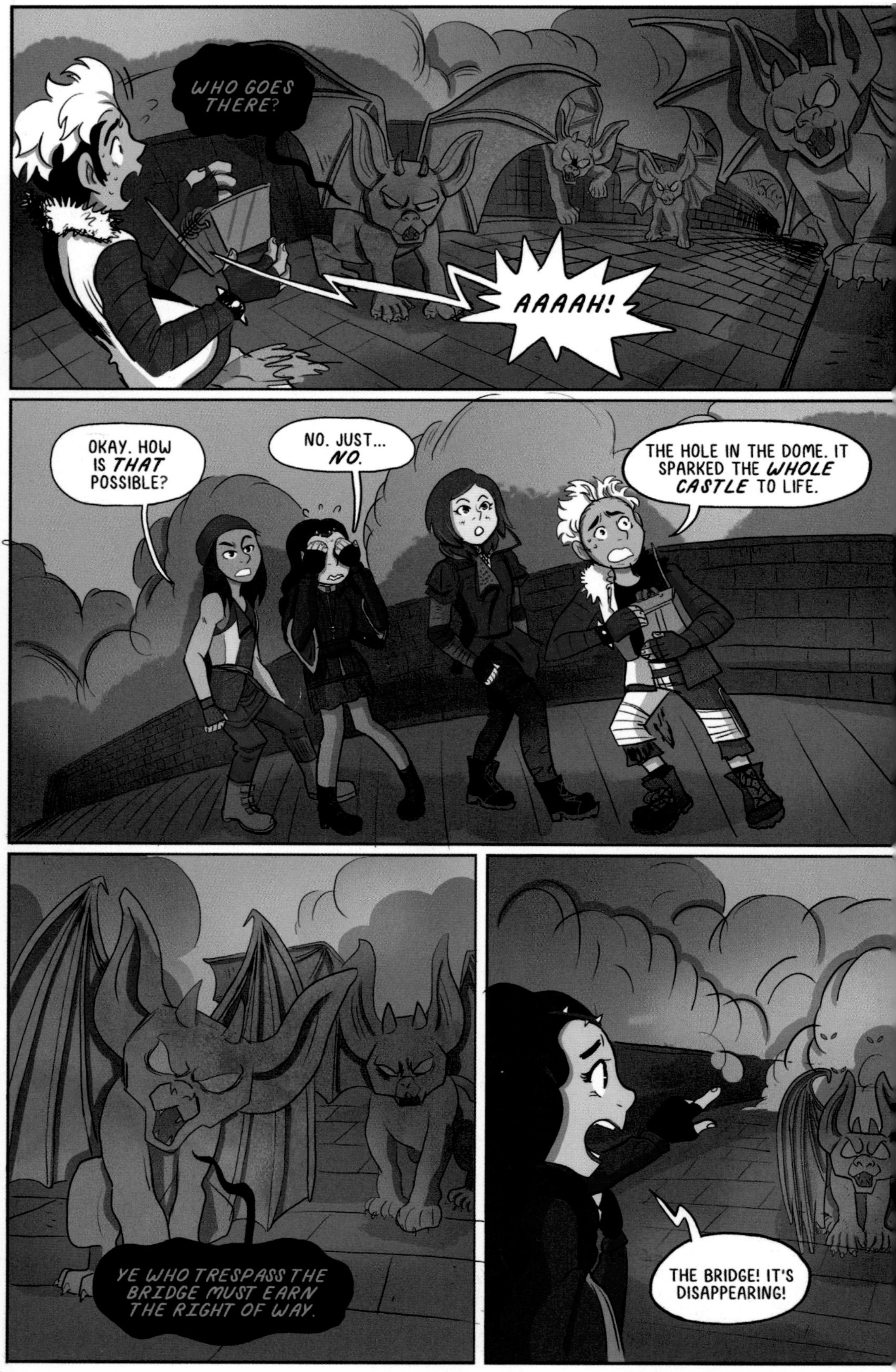
WHO GOES THERE?
AAAAH!
OKAY. HOW IS *THAT* POSSIBLE?
NO. JUST... *NO.*
THE HOLE IN THE DOME. IT SPARKED THE *WHOLE CASTLE* TO LIFE.
YE WHO TRESPASS THE BRIDGE MUST EARN THE RIGHT OF WAY.
THE BRIDGE! IT'S DISAPPEARING!

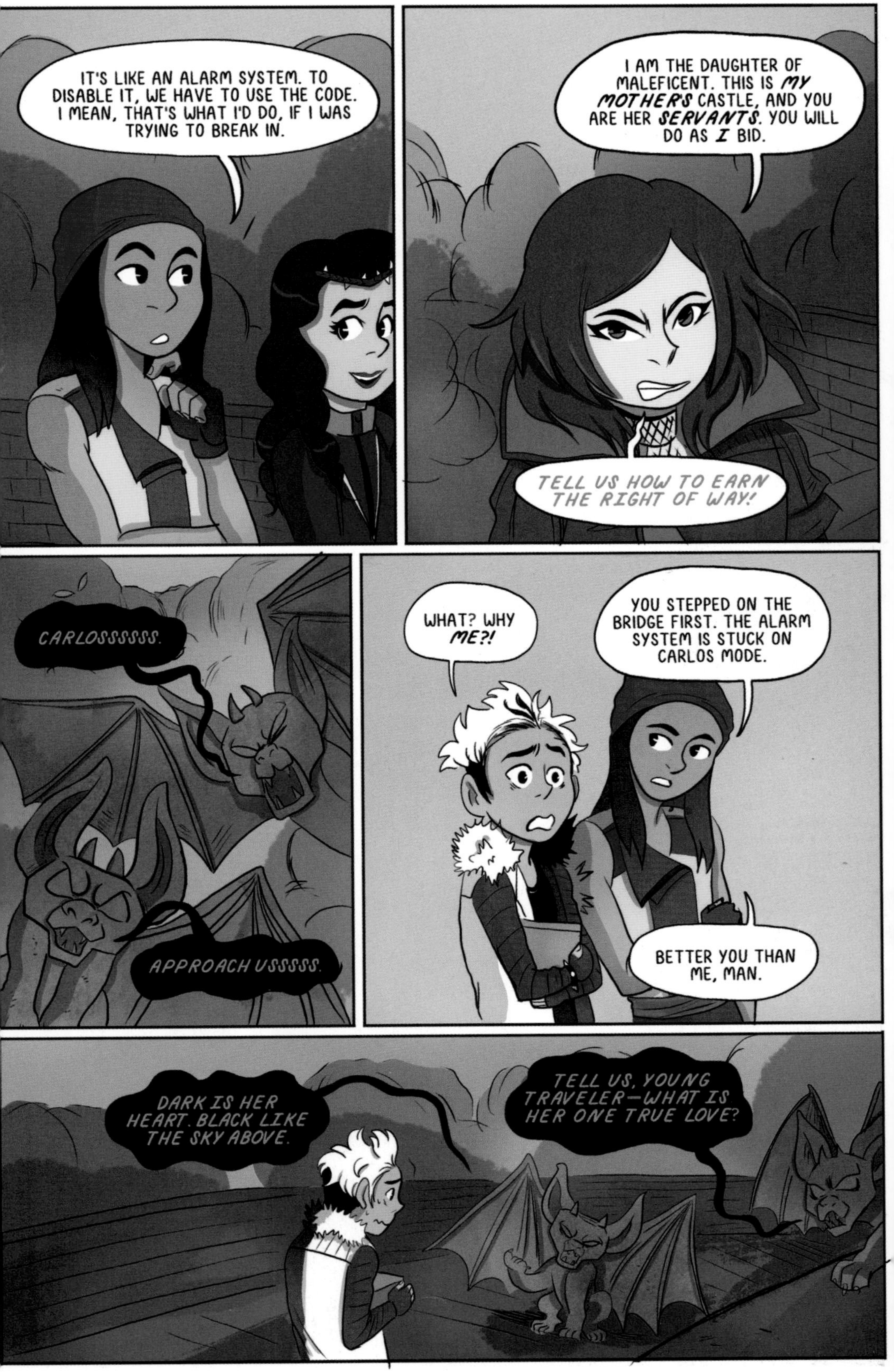
IT'S LIKE AN ALARM SYSTEM. TO DISABLE IT, WE HAVE TO USE THE CODE. I MEAN, THAT'S WHAT I'D DO, IF I WAS TRYING TO BREAK IN.
I AM THE DAUGHTER OF MALEFICENT. THIS IS MY MOTHER'S CASTLE, AND YOU ARE HER SERVANTS. YOU WILL DO AS I BID.
TELL US HOW TO EARN THE RIGHT OF WAY!
CARLOSSSSSSS.
APPROACH USSSSSS.
WHAT? WHY ME?!
YOU STEPPED ON THE BRIDGE FIRST. THE ALARM SYSTEM IS STUCK ON CARLOS MODE.
BETTER YOU THAN ME, MAN.
DARK IS HER HEART. BLACK LIKE THE SKY ABOVE.
TELL US, YOUNG TRAVELER—WHAT IS HER ONE TRUE LOVE?

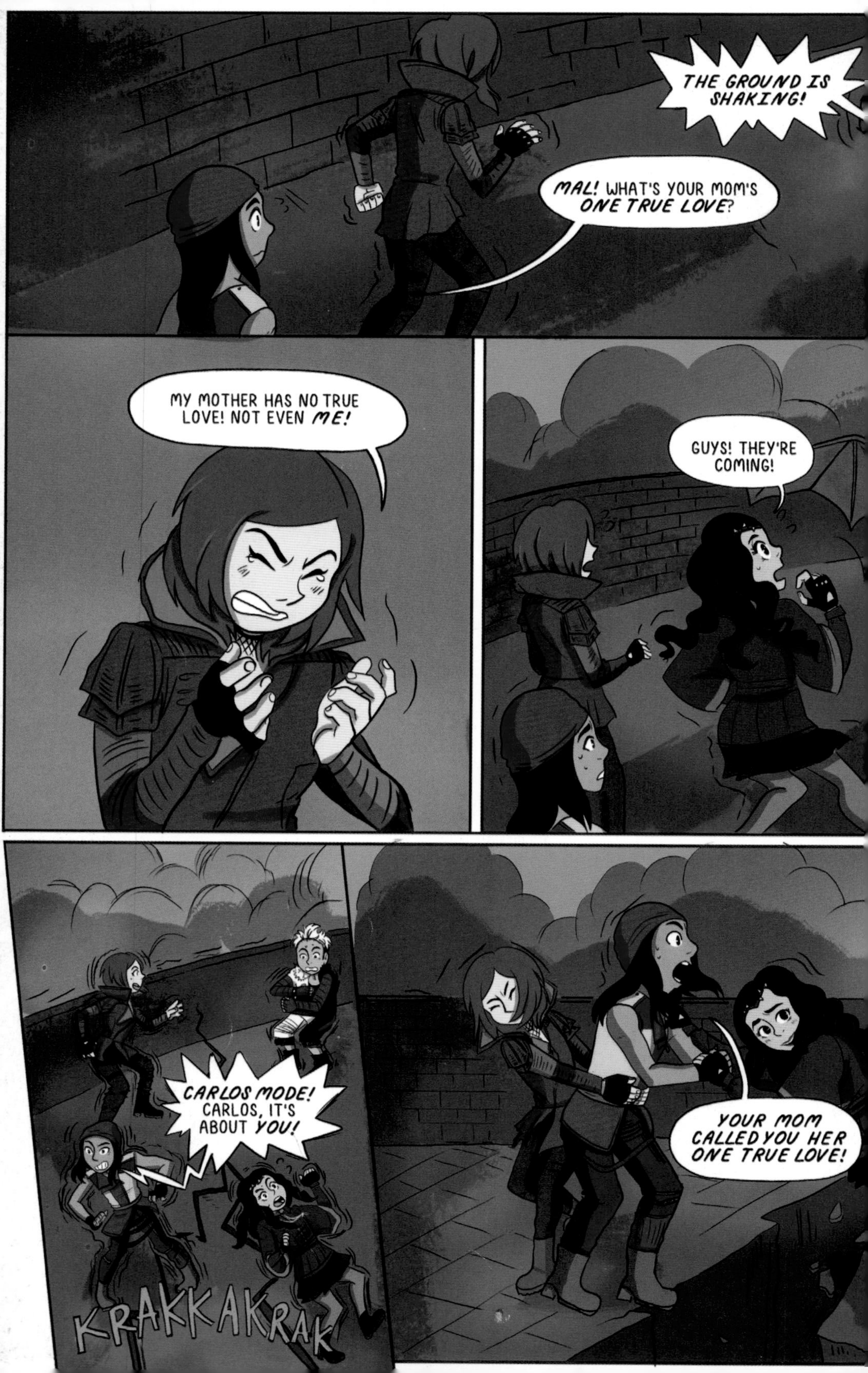
THE GROUND IS SHAKING!
MAL! WHAT'S YOUR MOM'S ONE TRUE LOVE?
MY MOTHER HAS NO TRUE LOVE! NOT EVEN ME!
GUYS! THEY'RE COMING!
CARLOS MODE! CARLOS, IT'S ABOUT YOU!
KRAKKAKRAK
YOUR MOM CALLED YOU HER ONE TRUE LOVE!

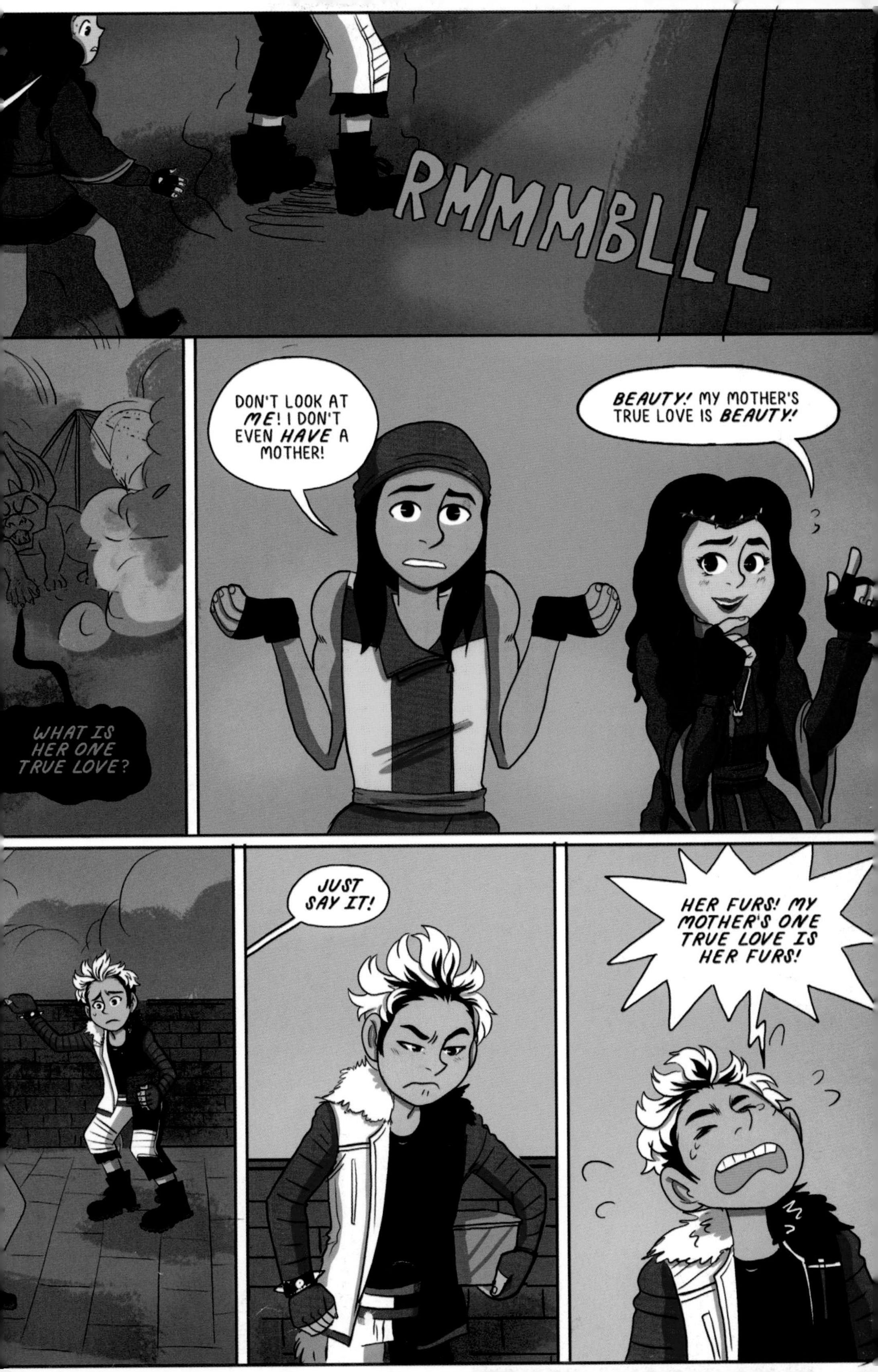
RMMMBLLL
WHAT IS HER ONE TRUE LOVE?
DON'T LOOK AT ME! I DON'T EVEN HAVE A MOTHER!
BEAUTY! MY MOTHER'S TRUE LOVE IS BEAUTY!
JUST SAY IT!
HER FURS! MY MOTHER'S ONE TRUE LOVE IS HER FURS!

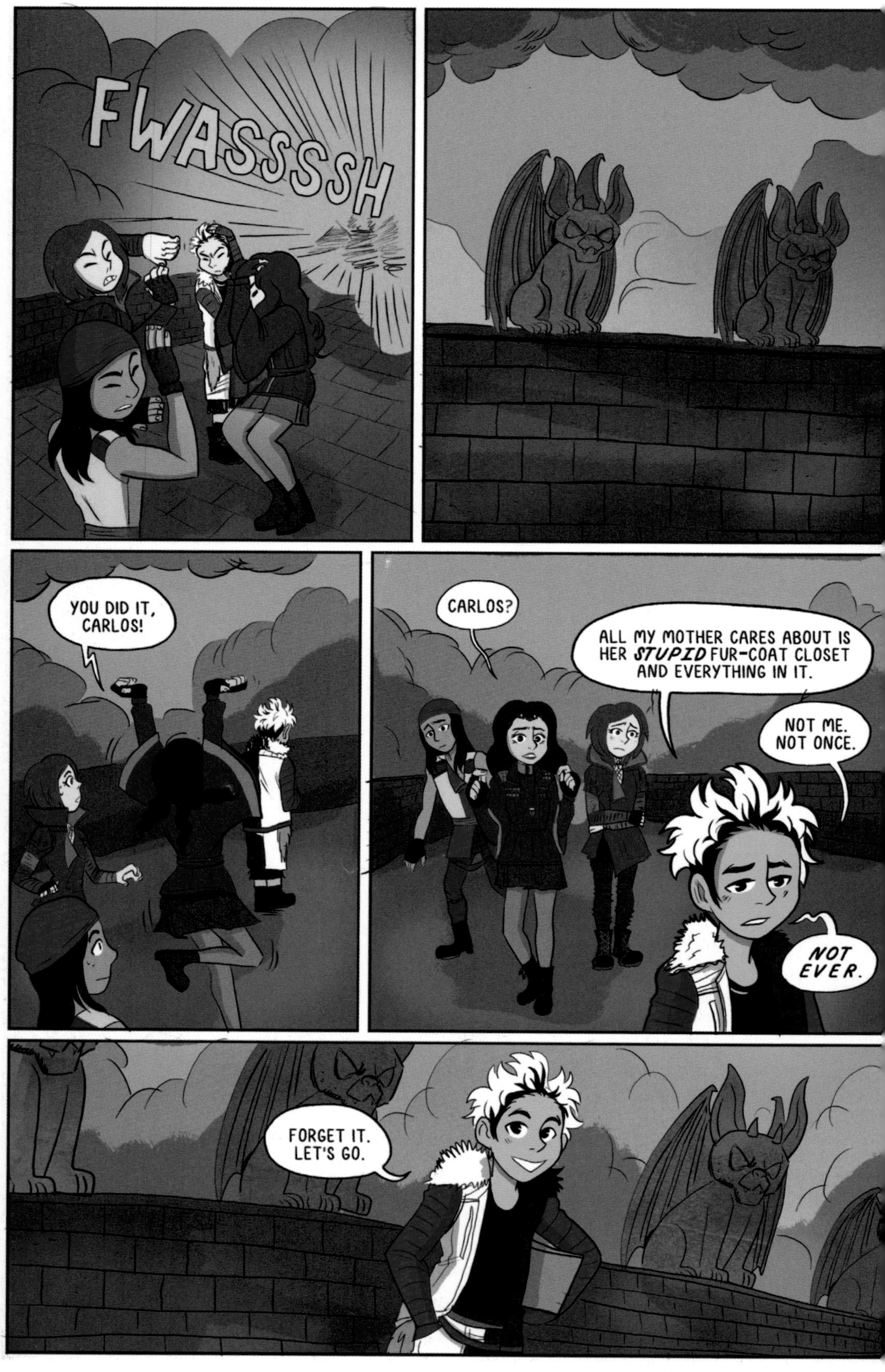
FWASSSSH
YOU DID IT, CARLOS!
CARLOS?
ALL MY MOTHER CARES ABOUT IS HER *STUPID* FUR-COAT CLOSET AND EVERYTHING IN IT.
NOT ME. NOT ONCE.
NOT EVER.
FORGET IT. LET'S GO.

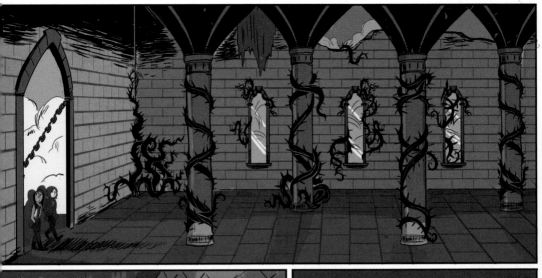

WELCOME TO MODERN CASTLE LIVING. TRADE IN ONE BIG, COLD PRISON FOR ANOTHER.

THE JUNK SHOP IS *COZY* COMPARED TO THIS.

THE REFRACTED ENERGY IS STRONGER HERE. I THINK WE'RE CLOSER TO THE SOURCE THAN WE'VE EVER BEEN.

BEEP BEEP BEEP BEEP

IN OTHER WORDS, WE'RE GETTING CLOSER TO THE DRAGON'S EYE.

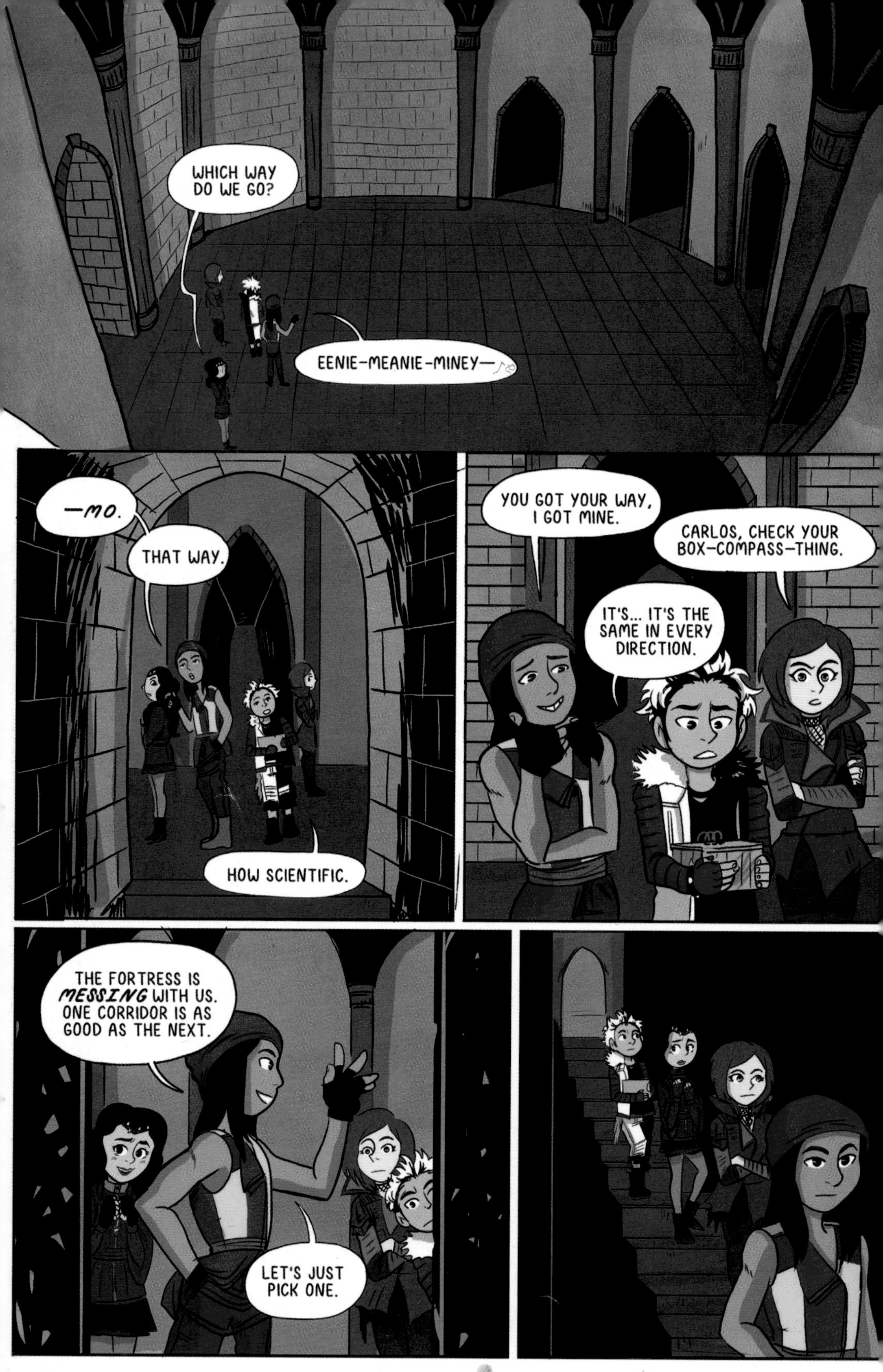
WHICH WAY DO WE GO?
EENIE-MEANIE-MINEY—
—MO.
THAT WAY.
HOW SCIENTIFIC.
YOU GOT YOUR WAY, I GOT MINE.
CARLOS, CHECK YOUR BOX-COMPASS-THING.
IT'S... IT'S THE SAME IN EVERY DIRECTION.
THE FORTRESS IS MESSING WITH US. ONE CORRIDOR IS AS GOOD AS THE NEXT.
LET'S JUST PICK ONE.

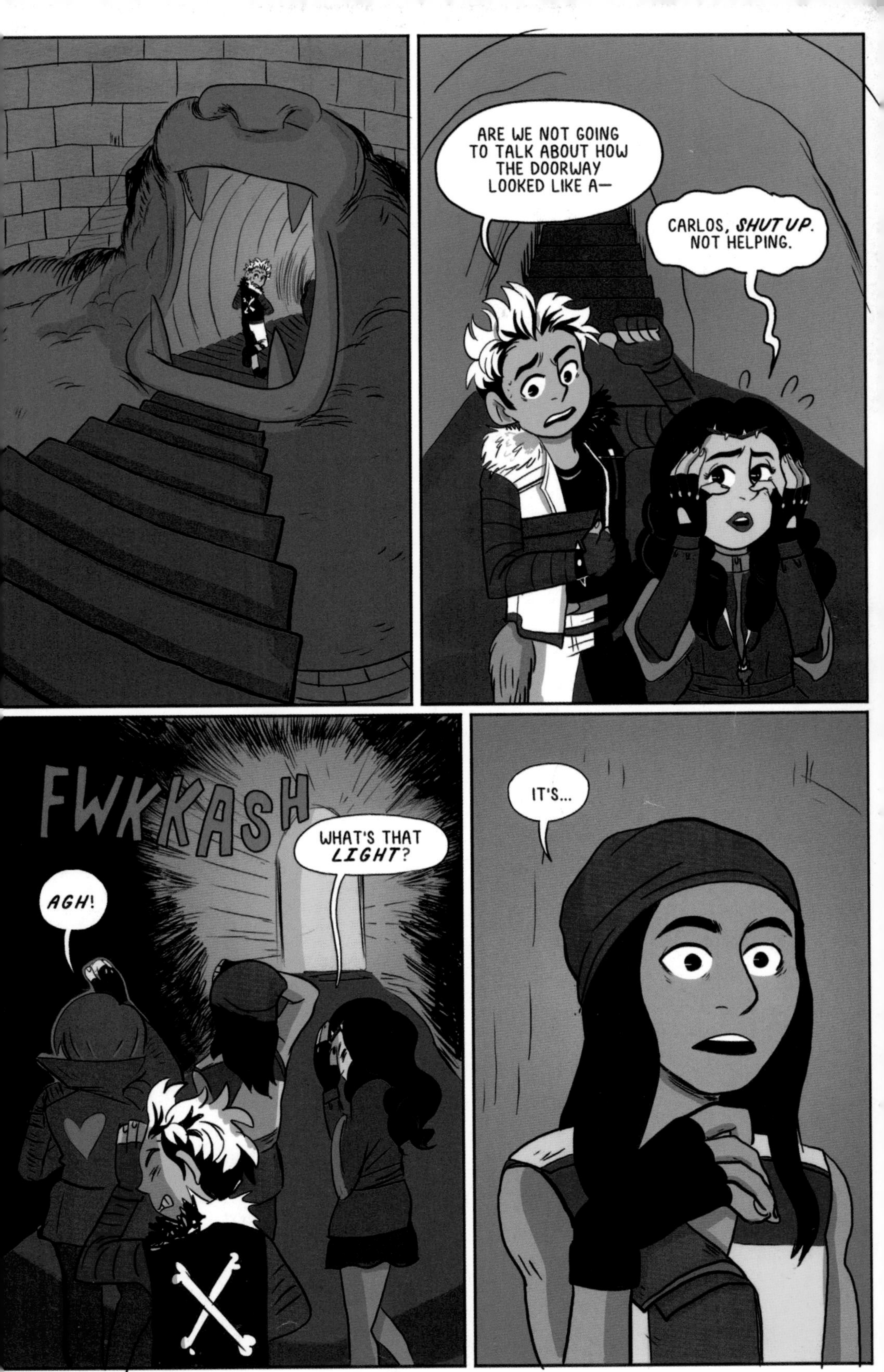

ARE WE NOT GOING TO TALK ABOUT HOW THE DOORWAY LOOKED LIKE A—
CARLOS, SHUT UP. NOT HELPING.
FWKKASH
WHAT'S THAT LIGHT?
AGH!
IT'S...

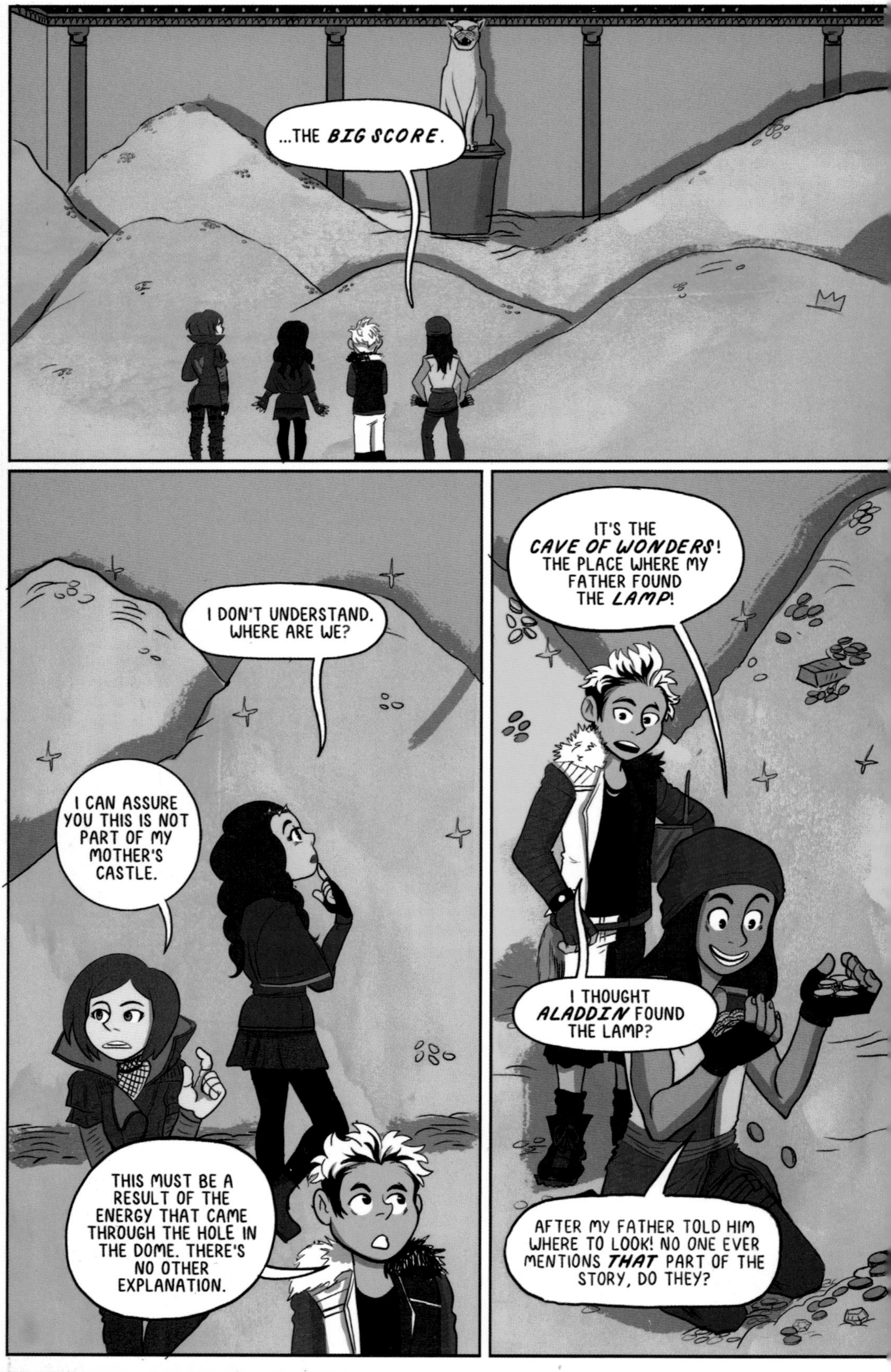
...THE BIG SCORE.
I DON'T UNDERSTAND. WHERE ARE WE?
I CAN ASSURE YOU THIS IS NOT PART OF MY MOTHER'S CASTLE.
THIS MUST BE A RESULT OF THE ENERGY THAT CAME THROUGH THE HOLE IN THE DOME. THERE'S NO OTHER EXPLANATION.
IT'S THE CAVE OF WONDERS! THE PLACE WHERE MY FATHER FOUND THE LAMP!
I THOUGHT ALADDIN FOUND THE LAMP?
AFTER MY FATHER TOLD HIM WHERE TO LOOK! NO ONE EVER MENTIONS THAT PART OF THE STORY, DO THEY?

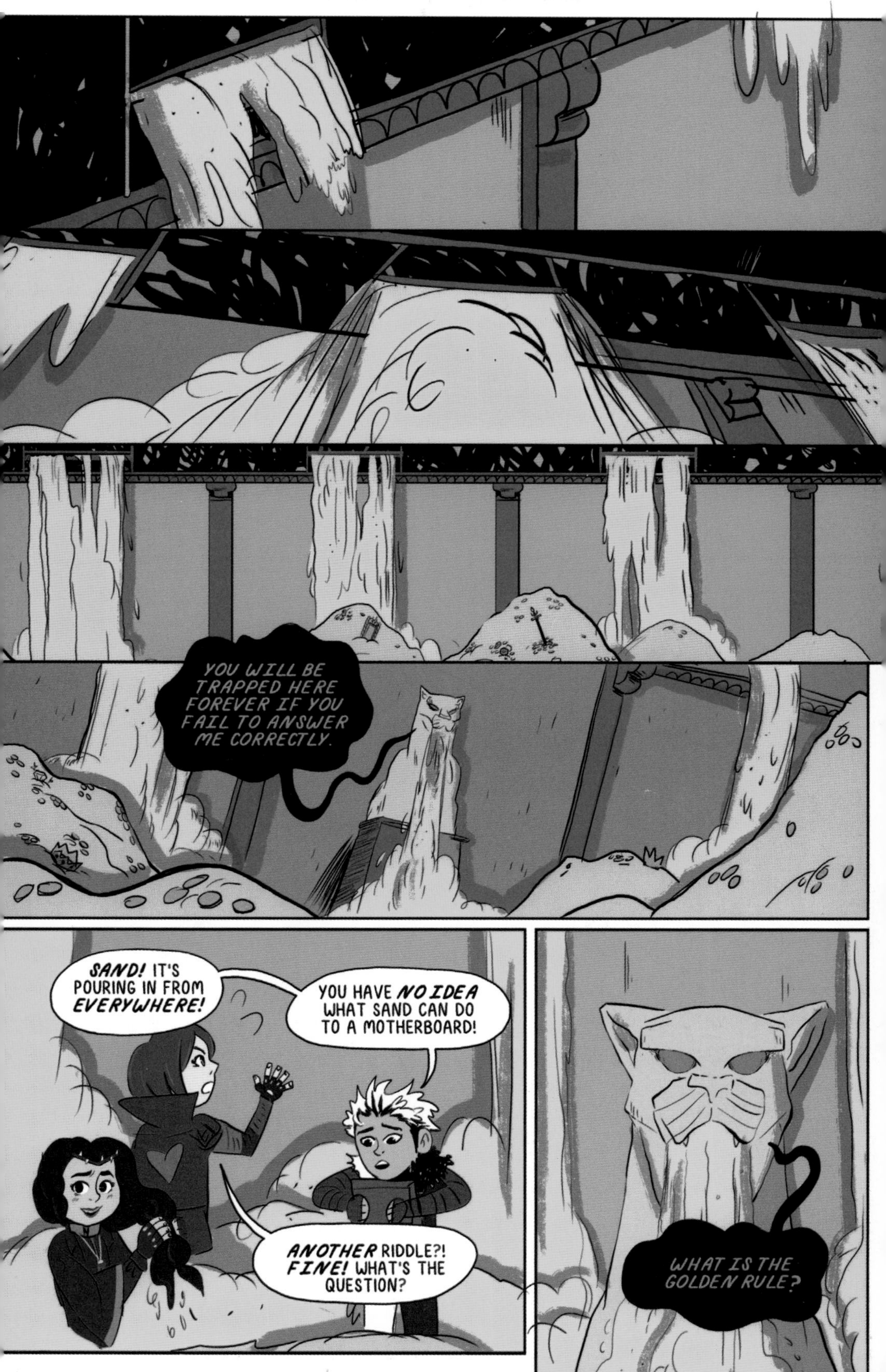
YOU WILL BE TRAPPED HERE FOREVER IF YOU FAIL TO ANSWER ME CORRECTLY.
SAND! IT'S POURING IN FROM EVERYWHERE!
YOU HAVE NO IDEA WHAT SAND CAN DO TO A MOTHERBOARD!
ANOTHER RIDDLE?! FINE! WHAT'S THE QUESTION?
WHAT IS THE GOLDEN RULE?

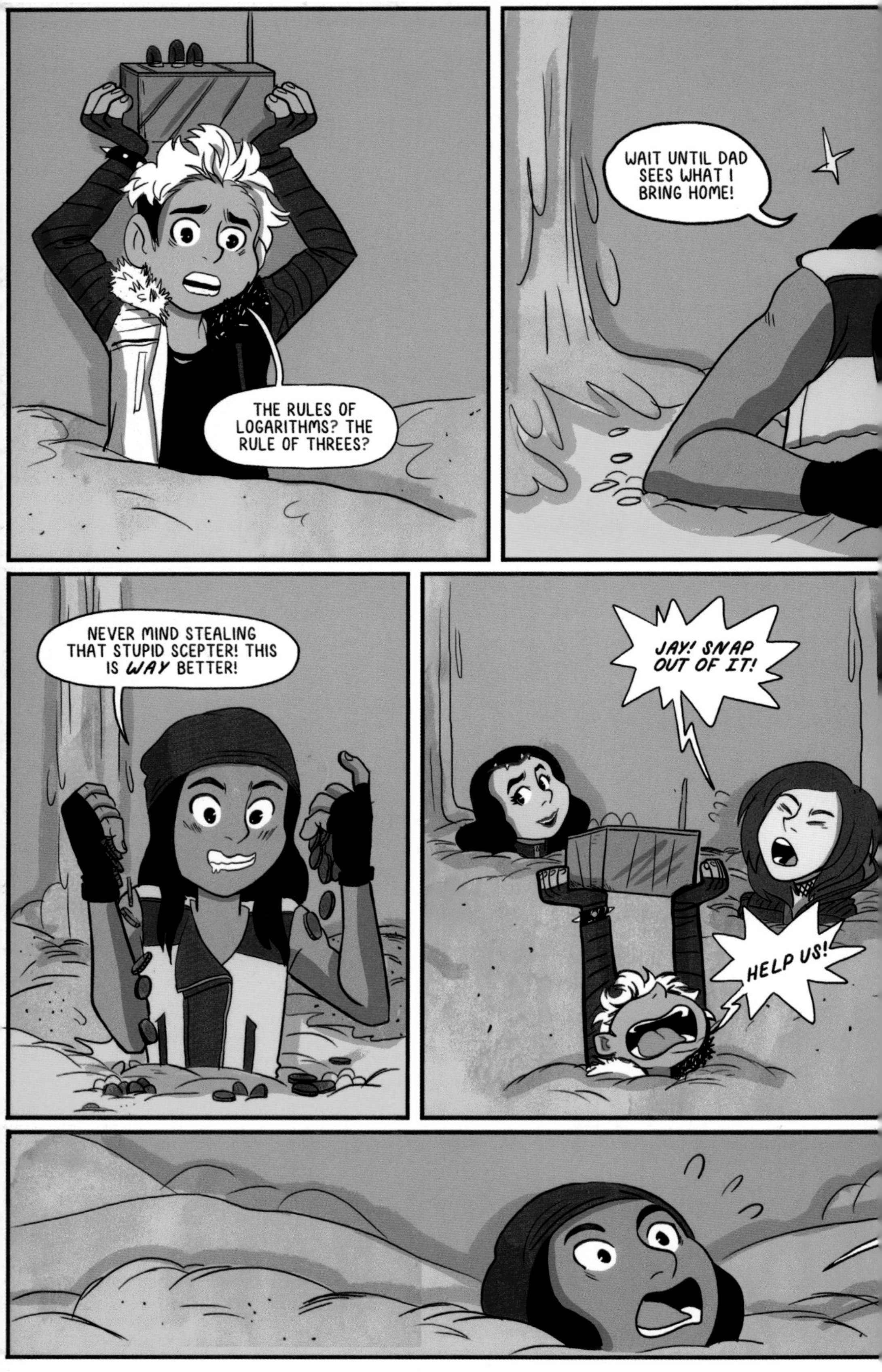
THE RULES OF LOGARITHMS? THE RULE OF THREES?
WAIT UNTIL DAD SEES WHAT I BRING HOME!
NEVER MIND STEALING THAT STUPID SCEPTER! THIS IS *WAY* BETTER!
JAY! SNAP OUT OF IT!
HELP US!

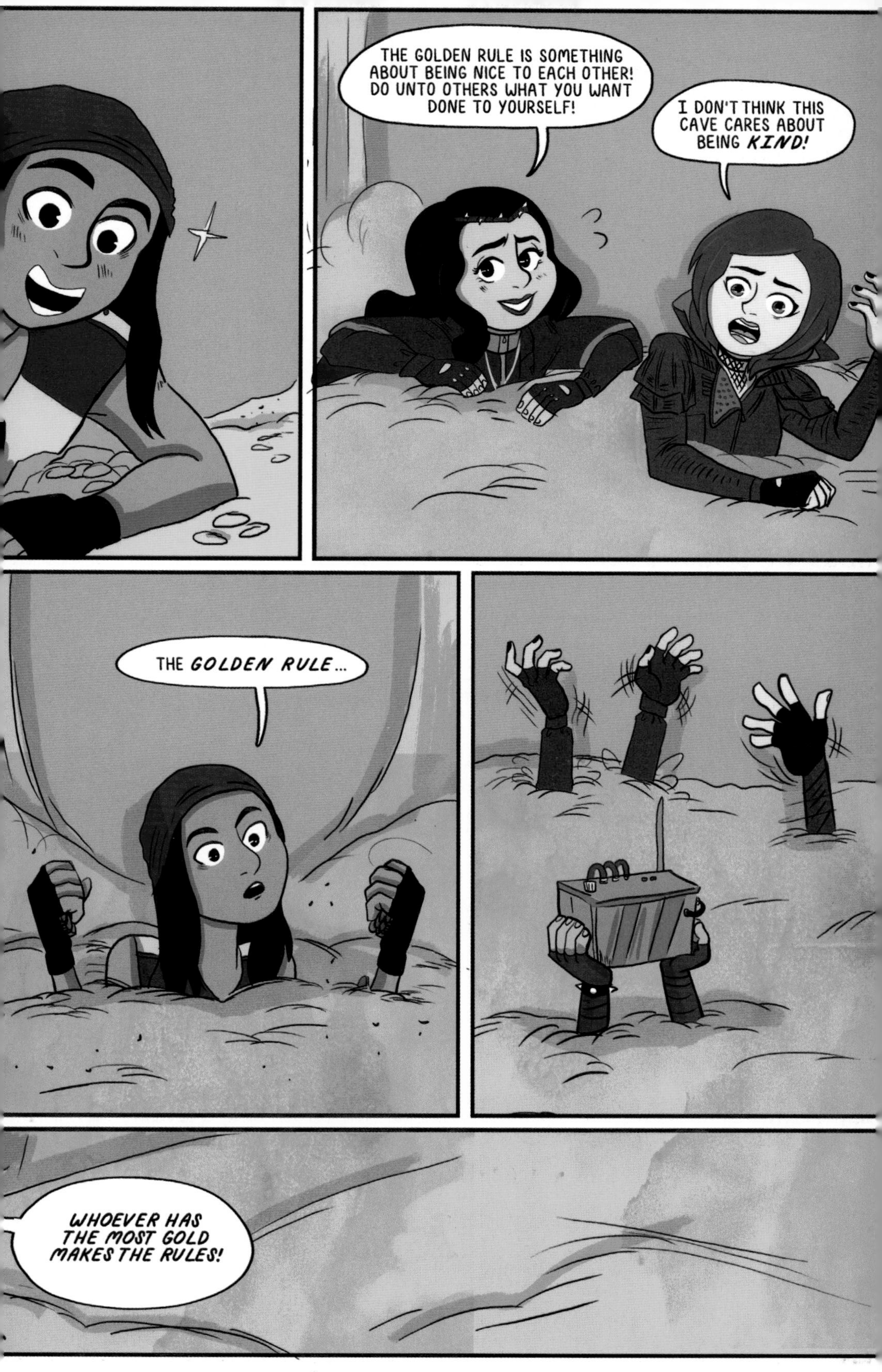
THE GOLDEN RULE IS SOMETHING ABOUT BEING NICE TO EACH OTHER! DO UNTO OTHERS WHAT YOU WANT DONE TO YOURSELF!
I DON'T THINK THIS CAVE CARES ABOUT BEING KIND!
THE GOLDEN RULE...
WHOEVER HAS THE MOST GOLD MAKES THE RULES!

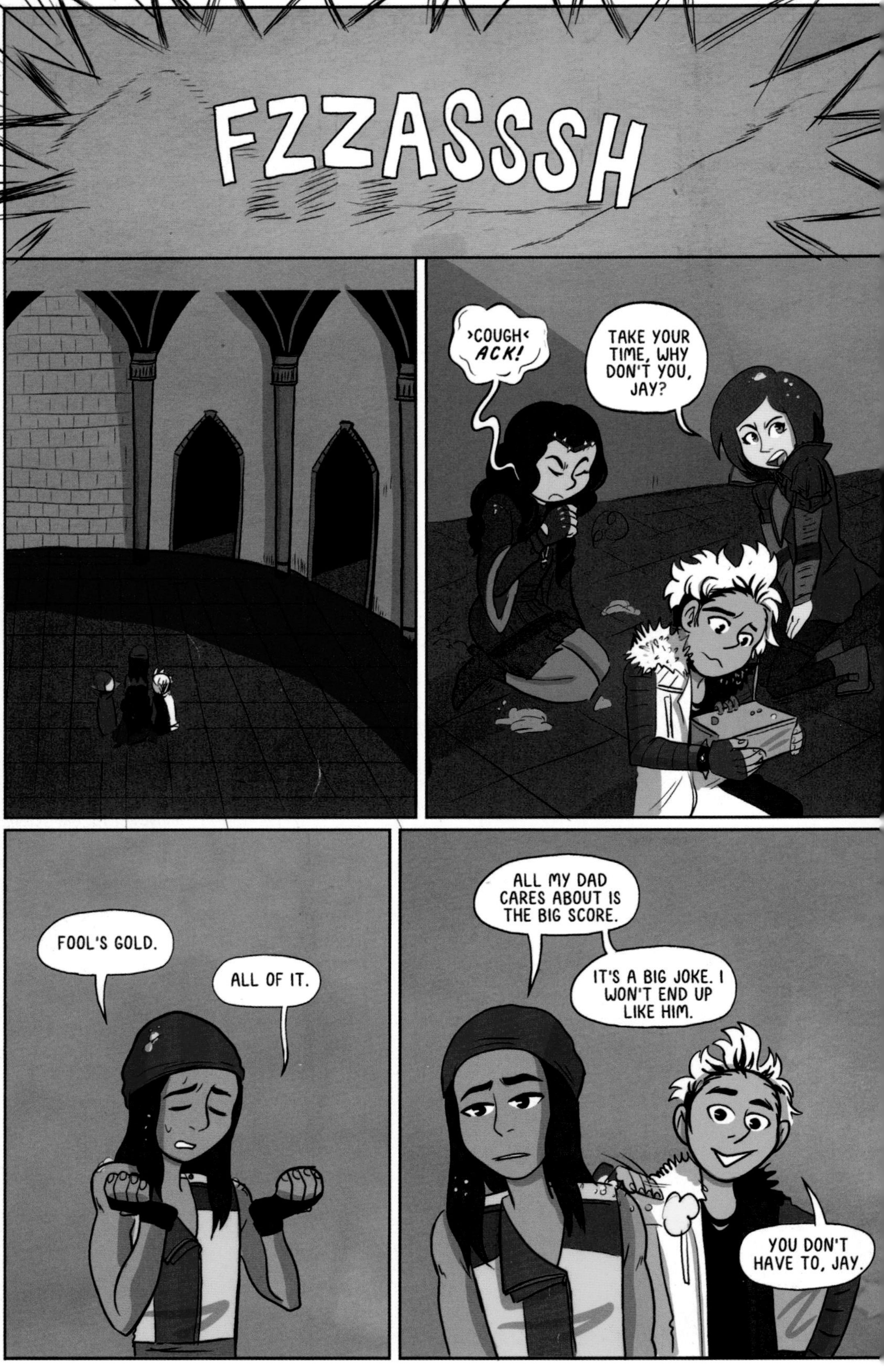
FZZASSSH
>COUGH< ACK!
TAKE YOUR TIME, WHY DON'T YOU, JAY?
FOOL'S GOLD.
ALL OF IT.
ALL MY DAD CARES ABOUT IS THE BIG SCORE.
IT'S A BIG JOKE. I WON'T END UP LIKE HIM.
YOU DON'T HAVE TO, JAY.

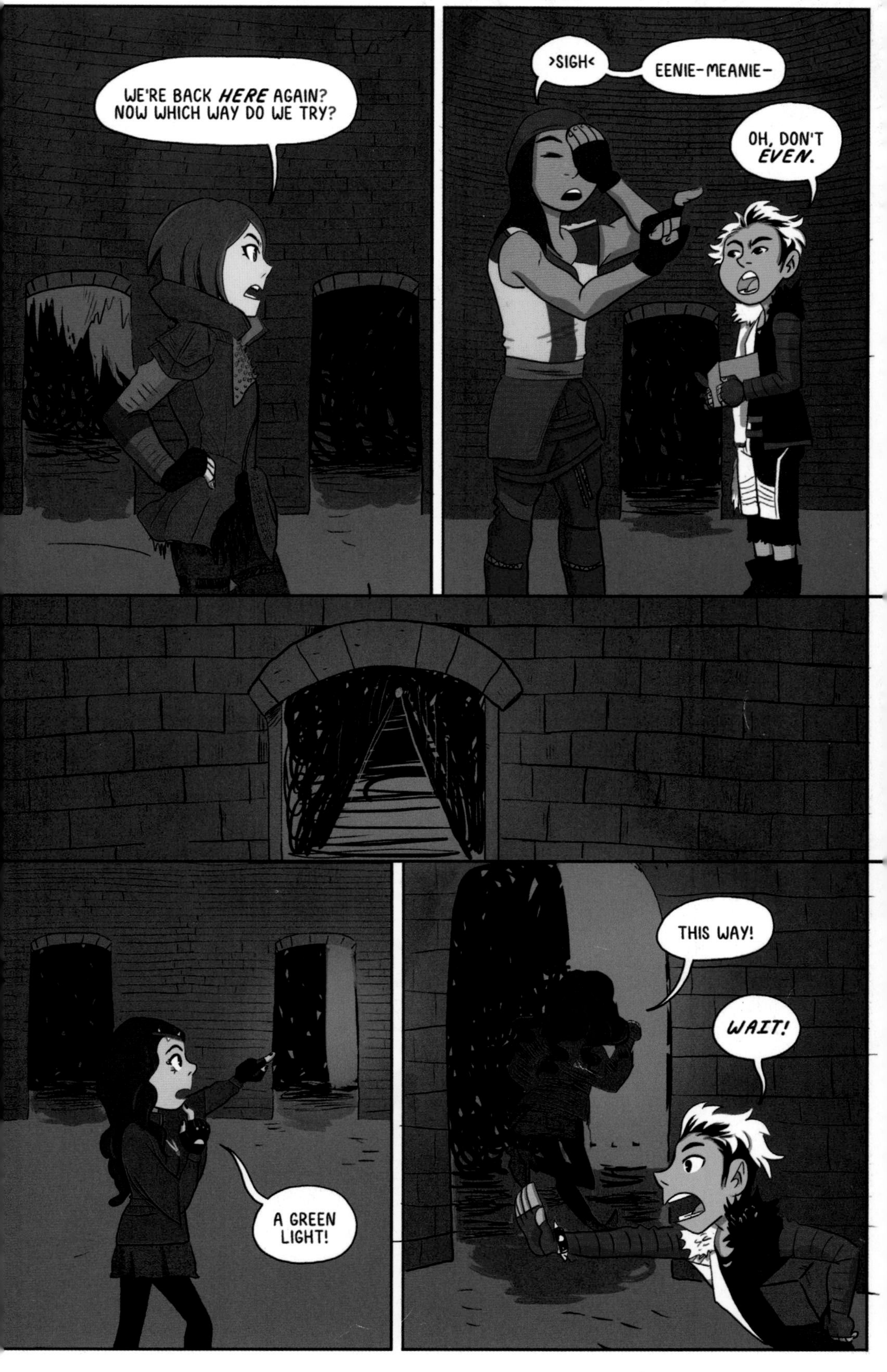
WE'RE BACK *HERE* AGAIN? NOW WHICH WAY DO WE TRY?
>SIGH<
EENIE-MEANIE-
OH, DON'T *EVEN.*
A GREEN LIGHT!
THIS WAY!
WAIT!

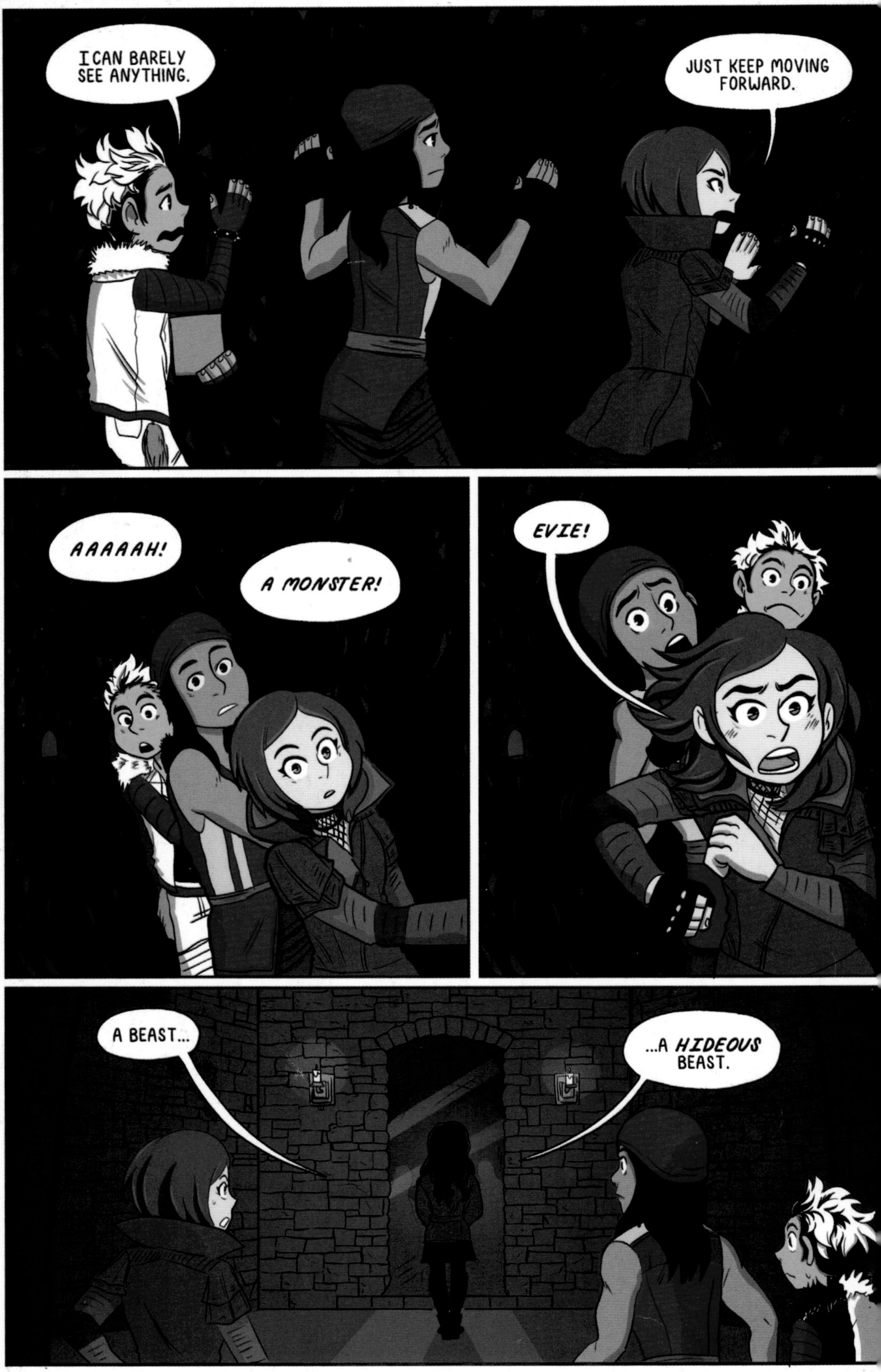
I CAN BARELY SEE ANYTHING.
JUST KEEP MOVING FORWARD.
AAAAAH!
A MONSTER!
EVIE!
A BEAST...
...A *HIDEOUS* BEAST.

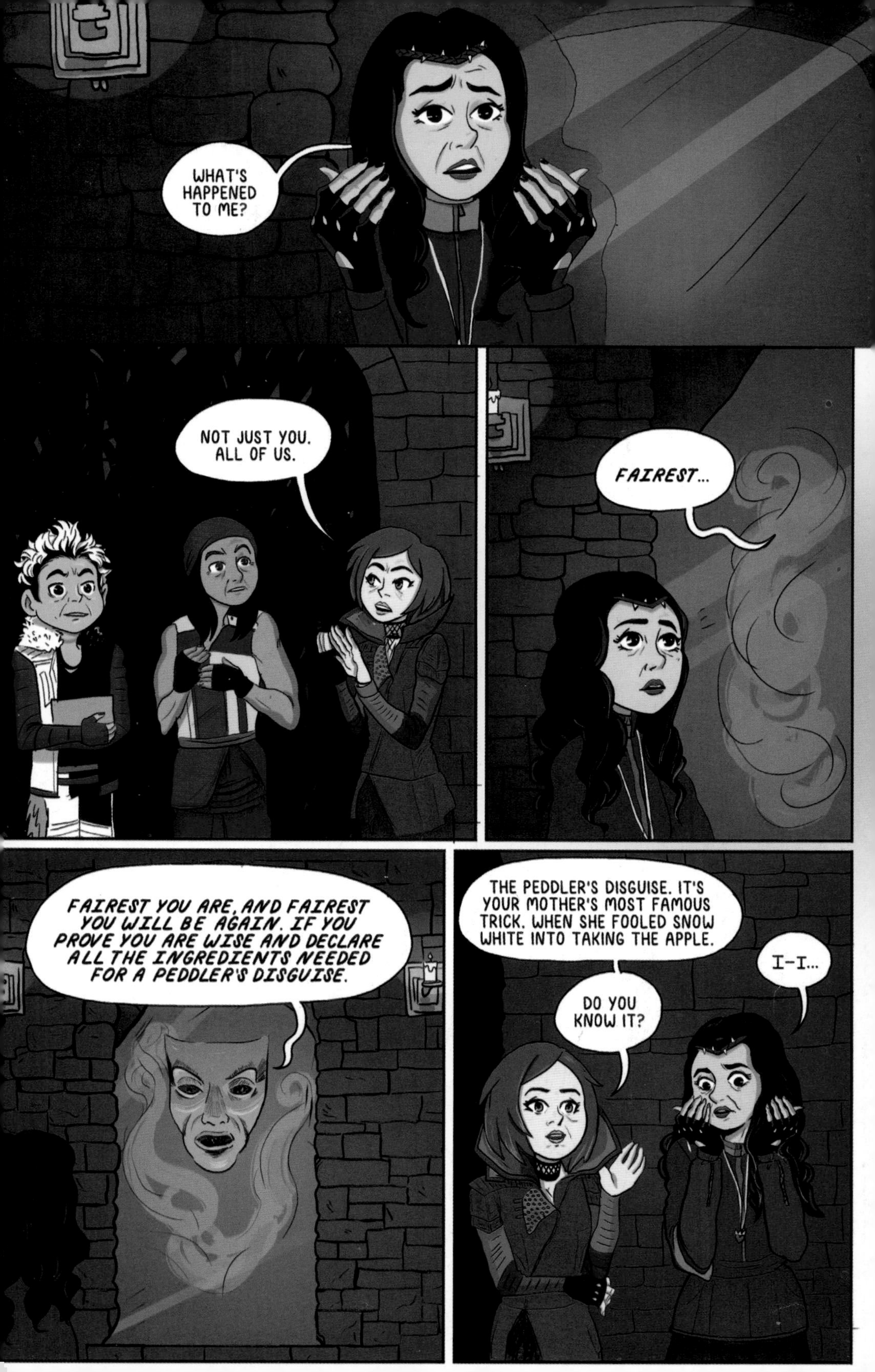
WHAT'S HAPPENED TO ME?
NOT JUST YOU. ALL OF US.
FAIREST...
FAIREST YOU ARE, AND FAIREST YOU WILL BE AGAIN. IF YOU PROVE YOU ARE WISE AND DECLARE ALL THE INGREDIENTS NEEDED FOR A PEDDLER'S DISGUISE.
THE PEDDLER'S DISGUISE. IT'S YOUR MOTHER'S MOST FAMOUS TRICK. WHEN SHE FOOLED SNOW WHITE INTO TAKING THE APPLE.
DO YOU KNOW IT?
I-I...

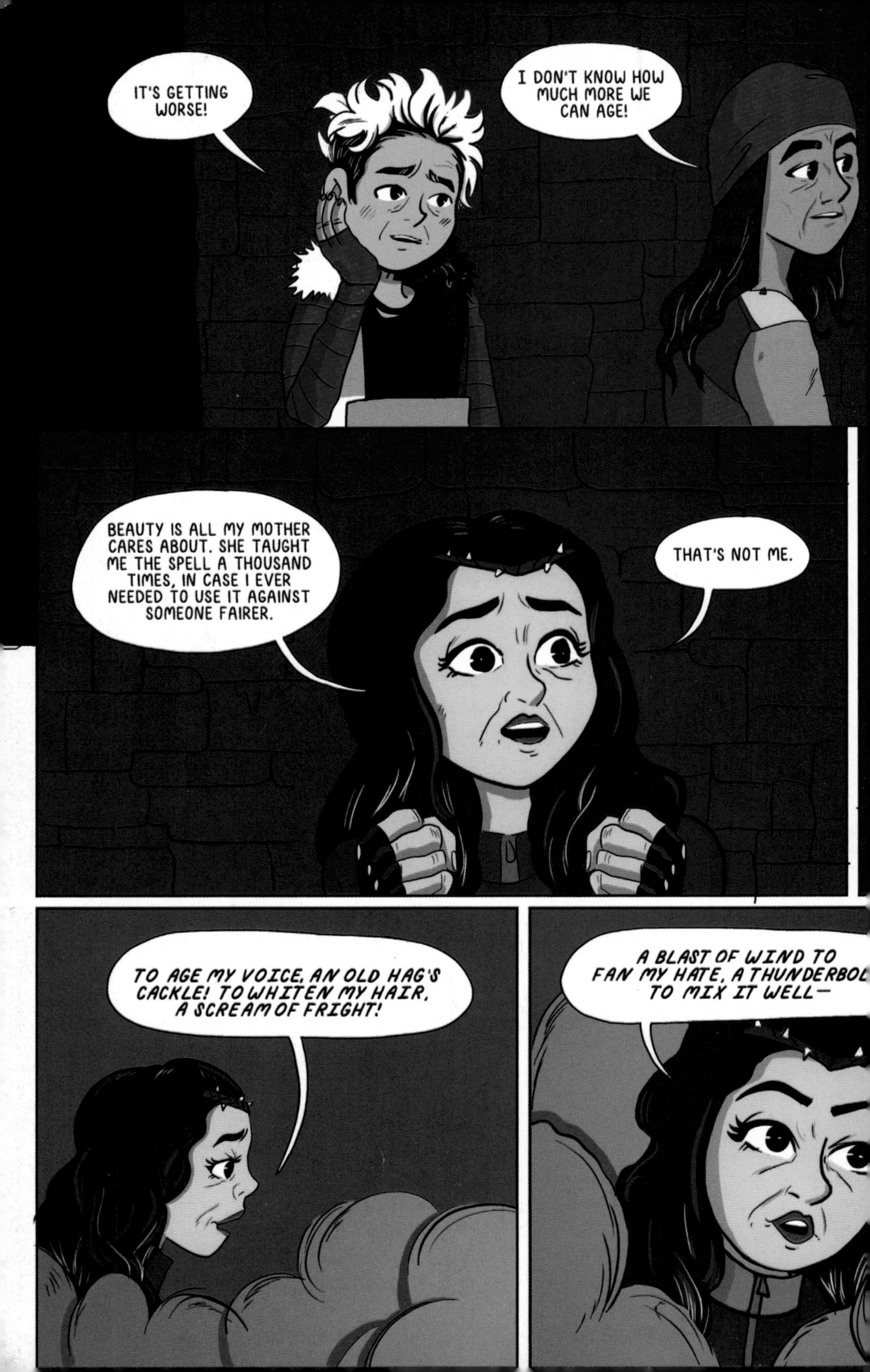
IT'S GETTING WORSE!
I DON'T KNOW HOW MUCH MORE WE CAN AGE!
BEAUTY IS ALL MY MOTHER CARES ABOUT. SHE TAUGHT ME THE SPELL A THOUSAND TIMES, IN CASE I EVER NEEDED TO USE IT AGAINST SOMEONE FAIRER.
THAT'S NOT ME.
TO AGE MY VOICE, AN OLD HAG'S CACKLE! TO WHITEN MY HAIR, A SCREAM OF FRIGHT!
A BLAST OF WIND TO FAN MY HATE, A THUNDERBOL
TO MIX IT WELL—

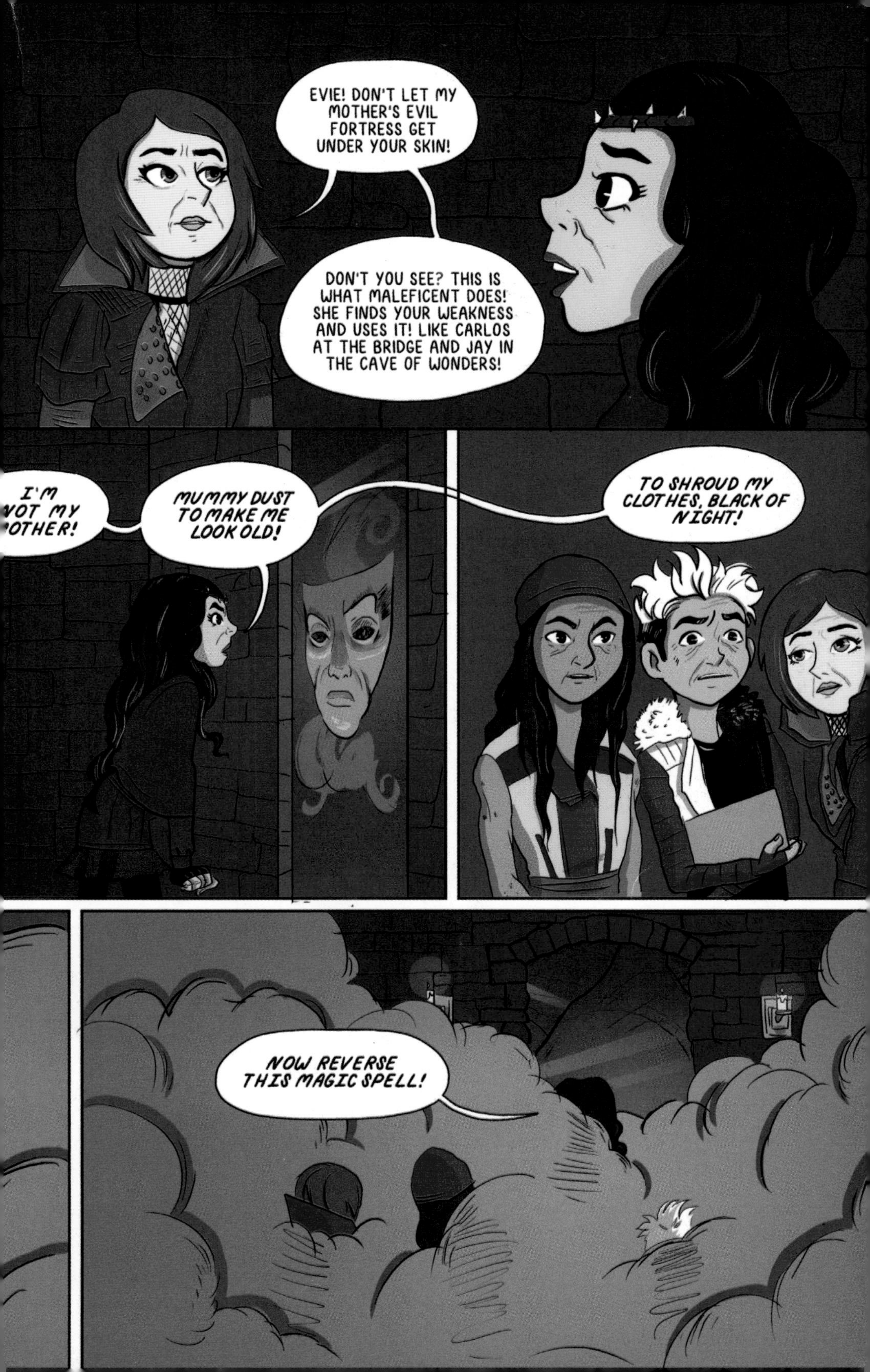
EVIE! DON'T LET MY MOTHER'S EVIL FORTRESS GET UNDER YOUR SKIN!
DON'T YOU SEE? THIS IS WHAT MALEFICENT DOES! SHE FINDS YOUR WEAKNESS AND USES IT! LIKE CARLOS AT THE BRIDGE AND JAY IN THE CAVE OF WONDERS!
I'M NOT MY OTHER!
MUMMY DUST TO MAKE ME LOOK OLD!
TO SHROUD MY CLOTHES, BLACK OF NIGHT!
NOW REVERSE THIS MAGIC SPELL!

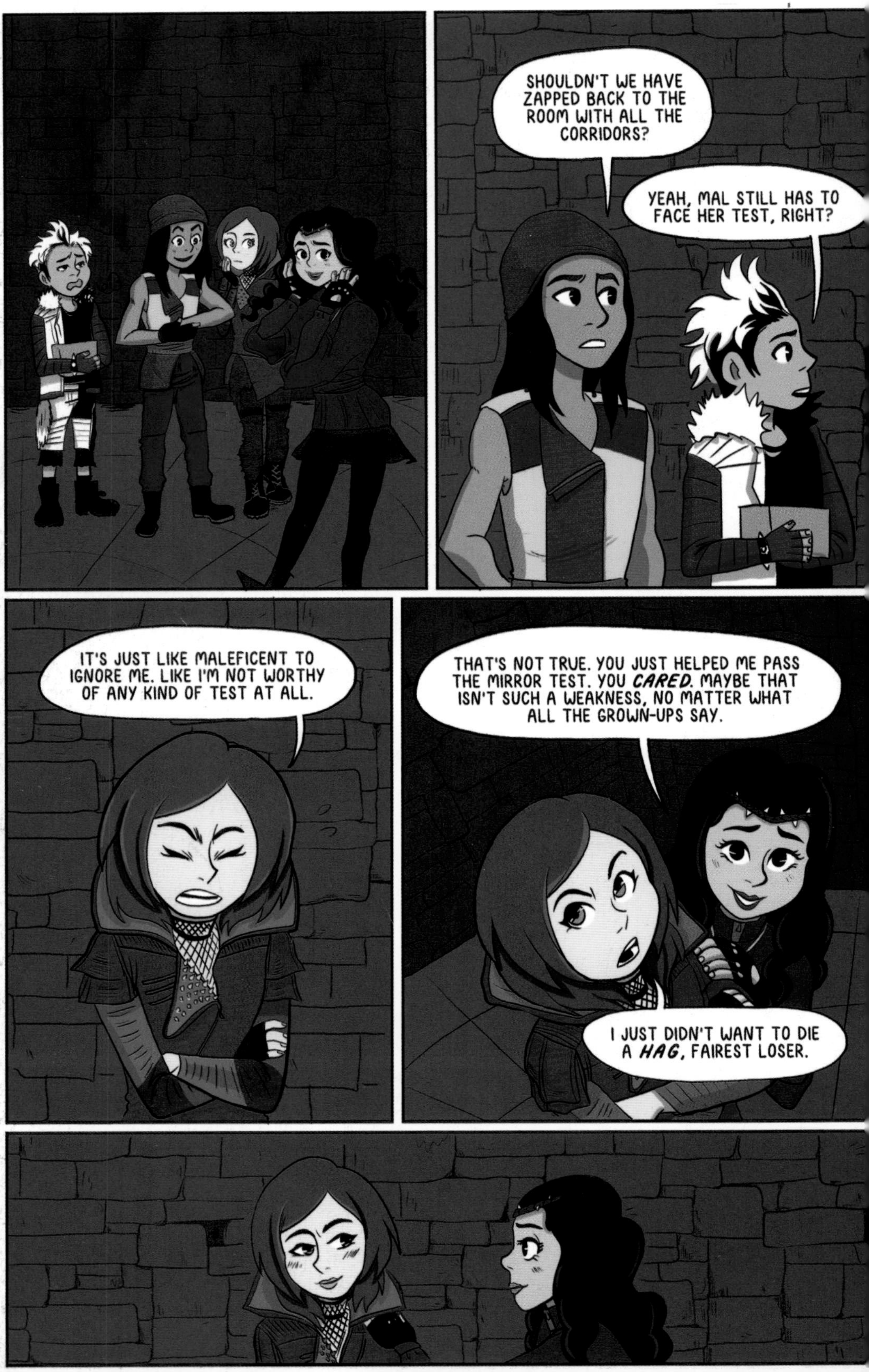
SHOULDN'T WE HAVE ZAPPED BACK TO THE ROOM WITH ALL THE CORRIDORS?
YEAH, MAL STILL HAS TO FACE HER TEST, RIGHT?
IT'S JUST LIKE MALEFICENT TO IGNORE ME. LIKE I'M NOT WORTHY OF ANY KIND OF TEST AT ALL.
THAT'S NOT TRUE. YOU JUST HELPED ME PASS THE MIRROR TEST. YOU *CARED*. MAYBE THAT ISN'T SUCH A WEAKNESS, NO MATTER WHAT ALL THE GROWN-UPS SAY.
I JUST DIDN'T WANT TO DIE A *HAG*, FAIREST LOSER.

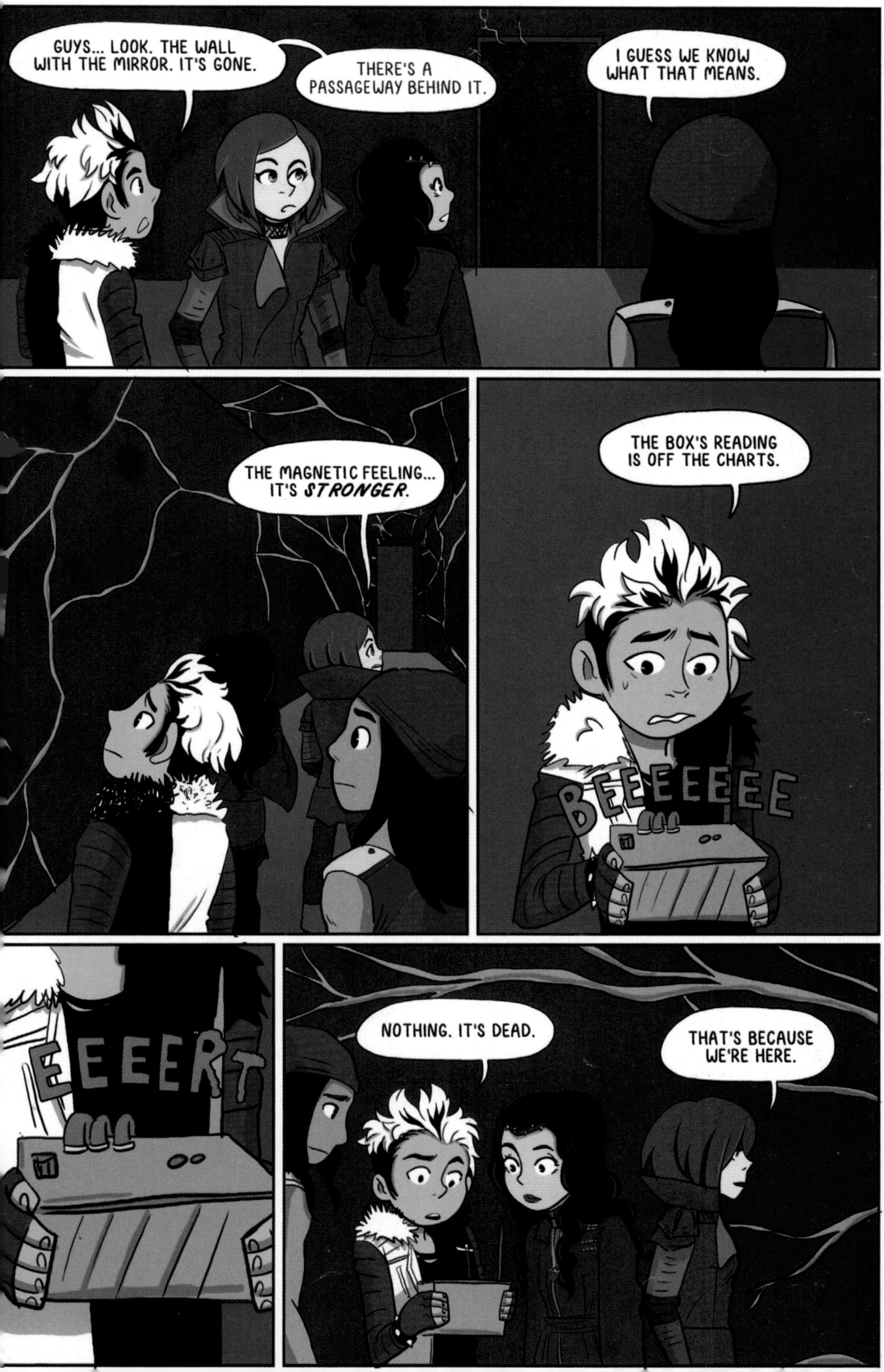
GUYS... LOOK. THE WALL WITH THE MIRROR. IT'S GONE.
THERE'S A PASSAGEWAY BEHIND IT.
I GUESS WE KNOW WHAT THAT MEANS.
THE MAGNETIC FEELING... IT'S *STRONGER*.
THE BOX'S READING IS OFF THE CHARTS.
BEEEEEEE
EEEERT
NOTHING. IT'S DEAD.
THAT'S BECAUSE WE'RE HERE.

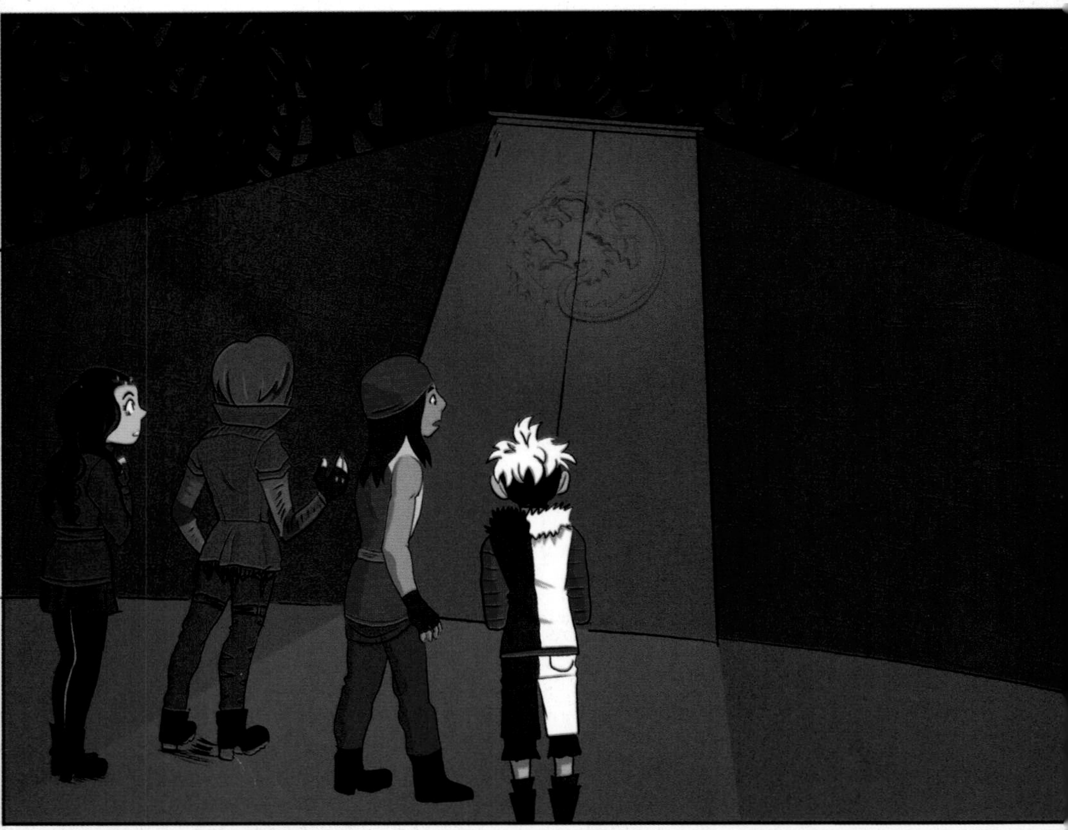

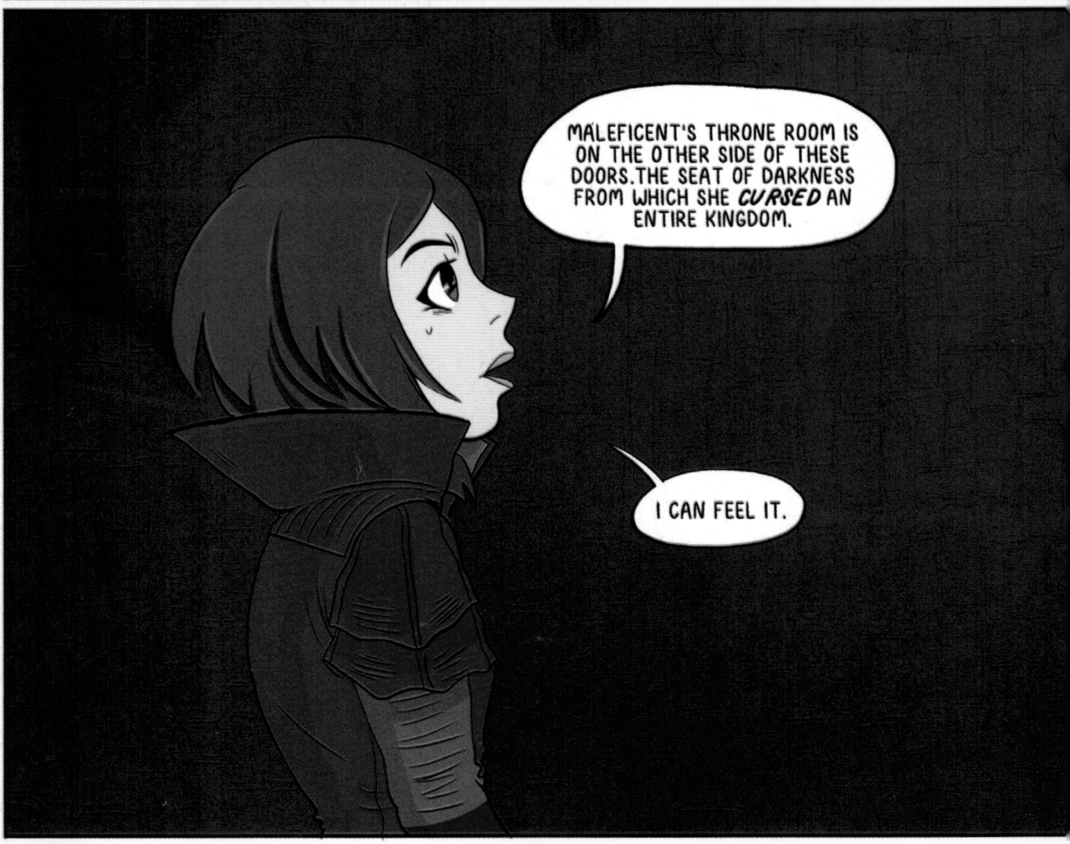
MALEFICENT'S THRONE ROOM IS ON THE OTHER SIDE OF THESE DOORS. THE SEAT OF DARKNESS FROM WHICH SHE *CURSED* AN ENTIRE KINGDOM.
I CAN FEEL IT.

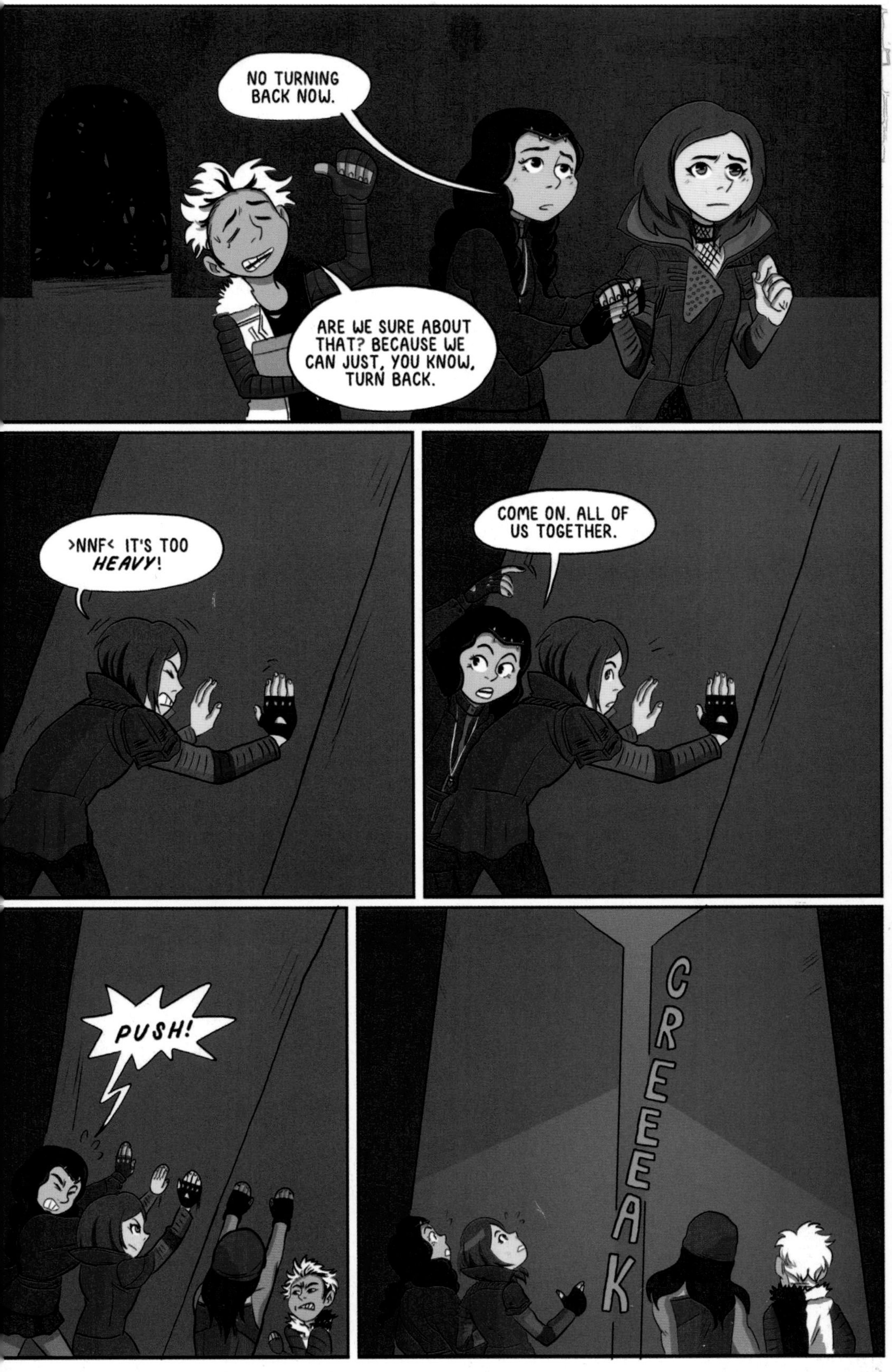
NO TURNING BACK NOW.
ARE WE SURE ABOUT THAT? BECAUSE WE CAN JUST, YOU KNOW, TURN BACK.
>NNF< IT'S TOO *HEAVY*!
COME ON. ALL OF US TOGETHER.
PUSH!
CREEEAK

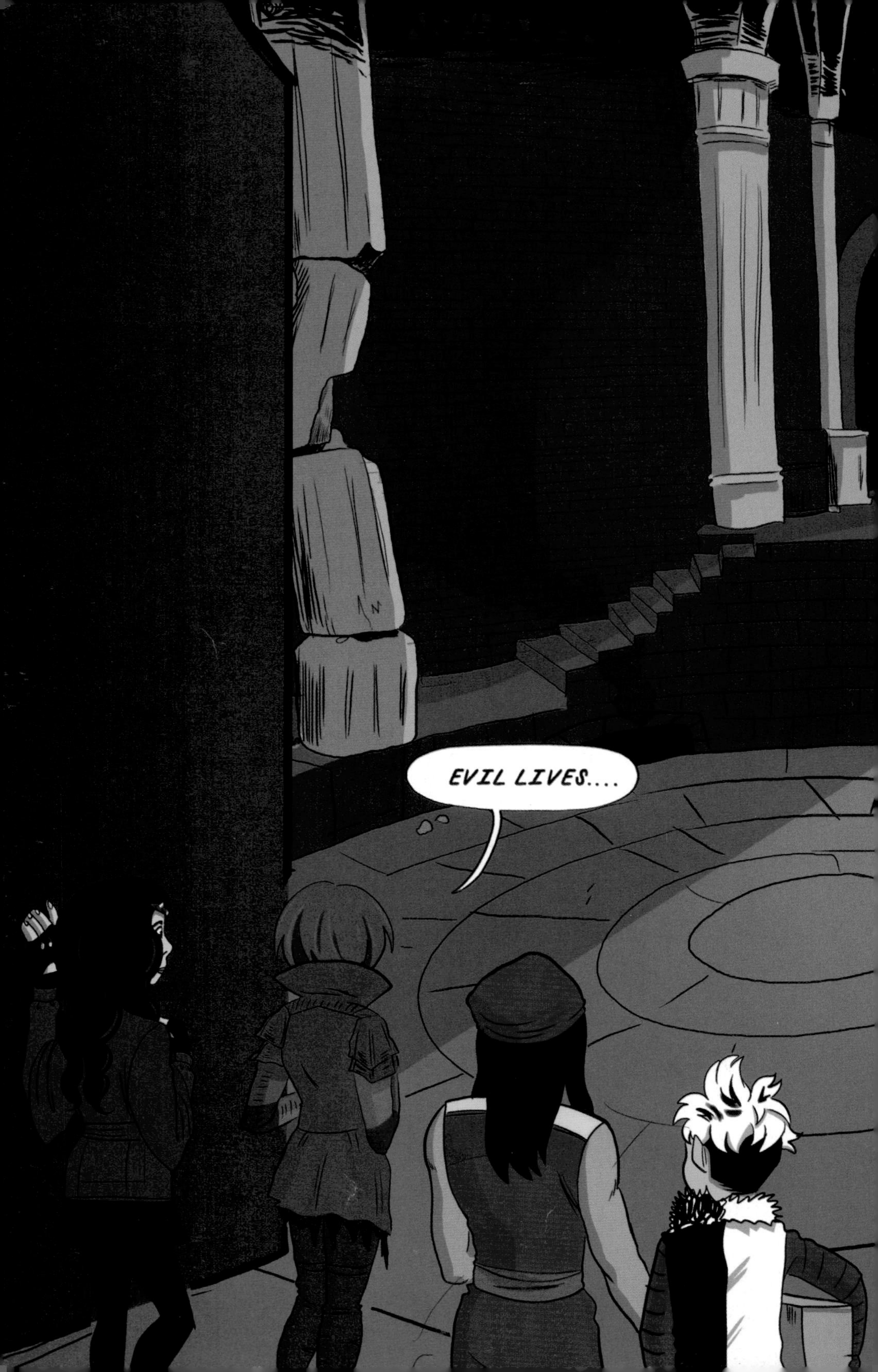
EVIL LIVES....

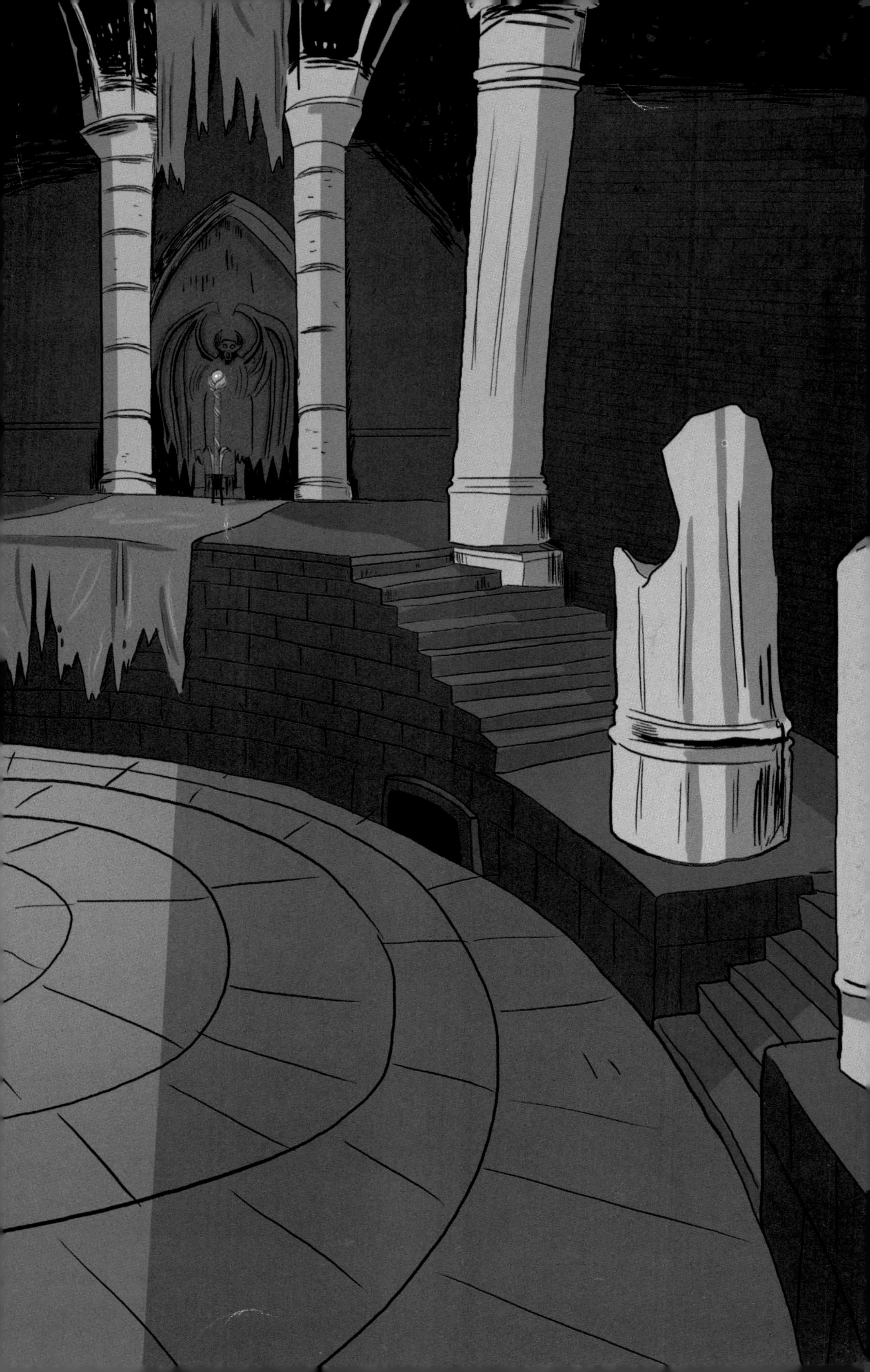

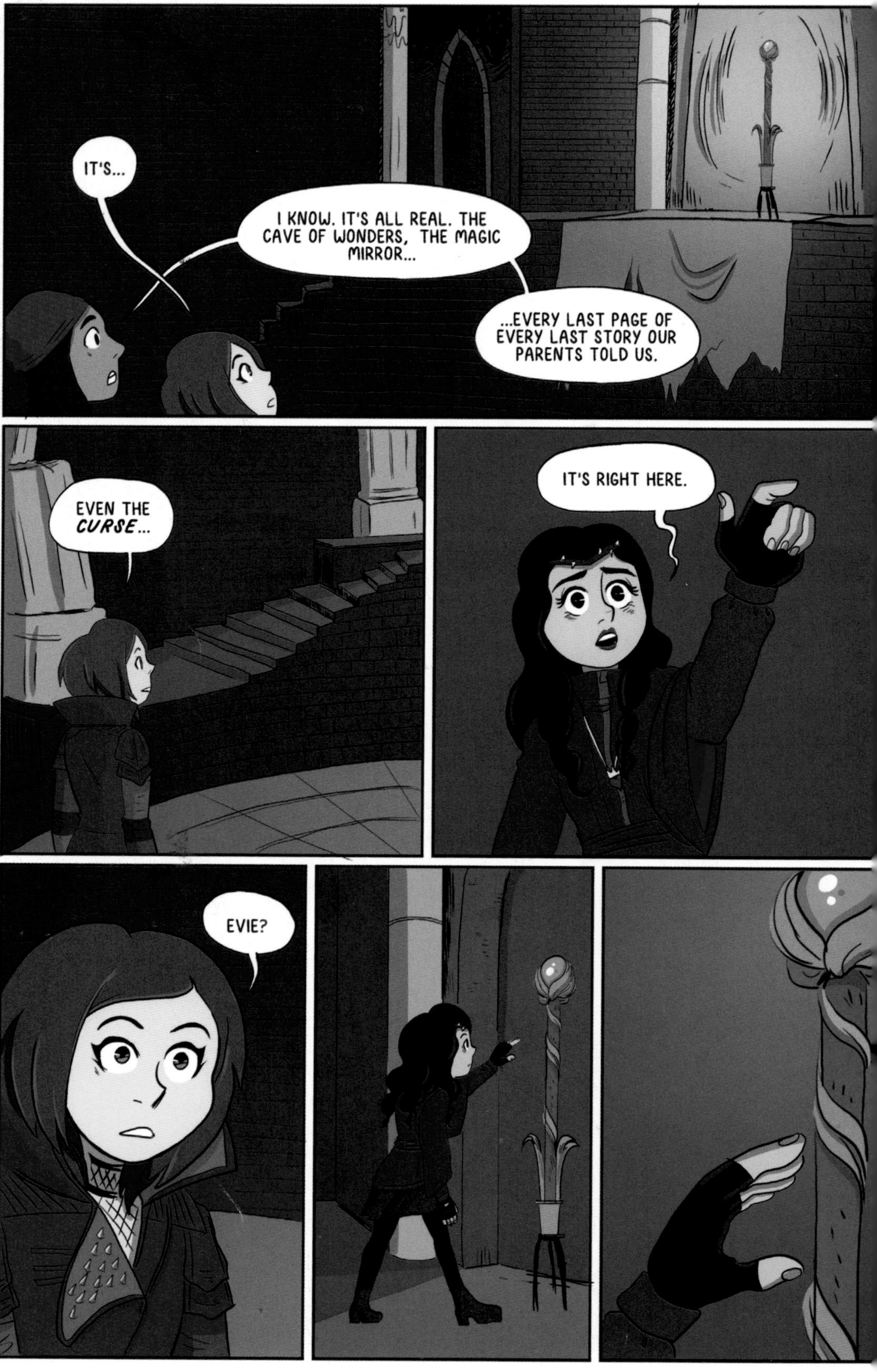
IT'S...
I KNOW. IT'S ALL REAL. THE CAVE OF WONDERS, THE MAGIC MIRROR...
...EVERY LAST PAGE OF EVERY LAST STORY OUR PARENTS TOLD US.
EVEN THE *CURSE*...
IT'S RIGHT HERE.
EVIE?

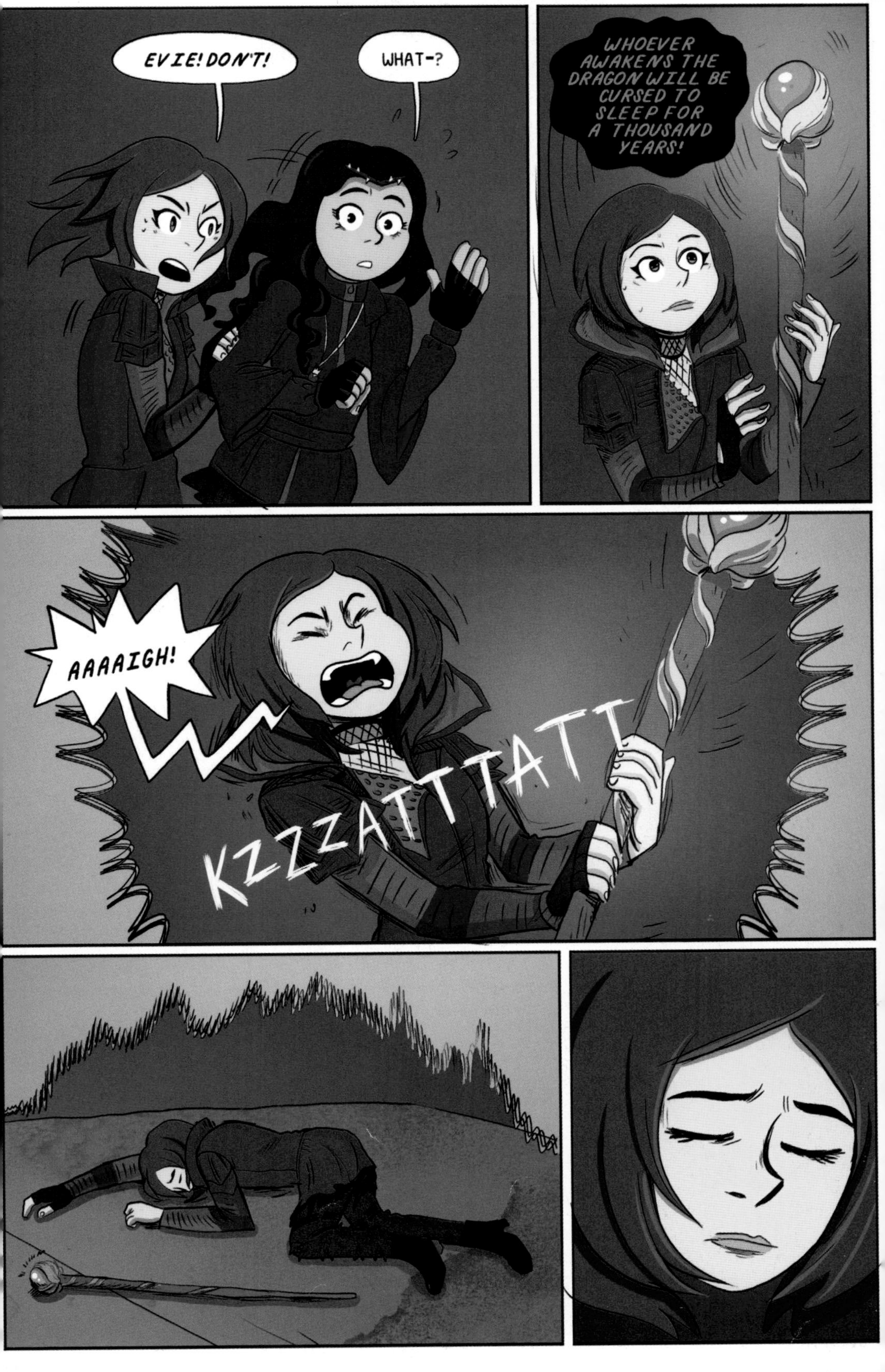
EVIE! DON'T!
WHAT-?
WHOEVER AWAKENS THE DRAGON WILL BE CURSED TO SLEEP FOR A THOUSAND YEARS!
AAAAIGH!
KZZZATTTATT

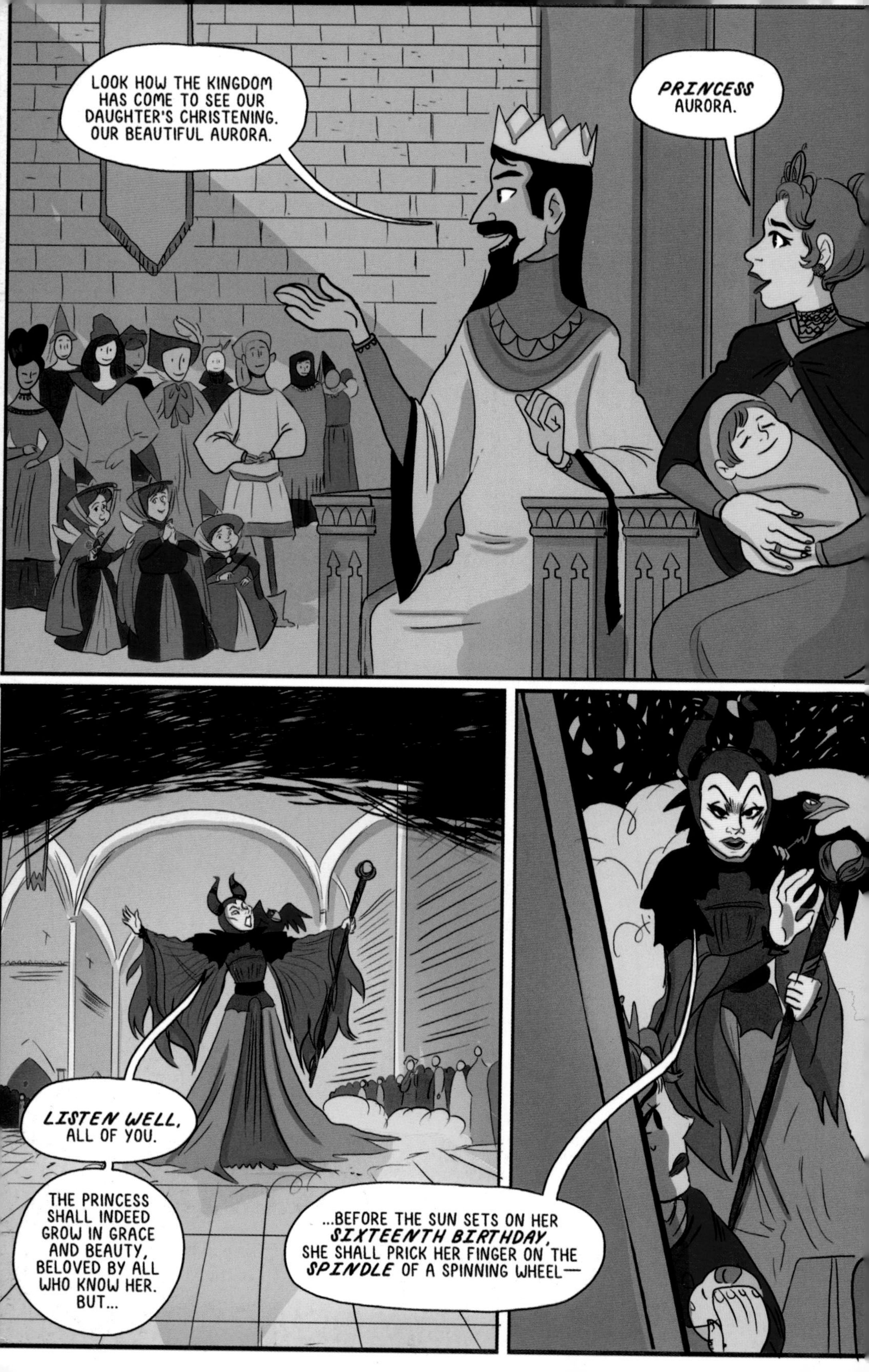
LOOK HOW THE KINGDOM HAS COME TO SEE OUR DAUGHTER'S CHRISTENING. OUR BEAUTIFUL AURORA.
PRINCESS AURORA.
LISTEN WELL, ALL OF YOU.
THE PRINCESS SHALL INDEED GROW IN GRACE AND BEAUTY, BELOVED BY ALL WHO KNOW HER. BUT...
...BEFORE THE SUN SETS ON HER *SIXTEENTH BIRTHDAY,* SHE SHALL PRICK HER FINGER ON THE *SPINDLE* OF A SPINNING WHEEL—

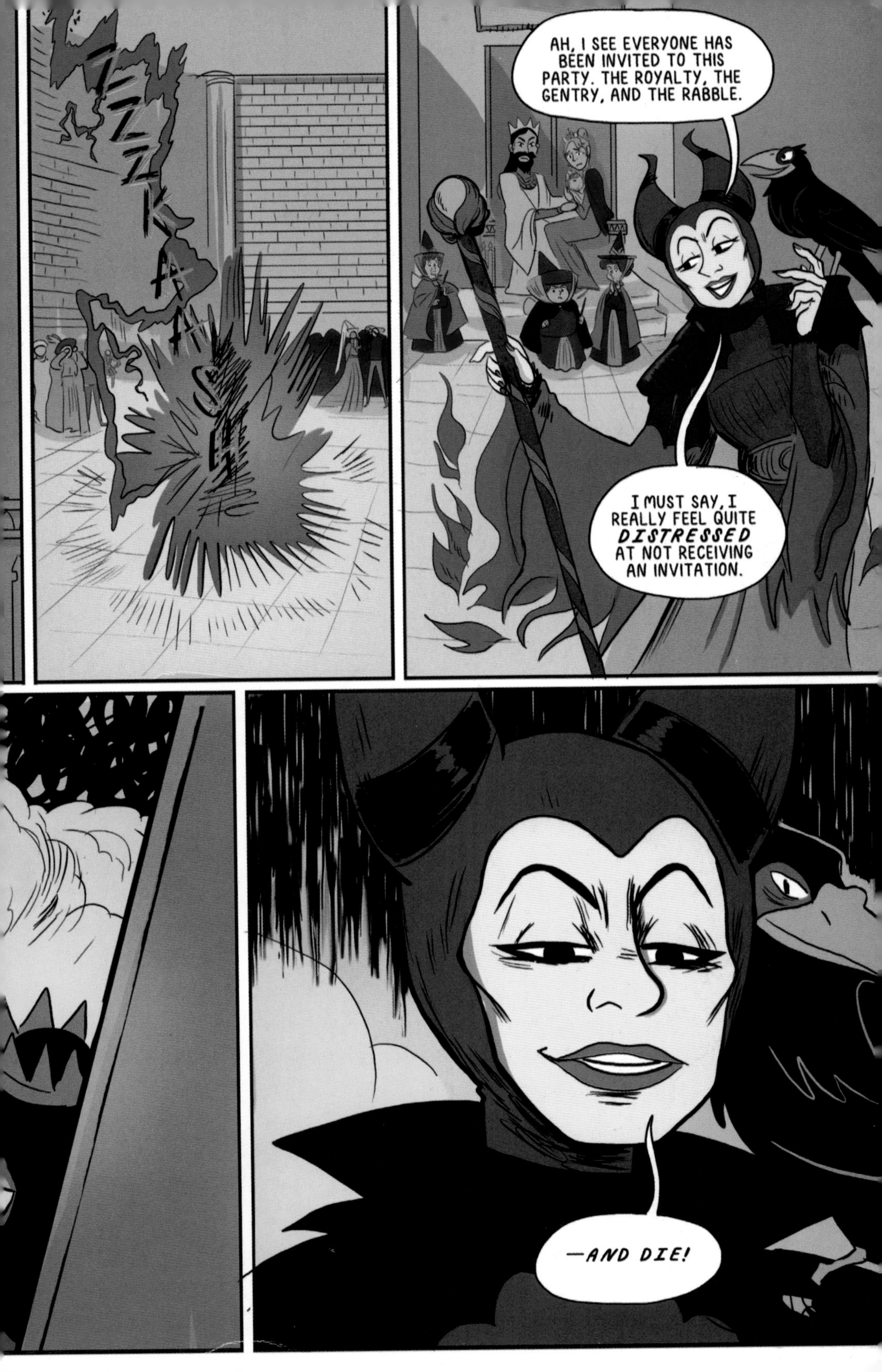
FIZZZKAPASH
AH, I SEE EVERYONE HAS BEEN INVITED TO THIS PARTY. THE ROYALTY, THE GENTRY, AND THE RABBLE.
I MUST SAY, I REALLY FEEL QUITE DISTRESSED AT NOT RECEIVING AN INVITATION.
—AND DIE!

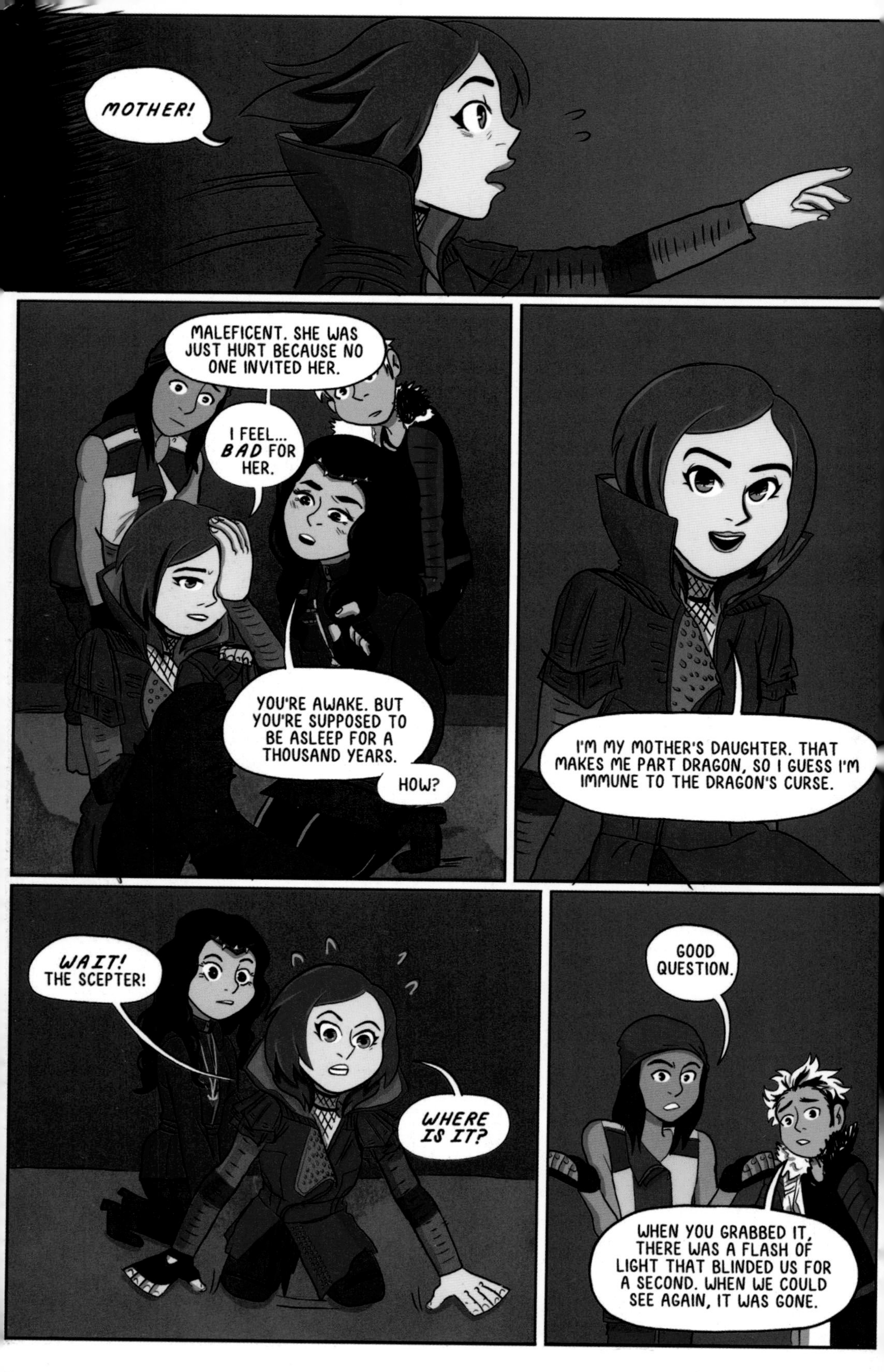
MOTHER!
MALEFICENT. SHE WAS JUST HURT BECAUSE NO ONE INVITED HER.
I FEEL... BAD FOR HER.
YOU'RE AWAKE. BUT YOU'RE SUPPOSED TO BE ASLEEP FOR A THOUSAND YEARS.
HOW?
I'M MY MOTHER'S DAUGHTER. THAT MAKES ME PART DRAGON, SO I GUESS I'M IMMUNE TO THE DRAGON'S CURSE.
WAIT! THE SCEPTER!
WHERE IS IT?
GOOD QUESTION.
WHEN YOU GRABBED IT, THERE WAS A FLASH OF LIGHT THAT BLINDED US FOR A SECOND. WHEN WE COULD SEE AGAIN, IT WAS GONE.

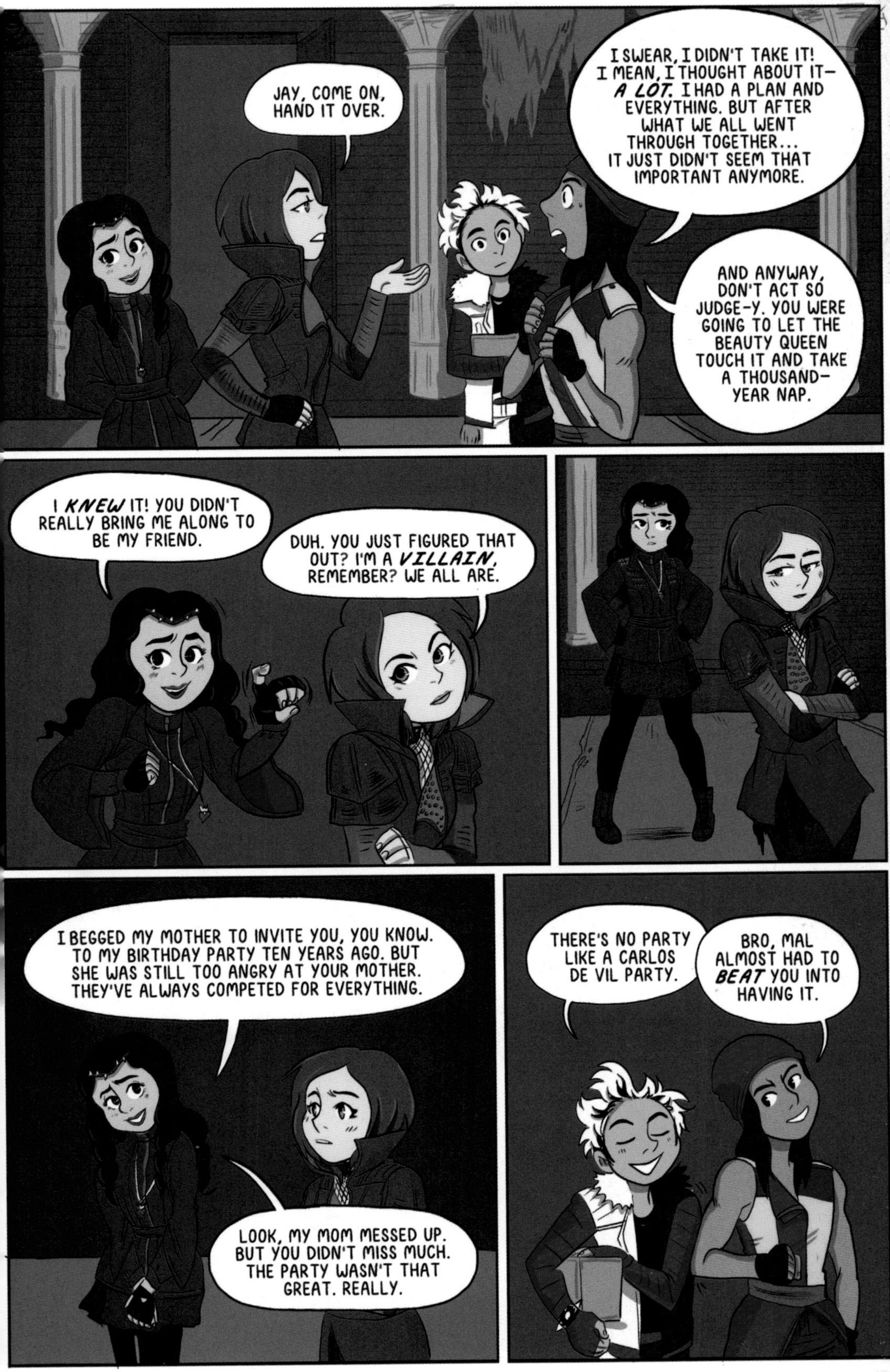
JAY, COME ON, HAND IT OVER.
I SWEAR, I DIDN'T TAKE IT! I MEAN, I THOUGHT ABOUT IT— A LOT. I HAD A PLAN AND EVERYTHING. BUT AFTER WHAT WE ALL WENT THROUGH TOGETHER... IT JUST DIDN'T SEEM THAT IMPORTANT ANYMORE.
AND ANYWAY, DON'T ACT SO JUDGE-Y. YOU WERE GOING TO LET THE BEAUTY QUEEN TOUCH IT AND TAKE A THOUSAND-YEAR NAP.
I KNEW IT! YOU DIDN'T REALLY BRING ME ALONG TO BE MY FRIEND.
DUH. YOU JUST FIGURED THAT OUT? I'M A VILLAIN, REMEMBER? WE ALL ARE.
I BEGGED MY MOTHER TO INVITE YOU, YOU KNOW. TO MY BIRTHDAY PARTY TEN YEARS AGO. BUT SHE WAS STILL TOO ANGRY AT YOUR MOTHER. THEY'VE ALWAYS COMPETED FOR EVERYTHING.
LOOK, MY MOM MESSED UP. BUT YOU DIDN'T MISS MUCH. THE PARTY WASN'T THAT GREAT. REALLY.
THERE'S NO PARTY LIKE A CARLOS DE VIL PARTY.
BRO, MAL ALMOST HAD TO BEAT YOU INTO HAVING IT.

THIS WHOLE THING WAS MY MOTHER'S TEST. A TEST TO SEE IF I COULD BRING HER BACK THE DRAGON'S EYE. TO SEE IF I'D MAKE EVIE GET CURSED.

A TEST TO SEE IF I'M WORTHY OF BEING NOT JUST MAL, BUT MALEFICENT. I GUESS I FAILED.

IT'S NOT LIKE I'M BRINGING HOME JAFAR'S BIG SCORE. AND EVIE REFUSED TO PUT HER LOOKS ABOVE EVERYTHING ELSE. CARLOS DIDN'T DO . . . WHATEVER WEIRD THING HIS MOM WANTED HIM TO DO.

WE *ALL* FAILED THE TEST.

OR MAYBE WE ALL PASSED. JUST BECAUSE WE AREN'T OUR PARENTS, THAT DOESN'T MAKE US FAILURES.

WELL SAID, CARLOS.

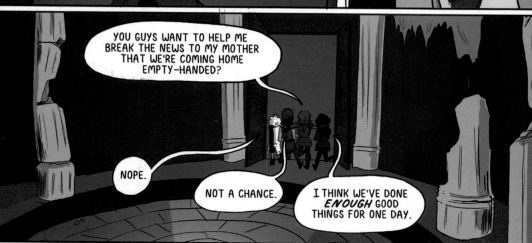

YOU GUYS WANT TO HELP ME BREAK THE NEWS TO MY MOTHER THAT WE'RE COMING HOME EMPTY-HANDED?

NOPE.

NOT A CHANCE.

I THINK WE'VE DONE *ENOUGH* GOOD THINGS FOR ONE DAY.

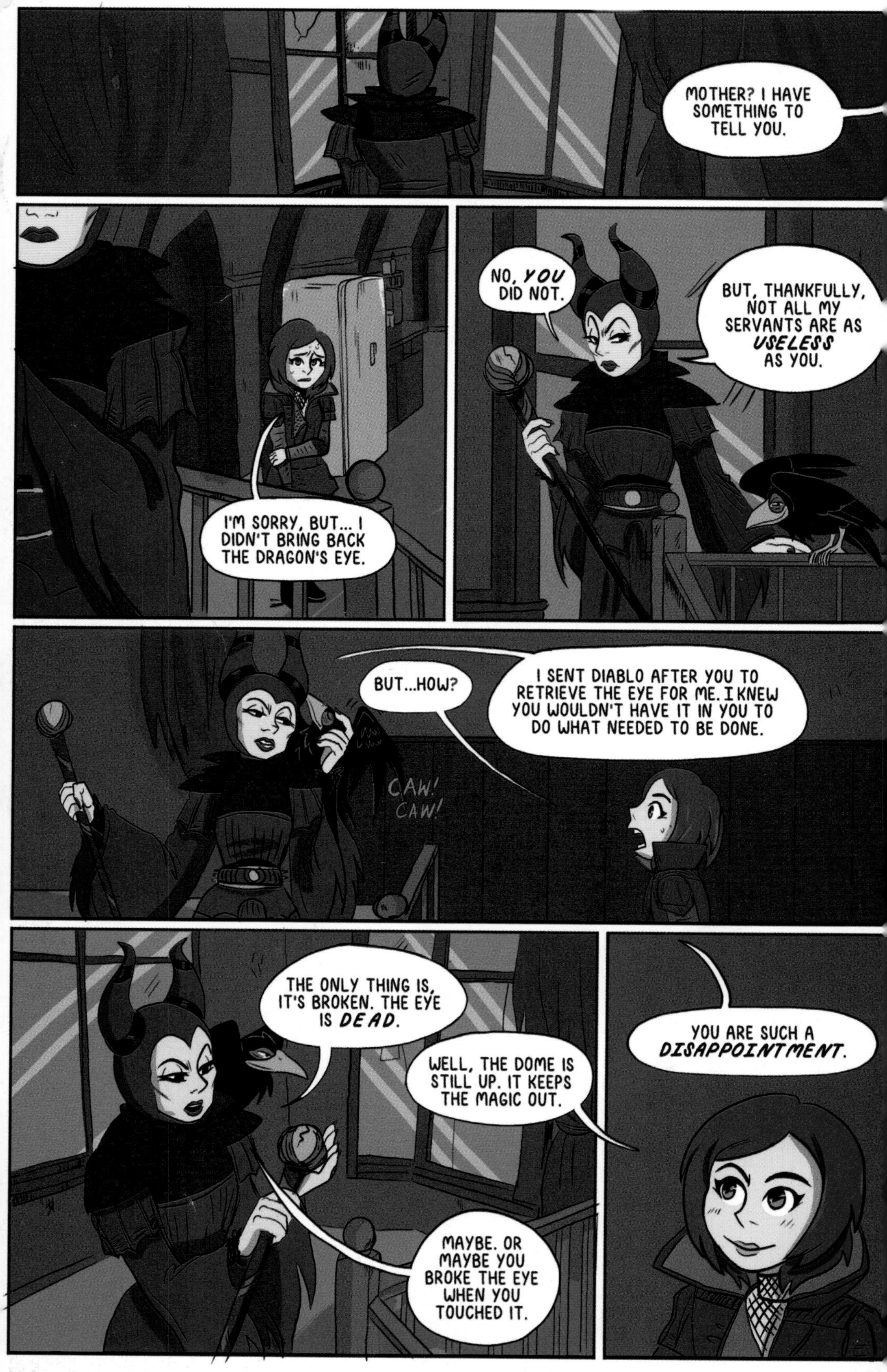
MOTHER? I HAVE SOMETHING TO TELL YOU.
I'M SORRY, BUT... I DIDN'T BRING BACK THE DRAGON'S EYE.
NO, *YOU* DID NOT.
BUT, THANKFULLY, NOT ALL MY SERVANTS ARE AS *USELESS* AS YOU.
BUT...HOW?
I SENT DIABLO AFTER YOU TO RETRIEVE THE EYE FOR ME. I KNEW YOU WOULDN'T HAVE IT IN YOU TO DO WHAT NEEDED TO BE DONE.
CAW! CAW!
THE ONLY THING IS, IT'S BROKEN. THE EYE IS *DEAD*.
WELL, THE DOME IS STILL UP. IT KEEPS THE MAGIC OUT.
MAYBE. OR MAYBE YOU BROKE THE EYE WHEN YOU TOUCHED IT.
YOU ARE SUCH A *DISAPPOINTMENT*.

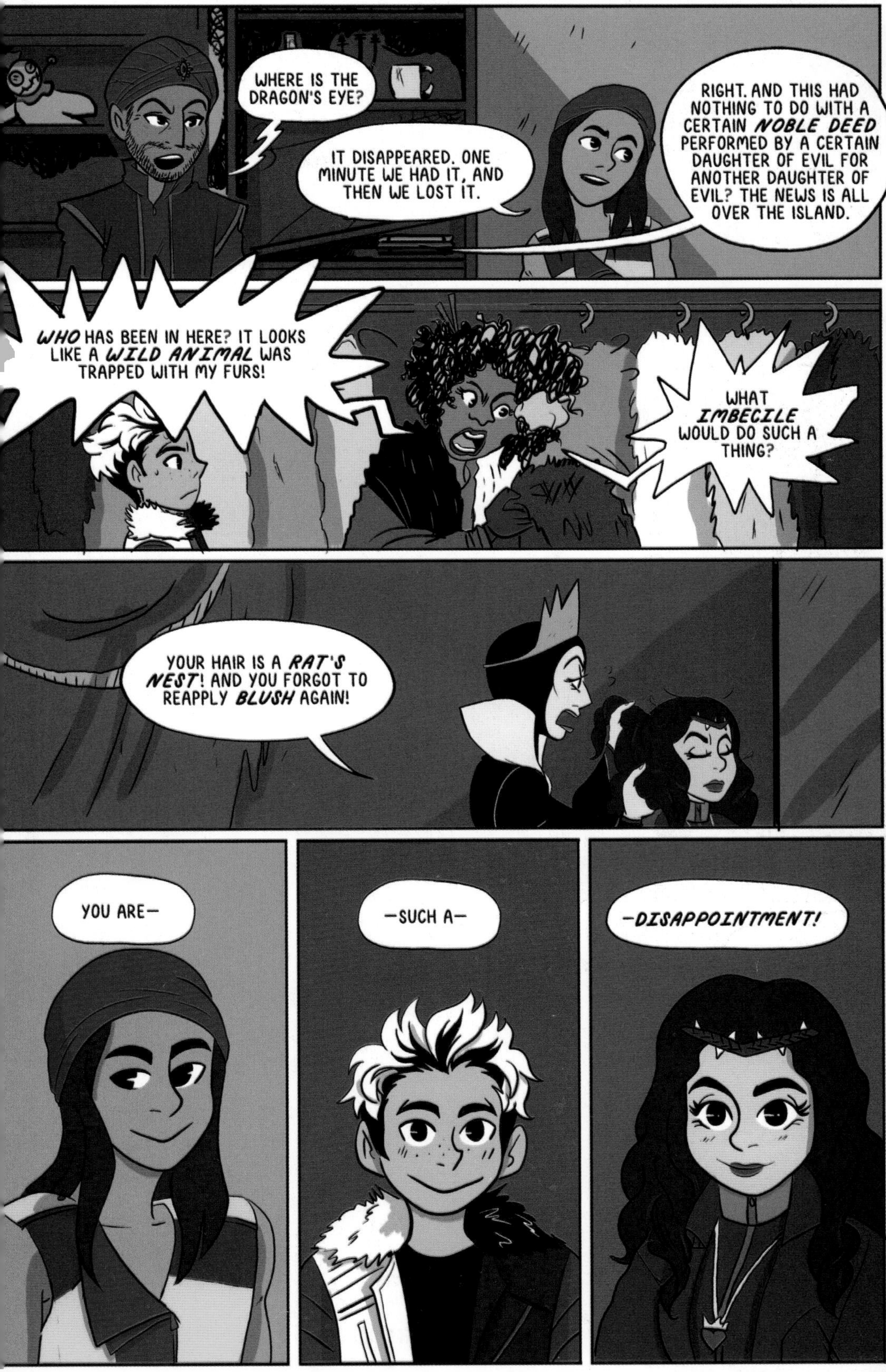
WHERE IS THE DRAGON'S EYE?
IT DISAPPEARED. ONE MINUTE WE HAD IT, AND THEN WE LOST IT.
RIGHT. AND THIS HAD NOTHING TO DO WITH A CERTAIN NOBLE DEED PERFORMED BY A CERTAIN DAUGHTER OF EVIL FOR ANOTHER DAUGHTER OF EVIL? THE NEWS IS ALL OVER THE ISLAND.
WHO HAS BEEN IN HERE? IT LOOKS LIKE A WILD ANIMAL WAS TRAPPED WITH MY FURS!
WHAT IMBECILE WOULD DO SUCH A THING?
YOUR HAIR IS A RAT'S NEST! AND YOU FORGOT TO REAPPLY BLUSH AGAIN!
YOU ARE—
—SUCH A—
—DISAPPOINTMENT!

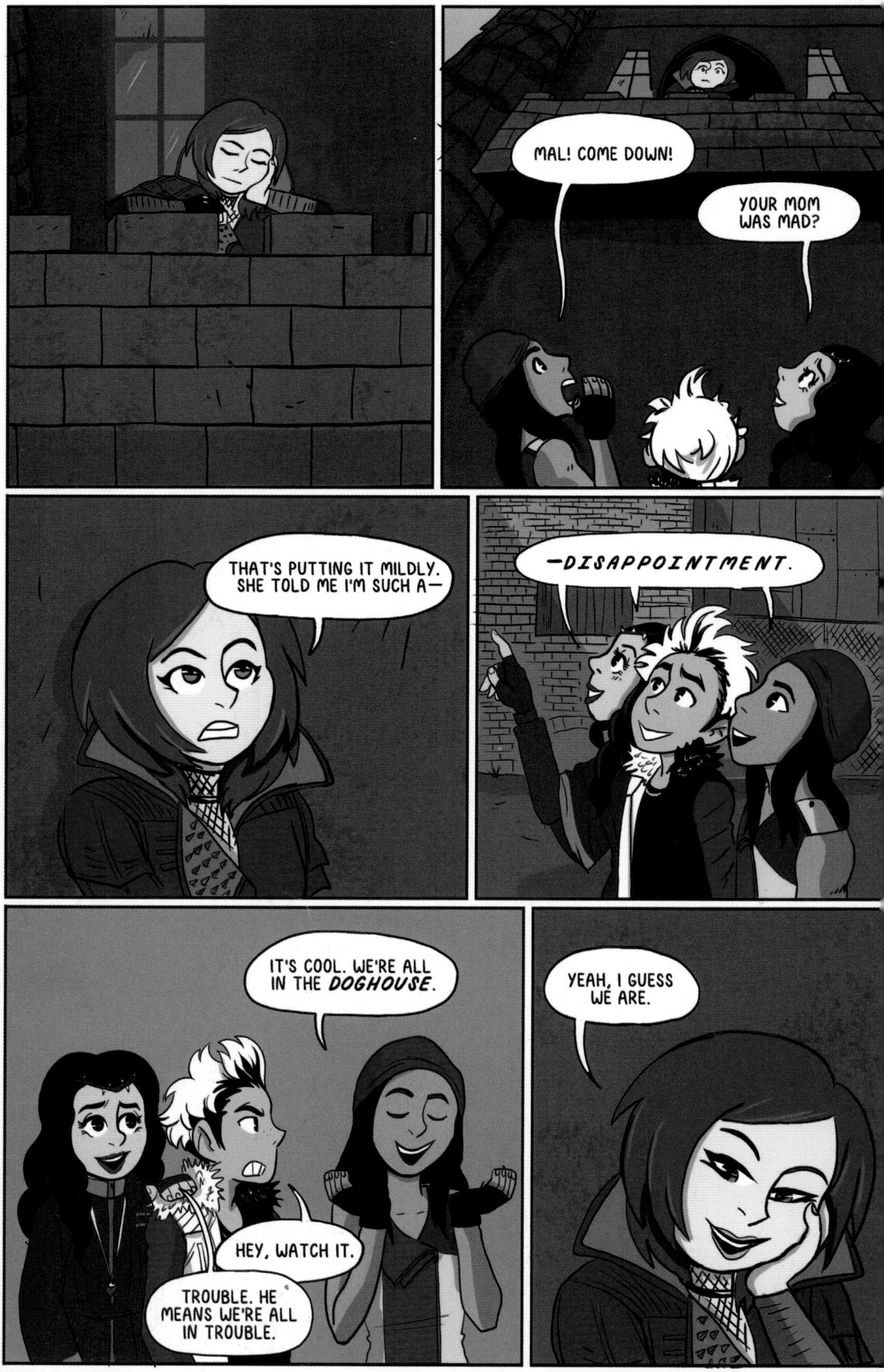
MAL! COME DOWN!
YOUR MOM WAS MAD?
THAT'S PUTTING IT MILDLY. SHE TOLD ME I'M SUCH A—
—DISAPPOINTMENT.
IT'S COOL. WE'RE ALL IN THE *DOGHOUSE*.
HEY, WATCH IT.
TROUBLE. HE MEANS WE'RE ALL IN TROUBLE.
YEAH, I GUESS WE ARE.

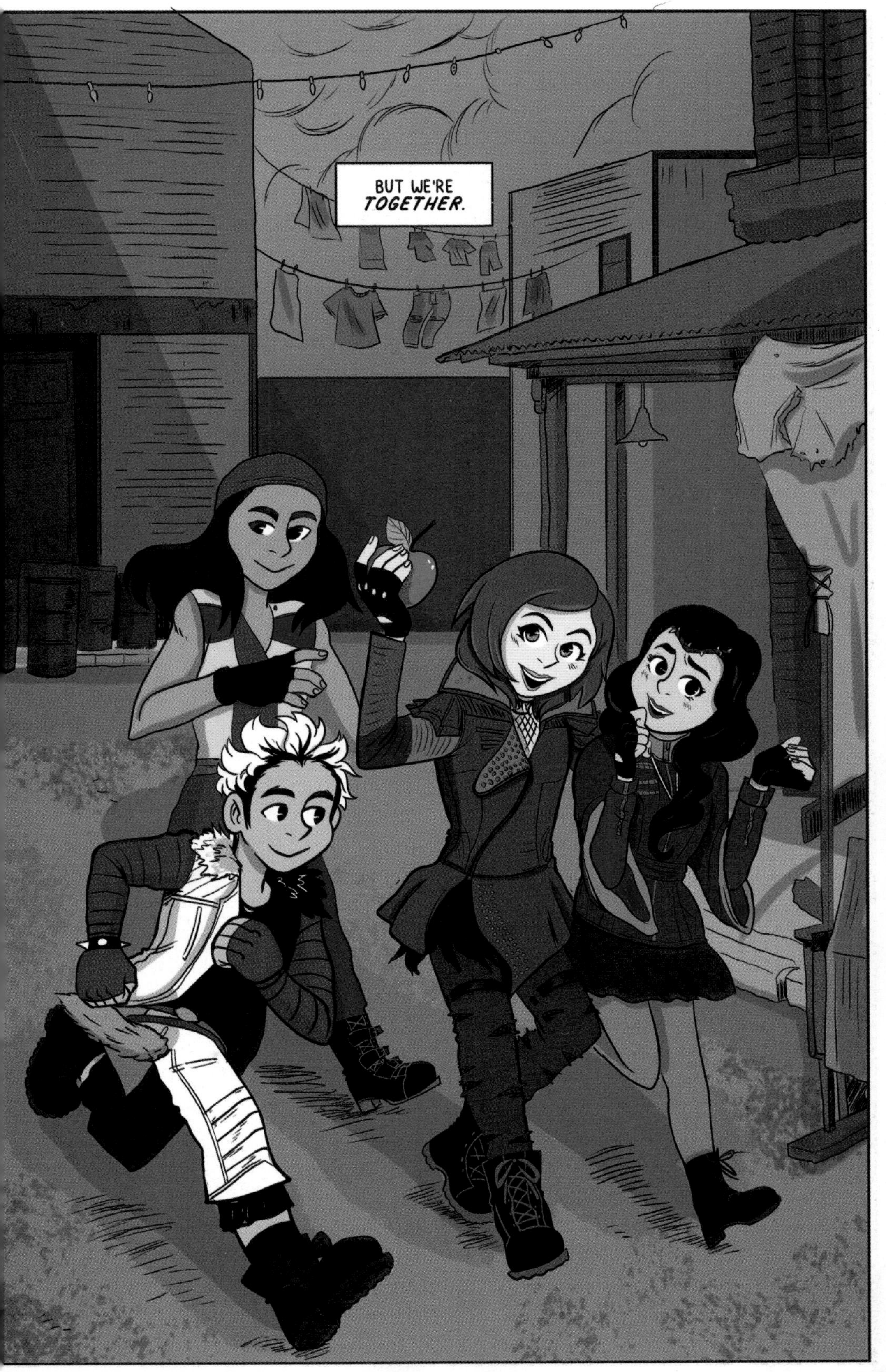
BUT WE'RE *TOGETHER*.

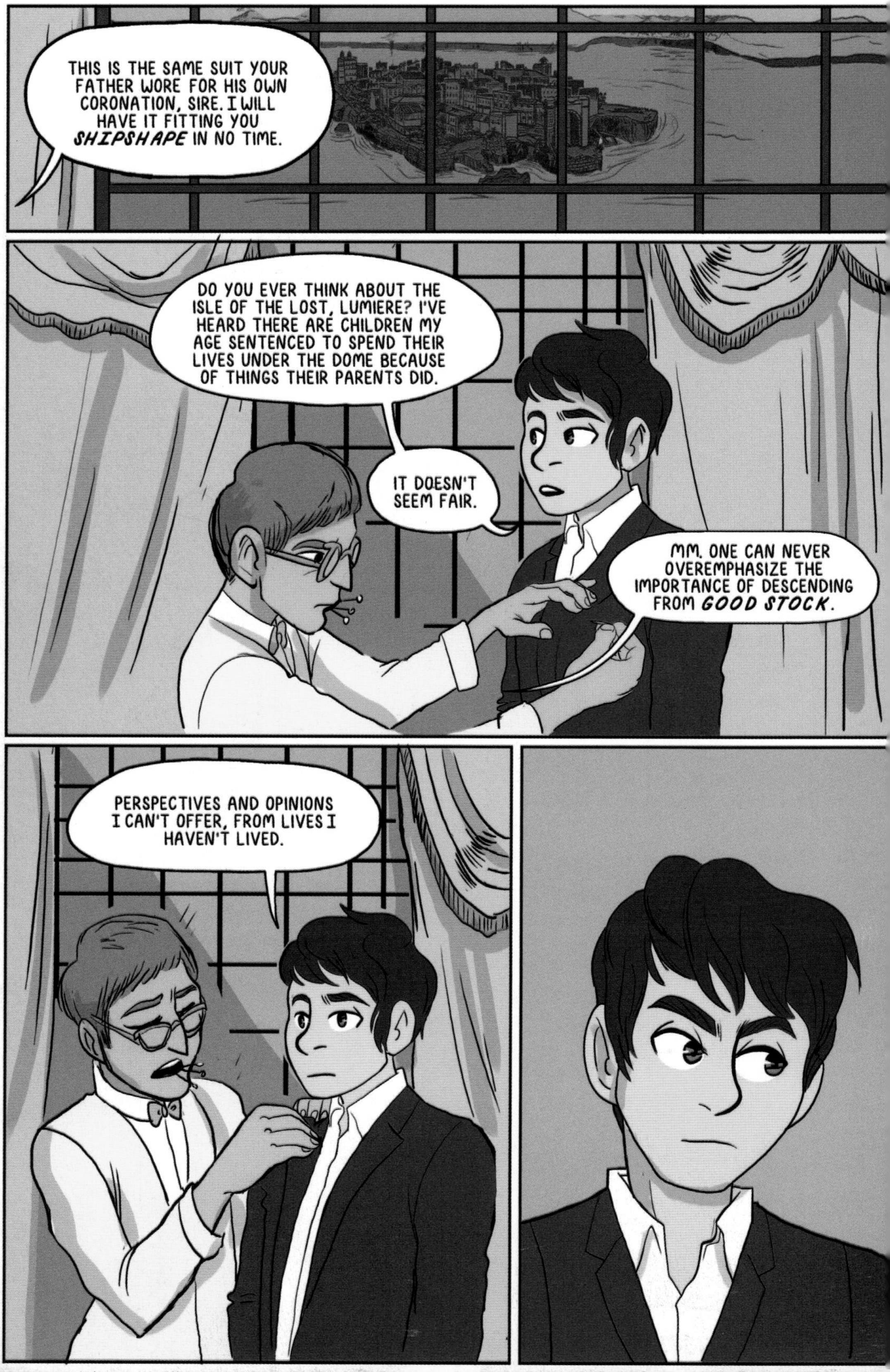
THIS IS THE SAME SUIT YOUR FATHER WORE FOR HIS OWN CORONATION, SIRE. I WILL HAVE IT FITTING YOU *SHIPSHAPE* IN NO TIME.
DO YOU EVER THINK ABOUT THE ISLE OF THE LOST, LUMIERE? I'VE HEARD THERE ARE CHILDREN MY AGE SENTENCED TO SPEND THEIR LIVES UNDER THE DOME BECAUSE OF THINGS THEIR PARENTS DID.
IT DOESN'T SEEM FAIR.
MM. ONE CAN NEVER OVEREMPHASIZE THE IMPORTANCE OF DESCENDING FROM *GOOD STOCK*.
PERSPECTIVES AND OPINIONS I CAN'T OFFER, FROM LIVES I HAVEN'T LIVED.

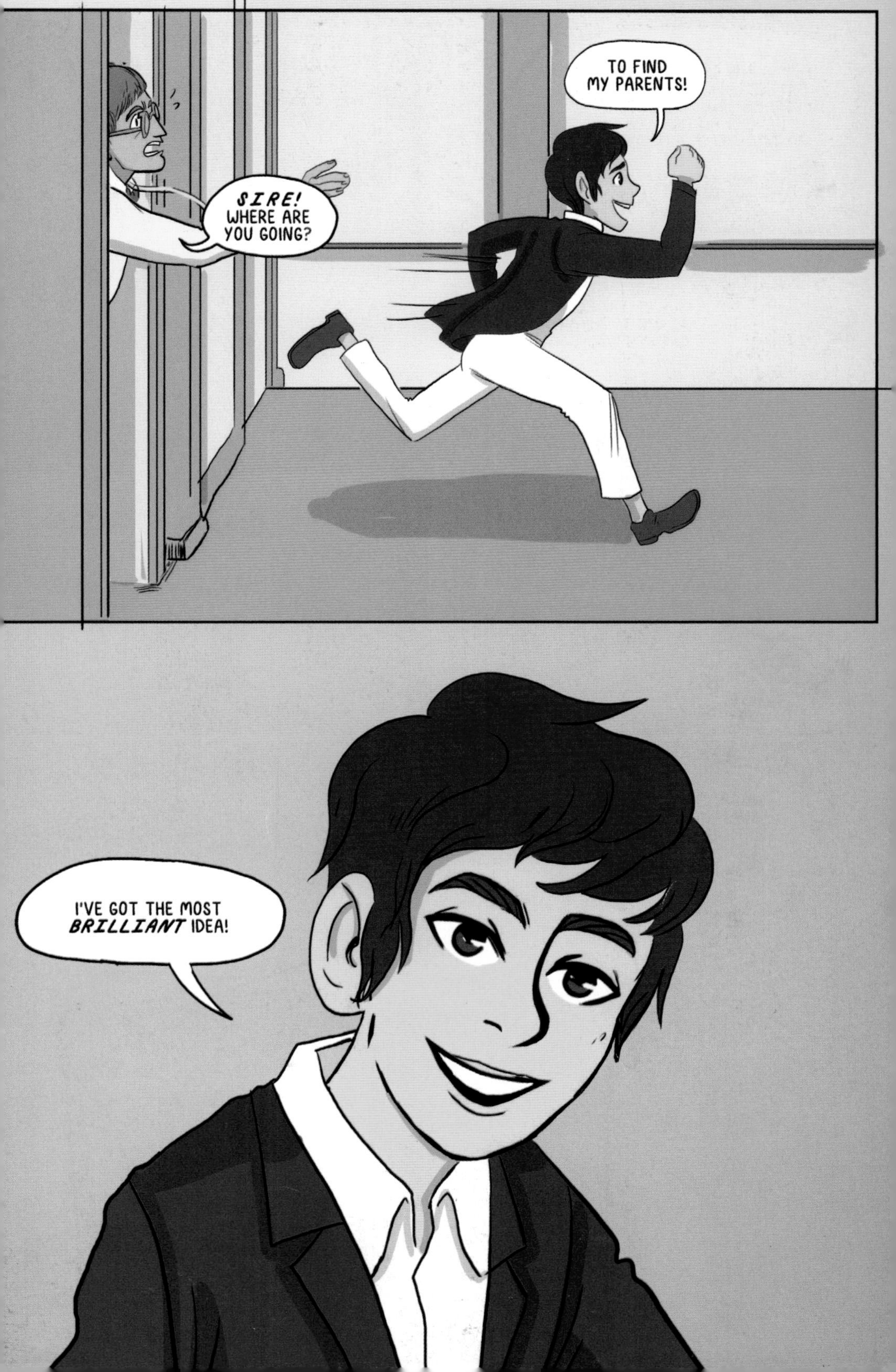
SIRE! WHERE ARE YOU GOING?
TO FIND MY PARENTS!
I'VE GOT THE MOST BRILLIANT IDEA!